Renegade Boys 4

Lock Down Publications and Ca$h Presents

Renegade Boys 4

A Novel by *Meesha*

Lock Down Publications
P.O. Box 870494
Mesquite, Tx 75187

Visit our website @
www.lockdownpublications.com

First Edition November 2019
Printed in the United States of America

Lock Down Publications
Like our page on Facebook: Lock Down Publications @
www.facebook.com/lockdownpublications.ldp
Cover design and layout by: **Dynasty Cover Me**
Book interior design by: **Shawn Walker**
Edited by: **Tam Jernigan**

Stay Connected with Us!

Text **LOCKDOWN** to 22828 to stay up-to-date with new releases, sneak peaks, contests and more…

Thank you.

Submission Guideline.

Submit the first three chapters of your completed manuscript to ldpsubmissions@gmail.com, subject line: Your book's title. The manuscript must be in a .doc file and sent as an attachment. Document should be in Times New Roman, double spaced and in size 12 font. Also, provide your synopsis and full contact information. If sending multiple submissions, they must each be in a separate email.

Have a story but no way to send it electronically? You can still submit to LDP/Ca$h Presents. Send in the first three chapters, written or typed, of your completed manuscript to:

LDP: Submissions Dept
Po Box 870494
Mesquite, Tx 75187

DO NOT send original manuscript. Must be a duplicate.

Provide your synopsis and a cover letter containing your full contact information.

Thanks for considering LDP and Ca$h Presents.

Chapter 1
Nija

I could hear what sounded like gurgling noises in the background. Then Kimmie screamed, "Ricio! Hold on, brah. Look at me! Don't close your eyes, look at me!" she was silent for a moment before her voice came through again. "I need an ambulance 9225 S. Sawyer Avenue. Hurry up because he's been shot!"

"Who's been shot, ma'am?"

"Get an ambulance here fast!" Kimmie screamed then the recording ended.

My hands were shaking and my heart was beating erratically. Tears streamed down my face and the only thing on my mind was Ricio laying in a pool of his own blood. The blast from the gun going off rang in my ears and I covered them to drown out the noise.

"I should've answered the phone! Dammit, why didn't you answer the phone, Nija!" I screamed out loud.

The sound of knocking interrupted my cry but not completely. I looked to my left and Tangie was staring through the window, a look of concern on her face. "Open the door, Nija," she said softly. Doing as she asked, I popped the locks and Tangie pulled the driver's door open. "What's going on?" she asked gathering me in her arms.

Knowing I wasn't alone allowed me to let my feelings out on her chest. I wailed like a wounded animal because my heart was aching. Crumbling her shirt in my fist with all my might, I cried until I felt like I couldn't breathe.

"Nija, you have to tell me what's wrong! Stop crying, hun so we can figure out how to fix whatever you're going through," Tangie said in a shaky voice.

"They shot him, Tangie! I should've answered the phone instead of trying to make him think I was with another man! He just buried his brother!" I cried harder.

"Who got shot, Nija?" she asked pushing me away from her to look into my face. "Breathe! Crying is not going to help me, help you! I know whatever happened is crippling you, but you have to think about the baby you are carrying."

When she mentioned the baby, I became lightheaded. My head slumped against the seat and I thought I was going to die. The tightness in my chest was intense and it felt like I was having an asthma attack. The car seemed to be closing in on me and I couldn't get a good stream of air in my lungs.

Tangie reeled back and slapped the fuck out of me but I didn't feel the impact of the slap but it caused me to breathe again. Yanking me out of the car by my arm, she wrapped her arms around me as she rubbed my back. With the breath of fresh air, I was able to calm down long enough to tell her what happened.

"I was listening to the voicemail that my child's father left and all of sudden gunshots rang out. He was shot, Tangie and it was all because of me! If he hadn't been on the phone, he would've seen what was about to happen. My best friend was there and she called for an ambulance. I haven't been able to dial on the phone to find out anything!" I cried.

"Where's your phone?" she asked assisted me in sitting down in the car seat. Glancing around, I spotted my phone on the floor of the car at the same time as Tangie. She bent down, grabbed it and handed it to me. "Call somebody, anybody to make sure he's okay."

My hands shook as I unlocked the phone and went straight to Kimmie's name. As the phone rang, I started biting at my nails. It was something I did when I was extremely nervous.

"Nija! Where are you? Ricio's been shot!" Kimmie screamed into the phone.

"I just heard everything on the voicemail. What hospital did they take him to?"

"They took him to Little Company of Mary Hospital but they are preparing him to be transported to The County by helicopter. I'm on my way there now. Nija, I need you to get to the hospital, sis. Where are you?" Kimmie asked.

"I'm at the Applebee's on 95th. I went to dinner with one of my coworkers and had Ricio thinking I was with someone else. I didn't mean to distract him, Kimmie," I cried.

"This is not your fault! Them niggas was gunning for him anyway, even if he wasn't on the phone. I think they were coming for me, because how the hell would they know to be at my house? This shit got Nihiyah written all over it and I'm fucking your sister up on sight! Hold on, Rodrigo is calling on the other line," she said before the line became silent.

A few seconds later she was back. "Sis, Rodrigo is on his way to pick you up. He went to Little Company of Mary instead of the County and he is right up the street. You don't need to be driving right now because I hear it in your voice, you are breaking down. Everything is going to be okay. Do you hear me?"

"It's not going to be okay, Kimmie! I heard him gurgling blood!" I cried.

"Stop it, sis! Ricio is going to be alright, I was there with him. There was no blood coming from his mouth, I swear. He was talking when they put him in the ambulance. The only reason they're transferring him is because The County specializes in gunshot victims. Nothing more, okay."

"I have to see him for myself before I can agree to anything, Kimmie. This is breaking my heart so bad," I wailed as a car pulled slowly into the parking lot. "Rodrigo is here. I'll see you at the hospital soon, sis."

"Nija, stop crying before you make yourself sick. I love you and I'll be waiting for you to pull up," Kimmie replied before hanging up.

Rodrigo pulled behind my car and jumped out along with Angel. "Nija we have to get to the hospital. Angel will drive your whip and you gon' ride with me."

"Okay," was all I could say as I turned to Tangie. "Thank you for being there for me. I probably won't be at work tomorrow—"

"Don't worry about that right now. Go do what you have to do and call me so I'll know you are alright. Keep your head up, Nija," Tangie said walking to her car.

"Nija, give me your keys," Angel said with a thick accent.

Handing over the keys, Rodrigo led me to his car and opened the door so I could get in. Knowing where we were headed, tears clouded my vision and the first drop landed on my arm. Rodrigo hopped in the driver's seat and pulled ahead so Angel could get my car out of the parking spot.

"Nija, let me prepare you before we get to the hospital," Rodrigo said solemnly as he pulled into traffic.

"There's no need, Bro. I heard everything as it happened. All I care about right now is knowing if Ricio is okay," I said wiping away tears.

"You heard everything, how?" he asked glancing briefly in my direction.

"Ricio was leaving me a voicemail because I refused to answer his call. If it wasn't for me, he wouldn't have gotten shot."

"That's far from the truth. Blaming yourself for what happened won't be good for you or the baby, sis. Those niggas were ready to get back at us, we just didn't know when. It's fucked up for them that it had to be my brother, but it could've been any of us. Play that voicemail for me."

"Rodrigo, I can't listen to that voicemail again," I cried.

"I'm not asking you to either. Go to the voicemail and hand over your phone."

He slowed the speed of the car when he put the phone to his ear. Rodrigo didn't miss a beat as he listened to what happened to his brother. He kept replaying the recording and he became angrier each time he started the message over. "This muthafucka!" he yelled as he tossed my phone in my lap.

"Tell me you recognize the voice, bro."

"I do and his ass won't be breathing too much longer. He better pray for forgiveness because his ass is mine," he snarled. "When we get to the hospital, I'm going in with you, but I won't be staying, I have shit to handle."

"We have to make sure Ricio is okay before you can even think about going after anybody."

"I'm not trying to hear none of that shit. Ain't nobody about to wipe out my whole muthafuckin' family while I sit back and do nothing! Sitting in wait is the reason my brother is laid up in a hospital now! The waiting game is over, Nija!" he exclaimed loudly as he entered the expressway hitting the gas.

I knew for a fact that things were about to get worse. There wasn't anyone on this earth that would be able to stop Rodrigo from getting revenge. Prayers were needed for everyone involved, including Rodrigo.

Chapter 2
Angel

My cousins and I had met recently, but one couldn't tell. In the short period of time, we'd become really close. With the shit that was going on with Max's murder, I was ready to go all in and help take the niggas who killed him down. The agitation was high because everybody kept saying, 'it's not the right time, we have to wait', and I didn't agree with it. Me myself would've attacked when my girl was targeted.

Rodrigo and I were at the warehouse that he and Ricio owned when we received the call that Ricio was shot. Cuz was weakened by the news, but only for a few minutes. He locked up and we jumped in his ride while he talked to Kimmie on the phone. Speeding through the streets like a madman, Rodrigo was on a mission to get to his brother's side.

Ending the call so he could concentrate on the road, Rodrigo gripped the steering wheel until his knuckles turned white. I knew how he felt because I was right there with him. When we were a short distance from the hospital, he called Kimmie and asked where she was in the hospital. She explained that Ricio was being transferred to another hospital and he needed to go pick up Nija because she wasn't in any condition to drive herself.

Now, I was trying my best to keep his car in my sights as he weaved in and out of traffic. Rodrigo was a loose cannon and his pistol was about to get a workout. I had his back with whatever he wanted to do. I saw Rodrigo hop two lanes and I was able to get over without tearing Nija's shit up to get over too. He made the next exit and so did I.

My phone rang and I answered it without looking because I couldn't lose sight of Rodrigo's car. "Yeah," I said into the phone.

"Angel, where are you?" my brother Javier asked.

"I'm on my way to the hospital, Ricio was shot."

"Why didn't you call to let us know? What hospital is he in?" he asked.

"It's called Cook County. I don't know the address, I'm trailing Rodrigo. The best I can at least."

"I'm about to look up the address and we'll be there soon."

Javier didn't wait for me to reply and I was glad because I didn't have any more answers for him if he had questions. Rodrigo pulled into the parking lot of the hospital and found a spot immediately. I, on the other hand, wasn't so lucky. I had to circle around and saw someone backing out. Cutting the engine, I got out and locked the doors.

"Thank God, y'all here," Kimmie yelled as she ran across the parking lot. "They rushed him straight to surgery and I haven't heard anything more on his condition."

"Anybody else here besides you?" Rodrigo asked.

"No. I didn't call anybody but you and Nija. I figured you would call everybody else," Kimmie said.

"It's cool, baby girl. Tell me what happened tonight."

"I was home watching tv when I heard a car door slam outside my window. Not thinking anything of it, I didn't pay it any mind. But, when it started sounding like World War III, I jumped up when I heard someone yell something and a car driving off the block fast. When I got outside, I saw Ricio lying on the grass in front of my house.

From what I could see, he was shot in both legs, and his left arm. I know for sure that one of his legs is fucked up. They rushed him to surgery as soon as he arrived."

"What was the gurgling sound I heard on the voicemail?" Nija asked.

"Sis, I didn't hear any gurgling when I listened. Ricio was grunting, that's about all," Rodrigo answered.

"He sounded like he was having a hard time breathing. I'm glad he wasn't seriously hurt. The thought of him being shot scared the fuck out of me. Hopefully we are able to hear something soon."

Nija was trying to be strong but she was nervous as hell. We all were actually but I knew Rodrigo wasn't trying to sit around waiting. Whatever he decided was cool with me because I was on the same shit.

"Nija, stop biting your nails, I'm out. Hit me up when bro comes out of surgery," Rodrigo said backing up toward his ride.

"Wait, where you going?"

"Nija, Call Beast and Sin. Tell them what's going on," he said as he paused ignoring Kimmie's question.

"Rodrigo, I know you hear me talking to you. If you going after whoever did this at least wait until we get word on Ricio. Shit, I wanna roll too because I believe the intended target was me! Ricio just so happened to show up."

"That's more reason for us to go after these fools," I chimed in. "I'm tired of them targeting females to get to men. That's hoe shit!"

"Ain't no more waiting, I can taste the blood as we speak and nothing will stop me from doing what needs to be done," Rodrigo said walking off. "Nija, make that call right now," he shot over his shoulder as he headed for his car with Kimmie on his heels.

"Nija, Rico will be fine. Don't worry about anything we will handle shit tonight," I responded trying to reassure her.

"Watch his back, Angel. Rodrigo is a loose cannon. He acts first and never asks questions."

"I got him. Make that call so someone beside Kimmie will be here with you. I have to go before cuz leaves me," I said leaving her standing there alone.

Javier's rental turned into the lot and sped up to Rodrigo. Cuz automatically drew his Glock aiming it at his head. Kimmie was right with him with her bitch in hand and Javier had two weapons in his face.

"Rodrigo, no!" I screamed across the parking lot as I made a dash in their direction. "That's my brother, cuz!"

"Shid, I see that now," he said lowering his piece. "You better make yourself known and don't roll up on me, fam. Shit could've been bad for ya."

"I see," Javier laughed nervously. "Ya girl was ready to pop my ass too!"

"She's not my girl, but that shit made my dick hard. Kimmie, what you doing with that?" Rodrigo asked.

"Never leave home without her," was her reply. "I still don't think you should go out tonight. Floyd is expecting retaliation."

"And he will get it! I don't give a fuck, he should know how the fuck I get down by now," Rodrigo yelled. "Go back in the hospital, Kimmie. I'm wasting time out here going back and forth with you."

Kimmie put her tool back in her purse and headed across the lot. Rodrigo caught her by the arm and hugged her from behind. I couldn't hear what was said, but the pat on her ass told me there was a little history between the two.

"What's up with you and Kimmie?" I asked when he came back to Javier's car.

"Ain't shit going on with us. I don't know what was going on with her and Sosa, but the way she upped that thang got a nigga wondering," he said glancing back at Kimmie and Nija. "Ain't nothing like a female that's down to get her hands dirty. I know I'm coming back alive so I can find out though."

"You wild, cuz," I laughed. "Aye, bro. Ricio is in surgery so we about to go pay these niggas a visit for the shit they pulled tonight. Follow us because they are about to get it like we do it back home."

"Hell yeah! I'm all for that," Javier said holding up his twin gold plated nine-millimeter berrettas.

"Those muthafuckas are sweet," Rodrigo said holding his hand out for one of the weapons. "How many shots you get with this baby?"

"Seventeen and I stay ready to pop another clip. I'm ready for war, what are we standing around talking guns for? Let's go blow some shit up," Javier said taking his piece back.

"You ain't said nothing but a word. Follow me. We have a stop to make, then it's game time," Rodrigo said jumping in his ride.

"Keep up, bro. This nigga drive like a drag racer," I said before joining Rodrigo. "Where are we going, cuz?" I asked once I closed the door.

"I'm going to scoop Psycho," he said pulling his phone out. "You didn't think we were heading out alone, did you? We killing everything moving around that bitch."

I listened as he called the rest of the crew while he pulled out of the parking spot and onto the road.

Chapter 3
Psycho

I was sitting at the crib chilling, smoking a spiff and sipping a glass of Remy slowly. My father was a weak ass nigga which didn't surprise me because of the people he held high on a pedestal. All the praising he did for the wrong muthafucka got his ass murked by his own son. The shit was on my mind constantly but I wasn't bummed about it.

It was time for us to move in on Floyd's ass because I had a feeling he was about to attack. Shit was too quiet. Unfortunately, the brother I knew nothing about ended up dead because his daddy led his ass in the wrong direction. At that point, I was glad I'd taught myself the way of the streets.

As I drained the last of my Remy, my phone started vibrating on the coffee table. Placing the empty tumbler on the coaster, Sosa's name displayed on the screen. "What up, fam?"

"Gear up I'm on my way to get you. Floyd caught Ricio slippin'. He's in surgery at the County," Rodrigo yelled into my ear.

"Say less. Pull up, I'll be ready," I said springing from the couch.

I was just thinking to myself that we needed to get them niggas and *BAM*, they did some stupid shit to set it off. Waiting wasn't my forte but Ricio needed to get better before we could make a move. Opening the closet door, I removed my gun case and pulled out my Glock .40 as well as my .38 automatic. I made sure both clips were full and grabbed a couple extras in case.

At some point I knew we were going to Floyd's traps to tear shit up. Once I was ready, AK called as I was slipping on my shoes. "Come outside, nigga. It's showtime," he said hanging up.

I snatched my keys from the hook by the door and locked up my crib. Felon, Fats, and AK was in AK's truck. Rodrigo and his cousin Angel were in his whip and his other cousins were in a car behind him. They pulled up on a nigga deep as fuck. Shit must've been bad for the big homie Ricio.

Deciding to hop in the back of Rodrigo's whip to even out the cars, he didn't wait to peel off. "What happened, bro?" I asked.

"Floyd shot Ricio outside of Kimmie's crib. The damage isn't life threatening as far as we know, but bro is going to be alright," Rodrigo replied.

"Hopefully he's all good when we get to the hospital. I can't wait to get at these niggas."

"Get ready because that's exactly what we 'bout to do. I hope you're strapped because we're about to fuck 76th Street up!" Rodrigo said savagely as he hopped on the expressway heading southbound.

"Yeah, I'm prepared," I said sitting back against the seat.

It didn't take long for him to get off the Dan Ryan and took a right onto 75th Street. The sound of clips being loaded and checked were heard throughout the vehicle. I was excited to finally be able to get payback in these streets. A phone rang and Rodrigo pushed the button on the steering wheel to connect it to the Bluetooth.

"What up, Beast?" He asked never taking his eyes off the road.

"Where the fuck you at? Nephew, don't do nothing stupid. Get back to the hospital, now!" Beast's voice boomed through the speakers.

Rodrigo laughed. "You got me fucked up. Yo' ass been soft as fuck around this muthafucka, Beast. Where is the heartless muthafucka that rode beside my father back in the day? I have yet to see his ass. All I've seen is a soft muthafucka that's always trying to be the fuckin' mediator.

How many of us got to be killed before yo' ass snap? The very hospital you are trying to get me back to, is the same one my brother is laid up in because of these niggas! I'm not trying to hear 'this ain't the time' because there's no better time than right now. If you didn't catch that, I won't be at the hospital until I send a few niggas to the morgue," he said ending the call without giving Beast a chance to respond.

Not even two minutes later his phone was ringing again and he continued to drive without answering. Instead he pulled into a vacant lot waiting for the others to join him. We all exited the cars and waited to hear what Rodrigo had planned.

"These Southside niggas don't know shit about us but it would be suspicious if all of us swarmed the block at once," Rodrigo stated. "We'll park in the back alley while Angel and Javier walk around the block to cop some green."

"Hold on, Rodrigo. I've been on this block," AK said interrupting. "When I told you they're getting money, they doing the damn thing. They don't pay attention to who the fuck they serve. Nobody gets turned away, that's gon' be their downfall tonight. I suggest we all drive through, but let Angel and Javier out and the rest of us keep watch until it's time to make our move."

"You right, fam. Everybody, keep your eyes and ears open, we really don't know what's going on over there but we ain't leaving. Angle, Javier, y'all pretend to make a purchase. Distract them, give 'em hell about the price, quality, or whatever. The rest of y'all, follow my lead," Rodrigo said getting back in his whip.

I had no clue how this mission would pan out because there was no real plan in play and that shit worried me. Traveling down 75th, Rodrigo signaled to turn left on Peoria Street. When he turned right on 76th then another right on Sangamon, AK was right. Business was good for them, but not for long. Rodrigo's jaw was clenched and his eyes were pinched.

"I don't give a fuck who didn't pull the trigga, everybody serving is getting this heat, understood?" Rodrigo said to no one in particular. "I'm getting up close and personal, fuck that. Angel, go ahead and make your move. I'm right behind you."

"I'll go with him. Call Javier and tell him to hold fast," I spoke up. "This will give me an idea of what we're working with."

"Sounds good," Rodrigo said calling Javier. "Cuz, stay put. Psycho's rolling with Angel," he paused. "Bet. Get ready."

"Aight, Angel. You locked and loaded, right?" I asked opening the back door.

"My shit stays ready," he said getting out.

As we walked down the street, there was nonstop movement in front of one particular house in the middle of the block. Easy targets were what those niggas were because the only thing they were worried about was money. Not one of them were watching out for anything to pop off. Taking my phone from my hip, I hit Rodrigo up. “This gon’ be smooth. Stay on the line until I start complaining about the green, then move in,” I explained.

“Aight.”

We could’ve walked up blasting but I wasn’t sure if there were any more niggas inside the house or camped out somewhere on the block. Being safe was better than being sorry for moving too soon. They were oblivious to what was about to happen on their turf. One of the dudes spotted us and hurried to finish the transaction he was conducting.

“What y’all need?” he asked quickly as we stood in front of him.

“My boy told me y’all had that fye green over here,” I replied.

“Who the fuck is yo’ boy? You know what? It don’t even matter. How much you talking?”

“Let me get an ounce. I’on want no weak shit either,” I clapped back at him.

“Ain’t shit weak this way, homie. Ya boy already told you I got that fire,” he said pulling a baggie from his pocket. “Smell this, nigga,” he boasted. “An ounce gon’ run you three hunnid.”

Taking the bag from him, I knew off bat the shit was bunk. There was no scent at all in the air. I didn’t smell nothing until my nose was practically inside the baggie.

“Nigga, y’all out here selling grass food! I can tell right now, this shit ain’t hittin’ on nothin’! You want three hunnid for some muthafuckin’ horse hay? Get the fuck outta here!” I said throwing that bullshit on the ground.

“Damn, fam why you gotta be disrespectful with the shit. I don’t know what you’re used to but that type of shit will get yo’ ass fucked up,” he said as he bent down to retrieve that weak shit he called weed.

I pulled my Glock and placed the nozzle to the back of his head. “Raise yo’ ass up and don’t try to be a super hero,” I growled.

“What the fuck! You muthafuckas jack boys?”

"Nah, we murderers', nigga. Floyd signed your death certificate, night night muthafucka!"

Boc! Boc! Boc!

Watching his body fall to the pavement, I heard feet pounding against the pavement and Angel's .45 creating a beat of its own as he backed up with his arm extended. I joined the party as niggas came out the woodworks with pistols blasting. I dived between two parked cars and took cover.

Tat! Tat! Tat! Tat! Tat! Tat! Tat! Tat! Tat! Tat! Tat! Tat!

I knew that sound oh so well. Precious was clearing the street with her crazy ass nigga standing ten toes behind her. Peeking out from behind the car I saw a nigga lying on the sidewalk with his brains splattered. My head jerked behind me as I heard a nigga running past the car I was ducked behind. Angel stepped out and immediately filled his stomach with lead.

It sounded like a war on that block and me and Angel ran back toward Rodrigo who was using niggas as target practice. In the distance sirens could be heard so we didn't have much time to get away from the scene. Out the corner of my eye I saw a nigga running towards Rodrigo. Me, Angel, and Javier unloaded our clips on him before he was able to get a shot off.

"Let's go!" Alexander yelled.

"This nigga ain't dead. I didn't kill his ass purposely, help me get him in the trunk of my car," Rodrigo barked. "AK, head to the warehouse! Get out of here!"

It took the three of us to throw his big ass in the trunk before we loaded up and sped off the block. Rodrigo slowed down a bit because there was a line of squad cars coming toward us in the opposite direction. Pulling to the right, he waited until they passed and hightailed it back to the expressway.

***

We rode for about twenty minutes before we pulled up to the warehouse. AK's truck was parked outside along with the car Javier was driving. Rodrigo parked in front and got out and walked to the steel door. When he entered, the huge steel delivery door started going up and he ducked down and came back to the car. Hopping back into the driver's seat, he drove his whip right into the warehouse and cut the engine.

AK was standing beside a table that was placed in the middle of the room. There were leather arm and leg straps attached to it as well as a smaller table with other tools sprawled on top. These niggas had set up a torture chamber in the small amount of time it took for us to get to the warehouse.

Rodrigo popped the trunk and the big burly dude jumped out swinging wildly. "Let me out of this muthafucka!" he screamed landing a punch to Rodrigo's head. The hit didn't faze fam one bit though. Head butting the dude, Rodrigo grabbed him by the throat and pressed hard on his windpipe.

"I will kill yo' muthafuckin' ass in this bitch, nigga!" he snarled as he watched the veins protrude from dude's forehead. "Walk yo ass across the room!"

"Ack. Ack," was all he could force out of his mouth.

Rodrigo pushed him in the direction he wanted him to go and followed closely behind him. Trying to catch his breath, the dude coughed and sputtered as if he was dying. I walked around the other side of the car just as he spun around and raised his fist. My Glock was in his face before he could throw that muthafucka forward.

"Don't even try it, nigga. Get yo ass on that table," I gritted.

"I'm not getting up there!"

"Oh, you not? We'll see," Angel said as he and Javier grabbed his ass and threw him on the table.

He was kicking and screaming as AK and Alexander buckled the straps around his ankles, while Angel held his arms so me and Javier could secure them too. After he was restrained, Rodrigo stepped forward and looked down at him.

"Where the fuck is Floyd?" he asked calmly.

"I'm not telling you shit, nigga!"

"That's cool. Yo' ass gon' tell me everything I want to know by the time I'm finished with yo' fat ass," Rodrigo laughed as he walked around the smaller table eyeballing the many tools that were lying upon it. Choosing an icepick and a scalpel, he twirled both around in his hands a couple times before walking back to the larger table. Rodrigo ran the scalpel along dude's pants leg, cutting the fabric up to his groin area. He did the same with the other pants leg and paused when he finished. "You want to tell me who shot my brother tonight?"

"Come on, man. Stop playing with that shit!"

"Who's to say I'm playing? My brother getting shot is not a game, muthafucka!" Rodrigo said carving a circle into his thigh.

"Arrrrrggggghhhh!" he screamed fighting to get out of the restraints.

"Now, do you want to tell me what I want to know?"

"Fuck yo' brother!"

"Wrong answer," Rodrigo sneered jabbing him repeatedly with the icepick. "Fuck my brother? Nah, fuck u!" he screamed with every movement of his arm.

"Arrrrrghhhh! Arrrrrggghhh! Don't fold Erv. Don't fold."

"We got a name, fellas!" Rodrigo cheered. "Erv, my man. I got all night to play pin the tail on the donkey."

Sweat was pouring from Erv's forehead as tears ran from his eyes into his ears. Whimpering loudly, he tried hard to free himself from the restraints but they were attached to his wrists tightly. "Please let me go! I—I don't know anything!"

I leaned over Erv and whispered, "You know something. Stop lying and tell us what we want to know. What. Happened. Tonight. Nigga!"

Erv didn't open his mouth, instead he opted to cry it out. His bitch ass was pissing me off because crying was not going to get him out of this situation. I held my hand out and Rodrigo gave me the scalpel.

"Let me give yo' pussy ass something to cry about," I said slicing his right ear off.

"AAAHHHH! Fuck! Okay, Okay!" Erv screamed fighting against the restraints. "I'll tell you!" he howled breathing heavily.

"Get to talking then!" Rodrigo growled.

"Floyd told me to drive to an address Nihiyah gave him to find her sister. We were only going to scoop her up so y'all would come looking for her. When he saw Ricio's car, he had me to speed down the street when he got out of the car and shot him. I didn't know he was going to shoot the nigga, I swear," Erv cried.

"I find that hard to believe, but whateva. Where is Floyd's bitch ass now?" Rodrigo asked.

"He had me drop him off at the crib. That's the last I've heard from him because I went to the trap to make some money."

"Give me names and addresses of the niggas that were involved in the shooting at the cemetery."

"All them niggas dead—"

"Lie one more time and I'll end your life right now, muthafucka! Only two of them niggas dead and one is in the hospital," Rodrigo yelled cutting him off.

"All three of them niggas dead, bro. Shake died Monday when I went to the hospital to find out his condition," I said correcting him.

"Sucks to be that nigga," he said laughing. "If you want to be next, keep that information to yourself. To live all you have to do is simply comply with what I asked for."

"I don't want to die! I got a family to live for!"

"And my brothers didn't? Nigga save that shit! You got five seconds to start talking. One. Two. Three. Four—"

"Rello, Quis, Kat, and Quake are the only ones left beside myself. If you found my trap, I'm quite sure you know about the others. All them niggas be at their shit faithfully," Erv blurted out before Rodrigo could get to five.

"Mateo, grab that notebook and write down the addresses he's about to give me. I'm listening nigga.

Erv recited the addresses for his homeboys along with additional information on family members and dip offs. I was proud of the nigga but laughing at his ass at the same time because he thought he was walking out of this bitch. He's from the streets and should've known better, but hey, wishful thinking works sometimes. Just not in this case.

Once he was done, Rodrigo patted him on the arm and turned away. Throwing the icepick on the table, he picked up a bottle of rubbing alcohol. Screwing the top off the bottle, he turned back around with his eyes trained on Erv.

Dousing the flammable liquid all over Erv's body, Rodrigo emptied the bottle and threw it on the floor. "What are you doing?" Erv screamed.

"Yo' ass wasn't as innocent as you portrayed yourself to be. Your hand was all the way in everything that took place, right along with Floyd. Oh, you thought you would live? Nigga, you thought wrong! All you muthafuckas gon' die by the hands of Rodrigo Vasquez!" he said pulling a butane lighter from his pocket.

"Tell Shake I send my regards, bitch!" he sneered throwing the lighter onto Erv's alcohol-soaked body.

Chapter 4
Floyd

Getting at Ricio was the best feeling I've had in a long time. When I went to the prison to deliver Big Jim the news about Shake's death, I didn't expect him to react the way he did. Big Jim beat the fuck out of me and I couldn't defend myself because I was higher than a muthafucka. I'd tried to call him but his phone was going straight to voicemail. That only meant he was in the hole behind my fuck up.

I had a strong chance of getting back into his good graces by handling that nigga Ricio. Erv dropped me off at the crib and I was chilling while fighting the craving of inhaling the white girl up my nose. Staring at the five lines I had on a plate, I picked it up and walked down the hall to the bathroom. Before I could get halfway down the hall, my phone started ringing back in the living room. It stopped ringing by the time I got to it but started ringing again soon after.

"What up, Rello?"

"Get over to Sangamon! Everybody is dead and we can't find Erv!" he screamed hysterically into the phone.

"What the fuck happened?" I asked scrambling around not knowing what I was looking for. "And what you mean you can't find Erv? That's his trap!"

"One of the regulars said some niggas came through blasting. They threw Erv in the trunk of a car and peeled out before twelve came through. I came right over and there's red tape and markers up and down the street. It's about a hunnid shell casings on the block. Bodies covered waiting on the meat wagon to pick 'em up."

"That muthafuckin' Sosa! I screamed throwing a vase into the wall.

"Them niggas in hiding, Floyd. What makes you think they had anything to do with it?"

"I shot his muthafuckin' brother earlier tonight! We're not beefin' with nobody other than them, niggas. I'm on my way, call everybody and tell them to close shop," I said snatching my keys from the coffee table.

"We're all here already, you just get here!" Rello said hanging up.

I destroyed my living room because I knew deep down Erv was dead. Sprinting out the door, I hopped in my car and pushed above the speed limit down the residential street. Every light I pulled up to turned red now that I was trying to get where the fuck I was going.

Finally making it to the expressway, the inside of the car was too quiet. Hitting the power button on the radio, the DJ on WGCI was talking about the shooting I was breaking the law to get to.

"Man, my city is out of control! Y'all listen to what I'm about to say and this shit is coming from the heart. Yeah, I'm cussin', might even lose my job behind it, but you mufuckas need to put the guns down! It's not my business what they were doing on the 9600 block of south Sangamon, ten people were killed at once! This hurts my heart that this has become a norm in Chicago.

Y'all making the funeral homes rich and leaving these babies out in this fucked up world without mother's and father's! Stop this bullshit! Go to commercial."

I felt where the DJ was coming from, but this shit was personal. It wasn't going to stop until everybody on one side or the other died. The only muthafucka safe in the situation was Big Jim. He couldn't be touched locked in a cell.

Nihiyah crossed my mind as I got closer to the Southside. Her hoe ass hadn't called to tell me anything about her sister. I gave her a time period and she'd been ghost. It was good because soon as I see her, I was going to beat the fuck out of her ass.

Traveling down 75th Street, traffic was thick so I knew folks were being nosy trying to find out what was going on. I turned down Peoria and the street were blocked off at 76th by police vehicles. Parking my ride, I decided to walk to Sangamon Street. The media was all on the story and they were eating it up. I stopped and hit Rello up on my phone but had to hang up because the two bitch ass detectives, Bradley and Cooper rolled up on me.

"Well, well, well. If it ain't Floyd Douglas. Why doesn't it surprise me to see you at a murder scene?" Cooper said.

"Man, what you want? All these people out here and you fucking with me! Go do yo' damn job cause y'all ain't investigating shit over here," I snapped.

"Why are you so hostile? You're guilty, huh?" Cooper laughed. "It's all good. We're going to allow you niggers to keep killing each other. Save us the trouble."

"Get the fuck away from me with that nigger shit, punk ass bitch! You real tough with that gun on your hip!" I was pissed because there were too many people around for me to kill his ass so I just walked away from him.

"Don't go too far, I'll be seeing you soon, Douglas," Cooper called out behind me.

Ignoring him, I kept walking to see what was really going on with my people. When I reached the corner of 76th and Sangamon a medical examiner's truck was driving away from the scene. A woman was fighting off a couple of people that were attempting to calm her down. As I got closer, I recognized her as one of the lil homies mama.

"Noooooo! They can't take my baby! Why did this happen to him? Somebody knows something! Fuck that no snitchin' shit, talk got dammit! My son is dead and I want justice!" his mama cried. "I'm tired of this shit! Y'all need to learn how to fight your differences out. Put the guns down, coward ass punks!"

Byron better known on the streets as Lil B was a tough nigga. I was all for his mother being distraught about him dying. At seventeen Lil B could out sell some of the vets when it came to weed and crack. He stayed strapped and knew how to handle whatever he chose to pack for the day. The media crowded around his mama and I knew she was feeding them a story about how he was a churchgoing young man that did no wrong. That was far from the truth, but whatever.

I heard the distinct whistle that we used to communicate in my ears and looked in the direction it came from. Rello was summoning me across the street along with the rest of the crew. Looking both ways before crossing the street, I jogged over to where they were waiting.

"What info you got for me?" I asked with my hands tucked in my hoodie.

"It was definitely Sosa. Jay was over at the trap picking up some work when the shit went down. They didn't pay him any attention I guess because he's just a kid. I asked was he sure it was Sosa and he said yeah because he remembered him from over on 26th street," Rello explained.

"Yeah, Jay had seen them niggas before, so he would know. Did he see them put Erv in the trunk of the car?"

"Nah, he said he ran down the street to get away from the gunfire. It was like a war zone according to him. Why didn't you keep us in the know about you poppin' this nigga's brother?" Rello asked angrily.

Glancing around to make sure nobody was within earshot of us talking, I responded to his question. "They didn't know shit about where the traps were out here. I didn't expect for them to come gunnin' for them."

"You have to expect the unexpected nigga! You were probably being followed every muthafuckin' day since the day we shot up the cemetery. Yo' ass supposed to be the head of this operation and you ain't doing a good job at holding your empire down. Big Jim picked the wrong nigga for the job."

"Don't start questioning me about how I handle shit, Rello. There's a lot to figure out and I'm on it. I have to move a certain way because the pigs are breathing down my back. They swear I was involved with this shit," I said rubbing my head.

"You are involved! This yo' beef! We didn't have shit to do with them niggas, we do now though. They won't eliminate us like they did them muthafuckas out west. I'm gon' find some shit out on my own. I refuse to be a sitting duck, waiting around for you to tell me what's going on. You've already proved that we're on a need to know basis and that don't sit well with me," Rello said heatedly.

"I got this don't worry," I said backing away.

"I'm far from worried but you should be. If anything happens to anyone in my family, I'm coming for yo' ass. Believe that shit."

Rello's words danced in my head as I headed back to my car. There was nothing more I could do standing around watching people cry and police moving around examining shit. This shit just went to a whole other level and I didn't see it stopping anytime soon.

Chapter 5
Sin

Beast and I were laid up watching television with Giovanni lying close by in his bassinet. We hadn't had a night of relaxation since Max's death and I welcomed it with opened arms. His hands were roaming up and down my thigh while I nestled on his chest. In my mind I wanted him to touch my lady parts but he was always worrying about the baby being in the room. It was time for me to talk to Madysen about spending more time with *her* baby because a bitch needed a dick down with no interruptions.

Shifting my body so my ass pressed against him. Beast turned his body and positioned his dick on my ass. I grabbed his hand and placed it on my kitty and his fingers immediately strummed my clit.

"Mmmmm," I moaned.

"Sin, you know the baby's in here, right?"

"Beast, I'm not trying to hear that shit. He won't remember nothing that happens in this room, he's an infant. Plus, he's sleeping. You better knock the dust off this pussy before I have a whole attitude tonight."

"Somebody been missing the dick, I see," he chuckled in my ear before slipping his tongue inside. "I guess I better put out that fire for you, baby."

He turned me onto my back and kissed me deeply while playing in my love box. I instantly came on his fingers and he brought them to my lips. Sucking his fingers like they were his dick, I got real nasty and it turned him on. The smaller Beast had awakened and I knew then, I would get what I'd been craving. Kissing my lips once more, Beast trailed down my body with his tongue.

Taking one of my ample breasts into his mouth and suckled while rolling the other between his fingertips. My body was hot and I wanted more than what he was giving me. Slightly pushing his head to go lower, he nibbled on my nipple but didn't move in the direction I was guiding him.

"Eat my pussy, Beast," I said seductively.

"That's what you want, Sin?" he asked staring into my eyes. "You want me to put my tongue deep inside this sweet shit?"

"Yes," I replied lowly as he rubbed up and down my slit as he moved slowly toward my kitty.

Beast took his time gliding his tongue repeatedly across my clit before taking it in his mouth and sucking roughly. He knew exactly how much pressure I liked applied and he delivered. My stomach muscles started clinching and I was on the verge of cummin' down his throat. My thighs locked around his head and he pushed them apart as he shook his head back and forth with my pearl between his lips. My back rose from the bed and my waterfall escaped with ease.

"Turn that ass over," he demanded as he got up on his knees stroking his joint as we waited to entered me from the back. Sliding into my wetness slowly, Beast was making love to the pussy but I wanted him to fuck me. Pushing back on his tool, I bounced my ass harder as he allowed me to take control.

"Oooo shit, baby!" I moaned grasping the sheets.

My ass jiggled with every movement I made and Beast smack me on my cheeks hard. "Yes, spank me, daddy!" I cried as I felt his dick in the crevices of my stomach. I reach between my legs and started rubbing my bud vigorously and he reached down and grabbed my arm pinning it behind my back.

"I got this shit, Sin. I don't need yo' muthafuckin' help! Now throw that ass back like I taught you."

I plowed my ass against his pelvis and he used his free hand to stick his thumb in my ass. He knew I loved that shit and it only made me go buck wild on his dick. I felt my nut coming to a head and the faster I bounced, the deeper his thumb went. "Ohhhh shit, Erique!" I screamed. He let my arm go and pushed me down further on the bed by my neck, making me arch my back even more.

Before I could cum. Beast snatched his dick and his thumb out of both holes simultaneously and I plopped face first on the mattress and I hadn't even released. Helping me turn over onto my back, Beast lifted my legs and pinned them behind my head. At times his ass forgets that I'm not that young nineteen-year-old he taught all those tricks to back in the day. He held my legs as he plunged in and out of my cookie jar. Every time he came out, my pussy farted and that shit felt good.

"Yeah, that muthafucka's talking to me. She knows what time it is." He was right because I was about to squirt all over his black ass and he better be ready. Beast leaned down and our tongues connected like magnets. "I can kiss you forever. I love the way your lips feel against mine," he said into my mouth.

He was fucking me hard and I held on the bottom of the headboard so I could meet him thrust for thrust. My phone started ringing but I wasn't thinking about it at that moment. Beast hit every spot in my twat and I was working up a sweat. My phone rang again and I was willing it to stop because it wasn't trying to fuck up my nut that had built up.

My phone was chiming continuously but I was almost at my peak. Beast was delivering quick deep strokes that hit my gspot repeatedly. The muscles in my stomach tightened and the dam broke on my tunnel of love, forcing my back to levitate upward.

"Aaaaaah shit, baby! Yes!" I screamed out as I clawed his back. My nectar spewed out and my sugary walls gripped his stick with an anaconda vice grip.

"Fuck, Sin," Beast growled softly in my ear as his body released his semen into my love box. His dick became flaccid and slipped out and my juices glided between the crack of my ass. "That should hold you over for a minute. Now see who's blowing ya shit up. It bet not be yo' side nigga, he knows not to interrupt my time. Check his ass," Beast said rolling over getting out the bed.

"You know damn well ain't nobody calling my phone that don't have no business doing so. Maybe I should go find a suitable side nigga to see how you'll really feel when he hit me up," I smirked.

"That would be the day you get fucked up. Don't play with me, Sin," he said with an attitude as he glared down at me.

"Now you want to get mad because I want to bring the bullshit you conjured up to life. Go wash your ass, nigga. Quit saying shit you know is false and your feelings won't be hurt," I laughed as my phone rang once again.

"Hey, Nija," I spoke into the phone.

"Sin, you and Beast need to get to the County hospital—"

"Are you okay?" I asked seriously.

"I'm trying to hold it together but it's not me you need to worry about, it's Ricio. Sin, he was shot. I haven't gotten word on his condition yet, he's still in surgery."

"What happened? Beast! Beast!" I yelled.

"He was getting out of his car by Kimmie's house and someone shot him. Rodrigo left with Angel and his other cousins. We tried to stop him but he wouldn't listen."

Giovanni started crying and Beast rushed out of the bathroom leaving a trail of water behind him. He went to the bassinet and patted the baby on the back to calm him. Tears escaped my eyes as I tried to find my voice to respond to Nija.

"Sin, who's on the phone and why are you crying?" he asked sitting on the edge of the bed.

"Nija, we are on our way. Call me the minute you hear anything if we aren't there. I got Rodrigo, hopefully I get in touch with him before he does anything irrational. Stay calm, I'm on my way, baby," I said hopping up from the bed and tossed the phone on the dresser.

"Sin, slow down! Tell me what's going on," Beast demanded standing to his feet.

I took a deep breath and wiped my face. "Ricio was shot and he's at the County. Nija and Kimmie are there right now. Rodrigo was there but left with them damn Vasquez boys. Beast I know they are about to kill anything moving out there.

"Fuck!" he yelled scaring the baby again. Giovanni wailed loudly and Beast reached down and picked him up. "How is he?"

"Nija doesn't know anything right now, he's in surgery. Call Rodrigo and talk him out of retaliating. The police are hot on his ass right now."

"Go clean up and get dressed. I'm about to take the baby downstairs, I'll be ready to go in ten minutes tops. So, move ya ass. I'll hit nephew and put a bug in his ear," he said grabbing his phone heading for the door.

"Um, baby. You may want to put some clothes on, your dick swinging freely around this muthafucka." Beast looked down and shook his head. Placing the baby in the bassinet, he pulled on a pair of jogging pants and threw on a black t-shirt. Scooping the baby and his phone up, he rushed out of our bedroom.

I hurried into the bathroom and jumped in the shower. Washing my ass good enough to cleanse the important parts of my body, I got out and dried off quickly. Gargling with mouthwash, I spit in the sink and rushed to my closet. Pulling a pink jogging suit from the hanger, I pulled the pants over my hips and walked to the dresser to get a sports bra and a pair of socks. After pulling the bra over my breasts, I put the sweatshirt on and pulled the socks onto my feet.

As I was slipping my feet into my sneakers, Beast's voice boomed through the hall. "Where the fuck you at? Nephew, don't do nothing stupid. Get back to the hospital now!" he said walking into the bedroom.

"You got me fucked up. Yo' ass been soft as fuck around this muthafucka, Beast. Where is the heartless nigga that rode beside my father back in the day? I have yet to see his ass. All I've seen is a soft muthafucka that's always trying to be the fuckin' mediator.

How many of us got to be killed before yo' ass snap? The very hospital you are trying to get me back to, is the same one my brother is laying up in because of these niggas! I'm not trying to hear 'this ain't the time' because there's no better time than right now. If you didn't catch that, I won't be at the hospital until I send a few niggas to the morgue," he said ending the call without giving Beast a chance to respond.

"No his ass didn't hang up!" I said stalking to the dresser to get my phone. Hitting Rodrigo's name in my recent call list, I listened to the phone ring several times before I got his voicemail. I was livid because he ignored my call purposely. "Beat his ass, Beast!"

"You don't have to tell me what to do. I'm three steps ahead of you on that one. Sosa has never been disrespectful like the nigga that's taking over for him out here today. But I'm fucking both of them up on account of his reckless ass."

Beast put on his shoes and we headed for the stairs. I tried calling Rodrigo several more times but got the same results. When I stepped off the last step, Madysen came out of her room carrying Gio in her arms.

"What's going on?" she asked.

"We are on our way to—"

"We have to make a run. Did you feed Gio?" I cut in before Beast could tell her the truth.

"Yeah, he's fighting his sleep but I came out to make sure everything was okay. I heard Beast yelling upstairs."

"I'm good. There's nothing to worry about. Give us a call if you need us and we'll head back. Me and Sin just need some fresh air."

"Have a good time, y'all deserve a break from me. Thanks for everything," she said smiling.

"You don't have to thank us, Madysen. We don't need a break from you, we are here to help you anyway we can," Beast said giving her a half hug. "Don't' ever think you are a burden, okay?"

Madysen shook her head yes. "I'll see y'all in the morning. I doubt I'll be awake when you return," she said walking back to her room.

We headed to the garage and Beast hit the button to open the garage door. Once we were settled into the car, he stared at me strangely. "Why did you cut me off in the middle of my sentence?"

"Erique, we are leaving her alone with Gio. Telling her Ricio was shot isn't the best thing to do. Her mind is already fucked up, the last thing I want her to do is panic and harm Gio or herself," I explained.

"Damn, I didn't think about that. Thank you for always thinking for both of us at the right time," he said squeezing my hand.

"I'll always have your back, baby. Can we leave now? My nephew needs me."

"Say less, beautiful one," he said backing out of the garage.

The way Beast drove we arrived at the hospital in twenty minutes. I was still unable to get in touch with Rodrigo. He done fucked up because Beast is pissed and there was no telling how this would play out. As we walked across the parking lot to the entrance of the hospital, Nija and Kimmie was standing out front.

"Have you heard anything about Ricio yet?" I asked approaching the two of them.

"Yes, the doctor just came out a few minutes ago. He said the surgery went well. They had to remove bullets from his left side and his leg. The wound in his shoulder was why they had to conduct surgery. Ricio was lucky because the shooter used a low powered weapon.

They had to repair his bloods vessels in the shoulder area, tissue and muscle damage as well. Ricio will have to undergo extreme physical therapy to prevent loss of mobility in that arm," Nija explained.

"Ricio is being moved to a private room and someone will be down once he is settled," Kimmie added.

"That's good to hear. Have either one of you heard from Rodrigo?" Beast asked.

"I've called but he's not answering," Kimmie said. "I'm scared because he's not himself.

Beast laughed, "he hasn't been himself in a while, but he gon' wish he chose his words carefully tonight. Come on before we miss the opportunity to see my nephew."

Chapter 6
Ricio

The pain that took over my body was one I'd never experienced in my life. Struggling to open my eyes I panicked when I couldn't complete the once simple act. A beeping sound rang in my ears uncontrollably, then something tightened around my arm.

"You're okay, Mr. Vasquez. Stay calm," an unknown voice spoke softly. "Your surgery was successful, now the healing begins."

"Surgery? What happened to me?" I asked. The beeping stopped and the pressure released from my arm. Another thing that got my attention was the woman never answered my question. Instead, moved the covers as if she was tucking me in.

I'll be back to check on you later. I know you can hear me, Mr. Vasquez, your family is in the waiting room anxious to see you," she said tapping my hand.

The door closed and I was left alone with my thoughts. Getting out of my car in front of Kimmie's house was the vision that played before me. I remembered calling Nija a couple times after talking to her on the phone. She didn't come out and say she was having dinner with a nigga, but she didn't have to. I already knew.

If it was a female, she would've said that shit. As I was leaving a message to Nija's voicemail, a car speeding up the street caught my attention. My slow reaction fucked me up though. The first shot entered my arm and it felt like hot coal on my skin. The bullets kept coming and I hit the ground dropping my phone in the grass.

"You's a dead muthafucka now!"

Floyd's voice rang in my ears vividly. I knew for a fact he was the person that shot me. He fucked up because he didn't wait around to see if I was dead. I wasn't stupid, I played possum and acted like I was just that, dead.

Kimmie is the one I owed my life to. She sprang into action by getting me the help I needed to get to the hospital. I have a problem with not knowing what was going on with me. Why I couldn't formulate a word from my mouth whereas it could be heard. Everything went dark instantly and sleep took over.

"His injuries are not life threatening. We are waiting for him to come to from the anesthesia we used to put him under to perform the surgery." I heard the nurse explaining. "Our main concern is the nerve damage in his shoulder. We had to make a long incision to repair the muscle tissue as well as the nerve vessels. Mr. Vasquez will have to undergo extensive physical therapy to strengthen his arm."

"Does it typically take this long for one to come down from the medication?" I recognized the voice off top as Sin's. "He hasn't moved since we've entered the room." I loved Sin because she wanted to know everything and whomever better have an answer for her.

"It actually depends on the patient. He may wake up in the next thirty minutes or it may be tomorrow, we won't know until it happens. It's after visiting hours and I will allow you guys to stay for an hour, then you all will have to return between 8am and 8pm."

"Thanks, we appreciate that," Beast said in his deep baritone as the nurse exited the room. "Nija, have you heard from Rodrigo yet?"

My heartbeat quickened at the mention of Nija's name. I tried hard to open my eyes to no prevail. Once again, the machines went wild.

"Nurse, come quick!" Kimmie yelled. "His heart machine is going off."

"He's okay," I heard the nurse respond. "It has been happening when he gets excited, he can hear you all but can't respond the way he wants. There's no need to worry." I wanted to tell them to chill the fuck out because they were panicking like a nigga was about to cash out.

"Ricio, stop fighting and let your body relax. We're here with you, baby." Nija said kissing the top of my head.

The machine went back to normal and Beast had jokes. "Damn, you got that nigga in check even when he's unconscious," he laughed.

"Beast, I'm really not in the mood to laugh. I don't have control of Ricio in anyway at all. We are still friends and we will have to be cordial for the next eighteen years when this baby is born. Other than that, there's nothing more to it," Nija threw back. "I just want him to come out of this situation close to how he was before he got shot."

"Back that up a couple sentences," Beast exclaimed with his hands up and head held back as if he was praising God. "Go back to the baby part. When the hell did this come about and do Ricio know about the baby?"

"Yes, he knows. I found out the other day when Kimmie forced me to take a test. I went to the doctor and it was confirmed that I'm almost two months along."

"Why am I just hearing about this?" Sin asked with her hand on her hip.

"I haven't told anyone. I didn't know what I was going to do about the pregnancy. Ricio getting shot changed my train of thought about getting rid of my baby. life is too short. I have to live with the choice I made for myself."

Nija made my will to fight that much stronger when I heard her say she was keeping our baby. If I was able, I would've wrapped her in my arms and hugged her tightly never to let her go again. She had my heart from the day I met her, it took something drastic to happen for me to realize she was the woman I wanted by my side for the long haul.

"It surprises me to know that you had doubts about going through the pregnancy, Nija. I understand you and Ricio has gone through your ups and downs lately and the things you refuse to tolerate, I agree with wholeheartedly. You stood on your shit and I'm proud of you for doing so. At some point, the two of you should sit down and talk like adults."

"Sin, I agree. When the time comes, I'll be all for it. But enough about me and Ricio, to answer your question, Beast I haven't spoken to Rodrigo. Maybe you should try calling one of the other guys, I'm sure somebody will answer their phone."

"I talked to him when I went to the bathroom earlier," Kimmie said lowly.

"You mean to tell me that nigga called you and not us?" Beast huffed.

"I actually called to check on him."

"You calling him don't make the shit no better. Sin's been blowin' his line up since Nija called about Ricio. He'll see me sooner than later—"

"Beast, it's not Kimmie's fault Rodrigo has been ignoring my calls. Jumping on her about his bullshit is wrong," Sin said checking her man. "Kimmie, I apologize for Erique's outburst. Thanks for letting us know that he's still breathing. If you speak with him again, tell him to call me, please."

"No problem and I will," she replied.

The door open and the nurse interrupted the conversation. "You guys have to leave now. I hate to make you all leave but it's policy," she said.

"We understand and it's all good. I want every faculty member to keep a close eye one my nephew. No one other than the people on the list I'm about to write out for you are allowed in this room. If there are any problems, call me as soon as possible. My name is Erique."

"Okay, I'll let everyone know that's working tonight as well as document it in his chart. I'll be his nurse for the night so nothing will happen to him on my watch. I'm Brittany by the way," she said flirtatiously.

"And I will beat your ass! Concentrate on the words he spoke upon and a little less on his appearance," Sin snapped.

"I—I'm sorry, I didn't mean any disrespect, ma'am."

"Don't be sorry, be careful. Let me leave this muthafucka before I catch a case," Sin said leaving the room and slammed the door behind her.

"Here's the list. I'm serious, take care of my family," Beast's voiced boomed through the room.

"I got him, you have my word on that," the nurse said.

A soft hand held mine and I knew right away it was Nija. Resting her head on my chest, I felt the warmth of her tears soak through the hospital gown I wore. I couldn't console her and that tugged at my heartstrings.

"I'll be back tomorrow. Open those eyes for me Ricio. Your heart is beating strong, but it doesn't compare to hearing your voice and seeing that sexy ass smile. I love you," Nija said covering my lips with hers and raised up off me.

"Be easy nephew, I'll see you later. When I get back, I want to hear you speaking to a nigga," Beast said tapping lightly on my leg.

The door opened and closed and the room became deathly quiet and I drifted off to sleep thinking about how I was going to kill a muthafucka for halting my movements.

Chapter 7
Latorra

Knowing James was in the hole eased my mind about not having to run into him at the prison. The way he tried to strong arm me pissed me off. I didn't give a damn if he was my father, his ass wasn't there for me my whole fuckin' life. How dare he threaten me.

My supervisor finally left me the hell alone and allowed me to work the front desk again. It was kind of slow and I was ready to take my ass home. The book *Flatline* by *KS Oliver* was helping the time pass. The story was based on true events and I couldn't imagine going through everything Kai had to endure.

The desk phone rang jolting me back to reality. It was four in the morning, "who the hell calling this muthafucka?" I asked out loud. Placing my book face down on the counter, I picked up the receiver and held it to my ear.

"Danville Correctional Facility, this is Latorra speaking. How may I help you?" I said in my best white girl voice.

"Bitch!" Tammy's voice screeched into my ear. "I got the tea, bih! —"

"Hold on, let me get somebody to cover my post and I'll call you right back," I said before she could say anything more on the recorded line. Quickly pushing the button on my walkie, "Smith to anyone available."

"Thomas here, Smith what do you need?"

"Would you come cover for me so I can take a thirty, please?"

"I'm on the way, standby," he responded.

Racing to the locked drawer where I kept my car keys. I scooped them up and waited until Thomas walked out the door that led to the Blocks. I didn't give him time to get into the room behind the desk before I made a beeline for the exit. Speed walking to my car, I had several missed calls from Tammy even though she knew I never took my phone inside the prison. Tapping on one of the missed calls I counted the number of rings it took for her to answer.

"Latorra! Shit done got bad on the Southside. Somebody went through 76th and Sangamon and aired it out! All them niggas dead.

The dude that runs the trap is missing and nobody has seen him since he was dumped in a trunk after the shooting. Word on the street is they know who did it, but ain't nobody saying no names. I was at the club sippin' after my last set when Chanie and Silk started talking about Ricio getting shot."

I went numb when she mentioned Ricio getting shot. My heart stopped beating for a split second and my air supply was cut short. Drinking from the bottle of Pineapple Crush that I had left in the cupholder, Tammy screamed my name.

"Latorra are you still there? Latorra!"

"I'm here. You caught me off guard when you said Mauricio got shot. When did this happen? Is he alright?" I asked.

"Everything happened last night. I don't know his condition or if he even made it. Being the Inspector Gadget bitch that I am, I've put two and two together. The trap that was hit belongs to Big Jim. Floyd and his people killed Ricio's brother, his burial got shot up and Shake and some other niggas died behind that. Now Ricio gets shot and one of Floyd's spots gets hit, Ricio's people did this shit, Latorra."

"You don't know that for sure, Tam. Don't go spreading rumors."

"I'd bet money the shit I just ran down to you is gonna be facts! Mark my words, boo. Find out where ya man is and check on him. I'm going to bed because I've been shaking my ass all damn night," Tammy said yawning. "I'll talk to you later, girl. Keep me posted."

Tammy hung up and I sat in my car for another fifteen minutes. Even though I felt Ricio did me dirty, I still didn't wish bad on him. Hopefully Tammy had her information misconstrued. Ricio and his family has been through too much already.

"Smith, are you alright out there?" Thomas asked over the walkie.

"Yeah, heading back in now," I said getting out of my car. I had an hour and a half before I could punch out and go home. Sleep was no longer on my mind, the only thing I wanted to do was call around to find Ricio and make sure he was alright.

***

At six o'clock on the dot, I was running out of the prison to my car. I stopped at the bed and breakfast spot and grabbed a cup of coffee to keep me awake for the two-hour commute to my house. With every song that played on the Cardi B station on Pandora, I jammed along with. *No Limit* by G Easy came on that was my shit, I rapped my heart out.

If I hit one time, I'ma pipe her
If I hit two times, then I like her
If I fuck three times, I'ma wife her
It aint safe for the black or the white girl
It ain't safe, it ain't safe, it ain't safe, it ain't safe
Tell the man pipe up, nigga, pipe up
Hunnid bands from the safe in your face
What'd yo say?
Money dance turn this shit into a nightclub

As I actually listened to the lyrics, it pissed me off because Ricio hit once and called it a day. I felt low all over again for coming on to him and getting played. Turning the radio off completely so I could have a clear head to think about how I would find out where Ricio was. I sent a silent prayer up to God that I didn't find him in the morgue.

Finally arriving at home, I climbed the stairs to the second floor and there was a box sitting in front of my door. The box was addressed to me but there weren't any postage marks nor a return address on it. I didn't trust that shit so, I picked it up and took it downstairs and sat it by the dumpster in the alley.

Curiosity got the best of me and I wanted to know what was inside. Bending down I placed my ear to the box and no sounds came from inside. Using my key, I cut the strip of tape and opened the lid. Soon as I lifted the flap, a bunch of small mice scattered about causing me to jump back screaming.

My hands were shaking as I moved to peek inside after all the rodents went about their way. The mama rat was lying lifeless on top of a plastic bag with her abdomen cut open. In her mouth was a piece of paper with the words 'read me' printed on it. I reached inside and ran back to my apartment.

Closing my door and applying the deadbolt, I stripped out of my uniform breaking my neck to get to the shower. "Who the hell would send someone a box of mice?" as I scrubbed my body under scalding hot water. The longer I stayed under the stream of water, the dirtier I felt. All I saw were the mice running around my house even though they never made it inside. The water turned cold forcing me to get out. I wrapped a towel around my body and another on my head before I walked down the hall to my bedroom.

Pulling the covers back to get into my bed I remembered the note that I'd left on the counter in the bathroom. I grabbed an oversized t-shirt, dried my hair, slipped my feet into the slippers that I kept by the bed and headed back to get the mysterious note. Unfolding the paper, I began to read it as I walked to my bedroom.

"I told you my reach is long. Don't fuck with me, I want that nigga's head on a platter. It's on you to make that happen. Life as you know it will never be the same. The choice is yours."

James Carter had the nerve to sign that shit 'Daddy', I wish I'd never crossed paths with him. The worse part about it all was the fact of not knowing who he had watching me. Telling him I didn't care about him knowing where I lived was true up until that moment. A bitch was petrified.

I spent the next two hours calling hospitals and the morgue trying to locate Ricio. The urge to give up was strong but I made one more call. The last hospital I tried was the County and I prayed they had him.

"Cook County Hospital, how may I direct your call?" The guy asked.

"Yes, I was wondering if there was a Mauricio Vasquez brought in sometime last night," I replied biting my bottom lip.

"Who am I speaking with? Only family is allowed to see Mr. Vasquez."

The only name I knew associated with Ricio was his brother Max and he was dead. There wasn't any way he would be on any list. "Do Nija know where you are, Ricio," popped in my head from the night Ricio and I went out. The female that tried to come from me mentioned that name as being her sister's. Her sister was Ricio's bitch, bingo!"

"Ma'am are you there?" the guy asked.

"Yes, sorry. My name is Nija, I'm his fiancé," I replied hoping he fell for the lie I'd told.

"Nija Foster, you're on the list. When you arrive come to the counter and obtain a visiting pass."

"Thank you, I'm on my way," I said hanging up quickly.

Hopping out of the bed, I threw on a pair of jeans and a long-sleeved grey t-shirt with my grey Pumas. I combed my hair into a ponytail, brushed my teeth and rushed out of the house. I wanted to get in and out to see Ricio before his real family members came to check on him.

It took no time for me to get to the westside. I had to hop off the expressway and take the street the rest of the way to the hospital. Pulling into the parking lot, I lucked up on a spot in front of the entrance and got out of my car. As I approached the desk, I waited patiently as the guy conducted business on the phone. From the sound of his voice, he was the same person I'd talked to earlier.

"Good morning," he said ending the call.

"Good morning. I called earlier inquiring about Mauricio Vasquez. I'm Nija," I said smiling from ear to ear.

"Yes, Miss Foster. You are his first visitor of the day," he said handing me a pass. I was praying he didn't ask for identification and it paid off. "Take the elevators on the right and he's in room 517."

"Thank you so much," I said scurrying away before he decided to follow the hospital's policy.

Stepping out of the elevator on the fifth floor, I found the room easily. The door was slightly ajar so I pushed it open wider and entered. There were machines attached to his body but upon further inspection, there was only a heart monitor and blood pressure sleeve in place. He also had an oxygen tank nearby.

Pulling a chair to the side of his bed, I sat down and held his hand in mine. "Hey, Mauricio, it's me, Latorra. You don't know the trouble I went through to find you. It's good to see that you are still with us in this dreadful world. You're gonna pull through because God isn't ready for you. I'm not supposed to be here but I had to make sure you were alright."

He didn't stir or make any sounds when I was talking. That wasn't a good sign to me. I didn't know what else to say to him because I didn't really have any experiences with him other than one date and one sexual encounter. It felt right for me to sit with him so he would know I at least took the time to check up on him.

"Who are you and how did you get in here?" An angry voice said as the door opened.

Glancing over my shoulder without releasing Mauricio's hand, I stared at the woman standing in the doorway. She walked further into the room and turned on the light, placing her hand on her hip. I won't lie, baby girl was gorgeous and her eyes were changing colors as her scowl deepened.

"I know you heard what the fuck I asked you. Oh, I know exactly who you are. Miss Smith, right?" she sassed as recognition kicked in.

"You got it, the one and only. Mauricio is my man, that's how I got up here." Turning my back to her, I continued rubbing my thumb along his hand.

"Your man, huh? It's funny that all of you females seem to claim him, but he acknowledges y'all as meaningless hoes," she chuckled.

"Hoe? I've never been anybody's hoe. Mauricio wasn't considering me a hoe when he was deep in this pussy," I shot back at her.

"And guess what? That's all it was, pussy. It comes a dime a dozen to that man lying in that bed, you ain't special, boo. If you think for one minute he's going to claim you as his woman, you are sadly mistaken. Mark my words. Walk away while you still have your feelings in check, the dick will have you seeing shit that's not plausible, hunni."

"Bitch—"

"Check your tongue, Latorra. That's the mother of my child you talking to," Ricio said groggily without opening his eyes. "I've laid here listening to you since you walked into this room. I had to make my presence known when you decided to lie through your teeth about being my woman. I was cool knowing you came to see about a nigga, but when did we discuss anything about being together as a couple?" He asked peeking out of his left eye.

It caught me off guard that he was able to speak. The words 'mother of my child' echoed in my mind repeatedly. Not only did he fuck me like the hoe his bitch spoke of, he impregnated her ass on top of it. I was ready to forgive him for the stunt he pulled, but all bets were off, fuck him.

"I'm waiting on a reply, Miss Smith," he said in a low voice.

"How many times must I tell you not to call me that?"

"Focus on the question, ma. When. Did. We. Make. Shit. Official. Between. Us?" he asked like I rode the yellow short bus or some shit.

"We didn't, okay! I came to check on you. When I heard you were shot, I called all over the city to find you. That should mean something to you," I said staring at him.

"How did you get in this room? That's what I'm trying to figure out. Strict orders were given, along with a list of names. Your name definitely wasn't amongst the ones given," ol' girl stated angrily.

I knew about the list because the employee told me. I wasn't about to explain shit to her though. Ignoring her question, she stepped to the left side of me and grilled me as if she was going to swing on me. I dropped Mauricio's hand and shifted my body just in case.

"Nija, baby come here." She didn't move right away and I was waiting on her to throw hands so I could beat her ass. Rolling her eyes, she walked to the other side of the bed and sat down. "I got this," he said pulling her down toward him and kissed her on the corner of her mouth. "Nothing is going on between me and her.

We've went out to eat, I've talked to her on the phone. Did I sleep with her? Yeah, I did that too, but it was only once and it won't go any further," he explained to his bitch and it pissed me off to the max.

"You're full of shit, Mauricio! How the hell you fuck me and say that's it? How the fuck does that work? What happened to 'You had something to do and you will be back'? The way it sounded to me was as if you were trying to get to know me better. It's niggas like you that fuck females up in the head," I sneered.

"Slow down lil choo choo, yo' locomotive running! Slow that shit down. You fucked yo'self, shawty, I told you from the gate what I was on. You played the innocent role of not being down, but deep down you wanted exactly what you received. I'm letting you know now. We're done."

"You got it, Mr. Vasquez. Get well soon." Mauricio was standing strong on what he said in front of whatever the bitch was to him and I had to respect it. I'd never let a bitch see me sweat over a nigga. He got one up on me, he'd be back and I'd be waiting too. Tapping his hand lightly, I stood and left the room with revenge on my mind.

Chapter 8
Nihiyah

Living out of my car was something I'd never thought I would ever have to do. Out of all the shit I'd done in my life, my mama never turned her back on me. Nija is the one to blame because she should've kept her mouth closed. Always looking for sympathy like the spoiled bitch she's been all her life.

I went to my mother's house and my key didn't work. I beat on the door until she came downstairs to open the it. So what it was damn near one in the morning, I needed somewhere to sleep.

"Nihiyah, why are you out here banging on my door at this time of the night?" she asked with her .22 caliber at her side.

"The real question is, why did you change the locks?" I asked with an attitude.

"Last I checked, the mortgage is in my name. The bills are paid by me and I don't have to explain anything to someone I pushed out. Now, what can I do for you, Hiyah?" she asked leaning against the door.

"I'm tired and I need somewhere to sleep for the night."

"Are you off that shit? If not, you won't be sleeping here. We've already discussed this the day you packed your things. You're grown and made the decision to indulge in the things you have going on. I won't enable you another day, it's time to be an adult and find your own way. What I won't subject myself to is a drug addict. I'm standing strong on my decision just as you're standing on yours."

"Bitch, you done lost your mind! You can't put me out of a home I've lived in most of my life!" I screamed walking up on her with my fists balled up.

Her left arm came up quickly and the gun she held was aimed at my head like I was an intruder. "Walk up on me if you want to, I'll put something hot in your ass. I brought you in this world and I'll take you the fuck out! You've lost your ever-loving mind calling me a bitch! After all I've done for you and you have the nerve to disrespect me! Get the fuck off my porch before I send your ass somewhere that will have three hots and a cot waiting on you."

"You gon' call the police on me? Mama or not, I will beat yo' ass, don't play with me!"

She laughed and placed the gun on the table by the door. "Take your best shot, Nihiyah. This will be the best ass whoopin' you've ever gotten," my mama said squaring up.

Underestimating the fact that she was of age, I lunged at her and was knocked on my ass. My mama snatched me up by the front of my shirt and punched me repeatedly upside my head. I couldn't get away from her because of the death grip she had on my collar. Tossing me to the ground, she reached to her left and I thought she was going for her gun.

"Get off my porch, Nihiyah and don't come back until you can apologize for the bullshit you just pulled," she said slamming the door in my face.

I held on to the railing and hoisted myself to my feet. If Patricia Foster thought she was going to get away with treating me like a stranger, she had another thing coming. Walking down the steps, I picked up one of the decorative rocks that lined the walkway and hurled it through the living room window. Crash!

"You gon' learn to keep your hands to yourself!" I screamed running back up the stairs. Beating on the door with my fist, I waited for my mother to open the door so we could fight heads up. When the door didn't open, I went back to get another rock. Before I could throw it, a squad car sped into the driveway.

"Drop the rock, ma'am," an officer said as he got out.

I forgot what part of the city I was in. These police didn't play where my mama lived. Doing as I was told, the door opened and my mother stepped onto the porch pulling her robe tighter around her frame. "You called the police! How dare you!" I screamed running up the stairs.

I was tackled from behind and hit the porch face first. I felt something glide down my face as I landed on the wood. My arms were snatched behind my back and the cuffs were fastened tightly around my wrists. Another officer came to assist his partner and both of them lifted me up by my armpits.

"Loosen the cuffs, they're too tight!" I yelled loudly.

"Stand on your feet and relax, ma'am. You have the right to remain silent. Anything you say can and will be used against you in a court of law. You have the right to an attorney. If you can't afford an attorney, one will be provided for you." The officer read me my rights as I was led to the squad car.

"What am I being arrested for?"

"Vandalism. You threw a rock into your mother's home, which is a criminal misdemeanor. A crime. You will be going to jail."

"My mama won't press charges against me. You're wasting tax payers money," I laughed.

"Lock her ass up and get her off my property," my mother said turning around to walk into the house.

"Ma, stop playing. This ain't funny!" I said no longer laughing.

"Life is not a game, Nihiyah. Maybe now you'll take it more seriously. Until you get your act together, you have to deal with the consequences of your actions. I'll no longer save you from yourself, I've been doing it for far too long and that's where I fucked up at," she said slamming the door.

"This is bullshit! Fuck you!" I screamed as I was placed in the back seat.

I'd been sitting in the cold ass holding cell with prostitutes and zombie like crackheads and refusing hard ass bologna sandwiches. It was till hard for me to believe my mama was the reason I was there. She didn't have to call the police. It wasn't that serious. I'd been in there for hours like a caged animal and they hadn't given me my phone call.

"Excuse me! When will I get to make a phone call?" I yelled through the bars.

"Bitch shut the fuck up, I'm trying to sleep," the woman I was in the cell with said from the corner she was balled up in.

"If you knew what was good for you, you wouldn't say shit to me. Mind the business that pays you before you get slapped," I retorted.

A heavyset officer wobbled her big ass over with an ugly scowl on her puffy face. “You’re not outside. You lost that privilege so, keep your voice down. Foster, right?” she asked.

“That’s me,” I said nicely.

“I’m going to allow you to use the phone,” she said unlocking the cell door. “You don’t seem like you belong here. I’ve read why you are here and not to preach or anything, you only get one mother. Disrespecting her by busting out the windows in her home is overboard. You owe her a huge apology.”

“No disrespect to you, *Mrs. Officer*, but you don’t know the situation between me and my mother. The only thing you know is what the officers documented. If anyone is owed an apology it would be me. All I want to do is use the phone to get out of here. How much is my bail?” I asked without being rude.

“Your bail is five thousand dollars. You have to pay ten percent of that which is five hundred to walk. If it makes you feel better, your mother didn’t press charges. You have to appear in court in sixty days, if no one posts your bail, you will have to sit until then,” the officer explained.

“I’m going to let you use the phone at my desk. Do not call your mother because she has made it very clear that she won’t be coming to get you out.” I nodded my head and followed her to her desk.

The first person I thought to call was Shake. I knew that wouldn’t work because he was still in the hospital and was in no position to bail me out. Jolie didn’t have a pot to piss in so calling her was out of the question. That left me no choice but to call Floyd because my mama probably already told Nija what I’d done. She wouldn’t piss on me if I was on fire anyway. Dialing Floyd’s number from memory, I waited for him to answer.

“Yo!”

“Floyd,” I whispered. “Would you come bail me out of jail?”

“Who the fuck is this?” he asked angrily.

“It’s Nihiyah. I wouldn’t have called if Shake was out of the hospital—”

“Shake is dead!” he snapped cutting me off. “What makes you think I would come get yo’ shady ass anyway? You didn’t do what

I asked you to do, so sit yo' ass there and think about that shit!" he said hanging up.

After he said Shake was dead, I tuned everything else out. I didn't realize he had hung up until the busy signal sounded continuously in my ear. Pressing the end button on the phone, I tried my luck with Jolie. What did I have to lose? She was my only hope, there was no way I was sitting in jail for sixty fuckin' days.

"Hello," she said slowly when the call connected.

"Jolie, it's Nihiyah. I need your help, boo."

"Where are you calling me from?"

"I'm locked up and my bail is five hundred dollars. Please come get me, I'll pay you back," I cried. Knowing this was my last resort brought me to tears. "I know you don't have it but I thought I would ask anyway."

"Don't worry, boo. I got you. Where did they take you so I'll know where I'm coming?" she asked.

"At the police station on 94th and Kedzie, please hurry. If you don't bond me out, I will have to stay her for two months."

"We can't have that. I need my bitch out in these streets with me. Let me work my magic and I'll be there soon."

The line went dead and I place the phone on the desk and stood from the chair I was sitting in. I felt a little better knowing Jolie was going to try to come up with the money. Being led back to the holding area, the officer put me in one that was empty instead of the one I was in previously. Lying across the bench, I fell asleep thinking about Shake.

"Foster, get up! Your bail has been posted, time to go."

Lifting my head off the hard bench, a string of mucus fell from my already wet forearm. I had no clue as to how long I had been asleep, but hearing I was free to go had me moving at full speed. Standing to my feet, my whole body ached from sleeping on what felt the floor.

"Wipe your mouth. You look like you been back here eating your own pussy. Get it together," she said rolling her eyes.

The officer that was standing outside of the cell wasn't the one I spoke with earlier, this bitch looked like Tricks from the *Players*

Club. Big lips and fucked up weave to match, I promise I wanted to roast her ass but I didn't want to give her any reason to keep me locked up. I let Tricks have that because I was blowing that joint. Using the hem of my shirt, I dried my face, neck, and ears where I had drooled like a river flowing. After collecting my belongings and signing off on paperwork about my court date, I took that shit and walked out the station a free woman.

Jolie's mama's car was parked out front and I didn't wait to jump inside. "Thank you, so much! I owe you big time, boo. How did you get the money so fast?" I asked clicking the seatbelt in place.

"You know these stupid niggas thirsty as hell. I caught one slippin' and got his ass. The power of the pussy is a muthafucka. Put his ass to sleep and made his pockets three stacks lighter. He'll have to explain why he can't account for this too," she boasted as she swung a sack of rocks in my face. "It's time to celebrate your release, bitch!" she screamed pulling away from the curb.

Chapter 9
Rodrigo

After killing Floyd's boy Erv, I had to go somewhere to clear my head. Sin and Beast was blowing my phone up, but I wasn't ready to talk to either one of them. The only regret I had was not going to the hospital to see my brother. Kimmie informed me that he was doing a lot better except the meds kept him groggy. It has been two days since he was shot, I'd call him later.

I didn't want to go home so I ended up at the La Banque hotel in Homewood. The reason I didn't go home was because I knew I could be found by my family. Yeah, what I said to Beast was wrong and I meant every word. Whenever we saw each other, it was going to be a downright brawl. I was automatically programmed to kill and I had to remind myself that Beast wasn't an enemy, he was family. One thing I would never have on my hands is the blood of my own on my hands.

What was the best way to ease a nigga's mind? "Come here, girl wit yo' lil thick ass," I said licking my lips as Kimmie sashayed toward me.

Kimmie had been calling to make sure I was good all week. As a matter of fact, she was the only person that could get hold of me. Our conversations started friendly then I confided in her about things I'd never told anyone else. She asked and surprisingly, I answered.

Standing between my legs as I pulled on the loud I was enjoying, she leaned forward pressing her lips to mine. I blew the smoke into her mouth and she inhaled before exhaling the smoke into the air. "You make that shit look sexy as fuck," I said as I cupped her lace clad breasts.

"We ain't about to do this, Rodrigo. I'm here as a listening ear, nothing more." she stepped back out my grasp and I choked on the smoke I had inhaled. "You good?" she asked patting me on the back laughing.

I cleared my throat and grabbed the bottled water off the nightstand next to the bed. After a couple of sips, I was good. "Yeah, you just tripped a nigga up."

"How?" she chuckled.

"You claimed to be here just to be a listening ear, but you're standing in front of me with yo' ass out. If that's the case, your clothes would still be on your body and your lips wouldn't have been on mine a minute ago."

"When I arrived, this room was hot as hell. It took entirely too long for it to cool so, I came out of my clothes. It's not like you've never seen me naked before," she stated climbing into the bed.

"Correction, I've never seen you without clothes. You're confusing me with that nigga I put in a box. We ain't the same, babe. His demeanor is passionate, I can only imagine him going easy on the kitty. Me on the other hand, I tear the pussy up!" I smirked pulling on the spiff.

"You're still the same person regardless of what name you use. Stop trying to down play your dick, it's still the same," she laughed blushing.

"Don'tttt youuuu believvvvvee itttt! You gon' be asking that nigga for this Rodrigo dick after all this shit is over and he ain't gon' have a clue as to what the fuck you talkin' about," I laughed.

I squeezed her thigh before I stood from the bed. The Remy that was stored in the mini fridge was calling me. After popping the top on the bottle, I poured a generous amount in the glass tumbler and threw it back. Refilling the glass, I sat in a nearby chair and stared at Kimmie over the glass.

"Rodrigo, you are so rude. Where's your manners? I can't have none of your Remy?" she asked rolling her neck. "You didn't even offer, nigga."

"You know damn well you can have something to drink. Just to inform you, closed mouths don't get fed. I'm not a mind reader either."

"I'll hold off on the alcohol for now, let me get one of your spiffs," she smirked.

Kimmie seemed like she was on some sneaky shit. Falling for her foolery would work for the other me, but her games were going to have her fine ass screaming my name from her soul. Along with clutching the sheets and cumming all over my stick.

Grabbing the mango zig zag that I had on the nightstand, I proceeded to roll her a fat blunt. I wasn't shit because I didn't roll the loud from earlier, I was giving her the fie purp. We were fuckin' and she was the one that would kick it off. Licking the paper nastily by gliding my tongue back and forth along the paper, Kimmie's face turned beet red as she watched.

I gave the spiff one last lick before I held it out for her to come get. She stood and took it from my hand before snatching the lighter and putting fire to the tip. She inhaled deeply, holding the smoke in then blowing it out her nose.

"That's not weak weed, ma. You better smoke that shit responsibly. I won't be held accountable for what it causes you to do."

"There's no weed on Earth that'd have me doing something I don't want to do. Believe that," Kimmie stated before taking another toke and holding it out to me.

"Aight, we'll see. I'm good, that's all yours," I said sipping my drink.

Admiring how her lips wrapped around the blunt, my lil nigga jerked in my basketball shorts, causing me to cuff his ass up. She walked over to the fridge and bent over with the spiff between her lips. The boy shorts she had on did very little with hiding her cheeks. When she bent down to reach inside, the crack of her ass smiled widely exposing her fatty.

"Damn, that muthafucka juicy," I said quietly. "You playing a dangerous game with a nigga, Kim."

"What?" I'm only making myself a drink. Erase sex from your brain because it's not happening," she giggled as she raised up to pour the liquid in the glass.

I sat back in the chair without responding to the bullshit she was spitting. As I waited for the herb to take effect, I thumbed through the playlist on my phone while I sipped my cognac slowly. Kimmie sat on the bed and pulled on the spiff as she rocked side to side to music only, she could hear. Her glass was almost empty, the spiff was almost gone, and her eyes were low as fuck.

Baby girl was feeling good as she sat with her legs gapped open slightly. Her mound was sitting right between her thighs and my tongue tingled. Visualizing her lying on the bed with my head devouring her sweet honey dew juices before massaging her sugary walls with my pipe.

"Lie back for me, Kim," I commanded huskily.

"I'm not sleepy. Why do you want me to lay down?" she slurred.

You're fucked up, ma. Get some rest and relax," I said continuing to thumb through my phone.

"No, I'm not!" she screeched looking down at the spiff. It had gone out and she reached for the lighter and relit it. She smoked until it was gone and got up and refilled her glass.

I let her do what she wanted. I wasn't trying to hear that shit she was talking, I had something for her hardheaded ass. Finding the song I was looking for, I looked up at her and smiled. She had a chance to sleep, now she was going to get put down under my command. First, she was about to put on a show for me. Pressing play, I watched to see her reaction to my song choice.

I got some good dick, come and get it
I could lick your pussy right if you let me
Come on now, don't be silly
All you gotta do is tell me that you with it

Wet by Bando Jonez filled the room and just like I expected, Kimmie hopped from the bed soon as the beat dropped. Gyrating her hips, she was sexually arousing me with every move of her body. Her eyes connected with mine and I knew I had her.

I'ma get you wet
I got you dripping from your panties
I'ma keep you wet
'Til your body get to shiverin'

She was all into the lyrics and her hand glided down to her plump mound, rubbing it slowly with her pretty manicured fingers.

I'ma turn you on, girl

I'ma fuck you 'til you cum all over me
So you can jump on top and ride this dick slow

At that precise moment she mounted my lap and proceeded to give me a slow, nasty, sensual lap dance. Placing my phone on the table, I palmed her voluptuous ass. "Don't start nothing you not gon' finish, Kim. When my pole starts beefin' up, he gon' be ready to dig deep."

Instead of responding with words, she grabbed my ear with her teeth and ran her tongue along my earlobe. Sliding both of my hands into her shorts, I traced the tip of my finger between her cheeks. As I caressed her asshole, she purred lowly resting her head on my shoulder. The strain of my dick was excruciating and he wanted out.

Planting my feet and gripping Kimmie's ass tightly, I stood up as her arms wrapped around my neck. Gently placing her on the bed, I never took my eyes off hers and I ran my hands down her chest to the top of her shorts. Slowly pulling them down, she didn't resist so I kept going until they were resting on the top of her feet.

I got down on my knees and pulled them completely off before I nudged her legs open. Her pussy looked even better without the fabric covering it. Parting her lower lips with my thumb and index finger, I ran my tongue over her bud slowly.

"Mmmmmm,' Kimmie moaned. Her clit protruded more with every flick of my tongue. She tasted good and I couldn't get enough. Concentrating on her bud, I wrapped my lips around it and sucked lightly. "Oh shit, yes! Just like that," she cried out.

Licking from her asshole back to her hole, she was wet ass hell. Juices was flowing and I wanted all of it. Pushing her legs toward her head, her ass and pussy were on display and wasn't shit she could do but take the tongue lashing I was about to put on her.

I dipped my tongue into her love box and fucked her good with it. With every stroke, she leaked a little more and I cleaned it up. "Hold your legs just like that and you bet not let 'em fall," I demanded. Once she secured her legs in position, I used both hands to spread her lips and dived in.

"Oh Sosa!" she moaned grinding into my mouth. I lifted my head and mugged her. "Why did you stop?"

"That ain't my damn name. Don't worry about it, get on all fours and arch that back," I said standing to my feet and pulled my shirt over my head. I pulled down my shorts, letting them fall to the floor at my feet. "You gon' stop playing with me when it comes to this nigga, Kim."

She was laying on her stomach as I covered my man with the Magnum XL I retrieved from the pocket of my shorts. Pulling her by her leg, I smacked her on the ass and she bucked slightly. "Get in position, on all fours with that back arched," I said licking my lips as I watched Kimmie assume the position.

Sliding my pipe along her slippery folds, I entered slowly. A nigga damn near busted from the tightness and wetness of her kitty. Rocking my hips back and forth, she parted her legs allowing me all access. I plunged deeper and Kimmie scooted forward a bit but I pulled her back.

"Don't try to run now," I growled as I pumped in and out of her gushy while holding her waist. "You still think this dick is the same?"

When she didn't respond, I reached between her legs and strummed her nub like a guitar string as I served some Grade A dick on a platter. Her juices coated my joint making it harder. With every stroke her ass gave off a ripple effect.

"Ooooo shit, you too deep," she cried out as she reached back pushing on my stomach.

"Move yo'muthafuckin' hand, Kim. You getting all this meat today, baby," I hissed knocking her hand away. "I told you don't start nothin' you wasn't gon' finish, didn't I?"

"Fuck! Sssssss!" she moaned. Hitting her with long deep strokes I gripped both of her cheeks as our bodies made music together. "Oh, gawd, Rodrigo, hit that shit!" she murmured throwing her ass back.

"Whose pussy is this, Kimmie?" I growled.

"It's yours! It's yours!" She cried out in ecstasy as she tried to get away from the pounding I was delivering to her guts.

"What's my name, Kim?" I asked as I slipped my thumb in her asshole. Her movements paused momentarily but she must've liked it because she bucked back on my dick and made his ass disappear. Going deeper wasn't a problem for her anymore, baby girl was taking it like a pro.

"Rodrigo, baby!" she screamed. "This is your pussy, fuck me harder." Easing my thumb out of her ass, "don't take it out, it feels so good," she all but begged.

My first thought was to give her this pipe in that dookie chute but I knew she wasn't ready for that. In due time, baby girl was gon' get it though. Inserting my thumb back to the spot she had grown to love in a short time, I slammed her kitty on my snake, hard.

"Aaaaaah yeah, just like that. Fuck this pussy, baby."

The tingle in my balls was strong but I was struggling to hold back my nut. Kimmie had a death grip on a nigga and I was ready to bust, but I wasn't a selfish nigga. She had to get that one big one first.

"Cum on this muthafucka, ma," I growled wiping sweat from my forehead, "This tight shit will have me bodying a nigga over it."

Spreading her cheeks apart. I pounded into her pink center as I felt her lady clamp down hard on my tool. The shit paralyzed me and my toes dug into the carpeted floor.

"I'm cummin' baby!"

"Let that shit go, Kim! I'm right behind you," I groaned.

Kimmie squirted over the bed and the shit was fascinating to watch. My desire to hold my nut failed and I filled the condom with my seed. She fell forward onto the bed and her twat was still leaking.

Being the freaky muthafucka I was, I had to taste that shit. I wrapped my lips around her nub and sucked hard. Kimmie squirmed around like a fish out of water trying to force me to release her clit from my mouth.

"I can't take anymore, aaaaahhh," she moaned pushing my head.

Lifting her leg up, I licked her pussy until she squirted for the second time. "Oh shit! Fuck!" she screamed bloody murder as I caught every drop.

"From this day forward, you'll remember my fuckin' name," I said standing to my feet. "Me and Sosa ain't the same, Kimmie," I smirked as I walked to the bathroom while she struggled to keep her eyes open.

Chapter 10
Big Jim

They had me locked down for seven days and I was finally back with general population. The time spent alone was much needed and I welcomed it. Getting in touch with Rod was on my priority list and I couldn't wait to get to my phone. As I entered my cell, my cellie June scrambled from his bunk.

"Where the hell you rushing off to and why you looking like you've seen a ghost?" I asked.

I uh, uh gotta go handle something real quick," he stuttered trying to slip in his slides. "Glad to see you back, Big homie."

He rushed past me but I caught his ass by the back of his shirt before he could make his exit. This nigga was up to no good and he wasn't going nowhere until he told me what was up. I pointed to the chair in the corner and he sat down without question.

"Tell me what's going on, June. You in here looking suspect my nigga," I said folding my arms over my chest. He couldn't look me in the eyes so I knew he did something he didn't have no business doing. I just didn't know what. "It would be in your best interest to tell me the truth. If I have to find out on my own, I'm going right back to the hole for killin' yo' ass. Now talk and stop stalling, muthafucka!"

June was fidgeting and breathing hard. "Aight, you were gon' and I was hungry. I ate all your snacks." He mumbled the last part and the only thing I caught was snacks.

Putting two and two together, I stormed to my locker and snatched the door open. Sho nuff shit, my honeybuns, ding dongs, chips and cookies were missing. This nigga even used all of my muthafuckin' hot sauce, leaving a corner in the bottle. I had eight cans of pop and now I only have two. June had a good ol' time helping himself to my shit.

I turned around and grilled his ass after inspecting my commissary. "Before I went to my visit a week ago, you asked me for something and I said no. For you to take it upon yourself to go in my shit, that's called stealing and I can't stand a thief," I said walking up to him. "Stand yo' ass up, nigga." He hesitated and finally stood. I lifted his head up and punched his ass hard in the face. June stumbled into the wall and I hit him again in the back of his head.

"Don't ever in your life steal from me! If I don't give yo' punk ass what you ask for, don't touch shit!" I said punching him in his ribs. "There won't be a next time, nigga. From this point on, you will sleep over there," I said pointing to the small spot by the toilet. "I need to be able to see everything you do from now on. If you got a problem with it, request a cell change, bitch! Get out!" I barked.

June moved slowly toward the door and I kicked him in his ass to hurry him alone. I wasn't worried about him saying anything about what happened because he didn't want to deal with the consequences of doing so. Closing the door behind him, I locked it and went to my locker and retrieved my phone and charger.

Waiting for my phone to power on, I thought about what I was going to do about Floyd and his lack of leadership. All the years he had been by my side, I'd never known him to use anything other than weed. Knowing he was on drugs pretty much told me what needed to be done but I didn't want to put my sister in harm's way. She would be the first person his bitch ass would go after.

I had to be careful how I came at him so I had to find out who was to be trusted since Shake was dead. My man Rod had to be grief stricken with the loss of his son. He loved that dude more than his other son and groomed him to dominate the streets of Chicago. The hit was for sure an eye for a fuckin' eye because Rod offed their dad personally. Now his son is gone.

The vibrations from my phone brought me out of my thoughts. Notifications started popping up nonstop and my stomach knotted as I waited for them to finish downloading. Taking a deep breath, I went to the oldest messages first and they were from Floyd and my sister. His ass was apologizing for holding information and I wasn't trying to hear none of that shit.

I bypassed all of his other messages and came across a name I hadn't seen in a minute, Rello. He was one of my top hittas from the Southside and if he was hittin' me up, we had a problem.

Reading his texts was something I wasn't ready for, but there was no use waiting.

Rello: Ayo, Big I wanted you to know that ya man Floyd is out here fuckin' up. He put us in a bad position and left us out here blind. Holla at me, nigga.

Rello: Bossman I need you to get at me. Your empire is crashing before us. This nigga ain't on his shit!

It pissed me off reading his words because my workers shouldn't be calling me about the person I left in charge. Whooping Floyd's ass wasn't enough for him to get his shit together, I see. Pressing on Rello's name, I listened to the phone ring several times before he answered.

"Just the man I've been waiting to hear from. What's goin' on? Is everything good in there?"

"Everything is Gucci. Your texts got me wondering if everything straight out there. Don't sugarcoat shit, tell me everything you know," I said keeping my cool.

"Aight. I don't know how much you know but your Westside traps are no more. Everybody is gone, dead. Floyd is fuckin' up big time, bruh. The bullshit that transpired between them and Rodrigo—"

"Who the fuck is Rodrigo?" I asked confused.

"That's the name that nigga Sosa goes by now. Word on the street is he's vicious. He got hold of Erv when him and his people hit the trap on Sangamon and he hasn't been seen since."

"Wait a damn minute! When did this happen?" I asked heated.

"It happened last week, Wednesday or Thursday. I can't remember. They aired the whole block out, killing all the soldiers. I believe Erv is dead too, honestly. Ain't no way they dumped him in the trunk and he lived. Floyd had the nerve to tell us after the fact that he shot Ricio. He had us out here blind, Big. Then he said he didn't expect them to come for us because they knew nothing about our spots. He's fuckin' up royally!"

Hearing Rello run shit down made me want to put a hit on Floyd's head. I knew I couldn't do that right away because he had access to my shit. A scared man would leave my ass high and dry without a pot to piss in. I had to move some shit around before I eliminated his ass for good. On top of it all, a crackhead would sell his soul to get himself out of hot water. I wasn't trying to be in prison for the rest of my life.

"Listen and listen good, Rello. Since Shake is dead, I have nobody out there that's strong like he was—"

"Not to cut you off, Boss, but what the fuck am I, chopped liver? I can hold shit down for you better than Floyd's pussy ass," Rello exclaimed.

"I don't doubt that, Youngblood. You were the only one that had the balls to get at me to let me know the business. I appreciate that shit. Write this shit down that I'm about to say to you, and it's for your eyes only!"

"Hold on a sec, I need to get something to write on," he said shuffling around. "Aight, let that shit ride."

"First and foremost, I need you to get in touch with Rodney Banks, my attorney."

"That's not possible, Big. Floyd didn't tell you?" he questioned.

"Tell me what?" I asked standing to my feet pacing back and forth.

"Rod was found in his crib burned to a crisp the same day Shake was shot. He had to be identified by dental records. You got to find a new lawyer, my nigga. The process is about to start from day one for you."

"He didn't tell me shit! Not one time before I beat his ass, did he tell me Rod was dead too. This shit setting me back and I was on my way outta this muthafucka."

"Calm down. We just have to get another lawyer. As a matter of fact, I have somebody that owes me a favor and he has gotten me out of a lot of shit. I'll hit 'em up and cash in for you, fam."

"Good lookin' because I got to get outta this fuckin' prison. My shit is crashing and ain't nothing I can do about it from here."

"You still have one loyal nigga on your side. I'm not gon' sit back and let you go down. Tell me what else you need me to do and I'm on it."

"Close down shop for now because obviously Sosa knows about the traps on the Southside. We can't make no money if they gunnin' for us the way you say they are. Then Floyd failing to inform a muthafucka wasn't the right move. What I want you to do is find out the status on Ricio. Better yet, get in touch with this female named Latorra.

She fucks with that nigga, she should know. Her number is 773-555-0908. Call her now and get back with me soon as you finish talking to her."

"Bet, I'm on it. Everything will be all good, Boss," Rello said disconnecting the call.

I dialed my sister's number and she answered on the first ring, as if she was waiting on my call. "Jim where the hell you been? I haven't heard from you in a week!" she screamed. "I thought something happened to you," she cried.

"Stop all that shit, Lynette. I'm good, sis. I was in solitary confinement for fuckin' Floyd up during a visit. My business is sinking because of his ass. I need you to go to the bank and take his ass off all the accounts."

"Floyd has been your right hand for years, James. What's going on?"

"Come see me Wednesday and I'll explain everything to you. Right now, I need you to do what I asked first thing in the morning. I have to get another lawyer too but I'll fill you in on that when I get the information. I'm only concerned with securing my money right now. Be careful, sis and don't let Floyd run game on you. He is not to be trusted. Shoot that nigga if he comes at you wrong and I mean that shit."

"I heard about Rod on the news already. That was the reason I was trying to get in touch with you. I thought you were laid up because somebody got close to you. People are dying left and right out here, big brother."

"Nothing's going to happen to me. I'm good. continue to hold me down and I got you. I appreciate you for not turning yo' back on a nigga. Now stop that crying, I love you. I'll call you later, I have to figure out how to get my shit back on track," I said hanging up.

I hated hearing my sister cry but I couldn't let her emotions lead me to a soft spot. Knowing Sosa was on a warpath I had to make plans to hit them harder than they hit us. My money was being compromised behind this war and it was time to put an end to it all. Latorra was the key to getting Ricio and using her to my advantage was key.

My phone vibrated in my hand and Rello was calling back. "Yo, what's the deal?"

"Man, I don't like baby girl's vibe. She's too juicy at the mouth for me. She said fuck you and I bet not call her phone no mo'. Who the fuck is she and do you want me to reach out and touch her muthafuckin' ass?" He was mad as hell and serious as a heart attack too.

"Nah, I got her. Keep ya phone on, I'll be hitting you up soon. For the time being, go do what I mentioned earlier and continue to follow Floyd's orders. Report any new information to me as soon as you see or get wind of it."

The door to my cell was being tampered with and I banged on Rello's ass and stashed my phone. "Carter, what the hell you doing in there?" Smearing some Vaseline on my hand, I walked over to the door and yanked it open.

"Minding my damn business! Nigga can't even jack his dick around this muthafucka! What the fuck you want, Thomas?"

"You a jacking lie," he said trying to see what was behind me.

"You want proof, huh?" I smirked and palmed his face with my greasy hand.

"That's nasty! I'll beat your ass, nigger," he snapped wiping his face.

"You ain't gon' do shit. What you want?" I laughed.

"The warden wants to see your black ass. Let's go, but wash your hands first. Nobody wants to be in contact with your bodily fluids. I'll be in the hall."

He stormed his punk ass out of the doorway with a swing in his hips. If he kept playing with me, I was going to bend his ass over just for the hell of it. Cleaning my hands even though I knew what was really on them, I left out of my cell still laughing.

Thomas' face was red and he was mad as hell, his expression told it all. When he saw me coming out of the cell, he walked off ahead of me leading the way to the warden's office. I already knew he wanted to talk about the incident that landed me in the hole. He wasn't getting no information so he could scratch that shit. Warden Fitzpatrick was sitting behind his desk with his hands folded in front of him when I entered.

"Have a seat, Carter," he said motioning me to sit with his hand. Once I was seated, he cleared his throat and continued. "What happened during your visit was a violation. I have no choice but to add an additional six months to your sentence. You should think about the choices you make from this point on.

Floyd Douglas is no longer allowed to visit this prison. I don't care nor do I want to know what the altercation was about, that type of behavior is unacceptable in my prison. The next time you get in some shit, you'll be in solitary confinement longer than a week. "

"I hear what you're saying Warden Fitzpatrick. I may as well tell you what's going on before it gets back to you. One of your employees, CO Smith to be exact, has been throwing herself at me. Word on the Block is she's having sexual relations with many of the inmates. Turning her down seems to have upset her and I don't' want any problems."

Yeah, I was putting her ass in a tough position, but so what. She should've played by my rules and not her own. Now, her only choice would be to come back to me. I specifically told her not to underestimate me and she didn't listen.

"When was the last time she approached you, Carter?"

"She was sent to check on me when I was in the hole. Once she saw I was okay, she offered to suck my dick when I told her I was stressed. I declined the offer and she told me I would regret it," I replied throwing her deeper under the bus.

"I will have a conversation with her and thank you for not engaging in the inappropriate behavior."

"I don't think it would be wise for you to mention where you got the information from. There's no telling who she has on her side in here to come for me. Remember. I have a sentence to serve in this muthafucka and I'm not about to be watching my back over bullshit."

"You don't have anything to worry about, Carter. Allow me to do my job and I will get to the bottom of this. You are dismissed, I'll handle everything from here, don't get in anymore trouble or I will make sure to hang your ass out to dry."

Rising from the chair I was smiling on the inside because all I had to do was wait for Latorra to call crying to me saying she needed my help. She had information that I needed her to deliver to me. If making her life hard was the only way to get it, let the hardship begin. I hope she saved some dough for a rainy day. Her ass was going to need it.

Chapter 11
Nija

Time seemed as if it was going slow as ever and I was ready to leave the place I called work. I didn't have any more clients for the day but I had plenty of paperwork to complete. It was better than dealing with the attitudes that I had to endure everyday so I was glad I had the time to get it off my desk.

It was raining hard outside and there was a tornado warning. We were in the heart of the city and I wasn't worried about a tornado touching down where my job was located. The sky was dark at two thirty in the afternoon and it looked like a scary movie as I looked out the window. The rain didn't seem like it would be clearing up anytime soon and I was glad I didn't have to drive home.

I had been staying at my mom's since Nihiyah took it upon herself to throw a damn brick through her window. The only reason I stayed was because I hoped she'd show her bad ass back up. Kimmie had been out looking for her but she hadn't been lucky as of yet. On one hand I was glad she didn't find her because Kimmie was ready to beat her ass. On the other I wish I knew if she was okay.

My office line started ringing and I picked up the receiver and exhaled slowly. "DHS, this is Nija speaking," I spoke into the phone wearily.

"You sound tired, Nija. Are you okay?"

"Yes, Ricio, I'm fine. How are you?"

"I'm going home today. Will you come over and take care of me?" he asked.

"Ricio, I don't have a problem with coming to over to help you out. I won't be staying the night because I have to stay with ma to make sure she's going to be alright in the house alone."

"Ni, you're using your mama as an excuse. Nihiyah ain't that damn crazy. I know you are still upset and don't want to fuck with me, but I'm a patient nigga. We have a baby on the way and he or she won't be raised in a household without both parents. What time should I be expecting you at the house?"

Glancing out the window, the rain was coming down harder than before. There was no way I was going to his house in that type of weather. "I'll come after work tomorrow," I replied.

"Rodrigo is picking you up from work, right?"

I heard the amusement in his voice and the close relationship that he and his brother had got on my nerves. They were always trying to team up to be on bullshit and I felt that day was one of the times. "Yes, he is. If he's picking you up, I can call Kimmie to see if she'd come get me."

"Nah, Kimmie's at work. I have someone picking me up from the hospital and it's not my brother. There are others beside my brother that drive. My cousins are still here, then I can also call Sin or Beast too."

"Don't leave out your hoes while you're naming people," I mumbled.

"There you go worrying about the wrong things again, Nija. There are no hoes. We've already had this conversation the day Latorra showed up at the hospital. I didn't lie about anything concerning the two of us. She was wrong for calling you out of your name and I checked her on it. How long are you gon' hold this shit against me?"

"I'm not holding anything against you. Sue me for stating facts," I said trying not to get upset. "She's not the only one, Ricio. She's just the one that was bold enough to come out and stake a claim in my presence. This pregnancy doesn't change anything between us. We will have to figure out how to co parent, that's all. I've waited long enough to be the only woman in your life and the moment is over."

"I don't want to discuss this over the phone. Come over after work so we can talk."

"That would be a no for me. I need time to adjust and I have to find a place to rest my head. Living with others isn't working for me. I need my own space. I also have to go over to the house and pack up my things and put them into a storage unit. For now, I have to finish this paperwork before I get out of this office. I'll talk to you soon, Ricio," I said ending the call abruptly before he could reply to what I said.

I worked almost two hours straight without interruptions when there was a knock on the door. "Come in," I responded without looking up.

"Miss Foster?"

"Yes." When I held my head up, there was a guy standing in the doorway looking like Pee Wee Herman's lost son. I had to hold back a chuckle that tried to escape my lips so I smiled instead. "May I help you?"

"I have a delivery for you. Where would you like me to place it?"

"Anywhere is fine," I said dropping my pen.

Lil Pee Wee disappeared and returned with a huge teddy bear that held a heart in its hands. I pointed at a chair in the corner and he sat the bear down and left again. He came back with three vases of flowers, balloons and a small blue bag. I knew that color from anywhere and I knew it was from Tiffany's. The delivery guy put the items on my desk as I reached inside my purse and pulled out a twenty-dollar bill.

"Have a nice day, ma'am. You don't have to tip me. I was compensated nicely already," he said leaving out of my office. "There's a card inside the blue bag," he shot over his shoulder.

Before he could get out the door good, Tangie was rushing in. "Damn, Nija! Who you got beggin' for your attention?" Tangie yelled in her best *Tiffany Haddish* voice as she danced her way into my office.

"Nobody," I said standing up from my chair.

The flowers were beautiful. There were red roses, a bundle of lilies, and the colorful arrangement was a slew of purple, orange, yellow and pink flowers that I didn't know the name of. Picking up the Tiffany's bag, I opened the box and inside was a platinum chain with a diamond encrusted key charm. It was beautiful and I loved it. I sat the box down and reached inside the bag to get the card that was inside.

I'm sorry for everything I've put you through. You have my heart, Nija. Once I deal with the things going on, I promise I will show you how much I love you. My words mean nothing right now, but I needed you to know where my love lies. I love you. -Ricio

"That's so pretty," Tangie said picking up the jewelry box. "I'm gonna have to get on my husband so he'd step his game up. I should be getting shit like this," she said laughing.

"His ass did all this out of guilt. It doesn't impress me at all and he knows it. I'll give him an E for effort but I'm not going to let this move me. I'm far from the gullible type and it would take more than material things for me to be happy. Would you mind giving me a ride home? I didn't drive," I asked changing the subject.

"Sure, I don't mind. I was coming in to tell you that Vera said we can cut out early because of the weather. Nobody's been through here in hours and I've been bored. When you're ready to go, come to my office and we can leave," Tangie said as she turned to leave. "Nija, hear that man out. I'm quite sure whatever happened can't be that bad. Y'all about to have a baby, think about it."

"I'm not trying to hear anything he has to say. He can save that shit for—"

Tangie left and closed the door before hearing the rest of my rebuttal. I didn't care what she thought about me not wanting to listen to Ricio. He'd had years to prove his love and now that I was done, he wanted to be lovey dovey. Fuck him! I was furious as I threw everything I needed into my briefcase. I could admit, the flowers brightened up my office so I decided to leave them right on my desk.

I grabbed the jewelry box and added it to my briefcase before picking up the teddy bear. It was so big I had to prop it on my shoulder like a baby. Making my way to Tangie's office, I had to kick the door because my hands were full.

"Girl you look like you're struggling," she laughed taking the bear from my arms. "Here, take the umbrella and I got this."

"I left my umbrella in my office. I'll get it on our way out," I said heading back.

After getting my umbrella, we walked through the lobby and out the door. Tangie locked the door and I opened the umbrella and walked down the stairs. A car pulled up to the curb and I noticed it was Rodrigo. Cursing myself something fierce, I forgot to call him to let him know I had a ride.

"Who is that?" Tangie asked from behind me.

"That's Rodrigo. My ride."

"I thought you didn't have a ride," she said confused.

"I forgot to call him so he wouldn't come. I knew he was going to get his brother from the hospital and I didn't want to ride with him." I explained.

"So that's baby daddy in the passenger seat, huh?" she laughed. "Gone and get in that car, Nija. Talk to that man," she said as Rodrigo exited the car.

"Hey sis," Rodrigo said walking up the steps.

"Your brother lied to me, again. He told me he had a ride and it wasn't you," I frowned.

"Nija, you should've known he was lying. Come on so we can get out of here. Hey, sexy. What's your name?" he asked turning his attention to Tangie.

"I'm Tangie and I'm married."

"I don't care about your husband. I'm trying to get to know you. Whatever y'all got going on is between y'all," he smirked.

"Rodrigo! Stop messing with that damn girl," I laughed. "Here, take this damn bag and get back in the car.

"I'm not a damn Chauffeur, Nija! I just came to take your ass home. And for the record, I was dead ass about what I said to Tangie with her fine ass," he said snatching the bag.

"Girl, thanks for offering a ride. There's no way he's going to let me leave in your car. I'll see you tomorrow." I opened the umbrella and took the teddy bear from her making sure it didn't get wet before I got to the car.

The bear took up most of the backseat and Rodrigo helped me get it into the car from the other side. As I got comfortable and snapped the seatbelt in place, Ricio turned around staring at me.

Ignoring him, he turned and sat back to enjoy the ride. I had nothing to say to him.

Rodrigo pulled from the curb after making sure Tangie was safely in her car. My eyes automatically closed from the rain beating on the hood. The sound alone was relaxing and I didn't realize how tired I actually was. Before long, I was in a deep sleep without a care in the world. I don't know how long I slept but I knew we should've been at my mama's house already.

When I opened my eyes and looked out the window, Rodrigo was pulling into the garage of Ricio's condo. Sitting up straight, I glared at the back of his head and if looks could kill, his shit would've exploded. "Rodrigo, what am I doing here?"

"Nija, take that up with ya baby daddy. I had nothing to do with none of this," he said pulling into the second parking spot reserved for his brother.

"I hope you know you're taking me home, right?" I asked furiously.

"Ni, just get out the car. Brah will grab your stuff," Ricio said opening the door.

I watched him place the crutches out of the door and slowly rose out of the car. Ricio was struggling to maneuver the crutches with his bad arm and his leg. I felt bad for sitting in the car without helping him.

"Ricio, let me get the wheelchair bro. Yo' ass can't walk on your leg and can't work the crutches because of your arm. You so damn hardheaded! Gon' bust a vessel trying to be Hercules," Rodrigo said slamming the trunk.

"I'm not using that muthafucka, man. I'm gon' beat this shit on my own. I can do this!"

The pain had to be severe because it was displayed on his face. Getting out of the car, I grabbed my briefcase and left the bear on the seat. Ricio didn't take many steps before he fell into the wheelchair, he didn't want to sit in. "I'll always have your back, even when you don't me to."

Rodrigo went back to the car and got the teddy bear out and plopped it on Ricio's lap. He had a duffle bag hanging from his shoulder and I bent down to pick up the crutches.

Following them to the elevator, a phone started ringing and Rodrigo checked his hip to see if it was his. Obviously, it wasn't because the sound continued. Ricio didn't bother to check his at all. The whole time we were on the elevator, Ricio's phone rang non-stop.

I got off the elevator and walked ahead to unlock and open the door. I went into his bedroom and placed pillows at the foot of the bed so Ricio would be able to prop his leg up. Rodrigo pushed him into the room and helped him onto the bed. Adjusting the pillows under his leg, I fluffed the ones behind his head and handed him the remote.

"You should be good from here. Is there anything you need before I go?" I asked.

"Go. Where are you going, Nija? I can't do this alone. I told you that on the phone earlier."

"I'm going home. Rodrigo can stay here and help you out," I grabbed my briefcase off the bed and walked toward the door.

"Nija, don't play with me. Brah, go where you're going and lock the door behind you."

"How the fuck you're going to tell me what I'm gon' do?" I asked turning quickly in his direction.

"Y'all figure that shit out. I think it would be best for y'all to talk so there would be a better understanding between y'all. There's a baby coming into this world and all this back and forth shit needs to be taken care of before it gets here. Nija, call me when you ready to go because I got shit to do," Rodrigo said walking out.

"I'm ready to go now!"

"Nah, you're not. Ricio I will be going to take care of that soon as I gather the team."

The front door slammed shut and Rodrigo was gone. I couldn't believe he left me after I said I was ready to go. At that moment I wish I had driven my own fucking car.

Chapter 12
Latorra

Ricio had me fucked up. The way he called himself checking me for his bitch was the wrong move on his part. Nobody dismissed me like that and got away with it. The only reason I didn't snap was because I didn't want to catch a case. Hearing that he had a baby on the way only put fuel on the fire. His ass said all that shit to pacify her anyway, I knew he would be back.

I'd had a chance to think about what happened and had calmed down tremendously. Duty called and I felt a lot better as I walked into the prison for work. We had a packed house and I knew it was about to be a day filled with drama. Unlocking the door to take my position behind the counter, I didn't get the chance to even sit down before my supervisor was in my grill.

"Smith, you're wanted in the warden's office, now," he said sternly.

"What's going on?" I asked curiously.

"You'll find out when you get there." Was all he said before stepping aside so I could exit. "Thomas, you will man this position for the day."

Thomas nodded his head and continued checking visitors in. I had no clue as to why the warden of all people wanted to see me. Usually when a CO was summoned to the warden's office there was a complaint. I hadn't done anything that would warrant me to be going in that direction. Deciding not to worry about it any further, I followed quietly without asking anymore questions.

The fact that I was escorted to the office like an inmate pissed me off because I knew I hadn't done anything other than the job I was paid to do. Warden Fitzpatrick was standing staring out the window when I entered his office. He turned with a grim expression on his face.

"Close the door, Smith and have a seat," he said pacing back and forth behind his desk. Doing as I was told. I folded my hands in my lap and waited for whatever he had to say. "You may be wondering why I asked you to come here today. I won't keep you in suspense any longer," he said picking up his coffee mug, taking a sip.

"Latorra you have been with us for a little over two years and I've never had a problem out of you. The amount of dedication you have presented in this prison has been superb and you have really impressed me," he paused.

In my mind I was twerking because he was speaking highly of me and I smelled more money coming my way. I'd worked my ass off to do my job over and beyond expectations and I deserved that shit. The smile that graced my lips was one that couldn't be hidden.

"I received a bit of information concerning you and I didn't like what I heard," he continued. The words he spoke puzzled the hell out of me and I didn't know where he was going with his speech. "Smith you do know that personal relationships with inmates are not tolerated in my prison, correct?"

"Yes, I know that," I agreed nodding my head slowly. "I learned about it in training my first week on the job," I said confidently.

"Apparently from what I've heard, you seem to have forgotten at times."

"What exactly are you implying, Warden? I asked inquisitively.

"I'm not implying anything. Like I said, it was brought to my attention that you have been doing some things that violate the rules. I've been told by several inmates that you have been engaging in sexual relations with them."

"Excuse me? Somebody is lying to you because I have never had sex with any of the inmates in this prison. I do my job and go home, nothing more," I fumed.

"I've investigated the allegations, Smith. I've interviewed inmates as witnesses and the ones that admitted to having sex with you. What reasons would there be to lie on only you? Why not one of the other female officers?" he questioned.

I didn't like his line of questioning because I knew it was a lie. Fitzpatrick already made up his mind that I'd had sex with one of the nasty muthfuckas in the prison. "I don't know why my name of all people would come up in some bullshit like this. I don't even hold a conversation with your inmates."

"I hate to have to do this, Miss Smith, but I have to let you go," Warden Fitzpatrick had the nerve to say.

"Let me get this straight. You are firing me based off he say she say shit? I bust my ass in this damn prison for y'all and this the thanks I get? I don't deserve this type of treatment when I know for a fact, I haven't done anything mentioned in here today."

"I understand your frustrations. There's nothing else I can do. I need you to sign this termination form and you are free to leave," he said sliding a piece of paper towards me.

Reading over the letter of termination, my eyes widened. He wanted me to sign this shit admitting wrong doing of sexual contact with an inmate. My blood boiled over and I couldn't hold back my anger.

"You want me to sign this stating I committed these violations? Nah, I won't be signing shit! I will not incriminate myself when I'm innocent!" I said balling up the paper and tossed it across the desk. You can kiss my ass! This is straight bullshit and you know it!" I yelled.

"Mitchell will escort you out the building. Retrieve your belongings and never return to this prison, Smith. I will have no problem having you arrested for trespassing. I will need your badge, keys, and walkie," he said calmly.

I wanted to knock everything on his desk onto the floor. Instead, I stood with my head held high as I threw everything on the desk in front of him and walked out of his office. Mitchell was outside waiting for me as I exited. He grabbed me by the elbow and I shrugged him off.

"I am capable of walking on my own, thank you," I sneered.

When I made it to the front desk, I walked right out the front door of the prison. Unlocking the door to my car, I sat inside and the tears started flowing. The thought of what I was going to do crossed my mind as I cranked up the engine and continued to sit. My job was all I had to look forward to and I didn't have that anymore. I had seven hundred dollars in my account after paying my bills for the month and I didn't have a fuckin' job anymore.

Wiping the tears from my eyes, I put my car in drive and slowly made my way home. Traffic was pretty good and I took the opportunity to reevaluate my life. I didn't know what I was going to do at that point, but I did know I wouldn't be down long.

About two hours later I was pulling up to my home and I felt a sense of relief. All I wanted to do was take a nap before I hit the club. I needed a stiff drink to get my mind right and there was no better place than club Money. I needed to see my girl Tammy. She was sure to take my mind off my problems for the night.

***

I slept the entire day after crying for hours when I got home. The realization of losing my job set in and I came to the conclusion that there was nothing I could do about it. I went into the kitchen because I was hungry as hell. Filling a pot with water for the fettuccini noodles I planned to cook. I rinsed the chicken breast I took out before I went to work and put the pot of water on the stove to boil.

Seasoning the chicken with seasoned salt, pepper, and garlic powder, I heated the skillet on a low heat as I cut up the broccoli that I was going to add to the pasta. Cooking was something I loved to do but rarely had the chance to since I worked so much. My dinner was ready within the hour and I was ready to eat. The garlic bread was golden and made my mouth water just from looking at it.

After cooking I wasn't quite as hungry as I'd thought, so I went to my bedroom to choose an outfit for the night. Shifting through the many hangers in my closet, I ran across a black bustier with silver rhinestones scattered about the front. I paired it with a pair of black skinny jeans I knew would cup my ass just right. I reached on the shelf for the shoebox that contained my open toed black knee boots with the silver heels.

Gathering my underwear, I walked out of my room and made my way down the hall to the bathroom. I plugged my curlers into the wall and turned the water on in the shower. My mood saddened when I thought about the bullshit that happened earlier at the prison. Thinking about it a little harder, I realized no one other than James

Carter could've been behind the malicious act. The guy that called me must've reported back to his evil ass and he decided to lie on me.

I couldn't let something out of my control ruin my night. It was time for me to have a little fun before I set out to get my life back on track. I hadn't been out in a while and clearing my head was what I wanted to do. Adjusting the water temperature, I undressed and pulled the shower cap over my hair before stepping under the stream of water.

The water fell over my body and I relaxed on impact. Washing thoroughly, I got out putting on the plush robe that hung on the back of the door. My stomach growled loudly and I headed straight to the kitchen.

I fixed a small plate. Just enough to coat my stomach so when I started drinking, I could tolerate the beating I planned to put on my liver. After eating, I packed the remaining food into Tupperware containers and left them on the counter to cool. After I finished, I made my way back to my bedroom to get dressed. The bustier had my girls standing at attention and just like I thought, my ass looked good in the jeans I had chosen to wear.

Walking back to the bathroom, I curled my short hair so it fell in a feathery flow on my head. Adding eyeliner and a bit of lip gloss, I was ready to hit the streets. I thought about texting Tammy to let her know I was coming to the club but decided to pop up on her instead. Slipping my boots on my feet, I grabbed my purse and cell-phone and left my apartment.

Cautiously I stepped out of the glass door and locked it before scurrying to my car. Once, seated I connected my phone to the Blue-tooth and *The Need to Know* by Wale blared through the speakers. I pulled the gear into drive and headed for the expressway with Mauricio on my mind.

I'm not tryna pressure you
Just can't stop thinkin' bout you
You ain't really gotta be my boyfriend
I just wanna know your name
And maybe sometime

We can hook up

We can hang out, we can just chill

Even after telling me we were done, I still found myself thinking about him. On top of it all, I didn't want to leave him alone. Picking up my phone I pressed his name and waited for him to answer. The voicemail came one and hearing his voice brought a smile to my lips. I hung up and tried again but he didn't answer and my feelings were hurt. It was dumb of me to think he would answer anyway.

I jammed to different songs until I pulled up at the club. Money was jumpin' according to the line that wrapped around the building. Calling Tammy was a must because I wasn't about to wait to get in. Lucking up on a parking spot not too far away from the entrance, I grabbed my phone and hit Tammy with a text. Exiting my car, I slung my purse over my shoulder and clicked on Tammy's name as I walked back toward the club.

Me: Hey I'm outside and the line is long as fuck!

Tammy: I got you boo. Come to the door, I'm on my way out.

Quickening my pace, I made it to the entrance as Tammy peeked her head out the door. She pointed in my direction as she whispered in the bouncer's ear. He waved me over and I hurried to the front of the line and walked into the club.

"You should've told me you were coming," she yelled into my ear so I could hear her over the loud music.

Wrapping my arm around her waist, I leaned in to talk into her ear. "It was a last minute decision. I've had a rough day and need to unwind."

The music lowered for a bit and Tammy took that moment to talk without yelling. "I just came off stage and have an hour before I'm set to go back on. Let's sit and talk about what's going on," she said leading the way to the bar.

As we made our way through the crowd, many men reached out trying to get Tammy's attention but she kept moving. With the peach thong she had up her ass, the matching pasties covering her nipples, and the clear stilettos that adorned her tiny feet. Every step she took someone was fondling her, making it hard for us to get through.

Who wouldn't try to shoot their shot with her? The job was one she chose and enjoyed. All the attention came with being a popular stripper. I was glad they weren't paying me any attention because I wasn't in the mood for the foolery.

"Damn, these niggas think because they make it rain on a bitch they can reach out and touch whenever. Thirsty muthafuckas!" she said rolling her eyes as she sat on one of the two open stools at the bar.

I sat down and waved the bartender over. She looked my way and continued smiling in the dude's face that sat in front of her. Before I could say anything, Tammy stood from the barstool and stomped over to where the bartender was standing. Within minutes she was standing in front of me to take my drink order.

"What can I get for you?" She asked rudely.

"I would like a strawberry long island, but don't think about doing shit to my drink," I said looking her dead in the face.

"She ain't stupid! Right, Pinky?" Tammy said snidely.

"Bring me a double shot of Henny and a bottled water," Tammy responded.

Tammy watched Pinky like a hawk while she made our drinks. I sat back and rocked to the music that was playing and watched everyone having a good time in the club. My drink was placed before me and Tammy stood from her seat bopping to *Clout* by Offset. I waited for my part and I was out of my seat to show how much I loved it.

Look, whole lotta people need to hear this
It's a lotta names on my hit list
Mouth still say what it wants to
Pussy still wet like a big bitch
I should run a whole blog at this rate
They using my name for clickbait
Bitches even wanna start fake beef
Just send a little wave in the mixtape
They know I'm the bomb, they ticking me off

Saying anything to get a response
I know that mean they traffic is low
Somebody just gotta practice to launch

Rapping along with Cardi, I shook my ass and drew the attention as I twerked. When I finished the end of the rap, I took a sip of my drink walking off before a tall sexy nigga could make his way to me. Tammy grabbed my hand leading the way to the private rooms in back. "Aye, Shawty," I heard him yell but I kept going because he wasn't getting any play with me.

Tammy opened the door and I walked inside sitting on the plush sofa. "Talk to me, Latorra. What's going on?" she asked as she joined me.

Sipping from my drink I thought about what I wanted to reveal to her. After a few seconds I decided to start from the beginning leaving nothing out. Taking another sip before I caught my friend up on what had been going on in the past weeks.

"As you know, I've been dealing with Mauricio. We had sex and I found out his bitch is pregnant when I went to the hospital to see him. The beef he has going on with Floyd has nothing to do with me but I'm stuck in the middle."

"How the hell you in the middle? Don't nobody know you fuck with him," Tammy said angrily.

"Floyd knows because the bitch Mauricio is with has a sister that likes to shoot off at the mouth. Obviously, she told Floyd that she saw the two of us together. Big Jim is serving time at the same prison where I work. Tammy, he knew my mama!" I said with tears in my eyes.

"Who, Big Jim?"

"Yeah. He and my mama used to date back in the day." Pausing to collect myself as the tears fell from my eyes.

"So, that don't mean shit, Latorra. Don't get caught up in that man because he's grimy. No good can come from you associating yourself with him. Okay, he knew your mama. Leave that right there and ignore him."

"It's too late. Hearing what he had to say about my mama, I heard him out. He's my daddy, Tammy."

“That’s bullshit and he knows it! Floyd told him about your dealings with Mauricio and he would say whatever it takes to get information on that man. Please don’t fall for his shit.”

“I took a DNA test and he is indeed my father. Now, he wants me to set Mauricio up. I refused and now he’s sending rats and shit to my house. He had someone call me and threatened me before I cussed him out and hung up on his ass.

To make matters worse, I was fired from my job this morning. Inmates are saying I’ve been having sex with them during my shift. I have never had sex with any of them muthafuckas! It’s ironic how it happened the day after I told the nigga that called me to kiss my ass. Big Jim is behind the accusations, I know he is.”

“Hold up! this muthafucka got you fired? His ass is fuckin’ with yo’ bread because he’s trying to get at somebody else! That’s some bitch shit. I’m so pissed right now. You’ve been saving your money, right?”

“After paying my bills for the month, I have seven hundred dollars to my name. I didn’t expect to get lied on and lose my job,” I said wiping my face.

“You’re going to be straight, I got you. While you figure out your next move, you can dance here for the meantime. The money is good and Bentley owes me a favor,” Tammy suggested.

“No offense but I’m not shaking my ass naked in this club. Do they have a bartender position available? I’d rather do that.”

“None taken, I’ll see what Bentley has available,” she said as the door swung open with force.

A big burley dude frowned at Tammy when he spotted her. “I’ve been looking all over for you and you back here lolly gaggin’,” he snarled. “I don’t pay yo’ ass to lounge around, Devine. You’re up next. Get out there so you’ll be ready!”

“Piped that shit down, Bentley. My girl needed me. We both made a grip the first time I popped my pussy on the stage tonight. Fuck you mean?” Tammy shot back at him. “While I got your attention, my girl needs a gig and no she ain’t taking off her clothes. Is there room for another bartender?”

"We'll discuss that later. I need you on stage, Devine." Bentley looked at me licking his lips. I knew I would have to come in the club, do my job and go home. "Devine will let you know what's up some time tomorrow," he said leaving out of the room before I could say thanks.

Tammy downed her drink and stood to her feet. "Go out there, find a seat and watch how I make this loot. Maybe you will change your mind about that low budget ass bartending shit. Let the small shit go and enjoy yourself. Like I said before, you good. Drink all you want, it's on me," she said hopping up from the sofa.

Making our way out of the private room, Method Man & Redman's *Da Rockwilder* beat had the club turned up. I was rocking my hips to the beat as I looked for a place to sit. Everyone was going wild because the beat was sick! Spotting a seat close to the stage, I made my way to it while dancing through the crowd.

There was a group of niggas sitting at the table next to me and they were talking loudly even though the music had been lowered. It was annoying because they didn't have to shout to be heard. Sipping from my drink I tried to tune them out without bringing attention my way.

"I can't find Ricio in none of the hospitals. His name is Mauricio Vasquez, right?"

"Yeah, that's his name. Did you try the medical examiner's office? Maybe that nigga dead," another responded.

"Nah, but I will. Bossman gave me the information on the bitch that knows shit on him. I tried calling her and the hoe was disrespectful as fuck. I would've slapped the taste out her mouth if she was within reach. When I get the chance to approach her in the flesh, I want to see if she gon' still be loose at the lip then."

"Damn, Rello. You wild boy!" His homie laughed. "We didn't come here for this. Let's make it rain on these hoes while they shake their asses in this bitch and have fun."

Rello. I had a face to put with the name. I pulled my phone from my purse and snapped a low-key pic of the table of men. The way Rello talked about me pissed me off. Ricio wasn't answering my calls but we were in the same predicament with these fools. I may as well give him a heads up and get as much information that I could. It may be my only chance.

The music became louder again letting everyone know the next dancer was on their way to the stage. Rello looked down at his phone and leaned in speaking to his boy. They dapped each other up and that was my cue to leave before he did. Speed walking through the club, I raced to my car and did a U-turn to get to the other side of the street.

Rello was opening the door to his car when I drove slowly down the street. I was looking out the rearview mirror to see what my next move would be. He too did a U-turn behind me and I pulled over acting like I was looking for something. As soon as he passed me up, I pulled out behind him. I was prepared to get him before he could get to me.

Chapter 13
Rello

Money was my spot and I loved going there but I just wasn't feeling it that night. The only thing I wanted to do was get at Ricio and his brother. When my girl Courtney hit my line with a text asking where was I, that gave me a reason to get out of there.

Tracking down Ricio was harder than I thought. He was shot and now the nigga was nowhere to be found. I didn't believe he was dead but my gut was telling me they were plotting. Jumping on the expressway heading home, I couldn't believe them niggas used to get money together and nobody knew where the fuck they laid their heads at night. It was unbelievable and would've never happened on my watch.

Tupac's *Wonda Why They Call U Bitch* filled my ride soon as I turned on the Sirius radio. It took my mind to the bitch that came at me when I called her phone. All I could think about was my hands wrapped around her fuckin' throat while I watched her life come to an end through her nose. My phone vibrated and I ignored it because I knew it was Courtney again. She could wait until I got home to talk to me.

I'd already ended my night early for her ass. What more did she want from me? I wasn't about to listen to her talk about me being in the street all the time. My mama didn't live in my house so responding to a muthafucka when they wanted me to was something I had never done.

I rolled into the parking lot of my complex and killed the engine. Checking my surroundings as I exited my whip, I skipped up the steps two at a time until I got to the second floor. Before I could insert my key, the door was snatched opened quickly.

"Rell, why didn't you answer your phone? You know I hate when you do that shit. Anything could've happened and you're ignoring my calls!" Courtney snapped.

Gently pushing her to the side, I walked to the kitchen and grabbed a Heineken out of the fridge. "What's the emergency, Court?" I asked using the bottle opener to pop the top on the bottle.

"You know better than to hit my line like you were. That's an automatic way to get ignored because the shit is aggravating as fuck. Again, what was so important that you couldn't shoot a text stating what you wanted?"

"I could've gotten hurt for calling you repeatedly. Floyd came by here because he said your money intake was short when Lil Man brought it to him. Rell, he was high as fuck screaming about wanting his money. When I told him you weren't here, he pushed his way inside and searched the apartment for himself. I threatened to call the police if he didn't leave and he told me he would slap the shit out of me."

That was all I needed to hear before I slammed the beer on the counter and stalked to the door. "Rell, wait! Don't leave!" Courtney screamed stopping me in my tracks.

"Fuck that! Who the fuck is he, coming in here strong arming my woman in my house? I'm the wrong nigga to fuck with and he didn't have the balls to call me up! He thought coming for you was the right thing to do instead! Nah, wrong move on his part. Don't open this muthafucka for nobody, I'll be back!"

"Rell!"

Ignoring her cries as she called my name, I was out of the apartment faster than Speedy Gonzalez. I snatched my phone off my hip and hopped in my ride. Cranking up the engine, I hit Floyd's bitch ass up. Listening to the phone ring as I backed out of the parking spot and sped out of the lot. Anticipating him not answering and the voicemail picking up, the nigga finally answered at the last minute.

"What up, Rello? What's crackin'?"

I looked at the phone briefly to make sure I called the right person. Floyd was displayed at the top of the screen but his punk ass acted like everything was cool. "Where you at, nigga?" I barked into the phone.

"I'm over on 75th at the trap, come through. There's something I wanna run by you."

"Aight, I'll be there shortly," I said bangin' on his ass.

Since he wanted to act like shit was sweet, I was ready to play the game with him. I put the pedal to the metal and cut through the

Southside streets trying to get to the trap. I hit Damen at 55th and made a left to go further south. Traffic was nonexistent and that made it even better for me to get where I wanted to be faster. Ten minutes later, I was parking in front of the trap.

There were four of the homie's cars parked so I knew we wouldn't be the only two people in the trap but I didn't give a fuck who witnessed what was about to go down with this nigga. As I walked up to the door it opened. Lil Man was standing with a weird look on his face.

"Just the man I want to see," he said.

"Give me a minute, fam. Where that nigga Floyd at?" I huffed. He pointed behind him and I stalked inside with Lil Man on my heels. I entered the dining room where Floyd, Quis, Quake, and Kat was sitting in deep conversation. All heads turned toward me as I stalked over to Floyd and punched his ass in the mouth.

"Yo, what the fuck, my nigga!" Quis yelled.

Floyd's head jerked back against the arm chair he was sitting in and I went ballistic on his face. He tried to cover his face but he was too slow. Somebody pulled me by my waist and I gripped that nigga's shirt bringing him along for the ride. He wasn't getting off that easily. Fucking up his ribcage, Floyd buckled and fell to the floor forcing me to let him go.

"Rello, you wrong man!" Quis said pushing me in the chest.

"Wrong? This muthafucka came to *my* crib threatening Courtney because I wasn't there. He had that shit coming because won't none of you niggas disrespect mine," I growled. Turning toward Floyd, he was getting up wiping blood from his lip and looked down at his fingers when a half-filled baggie fell from the pocket of his hoodie.

"Rello, I didn't come to your crib, man. Your girl got me mixed up with somebody else. I wouldn't do something like that."

"You need to stop putting that shit up yo' nose, nigga," I sneered pointing to the baggie of coke that fell from his pocket. "It's fuckin' up yo' brain cells. My first mind was to come in this bitch and blow yo' got damn head off, but I had a talk with myself. Seeing the shit you're into tells me I made the right decision. You gon' kill yo'self fuckin' with that snow.

"That's not mine! I don't get high, nigga!" Floyd buffed up with a mug on his face.

I laughed at his ass because his eyes were bucked and he looked deranged. "Yo' ass high right now muthafucka! Not to mention, I saw the shit fall from your hoodie. You don't have to lie to kick it, Pookie! If you a cokehead, own up to that shit. It explains why you fuckin' up this operation."

"Damn, Floyd, tell me this shit ain't true," Kat said sadly.

"I, I, I don't get high," Floyd stuttered.

"Man, stop lying! You muthafuckas been sitting here shooting the shits with his ass and didn't notice how many times he sniffed. The nigga ain't never had allergies so that shit bet not be a rebuttal from nan one of y'all. Fuck all that, whatever rocks yo' boat is on you. I want to know how the fuck the intake was short when it made it to you, Floyd? When the money left my hands, shit was on the up and up," I questioned.

"Wait a minute, you didn't mention shit about the money being short. What the fuck you on, fam?" Lil Man asked.

"My bad, I counted it again and it was straight. It was a mistake on my part. The counter must've malfunctioned."

"Malfunctioned my ass! You lucky I didn't malfunction your muthafuckin' life. I'm out of this bitch! That ass whoopin' should hold you over and maybe it will convince you to get ya'self together. I still gotta get this money with yo' punk ass so, don't be on no kind of get back shit because I won't hesitate to lay you down. Take that shit like a nigga that deserved it because it could've been far worse."

Leaving out of the trap with all of them standing looking stupid, I walked down the walkway to my ride. As I opened the door, everybody came filing out behind me. "Aye, Rello!" Quis called out to me. Waiting for him to get to my ride, I lit a blunt and took a deep toke. "Floyd apologized but still insists that he isn't on drugs."

"Believe that shit if you want to, he's lying. Look around you, Quis. Shit is falling apart before our fuckin' eyes! We were forced into a war that we didn't know shit about. Floyd brought this to our doorstep and now we're being hunted by niggas we know nothing about. The Westside niggas didn't make bread with us. The only thing we had in common was Big Jim and Floyd.

All that other shit had nothing to do with us. Now we are on their hit list because we all fell into the trap of helping Floyd out and he don't even have a plan to retaliate on these muthafuckas. I've been trying to track down Ricio since I was told he was shot by Floyd. The nigga is nowhere to be found and that's not good for us."

"What we gon' do?" Quis asked.

"Tell everybody except Floyd to be at my crib tomorrow at noon. We got to handle this shit on our own. The traps are shut down until this shit is over and done with so we have to figure out how to get at these fools. Ask Floyd questions to get some type of information on these niggas. We have to move fast because they knocking us off like bowling pins. Have something for me tomorrow, I'm out."

"Aight, I'm on it," he said dapping me up before I put my whip in gear and pulled off.

Deciding to head over to Wing Zone on 95th to grab something for Courtney and I to eat. As bad as I wanted to go back and beat Floyd's ass again, it wasn't even worth it because I'd be locked up for killing him. I rolled down 95th street and turned into the parking lot of the wing spot when I saw a dude walking out of the restaurant that looked like Sosa.

He was smiling down at a female and wasn't paying attention to what was going on around him. I pulled into the first spot I saw on the side of the building and jumped out with my Glock in hand. Peeking around the wall, Sosa's back was turned away from me so I pushed off the wall and took aim.

"Get down!" the female yelled as she pushed Sosa to the right.

I pulled the trigger too late because both of them were able to take cover behind a parked car. Sosa lifted his head and I fired another shot and missed again. Pissed at myself because I almost never missed my target. Seeing movement from the right side, I noticed Sosa easing toward me using the cars as coverage.

Out of nowhere, the female popped up and let several shots off in my direction and I got hit in my left arm. Shooting in her direction while I back pedaled back to my ride, I barely made it inside before bullets tore into my shit. Starting my shit while ducked down, I put it in gear and backed up without clearing what was behind me. The rear window exploded and I pressed on the gas and took off. I didn't know how far their car was from mine, I took the next right to get off the main street and made a left down another street.

My arm was leaking blood and hurt like hell. I took out my phone and hit the number two button. I yelled in the phone when the call was answered, "I'm on my way to your crib. I was shot and I need yo' help!" I said to one of my dips that was also a doctor before ending the call.

I had just made matters worse for us because I hesitated when I had that nigga right in front of me. I needed to get a plan in order because they were not going to let this shit go.

Chapter 14
Rodrigo

Kimmie hit me up to chill with a nigga. At first, I didn't want to meet up with her because all I could think about was her creamy center. She wasn't the type of female that I would want to beat down every time we were in each other's presence. There was something truly different about her and I decided to play it safe and get to know her on another level.

Even though she and Sosa had some type of relationship, I didn't want to fuck up whatever that was being the dirty nigga that I was. When I agreed to pull up on her, going inside wasn't an option because we for sure would've been fuckin' the minute I entered. Instead I opted to take her out to grab something to eat. When I hit her up and told her I was outside, she didn't take long coming out.

"What's up, big head?" she spoke sliding in the front seat. "You could've come inside, you know."

"Nah, I don't feel like being cooped up inside. You hungry?"

"I'm always hungry," she laughed.

"What you got a taste for, anything in particular?"

"Yeah, chicken! Let's go to Wing Zone," she suggested.

I gave her the opportunity to pick the restaurant and she wanted some muthafuckin' chicken. Any other bitch would've had me blowing bread on an expensive restaurant just to eat half the shit they ordered then, box the rest up for their friends. Kim was a keeper and I had plans to keep her occupied until that nigga Sosa came back from vacation.

When we arrived at the restaurant, I found myself opening doors for her and pulling out chairs and shit. That wasn't shit that I did. Kim was making a nigga soft for her sexy ass. We sat at a table in the back and the waiter wasted no time coming to the table with two cups of water.

"Welcome to Wing Zone, I'll give y'all a minute to decide what to order," he said cheerfully.

"I already know what I want. What will you have, Rodrigo?"

“The sixteen-piece boneless Hotshot buffalo wings are what I’ll have with ranch on the side,” he said.

“Would you like fries or kettle chips with that, sir?” the waiter asked.

“Kettle chips will be fine,” I replied.

“Scratch that order please,” Kimmie interrupted. “I want the same thing so instead of getting two sixteen-piece wings, give us a thirty piece with ranch and blue cheese on the side. I will also take the kettle chips as well as fries and onion rings. To drink I would like a Pespsi.”

“I would have a Pepsi as well since there’s no alcoholic beverages in this place,” Rodrigo said snidely.

“Okay, I’ll be back with your drinks after I put your order in,” the waiter said collecting the menus that we didn’t open.

Taking a sip from my water, I stared across the table at Kimmie as she scrolled through her phone. She was beautiful with her caramel skin and full lips. The shirt she wore exposed her cleavage and the image of her brown areolas came to mind. How her pussy gripped my piece hardened his ass up with the mere thought.

“Why are you looking at me like that?”

Damn, she caught my ass staring at her, I thought to myself. “I wasn’t looking at you,” I said blinking rapidly to clear my head. “Actually, I was wondering, what kind of relationship do you and Sosa really have?”

“It’s not a relationship at all, we have an understanding. We kick it, smoke, drink, and fuck on occasion. I don’t expect nothing from him and he don’t expect shit from me either. With Max passing I noticed the difference in his behavior but I took it as his way of grieving. Y’all are really two different people living in the same body and it’s bizarre to me because I’ve never seen this type of thing in real life.

Sosa is a thug nigga but you take the shit to a whole other level. You shoot first and ask questions later, while Sosa is the mediator type. It’s seems like you and Ricio have changed roles because he is trying to tone your attitude down before you explode. Not to mention the situation between him and Nija has his mind off what's going on in the streets," she explained.

I didn't think about how Ricio felt when I reacted until Kimmie informed me. Regret was something I didn't feel about my actions. Max was no longer here and muthafuckas were going to pay for that shit with their blood.

"Another thing, I think you should go talk to Beast. The longer you wait, the worse y'all relationship will be. He's pretty mad because you haven't reached out to them and it's been a week. Believe me when I tell you, I understand why you did that. Give Beast and Sin a chance to see where your head was at the time," she said sincerely.

Kimmie was the only person that actually told me that I was going about shit the wrong way without screaming in my face. She had a real nigga sitting back actually thinking about everything I had done and I wasn't mad at her one bit. Nothing she said was going to change how I moved but I was taking everything in.

"I will go talk to Beast, but those niggas still dying, baby girl."

"No doubt. They brought whatever you have planned on themselves. They fucked with the wrong ones. Y'all can't let what happened go," she said as the waiter walked up with our wings.

"Here you guys go," he said sitting the platter of wings in the middle of the table. "I brought a picture of ice water because those wings are beyond spicy. They are hot!"

"Ain't nothing wrong with a little heat, man. I can handle it because I love a kick in my food. She's the one you need to worry about because she's not gon' be able to hang with the big boys," I laughed.

"You want to put a wager on that?" Kimmie smirked.

"I don't want to take your money, it's not long enough to fuck with me."

"Well I'll leave you two to compete. Give me a holler if you need me," the waiter walked to a table behind us.

"Aight, bad ass, let's get this shit crackin'. You need a bib and some milk?" The way she glared at me was funny as hell.

"Why you trying to get off the subject? How much money you putting up, Rodrigo?"

"You still on that shit? I'm not taking yo' money, girl."

"It's all woman over here. Stop confusing that shit with the little girls you're used to fucking with. Now about that money."

"Since you are being so persistent, the wager is five hunnid and I want my money when you lose. The rules are whoever drinks from their cup first loses. Deal?"

"Leggo! Ain't nothing to it but to do it," she said while rubbing her hands together licking her lips.

I picked up the first wing and held it up. She did the same and we tapped them together and dug in. The buffalo sauce was hot as fuck and my eyes watered with the first bite. Usually I had the regular buffalo sauce but wanted to try something different for a change. Kimmie was on her second wing and I was still babysitting the first.

"What's wrong, it's too hot for you, Mr. Shit Talker?" she asked licking sauce from her fingers.

"Nah, I'm just getting warmed up. Stop talking and eat ya food."

We ate silently and I was fighting the urge to chug my glass of water. I was sweating like a nigga lost in the desert and Kimmie was eating with no worries. She had to have a cast iron stomach and no taste buds in her mouth because she was truly unbothered when it came to those wings.

After eating ten wings straight, I couldn't take the shit any longer. My mouth was burning like a muthafucka and my stomach wasn't no better. Placing the half-eaten wing back on the plate, I reached for my water and Kimmie's eyes lit up with anticipation. She stopped mid bite to watch my next move. Grasping the glass, I brought it to my lips and drank all of the water.

"Yassssss! Pay up, buddy!" she yelled with her hands above her head.

Kimmie wasn't talking about shit that I wanted to hear, I was trying to get more water in my glass. Drinking four glasses of water and my mouth was still tingling, had me feeling like a lame ass nigga. Her lil short ass was still eating those hot ass wings and I couldn't believe it. I didn't even have a comeback for the cheering she had done during the time I had to drink. There was nothing to do other than pay up like she said.

Reaching in my pocket, I peeled off ten one hundred-dollar bills and sat them on top of the table. I glanced at the pitcher of water and poured another glass. "You won fair and square. I had to throw in extra because yo' ass still eating and haven't drank a drop of water. You a trooper, shawty. You gon' pay for that shit later when you get home," I laughed.

"Why do you say that?" she asked wiping her hands and picking up her Pepsi. The only wings that were left on the plate was the five I didn't eat.

"Your ass is going to burn when you go to shit. I'd love to be a fly on the wall to see your face."

"I'm true to this, not new to this, it won't faze me at all. Thanks for the rent money, big spenda." She picked up the money and counted it before dropping the bills in her purse. "You ready to go?"

"We can get up outta here. You want a to go box?"

"That's your food. I ate mine."

Waving the waiter over I glared at her like she was out of her mind. "I'm not eating no mo' of that shit. They can throw it away for all I care, but it's not going with me."

The waiter came over with a carryout container and the check. He must've saw the remaining wings and wanted to be helpful. The thoughtfulness and his kindness earned him a hefty tip.

"I brought a to go box for you. Did you enjoy the wings?" he asked placing the check on the table.

"Thank you but we don't need it. The wings were good but very hot," I said putting a money in the billfold. The waiter picked up the billfold and opened it up.

"I'll be right back with your change, sir."

"Nah, we're out, it's yours. Thanks for the excellent service," I said.

"That's a lot of money for a tip," he said skeptically. Are you sure?"

"I'm more than sure. You deserve it, homie. Going over and beyond your job description gets you ahead all the time. Have a nice night," I said standing from my seat.

Kimmie and I walked out of the restaurant and I couldn't keep my eyes off her. She was so beautiful but she was like one of the niggas. Don't get me wrong, she was all female but I could see myself kickin' it with her more often.

"Why do you always look at me like that?" she asked stopping outside the door.

Looking down at her five-foot frame, I licked my lips. "Damn, I can't admire your beauty, Kim?"

She didn't respond and her eyes expanded and fear replaced the smitten look on her face. "Get down!" she yelled as she pushed me with all her might. A gunshot rang out and I dived behind a car that was parked.

Glancing around I searched for Kimmie and didn't see her. No more gunshots rang out so I figured whoever was shooting was gone. Lifting my head, I peeked over the hood and more shots came my way and I ducked down quickly. I removed my tool from my back and crept behind the cars to get closer to the son of bitch that was shooting at me.

My eyes were trained on the gunman as I aimed at him but shots came from nowhere and I ducked thinking he had help. When I peeked from behind the car he was back pedaling around the corner. Kimmie ran after him and I was hot on her tail. He made it to his car and we both started busting at the car. His back window exploded but he took off out of the parking lot.

"To the car! We gotta get his ass!" she screamed running for the car. By the time I drove onto 95th the car was nowhere in sight.

"Fuck! These muthafuckas getting bold as hell," I screamed hitting the steering wheel.

"Calm down. They gon' get what's coming to them," Kimmie said putting her gun away.

"Thanks for having my back. You hit that muthafucka and he bolted. That was sexy as fuck, ma. Turned a nigga all the way on. Where did you learn to shoot like that?"

"You taught me," she smirked. "I mean, Sosa taught me."

"I was about to say, I ain't taught you shit. But I have plans to teach you how to bust without missing. You fired three times and hit that nigga once."

"And you didn't get a shot off. Let me find out you getting rusty," she said jokingly.

"Nah, I was trying to figure out where you were. You proved that you can handle yourself, Kim. I don't want to have you out here bustin' at these niggas 'longside me. I'm about to drop you off and go handle some shit. I'll hit you later, maybe we can get together and Netflix and chill or something," I said pulling into her driveway.

"By the time you come back it will be late. If you do decide to come back, be prepared to dish out that dick," she said getting out of the car before I could respond.

Chapter 15
Sin

I was so glad that Ricio made it out of that shooting with minor injuries. Seeing him at home working hard with his rehabilitation aide, brought tears to my eyes. He was adamant about getting back in the streets to avenge his brother's death. His determination was higher because Floyd shot him without going for the kill.

It was quiet inside my home when I entered. The first thing I did was walk down the hall to Madysen's room. Knocking on the door, the sound of shuffling could be heard before she approached the door and opened it.

"Hey, what's going on?" she asked leaning against the doorframe.

"I wanted to check on you and Gio. You okay in there?"

"Yeah, Gio is in his crib sleeping. His navel cord came off earlier and I burned it like you told me to," she smiled.

"That's good," I said smiling back. The way she was guarding the door frightened me a little bit. "Let me in so I can kiss the baby goodnight."

Sighing loudly, Madysen stepped back and motioned me inside.

The room was a mess. There were clothes scattered about, food containers on the dresser, dirty diapers on the floor, and the room smelled like shit. One thing I didn't tolerate was a nasty ass house. I kept shit spotless and it wasn't going to stop because she wanted to live like a pig.

"Aht, Aht. This isn't how we live around here. Open the window, Madysen. You need to clean this tonight. You're a grown ass woman that's living in filth with a baby sleeping in here with you. On top of that, I don't have roaches and rodents in my house and I want it to stay that way.

"Sin, I'm not a child and I should be able to clean up when I feel like it."

"You sure acting like a child if I have to come in here and tell you this muthafucka stank! If this room smell like this, I can only imagine what the fuck your pussy smell like. You don't even go nowhere but there's clothes all on the floor. And these smelly ass diapers should be in the baby genie, that's what it was bought for."

Stalking over to the crib, Giovanni was sleeping soundly. First thing I did was checked his diaper. The diaper was soaked as well as his sleeper. I picked the baby up and walked across the room to the changing table and grabbed a stack of pampers and baby wipes.

"Where are you going with my baby?" Madysen screeched.

"He's going with me. His pamper is wet as hell and it didn't get this way recently. This shit happened over several hours. Clean this shit up before I put you the fuck out!"

"Give me my baby, Sin! I don't need your help!"

"Hold on, what's going on in here?" Beast's voice boomed from the door.

"Look at this muthafuckin' room! She's about to clean this shit up and she's going to do the shit now or we're gonna have a major problem!"

Beast's eyes roamed around the room before they landed on Madysen. I took the time to clean Gio up. "Madysen, clean the room up please. There will be no more food in any part of the house other than the kitchen. Get those dishes out of here. This is ridiculous and we shouldn't have to tell you to clean behind yourself."

"I'm tired of y'all trying to run my fuckin' life! I've been on my own for years before meeting any of y'all. The only reason I'm here is because of that damn baby. I'll clean this muthafucka up, but I'm going to find a shelter that can take me and my baby in. I will not continue to be watched like I'm a rebellious teenager."

"Madysen you can leave when you're ready. You ain't taking this baby to a nasty ass shelter though. His butt is red as hell from laying in this pissy ass diaper. When he develops a rash and he's crying because his ass is raw, you won't know what the hell to do for him."

"Sin, you need to go upstairs and make a baby of your own! That one right there is mine!" She screamed at my back.

"That's enough, Mads!" Beast snapped trying to stop her before she could continue. I sped up the process of cleaning the baby because she'd jumped bad at the wrong time.

"Nah, she don't know what I'm going through after having my baby. She don't know what it's like to be a mother but she's always dictating shit to me. Until she pushes out a baby of her own, you better keep her away from me!"

"Madysen, that's a subject we will not speak on."

"Don't shut her up now, she has said more than enough," I said laying the baby back in his crib. Snatching Madysen by the top of her head and whammed on her ass. She had been itching for me to put a beating on her and she was getting it.

Beast tried to get me off her to no avail. "Sin, let her go!" he screamed pulling me by my waist.

"I opened my house to you and this the thanks I get from your trifling ass! Bitch I will kill you in this muthafucka!"

"Let me go!" she cried out swinging her arms to hit me.

The doorbell sounded but I kept hitting Madysen in the top of her head. Gio was crying but I didn't care about any of that. All I was concerned with was beating some sense into her. Beast finally got me away from Madysen and she ran out of the room.

"I'm leaving, Sosa! I'm tired of this bitch thinking she's my mama," I heard Madysen yell. The front door slammed and I picked Gio up and ran out of the bedroom.

"I'll take you calling me a bitch, Madysen!" I said watching her wrestle with Rodrigo to get out of the door. "This bitch helped you when you had nobody else in your corner to do so. The only thing I asked you to do was clean up the fuckin' room!"

"Let me out of here, Sosa!" she yelled trying to bite him.

"Sosa ain't in this muthafucka and I will slap the fuck outta you if you bite me. Stop this shit, Mads! Where you trying to go?"

"Anywhere but here!" Madysen yelled still trying to get out of Rodrigo's grasp. "I'll sleep in a shelter before I stay here listening to bullshit!"

"If you think you're taking my nephew to a shelter where people don't give a fuck who they let sleep there, you outta yo' mind. You have all the help you need within us and you trying to struggle in the street. You need to think before you speak because you sound stupid," Rodrigo said pushing her away from the door. "All you had to do was clean behind yourself and there wouldn't have been a problem.

Can't nobody live somewhere for free but you got it made and making shit difficult! Do you need therapy? If so, I'll arrange that shit and pay for it myself, Madysen. In my opinion, you need it."

"Really, Rodrigo? You should be the last person talking about somebody needing therapy. Mr. Split Personality. Don't judge me when you're crazy in real life. I'm only going through a form of depression. What's your excuse?"

Rodrigo walked toward her and Beast pushed him back before he could do anything to her. "Madysen, you're not going anywhere except in that room. Go clean up like you were asked and please don't battle with me because you won't win."

Storming past me, Madysen bumped into my shoulder purposely but I let it slide because I had Gio in my arms. The door to the bedroom slammed startling the baby. I shook my head and walked to the kitchen to make him a bottle. When I got back to the living room, Beast and Rodrigo was nowhere in sight.

Climbing the stairs, I entered my bedroom and sat in the rocker by the window. As I looked outside Beast and Rodrigo were standing in the middle of the backyard engaged in a heated discussion. I cracked the window a little bit to be nosy. Grabbing a light blanket to shield the baby from the air, I sat listening while I fed him.

"Beast, I wasn't trying to hear I needed to calm down, wait it out. Them muthafuckas tried to kill my brother, the only one I have left! Where was the lie in anything that I said to you? It's been *me* putting in the work with these niggas! I'm the one initiating shit! There's no time to wait no mo', that's how Ricio got hit because y'all are too relaxed and worried about what the media will think. Fuck them!"

"I'm trying to keep you out of trouble, nephew! I understand how you feel and I'm just as upset as you—"

"Act like it then, muthafucka! Get yo' muthafuckin' hands dirty for once! I came over so you can get yo' frustrations out because after this, don't come to me with no mo' bullshit. I will put you in the category of people to fuck up, Beast. Whatever you're feeling, get that shit off yo' chest right now."

I looked down at Gio and he had finished all of the milk. Listening to Rodrigo and Beast arguing back and forth was giving me a headache. The bickering was only going to last so long between them before hell broke loose. I placed the baby on my shoulder and burped him as I stood to lay him in the bassinet.

Crash!

The sound of glass breaking was heard from the opened window and I knew the time had come, I'd spoken it into existence. Racing to the window, Rodrigo was jumping to his feet and my glass table was shattered to pieces. I wasn't surprised because I knew it was going to happen sooner than later. Going to the closet I pocketed my nine-millimeter and turned slowly to head downstairs. Stepping out onto the patio, they were fighting like there was something to prove and neither was going to get tired any time soon.

They were going blow for blow and it was a scary sight. Rodrigo charged Beast and was caught in a headlock. Forcing his head downward, Beast brought his elbow down repeatedly on Rodrigo's spine. It didn't faze him because Rodrigo used all the strength he had in his body to lift Beast off his feet and slammed him on the ground. When Rodrigo raised his foot to bring it down on Beast's head, I knew I had to put a halt to the battle.

Pow!

I let a single round off in the air. Both of them upped their tools without thought and aimed in my direction. "Enough of this bullshit! Y'all have beat each other's asses now kiss and make up!" I yelled with the gun at my side.

"Are you stupid? You almost got gunned up doing that shit!" Rodrigo exclaimed! Beast on the other hand stared at me angrily, but I didn't give a damn.

"No, but y'all are! Out here acting like enemies when in fact y'all family. Were you going to kill each other if I hadn't put a stop to it?"

"It's not that serious for us to go that far. Nephew disrespected and we handled it accordingly. A good street fight amongst family ain't never hurt nobody. If these pussy ass niggas learned to fight and take that L, there would be fewer dead bodies in the streets. Me and nephew good, go inside. I already owe you one for fighting in my house! Now that, was uncalled for," Beast growled.

"Your house? Whatever. I bet she won't try that bullshit again," I retorted as I went into the house.

Madysen better get her shit together and stay the fuck away from me. Nothing would stop me once I got hold of her ass the next time. I knew Gio had to be in my sights at all times because if she tried to take him, her ass was going to be found floating in the Chicago river.

Chapter 16
Angel

The day Ricio was shot my body went numb and my blood boiled on the inside. Once I saw that he was cool laying in that hospital bed, I called Rodrigo constantly without him responding. From the things that I've seen and heard about my cousin I knew he was out causing all kinds of havoc in the streets of Chicago. I didn't blame him because I wanted to be on the same shit but I didn't know the first place to start looking.

Instead I googled electronics stores so I could get the equipment I would need to get started on my investigation. I purchased two of the latest models of the MacBook Pro, and a printer from BestBuy and got to work. Instead of using the software that common hackers use, I sat for hours creating my own. When I finished my eyes were burning from staring at the computer screen for so long. Stretching my arms to crack my back, I heard cuz groan loudly.

Rushing to my feet I went to see what the hell was going on. Opening the door to the guest room I slept in, I made my way down the hall to his bedroom. There was a woman in a pair of scrubs standing in front of him. She didn't have on any panties because the scrub pants were caressing the crack of her ass.

"You good, cuz?" I asked walking further into the room.

"Hell nawl! This shit hurts like a bitch and she wouldn't let me take a pain pill before doing these funky ass exercises."

"Man, fuck them pills! You a savage around this muthaucka. The last thing you need is to be dependent on that bullshit. Brave this shit out, you got it and I'm here to make sure you get through it."

"I'm not trying to hear that! I still got stitches in my shit and I feel them stretching like they gon' pop."

"Mr. Vasquez, You're healing just fine. These exercises are to strengthen your muscles. The stitches will dissolve on their own and some of them have. You have to endure the pain and think about how this will help you in the end. You've only been going through the sessions for a week and this is the first time you've done it at home. I want you to work on the treadmill today.

"I'm not getting on the treadmill! Bending my leg is a job in itself and the shit hurts! I didn't ask you to come to my house any damn way!"

"Mr. Vasquez, If you refuse, I won't have a choice but to recommend you do your therapy at the facility four days a week to use the equipment there."

Ricio ignored her and didn't respond. Cuz was being more stubborn than a mule at that point and I didn't know why. "Can you give us a minute, Miss lady? I wanna holla at my fam for a minute. Maybe I can get him to cooperate with you," I asked nicely.

She walked to the door and was closing it behind her when Ricio yelled out, "And don't touch nothing that don't belong to you!" He huffed as he positioned his back against the leather headboard of his bed.

"What's really going on, cuz? You snappin' on ol' girl for trying to help you get better. If you didn't want to do physical therapy in your home, why did you agree to it instead of going to the hospital?"

"This was Nija's doing! I asked her to stay here to help and she refused. My first night out of the hospital she stayed but when Nija left for work the next day, I received a call stating the therapist would be here today at noon. I was so mad I cussed the woman out and she still showed up."

I looked down at him because he was giving this woman hell for something meant for Nija. On top of that, he was jeopardizing his ability to walk better because of it. "Clear yo' mind and get right, cuz. You can't let whatever the hell is going on with you and Nija stop you from getting back on your feet!

The niggas that shot you are still out there probably gloating about taking you down and here you are crying about physical therapy! You weren't built like this, cuz! We need you better so we can end this shit and live life comfortably without looking over our shoulders everywhere we go!"

"I don't need you fuckin' lecturing me! Save—"

"Somebody needs to tell you what it is! If yo' daddy was here he'd punch yo' ass in the chest for lying there acting like a bitch. That's yo' problem, you think everybody is about to pacify you and it's not gon' happen. I'm going to get baby girl and you will do the fuckin' exercises, right?"

"Man, go get the bitch! The only reason I'm lettin' this shit go is because you showed me the importance of getting better. Other than that, I'd shoot yo' ass for coming at me like a hoe ass nigga."

"Stop acting like one," I said leaving his ass sulking with his face balled up. Walking down the hall, I found shawty sitting at the bar with her head in her hands. "Aye, ma. Excuse my cousin, this shit is kind of hard for him to deal with. I'm Angel, what's your name?" I asked looking over her voluptuous body the best I could with her being seated.

Glancing in my direction, she rolled her eyes. "I'm Mona, nice to meet you, Angel. At least one of you were raised right. I understand what Mr. Vasquez is going through. I've been doing physical therapy for four years and have seen people in worse shape than him. If he does what I ask he would be up and about in two months at the most.," she explained.

"Stop calling that nigga Mr. Vasquez. His name is Mauricio. The way his ass talked to you back there, all formalities would've gone out the window and I would've walked out on his grumpy ass." Mona laughed at what I said but I was serious. "Tell me how I can help you with his pinheaded ass and make things a little easier for you."

"Mr.—Mauricio said he had a weight bench, treadmill, and elliptical machine here in the house, but he refused to use them. I can't get him to do something he don't want to do on my own. If you can get him in his chair and to the equipment, that would be more than enough help.

Mona looked defeated and I found her pouty lips sexy. Tearing my eyes away from her mouth, I cleared my throat. "Give me a minute to get acquainted with you and I'll get him to the exercise room myself. If you've been in this profession four years, I know you've had to get gangsta on a couple muthafuckas to make them do right.

Don't give Mauricio's ass any lead way, go hard on him. Push him far as you possibly can."

"What makes you think I want to get to know you? I'm here to do my job and go home," she said blushing.

"I don't think about much. What I stated was I wanted to get acquainted with you. Now, if that's not something you're interested in doing, just be real and say that shit."

"A little conversation wouldn't hurt. What would you like to talk about, Angel? Just so you know, I'm only supposed to work with Mr.—"

"What'd I tell you to call him?" I asked with a raised eyebrow.

"Whatever. It's the professional in me, don't kill me over it," she laughed. "Like I was saying, I'm only supposed to be here until two and it's already one o'clock."

"An hour is better than nothing at all. We can talk after you're finished with my stubborn cousin. For now, we have to get him on the path to recovery. I need him to be able to stand on his own before I'm forced to shoot his ass," I said seriously. The look on Mona's face was funny as hell because she looked terrified by what I said.

***

Mona stayed over for about two hours and I learned a lot about her. She was twenty-six years old and very surprised that I was only twenty-three. She was single but swore she wasn't looking for a relationship because she worked a lot. We would see about that shit the more she came to the house to work. I had plans to give that fatty a round of physical therapy of my own.

Before Mona left, we exchanged numbers and made plans for dinner the next night. After Ricio's extensive workout, he went right to sleep. Taking a shower, I threw on a sweat suit and sat back at the computer to dig deep into Sam. The feeling of deceit hasn't left my mental since we met up with him at the last meeting. There was a reason he sought my cousin out to buy from him and I'm not going to stop until I find out.

I heard Ricio's phone ringing loud and clear from down the hall. "Aight, I'll be there within the hour. Thanks, Staci, I appreciate you." Ricio's voice carried to the guest room. I left out and headed down the hall to find out where he thought he was going, and who the hell Staci was.

"Who is Staci?" I asked leaning against the doorframe of his bedroom.

"She's my realtor, nosy ass. I need you to help me get dressed and drive me to see this spot I've had my eye on."

"I think you should get in the shower before you put on clean clothes, cuz," I said walking into his room.

"How the fuck am I supposed to do that? *You* ain't about to help me shower, nigga. So just help me throw on a pair of sweats and a shirt. I'm not going to fuck no damn body, I'm good. Plus, a nigga ain't funky and I won't be gone too long."

"Aight, but I want you to know, yo' ass smell like a muskrat. You funky as hell," I laughed walking to his closet to get his clothes.

"Fuck you, Angel. Just get my shit so we can go. I'm not trying to impress nobody and we won't be gone long. After this you can get the fuck out my shit!"

"Oh, so now you putting me out? I'm not worried, you talking crazy as fuck right now but I'm gon' let you have it," I said helping him slip on his pants. Slightly lifting him up, I pulled the sweatpants over his butt.

"Nigga, watch yo' hands!"

"Ricio, ain't shit gay about me. I'm gonna have to call Nija or Sin to help you dress from here on out because it's not sitting well with me being this close to your musty ass. Put this shirt on best you can, muthafucka so I can help you into this chair."

"I can get in that chair on my own for your information," he smirked.

"You mean to tell me I lifted yo' heavy ass earlier for nothing!" I growled.

"Yep. The shit hurts like hell but it's not impossible. It's the exercises that take a lot out of me, not getting in and out of my chair," Ricio laughed as he put his arms through his shirt slowly. I watched his punk ass sit up and swing his legs out of the bed before holding on to the wheelchair to lower himself into it. "Let's go, I need to get back and rest up, I'm tired."

"You need to come back and wash yo' ass," I said following him out the room.

"Keep it up and I'll run yo' Spanish speaking ass over."

Once I had his incompetent ass seated inside my ride, I got in on the driver side and brought the car to life. "Where we headed?" I asked backing out of the parking spot.

"Go towards Sosa's crib and I'll direct you from there."

Twenty minutes later, I was passing Sosa's crib and had made plans in my head to stop over there after we finished Ricio's business since his car was in the driveway. "Pull up to the white house on the right," he instructed.

I parked the car in the driveway and the house was beautiful from the outside. Ricio was really stepping his game up. It was time for him to get out of the condo and buy a new home because he had a baby on the way. I just wanted him to be able to enjoy it without all the bullshit going on. A petite woman stepped out onto the porch waiting for us to get out of the car.

"That must be Staci," I said staring at her lustfully.

"Yeah, get my chair so we can check this crib out."

I opened the passenger door after retrieving the chair from the trunk and helped his grumpy ass out of the car. Staci had opened the garage which I was glad for because I didn't want to carry his ass up the steps. Rolling Ricio into the kitchen, I paused as I looked around at the granite countertops, the stainless-steel appliances, and the oak wood cabinets that were on display. It was very spacious. Any woman in her right mind would love to cook in that muthafucka.

"You like it?" Staci asked Ricio.

Instead of answering her question, he looked up at me and asked the same question. "This yo' shit, the question is do *you* like it?" I shot back.

"It's cool. I have to see the rest of the house before I decide."

Staci led us into the dining room and I noticed so far, the house was fully furnished. That was odd to me because usually a property is empty for a showing. The table was big enough to sit at least ten. I didn't voice my suspicions and kept pushing cuz throughout the crib. When we got to the living room, it was decorated in slews of blacks and greys.

The sofa was a black sectional with grey pillows and there was a charcoal black glass table that had a vase full of black and grey marbles inside of it. There was a flat screened tv mounted on the wall and a huge stereo system in a glass entertainment case. I looked down at the Vantablack carpet and noticed the huge 'AV' displayed in grey. It didn't take long for me to figure out that Ricio had purchased and furnished this house for me.

"Damn, cuz! Are you serious?" I asked happily. "You didn't have to do this."

"I know I didn't, it was something I wanted to do. Cuz, you are here with me and my brother and I told you we were gon' look out for you. The amount of money you got means nothing to me, but getting yo' punk ass out of *my* crib was a must," he smiled evilly.

"All you had to say was get out and I would've obliged. You didn't have to buy a muthafucka a house." Pushing the side of his head, I hugged him tightly because the appreciation was real. My own father didn't offer to buy me a crib. He demanded that me and my brother live in his home. That gave him more control over us and it felt good to be out on my own in America. I could now actually get to experience being on my own.

"There's four bedrooms, three baths, and a full basement in this muthafucka. Go ahead and check it out. I can't go with you because I'm in this chair, but I'll see it eventually."

I left Ricio with Staci and went to check out the rest of the house and I loved it. I couldn't wait to have my brothers and cousins together again while they were here. We were about to brainstorm and get this shit rolling without having to watch what we say in the hotel room. Taking out my phone, I sent a message to them with the address to the house.

Angel: Pack ya shit and get to this address ASAP! 4136 Cambridge Circle, Country Club Hills, Illinois 60478

Javier: What's going on, bro? Everything cool?

Alexander: Do we need to gear up?

Mateo: We on our way! Get ya'll shit together so we can go!

Nicholas: I agree. We'll be there shortly, cuz.

I knew Mateo was going to be the one that got them together by skipping over all the questions. Responding wasn't necessary because I knew they were going to be here in the next hour or so. Putting my phone back in my pocket, I walked from room to room and I knew I was going to give Ricio a fat check to cover this shit. The way I was raised, I was tired of handouts even though I knew my cousin meant well. Accepting it was something I wouldn't be able to do.

When I went back downstairs, Rodrigo was talking to Ricio and Staci was nowhere in sight. I was glad to see him because nobody had heard from him since the night at Beast's house. I noticed he had a few bruises on his face and I got heated and was ready to set some shit off. He looked up and smirked at me.

"You like the crib, cuz?"

"I love it. What happened to yo' face though?" I asked.

Touching the bruises, he kind of laughed it off. "Me and Beast had some shit we had to squash. Things got physical and we both left one another with a little gift. All that shit is behind us and we cool."

"So, I guess he whooped yo' tough ass, huh?" I smirked.

"He didn't do shit," he retorted. "Did we go toe to toe? Yep, until Sin let her bitch ride stopping us mid punch. We both pulled out on her ass because we didn't know what was going on. She let us box it out long enough to get shit off our chests. Sin was still pissed at Beast for breaking up the fight between her and Madysen."

"Wait, Sin finally beat the brakes off Madysen's ass?" Ricio asked.

"Yeah. Sin asked her to clean the room she's been staying in and all hell broke loose. I didn't see the actual fight but Madysen was trying to leave as I was about to ring the doorbell. She was talking stupid saying she was taking Gio to a muthfuckin' shelter. I almost slapped her teeth down her throat when she tried to bite me because I refused to let her go. We have to get her some help before she hurts herself or the baby."

"Man, if she does anything to my nephew, I'll send that bitch straight to hell. I'll look into some places because she is out of control if Sin had to put them paws on her," Ricio belted out angrily. Rodrigo sat on the sofa and we joined him. Well at least I did, Ricio sat in his wheelchair with a frown on his face. "I'm pissed at you myself, bro.

Don't ever go missing the way you did. Not knowing where you were had a nigga worried, lying in a hospital bed, on top of it nobody knew if you were good. We've already lost too much for you to do shit like that when muthafuckas coming for our heads.

"I feel what you saying, bro but I had to clear my head. We got at a lot of them muthafuckas the night you were shot. Them niggas didn't do it per say, but they were guilty by association in my book. The bigger fish is still out there and he gon' get his in due time. Word on the street is you're dead. We'll keep it that way for the time being. How's your therapy going?"

Turning toward Ricio to give him my undivided attention, I waited for him to shoot that bullshit to his crazy ass brother. He looked over at me knowing he bet not lie. I was ready to put his ass on blast.

"I started today. Nija set shit up so they would have a therapist come to the crib. Instead of her helping me out, she made it easy for herself. She's being real selfish right about now. I don't know what the fuck her problem is."

"Ricio, you're her muthafuckin' problem," Rodrigo growled getting in his face. I told you to stop playing with that girl, but you didn't listen. At least she still gives a fuck enough to make sure you were straight. If she didn't, yo' ass would be sitting around trying to figure out who would be taking you back and forth to therapy. What, you thought she was gon' go back on what she said because you got shot?

Then on top of that, one of the bitches you fuckin' with made it her business to tell her she was yo' woman. How the fuck did you expect her to act? Sis, looked out for you. Shouldn't that count for something? And stop trying to buy her, nigga! She ain't one of these materialistic ass hoes that yo' dumb ass is used to. You out here fuckin' with these bobblehead ass hoes and got a gem in your fuckin' face," Rodrigo snapped shaking his head.

Cuz, had a point. Some of these females wouldn't have done as much as Nija did. Ricio needed to concentrate on getting better and less on Nija. I didn't believe she was going anywhere personally. She was just teaching his ass a lesson.

"Back to this Ricio died shit," I said changing the subject to get the heat off cuz for a minute and onto something of importance. "Where'd you hear that from?"

"You remember Jessica, Ricio?" Rodrigo asked sitting back on the couch.

"Tell me that hoe ain't back in the picture, bro. Where the muthafuckin' weed at? I need to smoke." Rodrigo went into his pocket and came out with a sack and a pack of swishers. "My nigga!" Ricio's eyes lit up at the sight of the green.

"I don't even know this hoe," Rodrigo said breaking down the swisher on the coffee table. "She called with all the dramatics talking about she heard about my brother getting killed and she was sorry my family was going through so much. Not knowing how to respond, I stayed quiet because I didn't know what the bitch was talking about. She started calling that nigga Sosa's name then she asked if I was still there. I responded nope and hung up on her ass."

We all laughed because this nigga ain't never gon' believe that he and Sosa is the same muthafucka. Ricio stopped laughing as Rodrigo passed him the blunt. "How you know it was Jessica that called?" He asked putting fire to the tip.

"That's the name that came up on the phone. She texted saying her cousin heard a nigga named Quake talking about how they caught you slippin' and laid you down. I want them to keep believing that shit though. Angel, from this point on, all interactions with

Sam will go through you. He is not to know Ricio is alive, I'm not trusting nobody.

The only people who knows differently is our family. Oh, and Ricio's other lil bitch. I'll fill Nija in on what's going on, I already told Sin, Beast, and Kimmie." Ricio coughed on the smoke he had inhaled and glanced at his brother. "Don't say shit brah, you knew I was gon' smash shawty. She already had shit going on with that nigga Sosa anyway," he smirked like he took that nigga woman or something.

"Speaking of Kimmie, she blasted a nigga the other night when we were leaving Wing Zone. The nigga knew me but I didn't know who the fuck he was. Believe me when I tell you that his face is embedded in my mind. The way Kimmie made her tool crack bricked my shit up on sight," he said smiling.

"Them niggas getting bold. I'm cool with handling Sam. I bought all the equipment I need so I can look into Floyd, Big Jim, and Sam too. I already created software to get on it and I'll have something soon. I know Big Jim and Floyd got family around this muthafucka and I'm determined to find 'em. We got to hit them harder than we did on 76th. It seems they think this is a cat and mouse game. It's time for us to wipe their asses out like a battleship game, except we ain't giving them a chance to strike back," I said as the doorbell sounded.

"Who the fuck could that be? Don't nobody know about this spot but us!" Ricio asked pulling his gun from under the cushion of his chair.

"That's the clan. I texted them with the address and told them to pack their shit and come on," I said getting up to answer the door. "We're about to chop it up for a minute and figure shit out together. Get ready, it's about to be a long night, fellas."

Chapter 17
Nihiyah
Three months later

I hadn't been back to my mama's house since she had me arrested. Things were harder than ever for me and I was too shamed to go back and ask for help. My phone was disconnected and I was living out of my car. Jolie was providing me with drugs and a place to stay until her funky ass mama made me leave. Three hundred dollars came up missing from her purse and the first person she accused was me. I may indulge in drugs but stealing, wasn't my forte.

The temperature was cold and I didn't have a coat to keep me warm. It wasn't below zero cold but it had to be at least fifty degrees. I didn't know how much longer I'd be able to sleep in my car. My stomach felt like it was in my back because I hadn't eaten anything in three days. But I'd smoked enough crack to last a lifetime and still had that monkey dancing on my spine.

Going to my mama's house was the only place I had to go. It was taking everything in me to swallow my pride and ask her to forgive me for everything I had done. My hair was matted, my clothes were dirty, and I smelled like I lived in the garbage can like Oscar the Grouch.

I started my car and pulled from behind the church onto Madison Street and got caught at the light. As I waited for it to turn green, my gas light came on and started beeping. "Damn, what else can go wrong," I asked out loud. The light changed and I took my foot off the brake.

Boom! Boom! Boom!

The sound startled me and I almost took off down the street but it was a good thing I didn't. I looked toward the sound and Jolie was trying to get my attention. Popping the locks, she jumped in with a panicky look on her face.

"Go, bitch!" she screamed banging on the dash letting a bag fall to the floor of the car. I stepped on the gas running through the light just as it turned red.

"What the fuck is wrong with you?" I asked glancing at her quickly before concentrating back on the road.

"We need to get off the Westside. Bitch I just took a nigga's whole damn stash! This ain't the ordinary stash that I usually come up on, it's bigger than that shit," she said looking back out the window.

"Jolie, I thought you said you wasn't going to do that shit no more."

"I couldn't let that lick slip out of my grasp. Them niggas was fighting and the shit was there for the taking. Finders keepers bitch," she laughed as she rummaged through the bag. "Bitch, there's drugs and money in this muthafucka. Jackpot!"

"You would pull this shit on a night I'm running out of gas! What would you have done if you didn't see me at the light, Jolie?" I asked making a right on Pulaski Boulevard.

"Hell if I know. We don't have to worry about that now because I'm safe in this car with you." Jolie kept looking out the rear window biting her nails. "I don't think nobody saw me snatch the bag up. Everybody was watching the fight. I think I'm good. Go to the Citgo gas station so we can fill up and we hitting I290 to get off this side of the city."

"You want me to stop and get gas this close to where you just took somebody's shit, Jolie?"

"We don't have a choice! I'll get out and pay, you be ready to pump the gas. Just hurry up and get there to be on the safe side."

The gas station was only about a mile up the street and we were getting caught at every fuckin' light. I was paranoid and kept thinking we were going to get rammed from behind at any moment but it never happened. Pulling into the gas station I kept the car running while Jolie took twenty dollars out of the bag and hopped out. Frantically looking around I glanced down at the bag and saw a bundle of bills on the floor that fell out the bag. There was a hundred dollar bill on top and I could only imagine how many more was inside the bag.

My nerves were going a mile a minute and I wouldn't be able to drive in my condition. Jolie ran out of the gas station and straight for the pump. I guess she wasn't trying to wait on me to get out. I kept checking my surroundings because I had a feeling in my stomach and it wasn't because I was hungry. Something bad was about to happen.

"Jolie hurry up, bitch! I feel like something ain't right!" I screamed as I lowered the window.

"Look in the bag and get you a hit to calm yo' ass down. I got away with the shit," she boasted shaking the nozzle before hanging it back on the pump.

As soon as she got back in the car, I took off before she closed the door completely. Making a left on Pulaski I drove south signaling left onto Harrison Street and got on the expressway. Traffic was pretty light for a Monday night and I was glad there wasn't any construction going on. it didn't stop me from checking the rearview mirror every now and again to make sure we weren't being followed.

I relaxed a little bit as I merged onto I90E/I94E because in about ten to fifteen minutes I would be that much closer to my mama's house. Jolie was sitting back without a care in the world while deep inside I was ready to shit bricks. Exiting the expressway at 95th Street, I made a right and smiled because I was almost at my safe haven. Looking into the rearview mirror, I saw a midnight black car behind us and got scared.

"Jolie, I think that car is following us," I said with a shaky voice.

"You're paranoid, boo. There's nothing to worry about, just drive this muthafucka!"

Approaching Kedzie Avenue I made a right and so did the black car. When I got to 92nd street I lifted my eyes to the mirror before I signaled to turn left. The car went around us and I let out the breath I was holding and completed the turn. Pulling into an empty spot down the street from my mother's house, I put the car in park.

"Give me that package you were talking about earlier. I need something to ease my nerves before I go to my mother's door."

"To be honest, Nihiyah, I don't think your mother is going to let us stay in her house. We have enough money to stay at a hotel for the night, then we can look for an apartment tomorrow. This isn't just my come up, this shit is ours."

I believed everything Jolie said but I wasn't about to drive anymore that night. All I wanted to do was get high and pray my mother had a heart to let us stay the night. Stuffing the pipe with crack, I fished around for my lighter so I could finally smoke. A shadow in my peripheral caught my attention but it was too late.

A hooded figure hit the window shattering it in my face. My arms automatically covered my head but it didn't shield me from the bullets that entered my body. The burning sensation traveled throughout my body and I could vaguely hear the passenger door opening.

"Bitch stole from the wrong muthafucka and she paid for it in blood. Give me my shit!"

I tried my best to stay quiet but it was hard to breathe and blood was filling my throat choking me. I coughed while the mystery man collected what was rightfully his and he paused. Looking up into his face he smiled sinisterly and pointed the gun to my head, pulling the trigger.

Chapter 18
Nija

Being five months pregnant was new to me and it was killing me on an everyday basis. I wasn't used to being sick every minute of the hour and my body was tired. Ricio had been calling and I tried my best to be cordial with a him because he was the father of my baby. He wanted me to come live with him but I was comfortable in my own space.

I'd finally found a small house that I loved a couple blocks from my mama and Kimmie. Starting fresh was something I opted to do instead of risking going back to old my place to get my belongings. Of course, Ricio sent money through Rodrigo and Kimmie every chance he got and I put that shit in an account so when I decided to give it back, it would be there untouched.

"What the hell you over there thinking about?" Kimmie asked walking into the kitchen where I was sitting. She'd convinced me to come over for a girl's night of quesadillas and taco salad.

"Nothing really. I still can't believe I'm pregnant," I said rubbing my protruding belly. "Nihiyah has been on my mind a lot lately and deep down I really wanted her to reach out to me so I'd know she was okay."

"Girl, Hiyah's ass is okay. She will come around sooner than later because she's not going to be able to handle being out there when that hawk gets ahold of her ass. Winter's in Chicago ain't no joke so I'll bet money she'll be knocking on somebody's door real soon."

Kimmie sat down in the chair across from me and her phone vibrated instantly. She was cheesing from ear to ear so I knew it was Rodrigo. My best friend was smitten with his crazy ass and I couldn't understand how she tolerated him. When she told me they had been hanging out, I knew right away he had a lot to do with the funky walk she possessed at times.

"Nigga got you over there looking like a Cheshire cat around this muthafucka," I laughed.

"Nija, if you would stop being so stubborn, Ricio could have you looking the same way. I don't know why the hell you putting that man through so much turmoil. He's already apologized and still helps you out without being asked. Y'all have too much history to let shit end like this. You have to admit that he has never put any bitch above you and has given you the upmost respect.

The only thing he is guilty of is not solely committing to you. Sis, you ran along with the relationship y'all had for years. Don't get me wrong, you deserve more for the time and effort you put in with him but it can't be forced. I think both of y'all should let it play out as it may. That's my opinion though."

"I sat back so it could play out too long, Kimmie. Just because I'm carrying Ricio's baby doesn't mean we need to be together as a couple. True enough, he apologized when he was in the hospital but it was only because he got shot. It just so happened his hoe showed her ass at that precise moment for him to check her about the things she said.

Ricio had my heart for years and didn't know what to do with it. I'm not going to dedicate my time while he continues to neglect the love I have to offer. There's a man out there that would be willing to love me and only me while I'm sitting back waiting on him to get his shit together. Plus, I'll have a baby to think about in four months, I no longer have time for the bullshit."

"Nija, whatever you decide to do from here on out, I'll still stand by your side regardless. Are you going to work tomorrow?"

"No. You forgot I have an appointment to find out the gender of the baby, didn't you?"

"Actually, I didn't but I made provisions for my Godchild's father to be in attendance." Kimmie hunched her shoulders because she knew I was upset with her the minute she said that shit. "Come on, Nija! He has every right to be there."

"Maybe I didn't want—"

Pow! Pow! Pow! Pow! Pow! Pow!

Both of us dived on the floor taking cover with the sound of the gunshots that rang out too close for my liking. Hearing gunshots in the neighborhood where I was raised was uncommon but the way the city was going to shit, I wasn't surprised. My heart was racing because the shots seemed like they would never end.

"Did Rodrigo say he was coming over here?"

"No, he just asked what I was doing. There was no mention of him coming through." She said raising up just enough to grab her phone as the gunshots suddenly came to an end. A car speeding away could be heard outside the window.

"Hey, where are you?" she asked into the phone. "Where's Ricio?" she paused as she listened to his reply. "Okay, I'll call you back." Kimmie ended the call and stood up. "They are at the warehouse. Those bullets were for somebody else."

Sirens wailed through the once quiet streets and within minutes, flashing lights were illuminating the windows. I rose slowly and bile eased up my throat forcing me to run to the bathroom. Barely making it to the toilet, I threw up everything I'd eaten that night. Kimmie was by my side rubbing my back and it soothed me.

"I'm okay, bestie," I said as I flushed the toilet. When I stepped to the sink and looked in the mirror, I was alone in the bathroom. The confusion I was feeling turned into fear. "Kimmie!" I screamed rinsing my mouth out.

"You okay?" she asked appearing in the doorway.

"Were you in here rubbing my back as I vomited?"

"Nawl," she said disgustedly. "I was in the window trying to see what's going on outside. The whole damn police force is on this block. They have the street blocked off."

"Something was touching me in here! You have a ghost in this muthafucka," I said walking out of the bathroom. "Let's see what we can find out. Maybe one of the neighbors saw what happened.

I grabbed my jacket and put it on as I opened the front door. The street was flooded with police officers and people trying to see what was going on. As we walked down the steps, Miss Janice came running towards me.

"Nija, go check on your mother."

"Miss Janice, what do you mean?" I asked looking around.

"She's over there talking to one of the officers," she said pointing down the street.

I looked in the direction she pointed and noticed Nihiyah's car surrounded by police. My stomach dropped and I stumbled toward my mother. Kimmie grabbed my arm to steady me and we continued on together. Watching my mother's body language, I knew my sister was involved with the shooting that took place.

"Ma, what happened?" I asked.

"Who are you, ma'am?" The officer asked turning to me. I opened my mouth but no words came out. The only thing I could do was stare at Nihiyah's car. Seeing the officers leaning inside taking notes and walking back and forth, I was lost.

"She's my daughter," my mother responding on my behalf. "Nija baby, Nihiyah is in the car and she's been shot."

"Why aren't they getting help for her? She needs to go to the hospital!!" I screamed at the police officer. The look on his face was grim and I didn't like what I saw so I turned back to my mother. That's when I saw the tears running down her face. She pulled me into her body and hugged me tight.

"She's gone, Nija. They are waiting on the coroner so they can take her body away."

"No. No. No, this can't be happening. He My sister is not dead! She just needs y'all to get her to the hospital," I said trying to get out of my mother's arms. She held on tighter and I sobbed on her shoulder as the words 'she's gone rang in my ears.

"Nija, it's okay," Kimmie said hugging me from behind.

"I'm alright. I promise, I'm alright," I cried pushing off my mama.

She loosened her arms and I took off running toward Nihiyah's car. None of the officers were paying attention so I made it under the red tape that was put around the crime scene. "Don't let her get to that car!" the officer I was talking to yelled. I was grabbed as I approached the car and screamed from my soul at the sight of my sister motionless body in the car.

Nihiyah was slumped over in the driver's seat with holes riddled in her body. There was blood covering the left side of her face and her eyes were open staring blankly. The light in her eyes was nonexistent. The woman in the passenger seat had a visible hole in her neck and her head rested against the window with a huge blood shatter outlining it.

"Ma'am, I'm officer Haddon. I need you to go back on the other side of the barrier. You don't need to see this," he said pushing me back gently.

"That's my sister! Why the fuck is she out on display like that?! Shield her from view!" I cried hitting him in the chest.

"What's your name, hun?"

"Nija," I sniffled.

"Nija, we have to wait for the coroner to arrive before we can remove your sister from the car. The bodies have to be properly handled so we don't destroy any evidence that may be on the bodies or inside the car. I'm sorry for your loss but is there anything about your sister that we should know about?"

"No, there's nothing you should know about her."

"Are you sure? There was a crack pipe in her lap and a large number of drugs on the passenger side of the floorboard."

"Are you interrogating me about drugs I know nothing about or are you trying to find out what happened to my sister?" I snapped.

"Calm down, this is not an interrogation at all. Any information would be helpful in finding the persons responsible for this murder. We want to get on this as soon as possible seeming the shooting happened very close to where your mother lives."

Taking a deep breath to calm myself down. I glanced around trying not to look back at the car Nihiyah was still in, but it didn't help. A white van was let through the barricade on the other end of the street and I started tearing up again. Blinking rapidly, I turned back to Officer Haddon.

"My mother and I found out my sister were using drugs months back. We tried to get help for her but she refused. We haven't seen her in months and that's why this hurts so bad. The only reason she would've been on this street was to come to my mother's house. I believe in my heart she was coming to change her life. Whatever happened before she arrived, took place unexpectedly. Nihiyah wouldn't bring this type of drama to my mama's doorstep."

"Thank you for telling me what you could. Here's my card if any new information comes your way. I need you to go back on the other side of the tape please," he said grabbing hold of my arm.

Moving wasn't an option for me because I needed to see my sister before she was taken away. "I promise I won't move from this spot. All I ask is that I'm given the chance to see my sister before they take her away."

"I can't promise that, Miss Nija. You can stand here with me and watch from here," he said as I watched the coroner snapped a brown paper bag open and placed it on Nihiyah's hand.

It took well over thirty minutes for the coroner to secure the body before removing it from the car. Nihiyah's body was place onto the stretcher and the coroner started zipping the bag slowly. My feet moved in the direction my sister was lying and then I sprinted forward.

"Don't close her in there! No one can breathe in that thing, she's not an animal!" I screamed. "Please, listen to me!"

I was grabbed from behind for the second time that night before I collapsed to the ground. My body shook as I wailed loudly watching Nihiyah disappeared into the black bag. Fighting to get on my feet, the strong arms that were wrapped around my body only held on tighter the more I tried to get up.

"Let me up! I need to get to my sister!" I cried.

"It's okay, baby. I got you."

The sound of Ricio's voice soothed my soul but nothing could soothe my broken heart. All thoughts of being mad were gone in the wind once he was there to console me. We hadn't really communicated since I left his house the day he came home from the hospital after being shot. I called to check on him but I kept communication at a minimum. Nihiyah's death took me back to the day Max was killed times ten.

***

Officer Haddon and his partner followed us to my mom's house after the coroner's van drove off with Nihiyah and the other woman's remains. I sat on the couch with my head resting on Ricio's shoulder. Rodrigo and their cousins were scattered about the house but they stayed clear of the police.

"Mrs. Foster, first I want to give my deepest condolences to you," Officer Haddon said taking a seat in the arm chair. His partner sat on the couch next to my mother.

"Thank you," mama said picking nothing off her pants.

"Tell me what type of life your daughter lived. I want to figure out why this happened to two very young women," Officer Haddon said beginning his questioning.

"My daughter has been doing her own thing for the past couple years. I never had to question what she did outside of my home until a couple months ago. She admitted to using drugs but swore she didn't have a problem. After telling her to leave my home, she came back about three months ago and threw a brick into my window. She went to jail that night and I hadn't heard from her since."

I watched my mama from the time we were outside 'til that moment. The only time she shed a tear was when she told me Nihiyah was dead. The hurt was visible on her face but I believed my mama expected something to happen with Nihiyah. My mind went back to the day me and my sister fought in the very living room where we sat. The last thing she said was, her insurance is paid.

"Do any of you know anything about Jolie Hernandez?" The other officer asked.

"I've never heard that name before," I replied.

"No, I don't know her," my mom said.

"What about you, Mr. Vasquez?" Officer Haddon asked staring hard at Ricio.

"I don't know nothing about her and how you know *my* name?" Ricio shot back.

"Wasn't your brother Maximo Vasquez? He was killed and an investigation is ongoing for his murder as well as the shooting that took place at the cemetery. According to reports, you were shot on this very street a few months ago. I'm glad you recovered well by the way."

"What does any of that have to do with Nihiyah getting killed? Are you trying to insinuate this incident is connected to what happened to me and my brother? If so, you are barking up the wrong tree. The only thing that connects me to Nihiyah is this woman right here," Ricio said pointing his thumb at me.

"There has been a lot of bodies being brought to the morgue since everything happened. Not to mention, your brother Sosa was questioned as well but swore he had no involvement in anything. I find that hard to believe when revenge is the only motive I can see as a rebuttal," Officer Haddon said sternly.

"Maybe you need your eyes checked because that don't mean shit! You won't pin nothing on me and my brother. Didn't you mention to Nija that there was a large quantity of drugs and drug paraphernalia in the car?"

Officer Haddon and his partner exchange uneasy looks when Ricio revealed what he knew. "Yes, I did," Officer Haddon said quietly.

"Again, how the fuck did this shit get off course and end up over here with me and my family? Dig deeper and find out who did this bullshit!" Ricio was so mad the veins in his neck were thick as hell.

"You are a dealer in my streets, Mauricio. With the events that has taken place in your family, it's no coincidence that someone decided to hit closer to home to get at you all," the other officer cut in.

"That's where you're wrong. I *used* to be a dealer your streets. That shit is above me now and has been for a while. You can miss me with your assumptions and kiss my ass. My hands are clean. You can keep probing wasting time on me while the niggas responsible are out there celebrating for taking the life of a woman!"

Officer Haddon stared at Ricio with a smirk on his face. "I have one more question and I'll leave you guys alone. Do you, Mr. Vasquez recognize the item in this picture?" He asked sliding his phone across the coffee table.

Ricio patted my thigh for me to sit up straight and he leaned in to look at the picture. Sitting back shaking his head, "that would be what is called a brick on the street." Recognition was in Ricio's eyes and his jaw flexed as he sat back.

"Have you seen the packaging on the street before?" Officer Haddon pushed.

"I see you're deaf, blind, and stupid! How the fuck would I know about that? I told you I'm not in the streets like that no mo'. Go do your fuckin' job!" Ricio yelled.

"I'm trying to do my job! This package was found in the car with two dead women! You're covering up something and I will find out what it is," Officer Haddon stood and snatched the phone from the table.

Both officers walked toward the door with my mother behind them. Officer Haddon turned to face my mother, "Mrs. Foster, sorry for your loss again. Mr. Vasquez may be holding the key to your daughter's murder. He knows more than he's willing to tell."

"I've known him since he was a boy. He has never lied to me and I don't think he would choose this moment to start. If he knew, he wouldn't hold back anything from me. Have a nice night, Officer," she said walking past them and opened the door.

"If I hear anything, I'll contact you. Now, please leave my home. I have to make plans to bury my daughter." Officer Haddon took one last look at Ricio before slowly walking out the door. My mother closed and locked the door behind them and walked back to the couch and sat directly in front of us. "You know something, what is it?" she asked calmly.

Chapter 19
Ricio

When I saw what the fuck was on the officer's phone, it took everything in me not to react. I fought for every muscle in my face to stay emotionless so I wouldn't give anything away. Obviously, it didn't work because not only did the officer peep it, Miss Pat did too. I was glad she waited until they were long gone to question me and I appreciated that shit to the fullest.

"You know something, what is it?" she asked.

Letting out the breath I was holding, I was ready to keep it one hunnid with her. Miss Pat was right I'd never lied to her about anything and I owed her the same respect then. "The picture he showed me was of a brick I sold to only one nigga in these streets. How those drugs ended up in Nihiyah's car, I don't know but I'm gon' find out."

"Mauricio, there have been enough bloodshed. I know telling you to leave it alone is out of the question because ya'll are not going to quit until everyone who has done wrong to you is no longer walking this earth. You're about to be a father and I want you to really think about what's going on. The life you are living can only lead to one of two places, in the grave or jail. I don't want either option for you or your brother."

"Mama, you don't have nothing to worry about. I have to do what needs to be done in order for me and your daughter to live together in peace." I looked at Nija and she rolled her eyes. "Don't say anything negative. I know I have a lot of work to do before you will even consider being with me."

The love I have for you won't fade and I will fight until my last breath to win your heart again. I believe in the saying, 'if it's meant to be, it will be'. We were meant to be, Nija and I love you," I said kissing her on the forehead rising to my feet. "Ma, let me know the cost of anything you may need for Nihiyah's homegoing. I'm sorry this happened to her and I will find the muthafucka that hurt y'all."

I walked around the table and embraced mama Pat in a hug. “I love y’all and I’m sorry I hurt your daughter but I promise to make it right.”

“You better before I put your ass back in the hospital. I only have one child left Ricio, find them!” she whispered in my chest as I felt tears soak through the front of my shirt. I felt her hurt and even though I wanted to kill Nihiyah myself for the shit she put Nija through, she didn’t deserve to go out the way she did.

“Kimmie, stay here with them for the night.”

“I’m going with y’all!” she shrieked.

“You going where?” Rodrigo asked walking into the living room followed by my cousins.

“Wherever y’all going,” she sassed rolling her eyes.

“Nah, you ain’t,” Rodrigo said turning his attention to me. “What the hell did the pigs want to know?”

“We’ll talk about it when we get to your crib, bro.” I bent down in front of Nija and took her hands in mine. “I’ll call you later. Try to get some sleep and I’ll be here in the morning to go to your appointment with you.”

“Be careful, Ricio. We’ve lost too much already, I don’t know how much more I can take,” she cried.

“I’ll call before it gets too late. I love you, Miss Foster. Don’t ever forget that,” I said pecking her on the lips.

“Come on y’all, we got shit to figure out. It’s time to let these muthafuckas know they have fucked with the wrong niggas at the right time,” I said walking out the door with my family behind me.

I jumped in my whip and pulled off without waiting for anybody. The shit on my mind was scrambling together because shit was getting hectic and I didn’t have a clue where we would begin to correct the situation. Seeing my product on the police phone pissed me off because I didn’t know how the fuck Nihiyah got hold of it. A whole fuckin’ brick at that.

Pulling up into Rodrigo’s driveway, I rolled a blunt and took that shit to the head. My shoulder was stiff and I rotated it around a couple times to loosen the muscle. The doctor said it would be that way for several months until it's healed completely. My leg was cool and I was ready to get back out there to wreck shit.

Rodrigo and my cousins pulled in not too long after me and I got out and headed up the stairs to his house. When he got out the car, he started talking shit as usual because he thought he ran my ass since I got shot. I'd been letting his ass know that he was my little brother, not the other way around.

"Nigga, why the fuck you peel out like that?" He stomped up the driveway like he was scaring some damn body.

"The same reason you ran off after hearing them niggas shot me. Open the muthafuckin' door and shut the fuck up!" I said pulling on the blunt.

"Yeah, aight, keep playing. Don't think I won't shoot yo' ass because you my brother."

I laughed following him in the house going straight to his refrigerator. Taking seven bottles of MGD out, I put them on the table along with a fifth of Remy. Everybody took a seat not waiting to pop the tops of the cold beer.

"Now, tell me what the fuck them cops were talking about, bro. I didn't want to be around them dirty muthafuckas, they can't be trusted," Rodrigo said taking a sip from his bottle.

"As usual, they were trying to pin this shit on us. One thing I can say is they got something that ties us to their case," I explained.

"How the fuck is that?" he asked loudly.

"The bricks I sold to Sam was in Nihiyah's car. It's a must we find out who the fuck he sold them to and why the fuck he didn't change the packaging to something of his own."

"I told y'all I didn't trust that muthafucka!" Angel hollered. "Our meeting got cut short and I didn't get the chance to tell y'all what I found out. Sam is involved with Floyd, he's his nephew. That muthafucka knew exactly what he was doing when he called to hook up with you. He gets down with some lil nigga named Rello.

Rello is one of Floyd's lieutenants on the Southside. He oversees a trap house on 63rd and Loomis but they have closed down shop since that punk ass nigga Erv came up missing. I guess Floyd was bringing too much heat and got cut off from his connect and needed another distributer, that's when Sam hit you up."

"How the fuck you find this shit out, cuz?" I asked.

"Yesterday Sam hit me up and said he needed fifty more bricks. I told him I'd hit him when I was on my way. Me and Javier went to the warehouse and loaded everything up and headed to his warehouse. When I called him, he said his man Quake would be there to collect and give me the money. The name Quake stood out because that's the same nigga Rodrigo's bitch Jessica mentioned."

"That ain't *my* bitch, I don't even know her ass," Rodrigo said shaking his head no.

"Anyway, when we got there, the nigga Quake gave me the money and started unloading with two other niggas. Quake was bitching about how he had shit to do and Sam should've had his stupid ass uncle at the warehouse instead. One of the other dudes was like, fuck Floyd with his crackhead ass. He ain't been seen since Rello beat his ass. Pussy nigga hiding out.

Obviously, Sam didn't let them know he was copping from Ricio because they started talking about you like the shit wasn't gon' get back. They're still looking for you and don't believe you're dead. When they finished unloading, I heard one of them ask if they wanted to go to the strip club tonight. They all agreed to meet up there at ten o'clock."

"What strip club did they say?" Rodrigo asked looking at his watch.

"Money," Javier replied.

"Well, it's eight o'clock, who's down to go see some naked booty hoes shake that ass and pop that pussy?" Rodrigo smirked.

Let me hit up the rest of the clan, I think we're about to kick this shit off the right way tonight," I said sending a mass text to Psycho, Felon, Face, AK, and Fats.

Ricio: We going on a field trip, meet up at Psych's crib in an hour. Gear up

One of the messages came back as unable to deliver and that was odd. But replies started coming back within minutes.

Psycho: Bet.

Felon: Say less
AK: Me and Precious will be ready
Face: I'll be there

"Aight, we will be heading out soon. I just told these nigga's we'll meet up at Pycho's crib. Have you heard from Fats, bro?"

"Nawl, I hadn't heard from him in a minute. I know Face been going through some shit with his daughter and ain't been around but we've been communicating back and forth. But that nigga Fats ain't been around in a hot minute. Let me hit his line and see what's up."

Rodrigo put the phone to his ear and put it down to look at the screen. He dialed Fats number again and looked up with a puzzled expression on his face. "This nigga phone is disconnected. How the fuck is that even possible?" he asked.

"I think we should go by his crib to make sure he's cool. It's unlike him to go ghost and don't reach out to any of us," I said standing to my feet.

"Who's this cat?" Nicholás asked. "Is he somebody y'all trust?"

"Hell yeah! We've all been tight as fuck since the sandbox, nigga. Outside of Rodrigo, they all I got. And of course, you Dominican muthafuckas," I said laughing. "Let's go check on fam and see what's going on."

"He bet not be on no foul shit bro. I don't trust nobody in these streets no mo'. If he dirty, he getting' bodied, plain and simple. I don't want to hear shit when I put one between his eyes."

Rodrigo was serious as fuck about what he said and I hoped like hell Fats wasn't on bullshit. I loved him like a brother but there was nothing I'd be able to do to help him if he chose to go against us. Deception was something none of us could overlook. You turn your back on us, we deal with the shit accordingly, straight like that.

"We rolling in the Navigator and AK's truck. There's no need for everybody to be scrambling to get in separate cars. Plus, both of them muthafuckas will stop any bullet that comes our way. It's time for these niggas to see that a few bullets ain't never gon' stop Maurico Vasquez," I said going through the door leading to the garage.

Piling into the truck, I pulled out of the garage and headed to the expressway. Rodrigo turned the radio on and 2Pac's *2 Amerikaz*

Most Wanted blared through the speakers and brah started rapping like he made the song.

Now give me fifty feet
Defeat is not my Destiny, release me to the streets
And keep whatever left of me
Jealousy is misery, suffering is grief
Better be prepared when you cowards fuck with me
I bust and flee
"These niggas must be crazy what?"
There ain't no mercy, muthafuckas who can't fade the thugs
You though it was but it wasn't, now disappear
Bow down in the presence of a boss player

Bobbin' with the beat, I cruised on the expressway as we listened to hit after hit. No words were spoken because for me, I knew tonight was the night blood would be shed once again by our hands. I hadn't bust my shit and I was itching to get at a couple of these muthafuckas for old and new. Rodrigo was the one having all the fun lately, but with the two of us and the clan behind us, we were a force to be fucked with.

Floyd must've thought I was broken when they took my little brother or some shit. Nah, I was trying to let shit die down for a minute. All that shit changed when he put a few hot ones in my flesh and now, I had to return the favor. I pulled up to Fats crib and all the lights were off in that muthafucka.

Rodrigo got out and I followed him up the steps as he rang the doorbell. No one came to the door and I knew his ass had a tribe of kids that was always running around making noise no matter what time it was. Peeking through the window, the living room was bare.

"This nigga up and moved without saying nothing to nobody!" I said out loud.

"Y'all looking for Fats?" A young girl sitting on the porch next door asked.

"Yeah, you know where he at?" Rodrigo asked walking down the steps.

“A few months ago, him and Sandra got escorted out by the police. The kids went to DCFS custody and the police took all kinds of drugs and shit out of the house.”

“Aight, thanks for that information, shawty,” I said walking back to the truck.

“This nigga knows about every muthafuckin’ thing Reese left for us! I wonder if that is the reason them pigs were questioning me the way they were,” I said closing the door.

“That muthafucka ain’t stupid enough to tell them shit! To be on the safe side though, we have to clear out the warehouse. Ain’t no telling what the fuck they know. We got thirty minutes to get to the club and head to Psych’s crib. We got work to do,” Rodrigo snapped.

Chapter 20
Latorra

Big Jim had been calling my phone nonstop and I refused to answer any of his calls. I knew he was behind me losing my job and I didn't want shit to do with him. The night I followed Rello, he led me right to his front door. He didn't even know he was being trailed and I got the address and stored it in my phone. I even took down his license plate number and the make of the car he was driving.

I wanted to send the information to Ricio but I didn't want him to think I had anything to do with the shit that was going on with Floyd. Explaining how I got the information would lead me to telling him that Big Jim was really my father. That shit would seem like I was trying to set him up from the beginning.

I'd been working at Money for the past two months and I hated it. Bentley gave me the job as a bartender but he kept pressuring me to dance. The tips that I made were good but it wasn't shit compared to what I was making at the prison. I was behind in my bills and I was scrambling to make ends meet. There was no way I was shaking my ass in front of all the perverts that came in the club, I didn't give a damn how much money they were willing to spend.

As I set up my bar for the full house Bentley was expecting, a group of niggas came through the door. I watched as they filed into the VIP section and one of them looked like Mauricio but I wasn't sure. While I was stocking the ice, Tammy came rushing up to the counter smiling from ear to ear.

"Girl, did you see them fine ass niggas that just went upstairs?" she asked excitedly.

"Yeah, and?"

"That was Mauricio and his people. It's money in this bitch tonight! Not only is he in here but Bentley said Marcellus Devon is throwing his bachelor party in this muthafucka too!"

"Who the fuck is he?" I didn't know who the fuck Marcellus was but he must've had money because Tammy was about to have an orgasm from just letting his name slide off her lips. The shit didn't excite me because I came to do my job and go the fuck home.

"He's an NFL quarterback but I only know that because Bentley told me. Regardless, he is the reason all the ballers are going to be here throwing money around like water. I don't give a damn what any of them looks like, all I'll be seeing is green presidents. Fuck everything else. You should dance so you can get some of this money too, bitch!"

I thought about what she said and couldn't picture myself stripping. Even though the money would help, I was terrified. "Look, all you have to do is take a couple shots to ease your mind. Then get yo' ass up there and act like you fuckin'. Shit, keep your eyes closed until the music goes off. Whatever it may be, you got to dance before you get put the fuck out of your apartment," Tammy kept trying to persuade me.

"Nah, I'm going to pass on that. I'll figure out how to get the money. Until then I'll keep serving these drinks while I wait for someone to call saying I have a job."

"If that's what you prefer to do. In times like this, Bentley comes out and makes any available female on his payroll to dance or give lap dance to get more money. Be prepared to tell him no. He won't be as understanding as me," Tammy said walking away.

The club filled up quickly and the man of the night was the reason. He came in with about thirty niggas and they were immediately taken into what was called the pleasure lounge. He would have access to at least ten dancers and anything he wanted he could have. That included pussy and blow jobs as long as he paid to play.

"Hey beautiful, can I get a bottle of Dusse."

I looked up and almost shitted on myself. Standing in front of me was no other than Rello. With seeing Mauricio and his entourage come in earlier and now Rello, I knew some shit was going to go down.

"Yeah, sure," I said turning to retrieve the bottle of cognac he had ordered. "That will be sixty-five dollars."

"Can I get about seven plastic cups?" Handing him the cups, he left a hundred dollars on the counter and smiled. "Keep the change. There will be more where that came from, my niggas will be coming through to buy from you. What's your name, ma?"

"Michelle." The name rolled off my tongue quick as hell because I damn sure wasn't about to tell him it was Latorra. He may pull out a gun and shoot my ass in the face if he knew I was the woman he was looking for.

"Aight, Michelle. I'll make sure they come buy from you. I'll be back to see that pretty smile a little later. Maybe you can come give me a lap dance before the night is over. It would be worth every dollar."

"I don't do lap dances, I'm a bartender, nothing more. Enjoy your drink," I said moving to help the next customer at the other end of the bar.

About an hour later the club was in full swing and the music was loud and drinks were flowing through the club nonstop. The dancers were working the floor harder than the average night and Bentley was walking around smiling from ear to ear. He walked behind the bar and looked me up and down. I ignored him and continued moving about filling drink orders.

"Aye, I need you on the floor tonight. There's money to be made and I'll have the new girl Rachel to cover the bar for you," he had the nerve to say in my ear. I looked at him like he had two heads because he had me all the way fucked up. "Did you hear what I said? He asked.

"I heard you but that's not what I agreed to when I started working here. You hired me to be a bartender, Bentley. I'm not taking my clothes off for you or anybody else. It's either you want me to work this bar, or nothing at all."

"I guess you no longer work at Money then. That's what I'm about and there's money to be made and I want it. There's plenty of bitches that would love to come work and do what I want them to do and more," he sneered.

"You're firing me because I won't expose myself for profit? That's bullshit, Bentley and you know it. I need this job!" I said stomping my foot. The guys that were sitting at the bar turned and look in our direction and I was on the verge of crying.

"Well if you need this muthafucka you better take yo' ass to the back and put on something sexy and work this muthafucka like your life depends on it and get this money! If not, get the fuck out of my establishment."

Opening my mouth to respond to him, I took off my apron and walk around the bar towards the dressing room. Bentley probably thought I was going to change but I was only going to get my jacket and purse. He could suck my dick if he thought I would allow him to strong arm me into doing something I didn't have any plans to do. They didn't stop making jobs available when he opened that fucking brothel he's running.

As I put on my black leather jacket and slung my purse over my shoulder, gunshots rang out inside the club. It sounded like a war was taking place and I had nowhere to go. The sound of people screaming and crying out from apparently getting hit by bullets with no name, I peeked out the door to see if I could make it to the emergency exit safely. There were bodies scattered about and I wasn't about to be one of them.

I took the opportunity to make a dash for the door and was pushed to the ground the minute I stepped out of the dressing room. "Get yo' ass out the way, shawty!" a guy yelled running to the exit. Bullets followed his ass and I screamed at the top of my lungs and ducked my head under my arms.

"Aarrrrghhh!" the guy groaned as the sound of his body hit the pavement. Multiple gunshots rang out and I knew he was no longer breathing. The door slammed shut and I stood up quickly to get out of there. As soon as I turned around, I was face to face with Mauricio.

"Latorra, go the fuck home. Now!" he barked in my face.

Bullets hit the wall inches from my head and Mauricio grabbed my arm and pushed me toward the door as he shot behind him. I tripped over the body that was sprawled outside and my feet landed in the pool of blood that poured out of his head. Jumping to my feet, I ran as fast as I could to my car and stepped on the gas to get the hell away from Money.

Chapter 21
Rodrigo

Purposely getting to the strip club early, we stepped into the building like we owned the place. We were led upstairs to VIP but we had no intentions of buying shit. We didn't come to party. Our mission was to deaden a couple muthafuckas and get the fuck out of there. Half naked bitches came up shaking their ass for a buck, they weren't getting none of my money.

A thick bodied broad came up to me popping her pussy too close to my face and I pushed her to the side. She gave me the ugliest mug I'd ever seen and I laughed because she didn't miss a beat going to the next nigga. I got up and stood next to Angel as he scoped out the club below.

"Have you seen them niggas yet?" I asked just as a group of niggas entered the establishment.

"Yep, they just walked in. The nigga with the dreads is Quake. Dude with the beard was one of the ones that was helping him unload and the muthafucka in the wheat Tims was there too."

Following them niggas with my eyes, I waited for them to be seated so I'd know exactly where I was heading when I pulled the trigger. There were about nine of them but that didn't mean shit to me because one of my guns held sixteen shots. They settled down and got comfortable when the DJ announced that Marcellus Devon was in the building. He picked the wrong night to blow his money, I hoped he stayed far away from them niggas because I wasn't watching for his ass.

As I paid close attention to them popping bottle after bottle, I knew it wouldn't be long before we could bust the move. They were damn near fucking the bitches that were dancing for them, making it rain like they were Bill Gates in that muthafucka.

Once they stopped watching their surroundings and the bitches had them occupied, I made my way down the steps. "Aye, bro. Where you going?" Ricio asked as I descended the steps.

"I turned around and smiled." I'm going to play Grim Reaper, y'all coming?" Not giving them a chance to react because I work better alone anyway, I stopped one of the barmaids and whispered in her ear. "Aye, go get ya girls away from them niggas over there," I pointed. "If you don't want they ass to get hit. Keep ya mouth closed and get it done. If y'all ain't out of that area by the time I get there, y'all on ya own."

Her eyes widened with fear and she rushed to the section I'd sent her to. Her girls were pushing her away and tears were running down her face as I got closer. Whatever she said to them worked because they hauled ass towards the front exit and I kept walking as they passed me with my Glock 40 with a silencer at my side. My eyes were trained on the nigga Quake and I raised my tool and shot his ass in the back of his head. *Pew!*

His boys reacted slowly as his body fell forward onto floor. I let off another shot hitting another muthafucka in his neck. Blood squirted out and splattered his homies. Everybody around me was trying to get out the club as I continued to walk forward. The rest of their crew took cover and started shooting blindly, hitting everybody but me.

I saw Ricio raise his gun and let off a series of shots as one of the niggas tried to run up and be a hero. He was hit in the chest and his body dropped quickly. I heard a shot go off behind me and I ducked and darted forward to hid behind a chair. Glancing behind me, I saw Javier aiming his gun at a nigga he'd laid down not too far from where I had run from.

Looking over the plush chair, I saw Ricio chasing a muthafucka down a hall but I didn't see the other niggas that was in the section. "They went that way! Psycho shouted running in the direction they ran. I followed him when I heard three shots coming from my left. That was the way Ricio went so I went that way instead of following Psycho and Face.

"Go that way," I shouted to Javier and Angel as I went to check on my brother. As I ran gunshots could be heard the further I got down the hall. I burst through the door and saw him running after a car that was speeding out of the parking lot.

Running full speed, I ran in the opposite direction and emptied my clip into the car as it sped down the street. Ricio met me in the middle of the lot and the sounds of sirens could be heard. We jogged to the Navigator and everybody was waiting except Face.

"Where the fuck is Face?" I asked out loud looking around.

"He didn't make it, fam. He rushed out the door and the nigga bust soon as he opened the door and clipped him in the head."

Hearing Psycho utter those words broke a real nigga down. I started walking back to the side of the building but AK grabbed me by the back of my shirt. "Twelve is getting close, bro. We gotta go. There's nothing we can do for him, he's gone!"

The police sirens were loud enough that I knew they were down the street. We all ran to the trucks and peeled out. This shit was fucked up because Face was my brother and another one of us had died by the hands of these coward ass niggas. I couldn't sleep knowing there were still muthafuckas breathing behind all this bullshit.

"How many niggas was in that car Ricio? Do you know?"

"Nah, bro. I know you popped two, I got two, it's at least five of them left."

"Angel, will you be able to break in to the surveillance in the club?" I asked looking into the back seat. Angel already had his laptop in his lap typing away on the computer. My cousin didn't answer as he concentrated on what he was doing. I let him work his magic for about five minutes before I turned again. "Cuz—"

"Everything has been wiped clean. Not only did I delete the footage in the club, I deleted every camera in the vicinity as well as the blue light cameras."

"Wait a minute. Why did your nerdy ass bring your laptop?" Ricio asked.

"You have to be ready even if you're not ready. Y'all carry guns everywhere with you, I carry a gun and a laptop. The cops would've had everything they needed by the time we made it back to my house to attempt to erase anything from those cameras."

"You are one smart son of a bitch," I laughed. "Since we got that under control, Ricio, go to Big Jim's house because Floyd is about to take his last breath."

"I'm with that shit. That muthafucka has to go," Ricio said hitting the expressway.

It took twenty minutes to get to the westside and Ricio turned down the street Big Jim's house was on and went around back. Cutting the car off, Ricio took the keys out the ignition as AK pulled up behind us. The house was dark and didn't look like anyone was home.

"I'm going to kick this nigga shit in without a plan. We're going in blazing, hitting anything and everything moving. Shit don't change, I want y'all to cover me because I'm going in to get what rightfully belongs to us. I don't want the dope. I just want the money."

AK, Psycho, Mateo, and Javier walked up to the truck. Ricio opened his door and we all got out. "AK, do you still keep gasoline in your truck?" I asked.

"Yeah, you need it?"

"When I do what I have to do in this bitch, I'm burning this muthafucka to the ground."

AK went back to his truck and retrieved the gas can and we headed to the house. I walked to the door with my gun in hand and kicked the doorframe. It gave way with one swift kick. We all scattered about the house and searched every inch of it. As I thought, Floyd's pussy ass wasn't home.

I went to the basement and went to the safe and entered the code. The muthafuckas didn't change any codes at the other traps, why would his ass be smart enough to change this one too. As I expected, the safe opened up with no problem. It was filled with money from top to bottom and once again, I was taking my father's money with me.

I walked to the closet and grabbed three duffle bags and started filling them with money. I walked back to the closet to get another bag because I wasn't leaving shit. I wanted everything that belonged to me. "Aye, bro! somebody come get these bags and tell AK to start dousing this muthafucka."

There were propane tanks in the basement as well as gasoline for the lawnmower sitting under the stairs. I started unscrewing the top on the containers when Angel and Mateo came downstairs to grab the bags. "Y'all get out of here because this house is about to collapse like it was hit with a weapon of mass destruction," I said as I ran a trail of gasoline from the propane tank to the stairs. I doused everything I could with the first can but I still grabbed the other one and went upstairs.

"Did you get upstairs yet?"

"Nah, I didn't have enough. I'm getting it good down here and the rest will catch when the fire spreads."

"I found more downstairs and I'm going up to hit the top. I'll set the fire up there then start the one in the basement from the top of the stairs. Get something to burn because once I start the fire at the top of the basement, we gon' have to haul ass. There are propane tanks down there. So be ready to use muscles yo' big ass ain't used in a minute," I said laughing.

"Fuck you, Sosa," he smirked.

"Keep it up, I'll make sure yo' ass burn in this bitch too."

"I'm not worried, go do what you need to do, fam. We gotta get out of here."

I ran up the stairs and poured the gasoline over every part of the upstairs. As I walked out of the bathroom, I tossed a match into one of the bedrooms and it went up in flames. Racing down the stairs, I got the steps soaked and placed the cans by the back door. I looked at AK and he nodded his head for me to toss the match in the basement. AK lit a piece of fabric from the curtain and tossed it on the couch and I struck the butane lighter I had and it ignited the gas on the basement steps.

We both raced to the back door, I grabbed the cans and before we could get to the truck, there was a loud explosion that knocked both of us onto the grass. Debris was flying and a ball of fire landed on my leg and I rolled around until it went out. That stop drop and roll shit really worked.

"We're going to my house, get there. I said to AK as I hopped in the Navigator. When Ricio pulled off there was another loud explosion and I looked out the rearview mirror, the entire house was engulfed in flames. Mission accomplished. *Now, where that muthafucka gon' lay his head?* I thought to myself as I sat back against the seat.

Chapter 22
Big Jim

The day I told Warden Fitzgerald the lie about Latorra, she wasn't seen on the Block again. Some of the CO's gave me dirty looks and tried their best to give me a hard time in the prison. None of that shit mattered because I wasn't easily intimidated. It had been months since I'd heard from her because she refused to answer my calls. My plan seemed to have backfired. My intentions were for her to come back to me for help.

I was laying back in my cell after lockdown and decided to see what was going on in the streets. Putting my headphones in my ear, I went to the *Fox News* app and clicked on the live news tab. There was a breaking news segment on about a shooting at a strip club called Money. Turning the volume up, I waited to hear what happened.

"Ten people were reported dead including the owner of club Money. Partygoers were trying to escape the club during the shooting and it resulted in many injuries. Two of the victims were found outside the club and succumbed. Police are on the scene investigating the dozens of shell casings and questioning witnesses. The Citizens of Chicago are terrified of all the gun violence taking place around the city.

When will it end? The victims have not been identified but stay tuned for updates. In other news, firefighters are trying to control flames at a home in the Garfield Park neighborhood. Nancy, tell us what's going on out there."

When the scene changed, the first thing I saw was *my* muthafuckin' house burning to the ground. The sight before me almost made me throw my phone against the wall. Everything I'd worked for was inside that house and now it was gone. The flames were too big for it to be accidental, somebody intentionally set the fire. I backed out of the app without listening to what the reporter had to say.

Tapping Floyd's name on my phone, I listened as it rang and the nigga didn't answer. I tried a second time and he answered. "What up, Big?" He slurred.

"Muthafucka, you out there higher than a kite and my shit is burning to the ground! Where the fuck you at?" I yelled not giving a fuck if I was heard or not.

"Man, what you talking about?"

"I just saw my house on the fuckin' news and it's not gon' stop burning until there's nothing left of it. What the fuck you do, Floyd?"

"I'm not even at the crib—"

"You should be! Is this payback because I cut yo' dope fiend ass off? Is this your way of getting back at me, nigga?" I grilled.

"That wasn't nothing to me, Big. I had my own money and you know this. I'm gon' be straight out here," he sniffed. "But I would never try to destroy you the way you've done me. I still got yo' back out here. Now like I said, I don't know shit about the house getting burned down. I got a spot of my own when you cut off my access to every fuckin' thing. I haven't heard from you in months because you in your feelings about some shit I had no control over."

"It's all good, bitch! You dead nigga, you better watch your back, Floyd because you ain't safe because I'm in this muthafuckin' prison. You better watch yo'self out there in them streets, faggot ass bitch!"

He didn't respond and I took the phone away from my ear and he had hung up. I was madder than a muthafucka because he didn't have a care in the world about my shit. I hit Rello's name and waited for him to answer. He needed to get in touch with the lawyer that owed him a favor so I could get the fuck out of this prison.

"What's going on, Big? Talk fast because I'm dealing with some shit right now," he said when he answered the phone.

"What's the word on the lawyer, Youngin'?"

"He is scheduled to come see you on Monday. His name is Bryan Stewart and he was on vacation when I first contacted him. Your sister sent him everything he needed so he could look over your case. I didn't get any feedback from him other than he would come see you on Monday. We lost four of our soldiers including Quake tonight, Big. Ricio and his people aired the strip club out but we got one of them niggas too."

"That was *you* niggas? I just saw that shit on the news. Rello, I need you to do everything you can to bring them down. This won't end until all of them are gone. I'm putting you in charge. My muthafuckin' house is burning as we speak and everything was in that bitch. Guns, drugs, money, everything. We ain't got shit right now!" I said holding my head in my hand.

"It's all good, Boss. I don't know where Floyd is, hopefully his ass was in that house. I got some of the lil niggas working the blocks. I copped some of those thangs from Sam, he got that raw shit straight from the Columbians and it's selling like hotcakes. We had a little hiccup when two crackhead bitches got away with some work, but they paid for their mistake and we got all of the shit back. So, I'm ahead of you on that."

"I knew I made the right choice with you. Fuck Floyd, that nigga ain't one of us no mo'. When you see that nigga, gun his ass down on sight. I need you to call my sister Yvette. Meet up with her after you find out what's needed for the niggas that didn't make it out of that situation.

She will give you some bread to take to the families. Don't sleep on Ricio and his brother, they are unpredictable. Keep your eyes open, Rello. One more thing, Remember the bitch I told you to call awhile back? I need you to go to her crib because she's been avoiding me for months. Beat her muthafuckin' ass until she near death and make sure she knows that *I said* get Ricio to you! Don't have no mercy on her muthafuckin' ass either." I ordered.

"I'm on that as soon as I go give the bad news to Quakes family. This one is hard and it has hardened my heart to the bullshit going on with these niggas. They better hope I don't find out about anybody close to them because no one associated with them niggas safe. I'll get at you, Big Homie."

"Aight, cool."

I laid back on my bunk thinking about all the shit that has transpired in the matter of months. It had never been like this back in the day, my team ain't strong like I thought it was. Rello had to pull a miracle or I would be the last man standing and have to start over from scratch once I beat this case and walk out of this prison.

Chapter 23
Fats

Sitting back watching highlights of the football games on *ESPN* my phone started ringing and I knew exactly who it was. I took a deep breath before I answered. "Yeah."

"Come outside, I have something I need you to look at," the voice on the phone said before ending the call.

Standing from the chair I was sitting in I slipped my feet in my Nike slides and threw on my jacket. Leaving out the door I looked around before I made my way off the porch and walked to the car that was parked a few feet down the street. Opening the door, I got in without saying anything.

"I think we got them!" Detective Cooper said staring at the side of my face. "If you can identify the things in these photos, you will be a free man."

If he thought that shit was music to my ears, he was dead wrong. I actually felt like shit and knew the consequences of my actions. They were trying to give me ten years for the drugs they found, along with the guns. I have a whole family and I had to protect them.

"Do you know anything about this?" Cooper asked showing me a picture of a brick of heroin. I knew right away it was Ricio's. It was in the same packaging that Reese stored it in when he kept it safe for his sons. This was hard for me to do but I was already in too deep and there was no turning back.

"Yeah. It belongs to Mauricio."

"Are you certain it's his?" Cooper pressed.

"I'm positive," I said keeping my answers short.

He placed another photo in my direction and it was a photo of a female dead in the front seat of a vehicle. It actually looked like Nija's sister. Upon further inspection, I knew for a fact it was her. "Do you know this girl?"

"Is that Nihiyah?" I asked looking at him.

"So, you do know her."

"I know her. We went to school together and she never bothered anyone to the point they would kill her. I mean, she had her days of getting into disputes with females but nothing major. What happened to her?"

"That's what we're trying to find out. The drugs were found in the very car she died in. With you saying the drugs belong to Mauricio, that only means he's connected to Nihiyah's murder as well."

"Ricio would never kill Nihiyah! He loves Nija and her family like they were his own flesh and blood. There's no way he had anything to do with her murder. I know what I'm doing with y'all is true betrayal but I've known these people since I was young. They had no beef with each other. Nihiyah and Nija had nothing to do with our dealings in the streets."

"Who do you think had something to do with this then?" Cooper asked.

"The only person they have problems with is Floyd. Like I told you before, he killed Max and they were out to get revenge. From my understanding, the drugs haven't even made it to the streets yet. Ricio and Sosa was waiting until they settled the beef with Floyd before they made any moves on that. I don't know what's been going on because I've been in hiding."

A nigga felt like shit blowing the whistle on the very people that had my back through a lot of shit. I knew what happened to snitches and I feared for my life but I didn't show it in front of the detective. All I wanted to do was get this shit over with so I could move the fuck out of Chicago before Ricio found out I was involved.

"This is the last picture I have for you," he said handing me a photo. "Who is this?"

Looking at the image I almost broke down. Face was lying in a pool of blood and I couldn't believe they had got him. "That's Byron Hayes but we called him Face on the streets," I choked out as tears ran down my face.

"He was shot in shootout at club Money tonight. None of the witnesses are telling who's involved and there's no surveillance footage. Do you have any idea what happened?"

I glared at his ass and if looks could kill, he would be dead. "Muthafucka, how the hell would I know? I'm tucked away in bum fuck Egypt and you asking me about what's going on in the city? I don't have a way to communicate with anybody because *you* had me to turn my phone off! I don't know shit!"

"Where do Sosa and Mauricio live?" Cooper asked. When I didn't answer right away, his voice boomed louder, "Give me the fuckin' address, Darren!"

"Ricio lives 505 North McClurg Court in apartment 1305. Sosa lives in Country Club Hills. 4122 Cambridge Circle. Are we done?" I asked ready to go.

"Yeah. I want you to continue laying low and no one is to know your whereabouts. We are going to need you when it's time to testify against your buddies in court," he smirked.

"I didn't agree to testify! That wasn't part of the agreement!"

"It is now and I dare you to bail out because I will have your black ass locked up before you close your eyes tonight. I won't have a problem taking your daughters from you permanently," he threatened. "Now get the fuck out of my car and wait for my call!"

Exiting the car quickly, I hurried back into the house and slammed the door. I rested my back against it and cried for Face, Nihiyah, and the thought of dying by the hands of Ricio or Sosa. There was no turning back from the hole I'd dug for myself. I was fucked either way I looked at the situation.

"Darren, is everything okay?" My baby mama asked coming down the steps as I entered the house.

"This was a bad idea baby. I'm gon' die as soon as word gets out that I'm working with the police to save my own ass."

Chapter 24
Nija

I didn't get an ounce of sleep last night because I couldn't believe my sister was gone. Nihiyah had her fucked up ways but she didn't deserve what happened to her. I was worried about my mama because she'd been walking around as if Nihiyah was running around in the streets instead of lying in a cold freezer at the morgue.

The smell of bacon filled my nostrils as I stretched and climbed out of the bed. I went into the bathroom to take care of my hygiene and was shocked by what I saw in the mirror. My eyes were puffy, nose swollen, and there were red blotches scattered about my face. I'd never looked this bad in my life.

After taking a shower, I walked back into my bedroom and threw on a pair of black leggings and a green sweater that Nihiyah bought me for Christmas the year before. I had never worn it because it was too big. Now that my belly was getting bigger, it fit well. I didn't have to be at the doctor's office until eleven so I had about an hour to hang out with my mother. Leaving my bedroom, I went down the hall to Nihiyah's room to wake Kimmie but when I got to the room, she was already awake and dressed.

"Hey boo!" she said cheerfully. "Oh my, look at your face, Nija. We have to cover that up, come here so I can put some concealer on your face."

"Kimmie, I don't wear that shit. It will start clearing up at some point, I'll be fine. I didn't get much sleep, how about you?"

"I basically tossed and turned because I couldn't get in touch with Rodrigo at all last night. He eventually returned my call about five this morning. Something happened last night, he didn't go into detail about it though. Ma cooked let's go feed my God baby and see how she's doing," she said after putting on her socks.

We went downstairs and my mama was staring blankly out the window and she looked like she'd aged a couple years. The bags under her eyes were deep and the stress lines around her mouth stood out. I walked behind her and wrapped my arms around her waist as I laid my head on her shoulder. Patting my hand, she smiled a little bit when she looked over her shoulder.

"Good morning, ma."

"Good morning, baby. Kimmie, hey baby. Thank you for staying with us last night."

"No thanks needed, that's what family does. I'll stay as long as you want me to," Kimmie said walking over to give mama a hug.

"I know y'all hungry. Let me fix y'all plates." She opened the cabinet and grabbed a plate. It fell from her hand when she attempted to place it on the counter.

"Ma, sit down we can fix our own food," I said rushing to her side.

"Why didn't she accept the help we offered her," she cried finally breaking. "My baby is gone, Nija. She had so much potential and she got caught up with those drugs. I wish I could turn back the hands of time because I wouldn't have put her out. This is all my fault!"

"No, no it's not. The decisions that Hiyah made were hers to make. You raised us, ma and did a hell of a job. You taught us right from wrong and whatever we did to mess up, was not on you. I won't stand here and allow you to beat yourself up about something you had no control over."

"I should've forced her into rehab. Nija, I'm not supposed to be mustering up the strength to bury my daughter, y'all were supposed to bury me!" The tears ran down her face as she banged on the counter. "I don't even know how to tell your father that his daughter is dead."

To be honest, I didn't even think about my father because the bastard hadn't been around since he left us for his current wife. It wouldn't surprise me if he didn't give a damn. Kimmie grabbed the broom and dustpan and swept up the broken glass. I finally got my mother to sit at the table while Kimmie made plates for the three of us.

"Ma, I'll make the call to daddy if you can't do it," I said as I scooped eggs onto my fork.

"No, I'll call him. As a matter of fact, I'll call him now." Rising from her chair, she went into the living room and came back with her cellphone. Sitting back in the chair she'd vacated moments before, she pressed my daddy's name and waited for him to answer. The sound of someone talking loudly came through the phone and my mama's face scrunched up in a frown.

"Look, bitch! Now is not the time for your bullshit, put your husband on the muthafuckin' phone," she barked angrily. She looked at the phone and my daddy's wife must've hung up the phone. "I know her stupid ass didn't hang up on me!"

"Ma, give me the phone," I said holding out my hand. Sliding the phone to me, I pressed the button to redial my father and waited for the call to connect.

"What the fuck you want, Patricia? The girls are grown so there's no reason you should be calling Mark's phone."

"Tina, this is Nija. Put my father on the phone please. I'm not my mother so keep that bullshit to yourself. Believe me when I tell you, if she's calling, it's for a reason." I said calmly.

"What do you want?" she snapped ignoring what I had just said to her.

"I would like to speak to my father!" After a few seconds I heard Tina shuffling through their house, hopefully to give my father the phone.

"Hey baby girl, how are you doing?" My father asked.

"Not too good. You need to tell your wife to respect my mama. She's going to make me get on the next thing smoking and beat her ass. Why haven't you told her my mama is not a threat to your marriage?"

"Stay out of grown folks' business, Nija—"

"I am grown! We haven't seen you in years because of her!" I said crying into the phone. "You let another woman keep you away from your kids and that's some punk ass shit. I'll let you think about that shit, but that's not what I called for. I wanted you to know that Nihiyah was killed last night."

"What do you mean she was killed?" His tone changed to one of pure hurt and I knew he was regretting staying away from us for so long.

"Hiyah has been dealing with a lot over the years and drugs was one of the main things. We tried to get help for her but she refused treatment. The last time I spoke with my sister, we got into a fight and when ma asked her why she was using drugs, she said because you were never around. How many times did she call and you never got back with her?"

"Nihiyah hasn't called me at all. I was wrong for not calling more to see how y'all were doing and I apologize for my actions. Nija, I swear to God, I never had one missed call from you nor your sister."

"I think it's time for you to check ya bitch! If you don't have any recollection of my sister trying to reach out to you, that mutha-fucka was answering your phone and telling Hiyah whatever she needed to in order for you not to communicate with her. I'll bet money she erased any messages and the call log so you wouldn't know. Now it's too late for you to make things right because she's gone. I hate you! Stay the fuck away from me like you've been doing. Ma with contact you about the arrangements, and you better answer the phone!"

"Nija, I'll be there tomorrow. I promise," he said sadly.

"I'm a grown ass woman, I don't need you here. Your other child needed you the most and she's no longer here. You can't make this shit up, *daddy.* Wait on that call because I don't have shit else to say to you," I said hanging up the phone.

Placing the phone on the table, I cried like a baby because I knew his wife was behind him not keeping in touch with us. My father was weak as hell for that shit but Tina wasn't shit for the sneaky shit she did. I couldn't blame her for everything because his punk ass played a major part in the bullshit too. Nothing should've kept him away from us because we were his kids too.

"Baby, are you okay?" My mama asked coming to my side.

Wiping my eyes, I nodded my head. I was hurt on top of pissed but I couldn't let my father put a damper on my day more than it already was. My appointment to find out the gender of my baby was supposed to be a happy moment. It was hard to smile during this time but the saying goes, 'when one life ends, another begins' and I truly believed that.

My food was cold and it pissed me off because I was starving. I grabbed my plate and walked to the microwave to warm the food. Once the timer went off, I took the food out and sat back down and attempted to eat. Kimmie had finished eating and stared at me intensely as I struggled to swallow the eggs I had placed in my mouth.

"Sis, you don't need to stress over this. You have a baby to think about and you are already going through it about Nihiyah."

"I know," I said quickly. "Would you go upstairs and get my phone please? I need to call Ricio to see if he's coming over to go to the doctor with me."

Before she could get up from the table, the doorbell rang. Instead of going upstairs, she went to answer the door. Kimmie came back into the kitchen with Ricio on her heels. He looked good in his black Balenciaga shirt and jeans and a pair of black Timbs. The black fitted he had on covered his locs and shielded his eyes.

"Hey, mama Pat," he said kissing my mama on her cheek.

"Good morning, Ricio." She patted him on his cheek and hugged him tightly. "Thank you for being there for Nija."

"You don't ever have to thank me for that. I'm gon' always take care of my responsibilities," he said walking over to me. "How are you? You don't look like you got much sleep. Are you ready to find out what we're having?"

I was still upset with him and didn't want to fake the funk about the situationship we had going on. It would be a lie if I said him being there with me didn't feel good, because it did. "Sleep didn't come easy last night but I'm okay. The gender of this baby isn't important as long as the baby is healthy, I'm alright with whatever we are having."

"Okay, it's time for us to get on the road. Unlike you, I'm excited to find out the sex of our child," he said squeezing my shoulder. "Kimmie, you rolling with us?"

"I wasn't, but you got me anxious to know and I'm going now," she said getting up rushing upstairs. She came back down with my purse, phone, and both of our coats.

Standing to clear my plate, my mama placed her hand over mine. "Leave that there, I'll take care of the dishes. I'll call my family members and deliver the devastating news then we can start planning Hiyah's homegoing," ma said sadly.

"We can do that tomorrow, mama. Get some rest and I'll be back soon as I can." I hugged her and kissed her on the side of her face. "We will get through this together. I love you."

"I love you too, baby. Ricio don't let nothing happen to my baby, be careful."

When I stepped out of the house the cold air chilled me to my bones, I stuffed my hands deeply in my pockets and rushed to Ricio's car. He hit the locks on the doors and used the remote to start the car. Kimmie hopped in the backseat and fastened her seatbelt. Ricio pulled off as soon as he got inside the car and backed out of the driveway.

It took twenty minutes to arrive at the University of Chicago Hospital. Kimmie and I got out the car while Ricio went to find a parking spot. Texting the directions to the clinic, I led the way to the elevator so we could go to the third floor. It was five minutes to eleven when I walked off the elevator and stepped up to the counter. Giving my name, I was escorted to the back immediately.

Informing the nurse to allow Ricio to come back in the room, I sat on the bed and waited for the doctor to come in. There was a light tap on the door and Dr. Hayes walked in pushing an ultrasound machine in front of her. "Good morning, Nija. You are getting bigger every time I see you. What are you eating?"

"I don't eat too much really. This is one big baby I suppose," I chuckled.

"Well, we will see what's going on today," she responded setting up the machine. The door opened and Ricio entered. Dr. Hayes glanced over her shoulder and smiled. "You must be dad."

"Yeah, how did you guess?" Ricio smiled.

"I would hope you were, walking in this room without knocking," she smirked. "Okay, Nija it's time to see what's going on in this belly of yours. Raise your sweater and lower your leggings a little bit so the gel won't get on them." Doing as I was told. Dr. Hayes applied the gel and moved the wand around my protruding stomach. "There's our baby!" Dr. Hayes said happily.

She was about to turn the monitor around when she leaned in closer to the screen. Her expression was perplexed and I became nervous. She moved the wand in different directions very slowly before turning to me. "Nija, I want to go in vaginally to get a better look at something. I need you to remove you pants for me." Ricio moved to help me pull my leggings off and Kimmie rushed to the head of the bed.

"Hold on, bro I don't want to look at her snatch!" Everybody laughed at her crazy ass and Dr. Hayes moved the machine along with her as she sat at the foot of the bed. Raising the stirrups, I placed my foot in them and opened my legs. Ricio licked his lips as his eyes zoomed in on the kitty he hadn't had in months.

Dr. Hayes placed a latex covering over the wand and applied gel to it. As she inserted the wand into my vagina, I let out a low moan and Ricio smirked at me wickedly. This pregnancy had my hormones going wild but I refused to call Ricio for sexual relations. Self-pleasure was the way I got an orgasm in the past couple months.

The room was quiet as Dr. Hayes studied what she was seeing on the screen intensely. She occasionally looked up at me and I started to fear something was wrong. Ricio stepped closer to the monitor and whispered in Dr. Hayes' ear. Pointing to the screen, she murmured softly and Ricio smiled showing all thirty-two of his teeth.

"What's going on?" I asked shakenly.

"Don't panic, Nija. I had to go through vaginally to make sure what I saw previously was accurate. Your baby is healthy and is growing very well. You are twenty-two weeks into this pregnancy and I'm proud to say that you will be the mother of not one but *two* baby girls! You are having twins!" Dr. Hayes revealed while clicking on the mouse as she continued to move the wand around.

"Twins! How is that possible? We've only seen one baby all this time, where was the other baby?" I asked confusedly.

"It's not uncommon during pregnancy for one baby to hide behind another. During the first ultrasound, the second baby didn't want to be known, I guess," she laughed. "You will likely deliver mid-January."

I was shocked to find out there were two babies nesting inside my womb. Tears fell down the side of my face and I openly cried. Kimmie hugged and congratulated me. Ricio came around to the other side of the bed and kissed me on my lips when Kimmie let me go.

"Thank you so much for giving me two beautiful babies, Nija," he whispered.

"Why are you so emotional, Nija? This is a blessing," Dr. Hayes said removing the wand as she printed off the ultrasound pictures.

"Nihiyah was killed last night." The excitement disappeared immediately from Dr. Hayes' face and her head dropped to her chest.

"I'm so sorry to hear that, baby. How's Patricia doing?"

"She's coping," was all I could say.

"I'll give her a call sometime today. If there's anything you all need, don't hesitate to call," she said getting up to give me a hug. "We are all done for the day. I want to see you back in two weeks. Be sure to make the appointment with Gabrielle. My condolences to you and your mother. I'll see you on a personal level in a couple days," she said handing Ricio the photos of the babies.

"Thank you, Olivia."

I sat up while Ricio helped put my leggings back on. He bent down to slip my Uggs on before I stood to my feet and pulled my leggings over my butt. I took one of the photos from Ricio's hand and stared at the images before me. Seeing both my babies filled the void in my heart and I knew Hiyah was smiling down on me.

Chapter 25
Slim

The last three and a half months were the hardest of my life but I made it through. I felt like a new man as I walked out of the rehab center that changed my life. Not knowing where my life was headed, I walked into the Greyhound station, courtesy of the facility heading back to Chicago. When I was taken to the hospital the doctors said I wouldn't live through the night. My heart stopped and the doctors worked on me until it started beating again.

I was in a beautiful place surrounded by flowers and green grass. My mother came to me and expressed how disappointed she was in me. My mother had passed away over fifteen years prior and it was good to see her but it also hurt my soul that I had let her down. She was just as beautiful as the last time I saw her alive and well.

"Jerome, you have to go back. Your job is not done on Earth and God is not ready for you. Your second chance is being presented to you and I want you to go about life differently. All the bullshit you were indulging in has to stop. The drugs are not the way to go. I knew the first time you put that pipe to your lips that you were hurting from not only losing me, but from losing your friend Maurice.

We are both alright, Jerome. Now it's time for you to turn your life around. It won't be easy but I have faith in the Lord and you will fight this battle. Mama loves you baby, be strong." My mama disappeared with a blink of an eye and I was alone again.

I roamed around trying to figure out why I was in the unknown place. Seeing my mama and hearing her voice was something I'd wished would happen for years. At the moment I didn't think about getting my next high, as a matter of fact, I didn't feel like an addict at all. My body and mind felt free and refreshed.

The scene went black for a spell then I heard a voice I hadn't heard in over four years. "Get yo' ass up, nigga!" Reese was standing before me dressed in all white with a huge smile on his face. "Long time no see, Slim." I couldn't believe my eyes, the man I loved like a brother was standing before me with his arms folded over his chest.

"What the fuck you doing here, brah? This isn't a place for you."

"I don't know why I'm here. One minute I was in an ambulance and the next I was here."

"That shit you put in your body is the reason you're here. Haven't you realized you would never get the same high you got the first time you tried that shit? It would never come your way again, Slim. It's time to get right, fam. Stop chasing it because it has come and gone.

I'm gon' tell you like I told my son. I see everything and I don't like the road you've chosen for your life. Them niggas were able to touch me and I'm good up here. It's time to stop using my death as a crutch. It's time to settle a score in the streets of Chicago. You want the pain to go away, get yourself together and help bring their asses down," Reese said.

"How the hell can I go about doing that?"

"First and foremost, you have to cleanse your body so you can be level headed. That means getting that monkey off your back. The shit is old and you've experienced the rush already. I need you to tell my boys to keep an eye on the people they are doing business with. There's a snitch in their circle and they need to move carefully out there.

Slim, you are the one that can get to Floyd. He's in the same boat you are so his mind isn't sharp as it used to be. The difference between the two of y'all, you will be bigger and better than him. I have complete confidence in you that you will do the right thing and get clean before you set out to get Floyd. You will see me again, Slim because I'm going to help you through this. I love you, nigga. Do the right thing, take your life back."

There were plenty of other times Reese came and kept me company within that week I was unresponsive. He scared my ass straight from the grave and now I was on my way back to Chitown. When I made up my mind to go to rehab, I knew I wouldn't be able to successfully finish the program in Illinois. The doctor found a place in Tulsa, Oklahoma.

It was hard for me to settle in because the drugs were calling me and my body was craving it every minute of the day. Every time the thought crossed my mind, Reese showed up with a prep talk. Eventually the cravings went away and now I'm on the road to staying dry. As soon as I touch down, I'll get in touch with Ricio and Sosa.

The bus ride was sixteen hours and I was hungrier than an Ethiopian kid. Going into my bag, I took out the snack bag that was prepared for me by the kitchen staff and there was only an apple, banana, two packs of peanut butter crackers, and two bottles of water in it. That shit would have to last until we arrived at a rest stop or my ass was going to starve to death. I had twenty dollars for that purpose and couldn't wait to get some meat in my system.

"You want to share some of your food?" A guy sitting next to me ask.

"Ain't shit to share. This is all I have," I said peeling the banana.

"Give the nigga the apple, Slim," I heard in my head. *"You gon' be straight when you reach your destination, I promise."* Reese was getting on my nerves still serving as the good Samaritan from the grave.

"Here man. Eat that shit slow because ain't no mo'," I said handing him the apple.

"Thank you."

The muthafucka ate the apple so fast I don't remember when he took the first bite. Falling asleep I woke up to the driver announcing that we had twenty minutes at the rest stop. The bus stopped at a taco bell that was inside a gas station and I rushed to get off the bus to be one of the first in line for food.

"May I help you?" The cashier asked.

"I'll have six hard shelled tacos and a small drink." It didn't take long for my order to be ready. I grabbed the tray and found a table to sit at. The same guy came and stood over me looking like a lost puppy as I unwrapped one of the tacos. "Sit yo' ass down and eat this taco," I said tossing one across the table.

"I'm sorry if I'm bothering you, sir I just haven't eaten in so long. Can you tell me where the bus is going?"

I looked at him confusingly, "How the hell you don't know where we're going? Didn't you pay for your ticket?"

"Nah, I snuck on the bus to get out of the cold. I have no idea where it's headed. I've been homeless for almost a year and jump a bus every chance I get. You may as well call me a drifter because that's what I do to stay warm. I lost everything in a house fire in Wisconsin.

My wife, two kids, and my dog died in that fire. The police are trying to pin a murder charge on me so I went on the run instead of turning myself in. I'm not going to jail behind that shit man, you know."

This cracker muthafucka done killed his whole family then he ends up sitting next to my black ass on the bus. How ironic is that? The wheels started turning in my head and I had big plans for his ass in the Windy city.

"The bus is going to Chicago. You can roll with me when we get there. Do you smoke dope?"

"Hell yeah, you got some? We can go around the side of the building and fire up," he said rubbing his hands together forgetting about the food I placed in front of him.

"No, but I'll be getting some as soon as we touch down," I said eating my food fast so we could go back to the bus. The bus driver had walked out of the restaurant and was heading back to the bus. "Come on, the bus is about to take off."

We got back on the bus and I slept the rest of the way to Chicago. I could hear Jake murmuring to himself about how he was sorry for killing his family. I kept my eyes closed to hear what he would reveal. He was talking to God, asking for forgiveness. There wasn't any way to forgive him for what he had done to his children. When I opened my eyes, the skyline was beautiful and I knew we were about fifteen minutes from getting off the bus. I looked over and Jake was looking out the window wide awake.

"This city is beautiful. I've never been here before," he said never turning around.

"Man, looks can be deceiving. My city is treacherous and deadly. I'm Slim by the way, what's your name?"

"I'm Jake. Jake Sanders," he said lowly.

This dude actually told me his full name like he wanted somebody to tell the cops on his ass. I made sure to store the information he gave in the back of my mind. Jake Sanders, wanted in house fire that killed his wife and kids in Wisconsin. As the bus came to a stop, I stood and exited quickly out of the back door.

Walking across the street to Union Station, I went inside and pulled Sosa's business card from my pocket. Looking around for a spell I spotted a payphone and headed straight for it. Jake was right behind me like he was my shadow. It was almost midnight when I picked up the receiver and drop the coins in the slot and dialed the number.

"Who the fuck is this?" Sosa barked through the phone.

"It's Slim," I replied.

"Slim? Nigga I've been looking for you, where you at?"

"I'm down at Union Station. Just got off the bus from Oklahoma."

"Stay put, I'll be there in twenty," he said ending the call.

Placing the receiver back on the hook I sat in an empty chair and waited for Sosa to arrive. I thought of a story about who Jake was by the time he showed up.

***

Walking outside to wait for Sosa, Jake and I fought against the cold air that bit through our clothing. A black Benz pulled to the curb and the window came down slowly revealing Ricio in the passenger seat. "What up, Slim?" He said smiling as he got out of the car. "You lookin' good as hell, homie."

"Thank you. I had to go away to get right, you know what I mean? It's time to make shit right for your pops." Dapping the young Reese up, I leaned down waving at Sosa. "What's good, Sosa?" The nigga didn't say anything back so I thought he didn't hear me so I repeated myself. "What's good, Sosa?"

"When I see that nigga, I'll ask him. Get the fuck in the car, this hawk ain't playing out here and y'all want to chit chat and shit," he growled.

I pulled the handle to get in the car and Jake was right behind me. Scooting all the way over behind the driver seat, Jake attempted to get in and was stopped with one foot in the car. "Who the fuck is you?" Ricio asked smugly.

"I'm a friend of Slim's. My, my name is Jake," he stammered.

"Slim ain't got no muthafuckin' friends. Get out the fuckin' car, Slim and explain who the fuck Jake from State Farm is before he needs some muthafuckin insurance to save his life around this bitch. You know we don't embrace nobody we don't know," Rodrigo said throwing the car in park and got out.

I got out and Jake looked like a deer caught in headlights as the two brothers sandwiched him. In spite of the cold weather, Jake was sweating bullets. He tried to turn his head in my direction and it was snatched forward by Ricio.

"He good, I met him on the bus and told him I would help him out."

"How the fuck you going to help him when you ain't in position to help yo'self! Go yo' white ass over there somewhere while we talk this shit over with fam," Rodrigo barked at Jake.

"I don't do the racist shit, man—"

"I don't either so just think as it being yo' lucky day because I hate you muthafuckas personally. Now, go the fuck over there somewhere before I shoot yo' goofy ass!" Rodrigo pointed toward the Union Station building. Jake looked at Rodrigo but didn't make a move. Before we knew it, Jake was staring down the barrel of his Glock. "Step before I drop yo' wack ass!"

"Bro, put that shit away and calm the fuck down," Ricio said grabbing his hand. "Yo, my man, let us talk to Slim." Jake walked down the street and started pacing back and forth talking to himself. "Who the fuck is this nigga, fam and what the hell were you doing in Oklahoma?"

"Like I told you before, he's someone I met on the bus. I figured I could use him to get to Floyd since his ass gon' die or end up in jail anyway. He's wanted in Wisconsin for the death of his wife and kids."

"Nigga, that's heat we *don't* need right now! I thought we had an agreement that you would clean yourself up and leave that bull-shit alone. Your friend Jake looks like he's on that shit, fam." Ricio snapped.

"That's why I was in Oklahoma. I've been clean for over three months and that life is behind me. With all the nights Reese came to me in my dreams, I'm done. He told me to help ya'll get to Floyd and Jake stepped to me at the right time. Ain't nobody looking for his ass but the pigs.

Since I don't use drugs no more, he would be the perfect guy to cop some dope from them niggas because I'm not doing it. Reese died because of Floyd and Big Jim's greed. His blood is on their hands as well as Max's. They set him up the night he was killed by calling him to the westside to pick up some money.

Big Jim made the call but Floyd was the one that was there to supposedly deliver the money. Rod was the one that ran up on Reese from behind and shot him in the back of the head. I was across the street in the alleyway because I had just copped some dope from Floyd," I said glancing up at Ricio. "Youngblood, it broke my heart to see you holding your father for the last time that night.

"Why didn't you say nothing, Slim?" Ricio asked.

"Floyd and Big Jim rolled down on me and threatened to kill me if I talked. They fed me drugs like tic tacs to keep me quiet and that's how my drug addiction spiraled out of control. I was on 26th Street every day to keep an eye on y'all. After that night, I didn't want nothing to do with them niggas.

I saw the change in Max but I didn't know what the issue was at the time. I didn't put two and two together until I was in Oklahoma. Floyd and Big Jim had been creeping behind closed doors for years and I think they were forcing that gay shit on him. I don't know for sure, but I truly believe that's what was going on." Pausing for a moment, I looked around at nothing in particular and turned back to Ricio.

“There’s a mole in your circle. I don’t know who it is, but watch your back, Youngblood.”

“How you come up with that conclusion?” Rodrigo asked.

“You may not believe me but Reese told me. Back at the hotel I thought you were just trying to scare me, Ricio. When you kept say Reese told you to find me and clean me up, I thought you were going crazy until my nigga came to me every night for one hundred and fifteen days. he kept me company until the drugs were out of my system.”

“Go get ya boy. We have to find Floyd quickly because Jake ain’t gon’ be around us for long because I don’t trust a muthafucka that would kill his own family. I have a bullet with his name on it as soon as he does what we need him to do,” Rodrigo said walking around the car with his phone to his ear. “Find out where Floyd is laying his head, ASAP!”

Chapter 26
Latorra

Being in the mist of a shootout was something I'd never experienced a day in my life. My life flashed before my eyes when that guy pushed me to the ground. Seeing Ricio shoot him in his back actually made me piss on myself. I knew crazy shit happened in clubs I just didn't think it would happen while I worked at Money.

Big Jim was steady blowing up my phone and I still hadn't answered his calls. I was done with his stupidity and wouldn't allow myself to get wrapped up in what he had going on. I was at home pacing back and forth because I couldn't get in touch with Tammy. I'd called her so many times that I already knew she was one of the people that died in the club. It was almost two in the morning and I didn't want to call her mother because I wasn't sure if she was okay or not.

Sitting on the couch, my phone started vibrating on the coffee table and I scooped it up quickly. "Hello," I said slowly.

"Latorra?" the female voice on the other end replied.

"Yeah, this is she."

"This is Tamara's mom. Sorry to call you so late, I didn't want to wait until morning. Tammy was killed at the club tonight. I know how close you two were so I wanted you to hear this devastating news from me. The police just left my house, Latorra. My baby is gone."

I couldn't speak due to the gut wrenching cry that escaped my mouth. Thinking back to the club, Tammy was on stage dancing when the mayhem broke out. I was hoping she got out or hid until the shooting stopped but her mother confirmed my worst nightmare. My best friend was no longer on this earth with me.

"I'm so sorry, Miss Ross. She didn't deserve this," I cried into the phone.

"It's not your fault baby. I've been trying to get Tammy to leave that club alone for the longest time. She wanted to make the fast money and I had to allow her to do what she thought was best for her. These streets are vicious and our city is not like it used to be.

The violence is at an all time high and it's not going to get any better no time soon.

I want you to be careful out there. You lived a different life than my daughter but a bullet doesn't have a name. I will keep you posted on the funeral arrangements. We won't cry for my daughter. It will be a celebration because she lived a good life. Get some sleep, baby and I love you."

"I love you too, ma."

After hanging up from talking to Tammy's mother I cried until my tear ducts dried up. I rose from the couch with my phone in hand and went to my room. Laying across my bed, I thought about all the good and bad days Tammy and I had throughout the years. Some brought tears to my eyes but majority of them put a smile on my face. We were supposed to be two old women sitting on the front stoop cussing out the neighborhood kids.

I fell asleep with an image of Tammy's face in my mind. Seeing her lying lifeless in a casket was something I wasn't prepared to do. But I saw the scene in a dream and jumped up running to the bathroom to throw up. As I was leaned over the toilet, I heard a noise coming from the front of my apartment. Knowing I was home alone I eased up and grabbed a towel to wipe my mouth.

Trying my best to get back to my bedroom without making any noise, I tiptoed down the hall. When I made it to the doorway of my room a felt the nozzle of a gun in the back of my head. Every muscle in my body became rigid and I was instantly paralyzed.

"Bitch, you thought I wasn't gon' find you, huh?" a male voice said behind me. "If you scream, I'm gon' blow yo' muthafuckin' head off." I glanced at the time on the clock that hung on the wall above my bed and it was a quarter to five in the morning. "Turn the fuck around, hoe!"

Hesitating to do as he demanded, I slowly turned and came face to face with Rello. He had a sinister grin on his face and I was scared shitless. Before I could open my mouth to speak, I was hit across the face with the butt of his gun. I fell to the floor hard on my wrist and I wailed loudly from the pain that traveled up my arm.

"Bitch, shut the fuck up!" Rello kicked me in my ribs and I balled up in a fetal position. He grabbed me by my hair and I felt it ripping from my scalp. I tried my best to get out of his grip but in return he slammed my head against the corner of the dresser. Blood ran into my eyes and blurred my vision. I was dazed for a few minutes but my legs couldn't hold my weight.

Falling to the floor, I was yanked back to my feet as he tightened his grip on my hair. Trying to focus on the items on my dresser, I was met with his fist pummeling me in my eye. A white light flashed in my eye and I squeezed it shut again. The swelling was instant and I was afraid to fight back.

"You will do what the fuck you were told to do next time won't you?" He barked as he punched me repeatedly in the top of my head. "I don't hit women but I fuck up hoes!" He said throwing me face down on the bed as he raised my gown over my ass. "I'm about to get some of this pussy before I leave your ass lying in here motionless.

"No! Please don't do this to me. Do what you came here to do. Kill me if that's what you have planned, but please, don't rape me!" I yelled kicking my legs trying to get to my feet.

Rello swung his arm and hit me once again with his gun. I was going in and out of consciousness as more blood squirted from the gash on my forehead. Hearing him rip open a condom, I couldn't move to save my life. Feeling defeated, I laid on my stomach and waited for him to finish whatever he was going to do with me. When he ran his hand over my kitty, I cringed.

"Yeah, you want this shit because you wet as fuck," he mumbled as he positioned himself between my legs. I tried to close my legs and he snatched them back open forcefully. My hip bone popped and I yell out in pain. "Didn't I tell you to shut yo' fuckin' mouth? You're a hardheaded muthafucka I see. I got something for your ass."

Rello shoved his dick roughly into my love box and I cried out in pain because he was aiming to hurt me. With every stroke, he punched me in the face. "Damn this pussy good." *Bam*! "You could've been my bitch with this good shit." *Bam!* "Now I hate I had to do this to you." *Bam!* "Fuck!" *Bam!*

The nigga had to be high or bipolar if he was enjoying what he was doing to me. I felt violated and dirty with him humping me like a dog. "Moan or something bitch!" he screamed pulling out and whamming on my face. I felt my face swell after every punch and passed out. Rello poked me in the head with the butt of the gun but I played possum and didn't move.

He turned me over and I held my breath as if I was swimming to make my chest stop moving. Placing his hand on my neck, he checked for my pulse. Shuffling around quickly, he started knocking things around. I let out the breath I was holding slowly but obviously it wasn't slow enough. Rello spun around and caught my eyes open and raised his arm and shot me in the stomach.

"Sneaky ass, bitch! Now yo' dumb ass dead dead!"

I heard him leave my bedroom and the front door closed a few seconds later. Struggling to get to my phone, I grabbed my stomach and blood spilled through my fingers. If I was going to die, somebody had to know who did this shit to me. I was finally able to climb onto my bed to get my phone. My left eye was swollen and the right one was barely open. I pressed the button and waited for someone to answer.

"What's up?"

"Ricio, I've been shot. This guy named Rello—"

"Where you at?" he screamed into the phone.

"At home. I'm gonna die Ricio. Rello did this shit to me," I said dropping the phone.

"Latorra! Latorra! Latorra!" was all I heard as I lost consciousness.

***

The sound of the machines had me fighting to open my eyes but I couldn't. The last thing I remember was telling Ricio what happened to me before I blacked out. I don't believe I survived the shit

I was put through. One of the machines started beeping uncontrollably and the sound of the door opening got my attention.

"Miss Smith, you are okay. You're safe now and I'm going to make sure you stay that way. I'm your nurse for the night and my name is Carmen. Don't try to open your eyes because they are swollen shut. The police have been here to question you but I told them to come back in a couple days."

"How long have I been here?" I asked barely opening my mouth.

"You were brought in by ambulance yesterday morning in pretty bad shape. You were rushed straight to the operating room for emergency surgery from a gunshot wound to the stomach. God is all I can say about your condition. The bullet didn't hit any vital organs but you have staples in your head, stitches in your face and stomach. You are one lucky woman, Miss Smith. Whoever did this to you, left you for dead. If it wasn't for your friend, you would've died," Carmen said as the door opened.

"Speaking of your friend, he's right here and has been by your side since you got out of surgery."

"What friend are you talking about?" I asked in a shaky voice.

"It's me, Latorra." Hearing Ricio's voice brought tears to my eyes. "You gon' be alright baby girl. I got her from here, Carmen. Thanks for everything," he said rubbing my hand.

"No problem. Press the button if you need anything. I'll be back to check your vitals in about an hour."

"Thank you," I mumbled as I felt something cold being placed over my eyes and the door closing softly.

"Latorra, I need you to tell me what happened to you yesterday."

"I came home after leaving the club and tried calling my friend Tammy to see if she was okay. Tammy didn't answer and I got a call from her mother saying she was one of the people shot at the club. When I got off the phone with her, I got in bed and cried myself to sleep. I had a dream that made me sick to my stomach. Rushing to the bathroom I heard a noise somewhere in my apartment and tried to get back to my room to get my gun. I was hit in the back of the head by this dude named Rello."

"What is your relationship with Rello, Latorra?" Ricio asked.

Telling him what happened from the day I met Big Jim 'til yesterday, I waited for him to say something about what I'd just told him. My eyes wouldn't open and it bothered me because I wanted to see the look on his face. Ricio was probably thinking the worse of me at that moment because the shit I'd been going through sounded fishy as hell.

"Why didn't you tell me about Big Jim being your father and how he was trying to use you to set me up? That shit wasn't important enough to share with me, Latorra?"

"I wanted to tell you but I didn't know how. Big Jim was calling me and I refused to answer him because I figured if he couldn't talk to me, he would leave me alone. Instead, he sent somebody to my house to kill me even after he had me fired from my job."

"So, you mean to tell me that for months you didn't know what type of nigga Big Jim was? His ass got a motive for everything and he reeled yo' ass right into his web. What else do you know about this Rello cat?" Ricio asked.

"I have his number in my phone but I doubt if they picked it up off my bed before bringing me here."

"I got your phone. What's your code?" he asked.

"6689 is my code. Go into the note's app, I have his address stored in there. I followed him home the night I got fired from my job. I was going to tell you but so much was going on in my life and I was trying to save money to move away from here," I said sadly.

"Latorra, I didn't mean to be harsh with you when you came to visit me at the hospital. The things you said to my woman was uncalled for so I had to tell you how it was. I would love to still be friends but we both know that wouldn't be good for my relationship. I'll give you some money so you can move and start a new life wherever you decide to go. But I meant what I said, we are done."

"I understand and I appreciate that, Ricio. Keep your money, I have enough to get by on. If I stay here Big Jim will find a way to kill me once he finds out I'm still alive. I'm sorry if I caused any trouble in your relationship."

"It's all good. I played a part in what went on between the two of us and I owned it. I chose my woman and that's the bottom line. You don't have anyone to help you out here and I'm gon' be there for you so you can get away. Thank you for the information on that nigga Rello and I will make sure you have protection here at the hospital at all times.

Carmen told me the police was up here trying to talk to you yesterday. Don't tell them shit! The only thing they need to know is, somebody broke in your house and attacked you. Nothing more, nothing less. I'm gon' take care of this nigga myself. Understood?"

"I understand and thank you so much. Would you buzz the nurse and tell her I need something for pain?"

Ricio pressed the button and waited for one of the nurses to respond. "Miss Smith, what can I help you with?"

"Can you tell Carmen to bring me something for pain?" I asked nicely.

"I'll be right there. I have to check your vitals anyway."

Ricio stood from the chair, "I'm heading out but I'll be back to check on you. Here's your cellphone, hit me if you need to and my security will be here within the hour to sit with you." Nodding my head in response I exhaled. Carmen walked through the door and Ricio walked out.

"That young man cares about you. You are so lucky to have him in your life," Carmen said as she shot the pain medicine into my IV.

"Nah, his woman is the lucky one," I replied relaxing as the medicine took effect.

Chapter 27
Ricio

Leaving Latorra in the state she was in had me feeling bad. Not because I have feelings for her, but because I was part of the reason the shit happened. Big Jim was on some fuck shit for sending a nigga to violate a female, especially his own daughter. I was glad Latorra got vital information on the nigga that beat and raped her. Rello is going to get what's coming to him, old and new.

Jumping in my ride I peeled out of the hospital parking lot and headed straight for Beast's crib. He and Sin had been quiet lately and I knew it had a lot to do with them keeping an eye on Gio. Today was the day for him to step out and get his hands dirty. I connected my phone to the Bluetooth and dialed up Nija.

"Hello," she said when she answered.

"How you doing this morning, baby?"

"Not too good. Ma and I just got back from the funeral home. The services will be this Friday," Nija sniffed. "I don't know if I'll be able to do this, Ricio."

"You will because I'll be right there with you. Nihiyah is not hurting anymore and she is in a far better place than we will ever be in. She's at peace and wouldn't want you crying for her. I know it's hard for you right now, but it will be alright. I'm out taking care of business and I'll be over there soon after. I love you."

"Okay," she said hanging up. I stared at the display screen and wanted to punch a hole in it. Nija still wasn't budging on being back with me as a couple. She was standing strong on this co-parenting shit and it wasn't sitting well with me.

However, that didn't mean I was going to give up, patience was the key. I would sit back and allow her to have her moment alone but it didn't mean I wasn't watching from afar. Pulling into Beast's driveway, I threw the car in park and got out. As I walked up the steps the door swung open and Madysen hurried down the stairs.

"Aye, where you going?" I yelled at her back. Madysen ignored me walking toward her car. "Mads, I know you hear me talking to you!"

"Leave me alone, Ricio," she said getting in the car pulling off.

I shook my head and went into the house closing the door behind me. It was awfully quiet and the feeling in the pit of my stomach told me something wasn't right. I ran up the stairs two at a time and searched each room. Beast and Sin wasn't there. Going back downstairs frantically looking around, I entered Beast's office and it too was empty.

Creeping to the guest room that Madysen used, I hesitated before I placed my hand on the knob and turned it. Not knowing what I would find when I entered, the room was empty. Walking to the crib, I looked down and Gio was crying behind a thick layer of tape. His small face was beet read and tears slid down the side of his face. Removing the tape slowly, his wails filled the room and I lifted him up in my arms.

My blood boiled over and I snatched my phone from my hip. "Where y'all at?" I snapped soon as Beast answered his phone.

"We went to have breakfast. Everything okay?"

"Hell nawl, everything's not okay. I'm at yo' crib and this bitch Madysen left Gio in the house by himself! I had just walked up when she stormed out the house but I didn't think anything of it until I got inside and nobody was here except a four-month-old with his fuckin' mouth taped!"

"I know you lying!" He barked into the phone. "Sin, we gotta go!"

"What's going on, Erique?" I heard Sin asked in the background.

"I'll explain in the car. Ricio, stay put, we're on our way."

"I don't have a choice but to stay here! Gio can't take care of himself!" I said ending the call.

Madysen was dead wrong for leaving my nephew alone in this muthafuckin' house. When I saw her ass again, she was getting fucked up on sight. That was on my mama. The bitch needed psychological help. Beast and Sin knew better than to leave her crazy ass alone with Gio. My shirt was soak and wet from his diaper.

The diaper was so wet it seemed Gio hadn't been changed since the night before. I was seething with anger because what Madysen did was fucked up. I placed Gio on the changing table and he was still wailing loudly as I removed the diaper. The sight before me almost dropped a real nigga to his knees. Gio had several burn marks on his private area and on his little butt.

Cleaning him up the best I could without hurting him. I smoothed Vaseline on the burns and dressed him. I'd never handled a baby before but I learned quickly as I wrapped him in a blanket and put him in his car seat. Practically running through the house, I snatched the spare house keys from the wall and locked up before heading to my ride.

Once I had Gio strapped in I jumped in and pushed my whip to the Ingalls hospital. I grabbed my phone to call Beast and he answered on the first ring. "I'm almost there, nephew," he said quickly.

"Go to Ingalls on Governor's Highway, this bitch done burned this baby with a cigarette or some shit all over his dick and ass! I'm killing that bitch Beast and ain't shit you can do to stop me!" I yelled over Gio's cries.

"Fuck! Okay, we'll meet you there."

I was driving fast as hell trying to get lil man to the hospital but my mind was on all the ways I was going to choke the fuck out of his mammy for the shit she did to him. My hands were gripping the steering wheel tightly as I whipped into the parking lot of the hospital and I hopped out and grabbed him from the back. Entering the emergency room, I walked up to the counter and the nurse sitting behind the desk put her pen down as Gio wailed uncontrollably.

"May I help you?"

"Yeah, I need somebody to look at my nephew. He was burned with a cigarette, I believe." Without hesitation the nurse stood and told me to follow her to the back. She put us in a room and told me to unwrap Gio so she could take a look. Stripping him down to his diaper, I opened it up and stepped to the side so she could examine him.

"Oh my God!" she shrieked in horror. The burns had turned to blisters and looked worse than back at the house. "What happened to this baby?" The nurse glared at me.

"It looks like cigarette burns and I believe his mother did this to him."

"You believe? Are you the father?" she asked wetting a towel.

"No, this is my nephew. When I went to the house, his mother was leaving. When I went to change his pamper, I saw the burns. After changing his diaper and applying Vaseline, I brought him straight to the hospital."

"Where is his mother now?"

"I don't know! Help my nephew because he is in pain, all this other shit can wait until he's comfortable."

"I'm going to leave this cold compression on his bottom and groin area. Give him a bottle to try to calm him and I'll be right back," she said leaving the room.

Getting Gio to the hospital was my main focus and I forgot to grab his diaper bag and bottles. Taking my phone out, I called Beast back and he answered on the first ring. "Ricio, I'm parking."

"I didn't pack a bag for the baby. He don't have diapers or bottles. Y'all gon' have to go get that shit because he won't stop crying," I said over Gio's cries.

"We have an emergency bag in the trunk. Where are y'all at?" He asked slamming the car door.

"We're in the emergency department, room eight," I said trying to calm Gio down.

"Okay, I'll see you in a minute." Beast ended the call and he and Sin was walking through the door minutes later. "Tell me what happened," he said sitting the diaper bag on the bed. Sin went to Gio and inserted the bottle in his mouth. His little tear stained face was red and he grabbed her finger with his.

"I was coming over to talk business when Madysen opened the door and stormed to her car. I called out to her but she told me to leave her alone before she got in her car and pulled off. The thought of her leaving Gio in the house without supervision never crossed my mind. When I saw him lying in a soiled, soaked diaper with his mouth taped shut, I almost broke down.

Thinking he was just wet, I proceeded to change him. When I opened the diaper, I saw that he was burned with a cigarette or something. I had found the cause of his crying and I was ready to find Madysen and put one between her fuckin' eyes."

Sin took that moment to pull the cold compression back and her mouth hardened into a thin line. Beast looked over and snatched his phone from his hip. Whoever he called obviously didn't answer. There was a knock on the door and a tall Caucasian doctor entered the room.

"Hello, I'm Dr. Gretowski and I'll be handling the care of this precious baby today," he said looking around the room. "You must be mom," he said glaring at Sin.

"No, this is my great nephew. His mother is not present," she shot back.

"Well, I need one of you to fill out the paperwork for the little fella."

"His name is Giovanni and I will do the honors," Sin said taking the papers he held out.

"In cases like Giovanni's, it's imperative that we inform law enforcement. The injuries the baby has sustained was done by someone and it's child abuse. We also had to contact Child Protective Services because the environment is deemed to be unsafe for him."

"Now wait a muthafuckin' minute. Giovanni is safe in my home," Beast snapped. "His mother has been going through a lot in the past couple months. We took her in before she even had the baby and things has been better, so we thought. The one time we leave her alone to care for Gio, she did some stupid shit. There's no goddamn way I'm letting y'all take him from us!"

"Sir, you can plead your case with the case worker that will be here any minute. That's not my line of business," he stated walking over to Gio. Removing the compression, Dr. Gretowski examined the wound and shook his head. "The burns aren't life threatening and will heal over time. We will provide an ointment to apply to the burns. This doesn't mean the situation will be overlooked." He rolled Gio over and examined his back exposing his little butt.

Beast drew in a deep breath and let it out slowing drawing Sin's attention from the papers she was filling out to the baby. Tears formed in her eyes and she held her head down. I had to turn my head because he didn't deserve the pain he was enduring by the hands of his own mother. There was yet another knock on the door and in walked two uniformed officers and a young woman dressed in a business pantsuit.

"Dr. Gretowski?" she asked stepping further into the room. He looked up and smiled. "I'm Mrs. Pamela Howard from DCFS. What do we have here?"

"Nice to meet you, ma'am. We have a case involving—" he paused and picked up the papers Sin had finished filling out. "four-month-old Giovanni Vasquez. He was brought in with burns to his groin and buttocks."

"Who are you guys?" One of the officers asked.

"I'm Erique Haley and this is my better half Sincere," Beast spoke giving the cop the side eye.

"And who are you, sir?"

"Mauricio Vasquez." Keeping shit short and simple but I saw the quick exchange between the two cops.

"What do you know about what happened to the baby?" The caseworker asked. I recited the events from earlier and everyone listened as I spoke. When I was finished, I looked over at Gio and he was sound asleep. "What is the mother's name and where can we find her?"

"I don't know where she is. Madysen Hook, the mother of Gio got in her car and drove off," I explained.

"I've been calling her since we received the call from Ricio but she hasn't answered or returned my calls. Madysen knows what she has done was wrong and don't want to face the consequences," Beast chimed in. "She has been staying with me and Sincere since she told us she was with child. As far as I know, she doesn't have any family here in Chicago. Madysen could be anywhere by now."

"I'm glad that you guys aren't trying to hold back any information to protect your loved one. I've seen many family members try to cover-up abuse and it only made the situation worse. We are going to take baby Gio—"

"Over my dead body! This baby doesn't need to go into the fucked up system when he has family that's able and willing to take care of him. The first thing y'all want to do is put a child in foster care before even considering immediate family! I understand what Madysen did was wrong and she deserves whatever happens to her. Giovanni doesn't deserve to be taken away.

Madysen is not welcome in my home after the shit she pulled today. Her rights to Giovanni are gone! I will raise this baby and he will not have to worry about a next time because there won't be one," Sin argued.

"Ma'am I understand your hurt but the child's safety is our main concern," the officer said calmly.

"Hold on a minute, Officer. Sincere, I see how much you care for Giovanni and you are correct. If I could finish what I was saying, you would understand a little better. We are going to take Giovanni to foster care *if* there's no one in the family that would be capable of caring for him. Since you are willing to care for the child, I don't see the problem in allowing you to do so.

There will be weekly visits to make sure Giovanni is being well taken care of and there can be no visits from his mother. The minute Miss Hook or you violate this agreement, the baby will be removed and placed in foster care. Do you agree with the terms I've laid out with you?"

"Yes. Yes, I agree. I need her found, arrested and I have no problem pressing charges. Madysen needs psychological help badly and I would like to file a restraining order on her."

Sin wasn't bullshitting when it came down to Gio. She was laying it on thick for the police and the case worker, but I knew her better than they ever would. Sin was covering her tracks because Madysen was good as dead if she showed up at their crib.

***

We were in the hospital for several hours with Giovanni getting paperwork and the temporary custody situation completed. Sin used her legal connections so they could adopt Gio without having any legal issues. Rodrigo rushed to the hospital when I called after the cops left and he was ready to tear the city up looking for Madysen. When we were finally able to leave, everybody went to Beast's crib. Sitting in the family room, I sipped on a glass of Remy while Rodrigo, all the cousins, Beast, and Sin congregated around.

"So much shit has happened in the past couple months and my body is tired," I said placing my glass on the coaster. "Beast, I know you haven't been hands on in this because of Gio but Unc, I need you to come out and have some fun." Glancing in his direction, he nodded his head with understanding.

"Fill me in, nephew."

"Nija's sister was killed the other night and there was a brick found in her car that belonged to me. The police was all over my ass about that shit but I denied knowing anything about the product. The only person that would have that the shit on the street is Sam. Angel found out he was Floyd's nephew when Sam reupped with him. Floyd has to be in the dark about what's happening in his empire because all transactions is going through a nigga named Rello. We caught them niggas slipping at club Money last Friday and aired that muthafucka out.

"You do know that shit was caught on surveillance, right?" Beast asked sitting up.

"Not when you have a computer genius on yo' team it's not. Angel erased that shit with a few clicks. Anyway, we lost Face in that shootout but they lost more than we did. I got some lucrative information on the nigga Rello and his ass is going down for the shit he did. I found out Big Jim sent him to kill the correctional officer that I was fuckin' with but she lived."

"I told you to be careful with that bitch!" Rodrigo sneered.

"Yeah, I told you the same thing. The bitch worked in the same prison Big Jim is serving time in. I knew he would get to her ass sooner than later," Beast added.

"It didn't go down the way y'all think. She became a target when she wouldn't play into his hand. He tried to use the fact that he was her daddy to get my head on a silver platter."

"Her daddy! That hoe lying to you, fam! She knew about y'all beef all along and is playing off that shit. Ain't no muthafuckin' way she didn't know who the fuck you were before she came at you," Angel yelled.

"First of all, I came at her. Secondly, she didn't know until they took a DNA test to confirm the shit. That's when she said he started requesting for her to set me up,' I paused.

"Yeah, I aight. You need to walk away from her ass and leave it at that. The bitch can't be trusted. In my eyes, she playing both sides but you can't see the shit because the pussy blinded yo' ass."

"Fuck you, Rodrigo! I'm not even fuckin' with shawty like that. When I told Nija I was done with the bullshit, that's what I meant. You can stop with all the extra shit because you don't know what you talking about! Why the fuck am I explaining anything to yo' ass anyway?" I said getting heated.

"You explaining because you know your actions is gon' get you fucked up! Stay the fuck away from the bitch, Ricio!"

"As I was saying, after we blew up Big Jim's crib, Floyd was my focal point. Once again, Angel tracked his ass down and he's staying in an apartment right on 26th street. My plan is to have Slim and his dude go over there to cop some dope. However, Slim has been clean for months so it will be on his guy Jake to make shit believable since he's actually looking to score and use."

"You gon' let two drug addicts set somebody up for you, Ricio? How smart is that?" Beast asked seriously.

"I believe it's a good idea because Floyd ain't looking for Slim to cross him. As far as he knows, Slim is still the same ol' crackhead looking for a hit. Trust me, it'll work."

"If that man dies behind yo' bullshit, I hope Reese haunt yo' ass in your sleep. Get ready to have many sleepless nights because shit ain't looking good from where I'm sitting. But I'll let you handle that. What you need me to handle?" Beast asked sitting back against the pillows crossing his foot over his knee.

"Sam is your mission. I need you to pick his brain to see what he's on. I think he was mixed in this from the gate."

"Ricio, when we sat down with Sam, I followed him for days and he didn't seem like he was on any type of bullshit. Maybe he doesn't know what's going on but I will find out. I'll set something up for tomorrow." Beast looked over at Sin briefly when she adjusted her body on the couch.

Sin wasn't speaking on anything. She just sat back taking everything in quietly. In the back of my mind I knew she was plotting. It wouldn't be her if she wasn't. There was no way she would be able to act on her thoughts with Gio keeping her occupied. Knowing Sin, her ass would find a way.

"Sin, what's on your mind?" Beast asked trying to pick her brain.

"Ohhhh nothing," she sang standing to her feet. "I think Gio needs me." The smirk on her didn't go unnoticed.

"Whatever you're conjuring up, forget it! You're a mother now so all that street shit has to come to an end indefinitely." Beast said to her back as she walked away.

Ignoring Beast's rant, she paused with one foot on the bottom step and turned her head to look back at me. "Ricio, when is Nihiyah's funeral?" she asked changing the subject.

"Friday. I'll find out the details tomorrow and let everybody know. We must be there for Nija the same way she was there for us."

"You didn't have to stress that. We as a family know what needs to be done. I'll call her in the morning. Until then, you boys be good," Sin winked and climbed the stairs.

Waiting until Sin was out of sight, I turned to Beast. You better watch her ass, she's up to something."

"I'm two steps ahead of you on that," Beast replied running his hand over his head. "Let's get back to business."

Chapter 28
Rodrigo

We spent several hours at Beast's house coming up with a plan. I was tired as fuck and needed to get some sleep because I had plans to kill before the sun came up. Driving down 183rd Street, it was a little after one in the morning. I turned right onto Crawford Avenue and noticed a set of headlights behind me. Continuing down the road, I signaled to turn left on 177th Street and the car was still behind me.

I made a right slowly down Sycamore Ave and blue and red lights flashed behind me. When I pulled over, a Crown Vic pulled up behind me and I knew right away it was those two crooked ass detectives that arrested me. Throwing the gear in park, I sat back waiting for the hoe ass pigs to get out. To my surprise, there was only one person in the car and it piqued my curiosity.

As the cop got closer, I realized it was Detective Cooper and my blood started boiling because I knew he was about to be on bullshit. I pressed the button to let down the window when he got to the back of my ride. "Step out the car, Mr. Vasquez?"

"What was I stopped for?" I asked placing my hands on the steering wheel. This muthafucka had no business fuckin' with me in the suburbs unless somebody told him where I laid my head.

"I have my reasons. Now step out the fuckin' car!"

Reaching over I pulled the lever and opened the door. I didn't worry about being arrested because officer racist bitch didn't have shit on me. He was adding to the reasons I already had to kill his punk ass. Soon as I got out the car I was slammed against the side of my vehicle.

"Where's the money and the drugs, Sosa?" Laughing immediately, my head was slammed into the door. "There's nothing funny, nigger! You are going down right along with your brother Mauricio. There's evidence that you are responsible for the murder of the woman in Evergreen Park."

"I haven't killed no muthafuckin' body!"

"According to my informant, you did," he whispered in my ear.

"Nigga, get the fuck out my ear! That's the way you talk to a bitch and I ain't that. Gay ass muthafucka. I don't give a fuck what yo' informant got you thinking is facts. Whoever's feeding you bullshit, don't know shit about me. the intimidation shit don't work over here."

"Oh, it will work, Sosa—"

"That nigga ain't here! I've told you before my name is Rodrigo, don't make me say it again, Officer Coop Poop!"

"Nigger, I don't care what you call yourself. What I care about is the fact that I know you're going to jail for a very long time." It was his turn to laugh and it irked the hell out of me.

"Where's your proof?" I challenged.

"Darren Cobbs," he said sarcastically. When I heard Fats government name, murdering him was the first thought that popped in my mind. The nigga had turned into a snitch and was using me and my family to save his own ass. That was the reason nobody had seen his punk ass.

"You don't have shit to say now, huh? Your smart ass is feeling really dumb, now aren't you? This should teach you to evaluate your friends from now on because they would turn on you at a drop of a dime. I'm watching you, boy. Your time on the street it limited. You will be locked away for life real soon."

The muthafucka got in his car and backed up the street and drove off. Holding my bottom lip between my teeth, I snatched my phone off my hip as I hopped back into the driver seat. I waited for Ricio to answer the phone with steam coming out my ears.

"What up bro?" he said roughly indicating he was blowing something.

"Find Fats! That nigga's running his mouth. That crooked ass cop Cooper just pulled me over down the street from my crib and said we are going down for Nihiyah's murder. We gotta take the garbage out. Get Angel to find whatever he can on Fats and fast."

"That bitch ass nigga! I'm gon' hit cuz up right now. Go in the house and don't move, brah. This shit ain't good. We have to figure out something and fast."

"I agree. Hit me later with any information y'all get on that muthafucka. After all we've done for his fat ass, psst. Aight, I'm gone, brah."

Pulling into my driveway, I got out and rushed up the steps and into my house. The shit Cooper said to me rang in my mind and I couldn't believe in a million years that someone we did so much dirt with would turn informant. I didn't give a fuck if they were throwing football numbers at his ass, he should've kept his mouth shut! But what's done was done and his day was coming. Fats knew what the consequences were for crossing a Vasquez brother.

Cooper must've fed him some bullshit that was sweet in his mind. All along, he got played like a side chick that thought she would be taking the place of the main bitch. Flipping the switch to illuminate the foyer, I headed upstairs to wash away the bullshit I'd endured. Walking in the bathroom I turned on the shower and let it run because I had the urge to smoke.

Going back into my bedroom I sat on the side of the bed and pulled my personal stash of dro out of the top drawer of my nightstand. I broke down the and rolled up a spliff before lighting up and inhaling deeply. Realizing I didn't set my alarm, I took another drag and put it out in the ashtray on the nightstand. Standing up from the bed, I made my way across the room and paused because I heard a noise coming from downstairs.

Carefully grabbing my Glock 50 from behind the TV, I quietly checked the magazine to make sure it was full. I eased out of the door peeking along the way because whomever had the balls to enter my shit better be ready to meet the reaper. They picked the wrong muthafuckin crib on the right day.

"Don't you hear the water running? His ass in the shower." Whoever was in my shit was whispering and I couldn't make out the voice. "I'm going upstairs, he won't see us coming and I know damn well he can't hear us over the water. I think we should make our move now!"

"Aight, we can't give this crazy fucker a chance to grab a weapon to defend himself. He has to die tonight."

Both voices didn't sound like they belonged to any hood nigga I've ever met, but I still didn't know who the fuck was in my crib. Knowing they were coming up to murk me while I was supposedly in the shower, I stepped into the linen closet and waited for these pussy ass niggas to make their move. I watched patiently as they crept up the stairs through the slots in the door. My finger caressed the trigger of my Glock in a lovingly manner and I couldn't wait to let loose.

"You go in and fill his ass with holes. I'm going down here to plant the drugs. This nigger is going out as the Kingpin he wants to be. He doesn't deserve to be locked up for years, he needs to die just like his father."

"One less nigger we have to worry about, sir."

The word nigger is what caught my attention and I knew right then they were definitely white muthafuckas. Once I heard furniture moving downstairs, I eased out the closet and hurried into my bedroom behind the dude that entered and slowly closed the door. The sound of the perpetrator snatching the shower curtain open echoed off the walls and I entered hitting him in the back of the head with my gun. I grabbed him around the neck before he fell forward into the tub and snapped his fucking neck. Easing him onto the floor, I raised the ski mask that covered his face and didn't know who the fuck he was.

I decided not to dwell on his identity because I didn't know him even if he passed by me a thousand times in the street. Leaving him and his gun lying in the middle of the floor, I went downstairs in search of the other muthafucka that had invaded my privacy. He was doing exactly what he said he would do and was putting bags of dope throughout my living room.

"Did you get his ass, Jasper?" He asked without looking up.

"Nah, he missed, bitch." Stepping off the top step, he looked up, and pulled his pistol from his hip. My hands instantly went over my head showing him I was unarmed. "Who sent you and what you doing in my crib?"

"You going down, Sosa! I want you off the street and jail's not an option. You have to die, tonight." The more he talked, the more his voice became familiar. I knew exactly who the asshole standing in front of me was. He sealed his own fate when he came for me on some sneaky shit. This was going to be one of the happiest days of my life.

Lowering my arms and crossing them behind my back, I smirked at him as he kept his gun trained on me. "You may as well take the mask off muthafucka, I already figured out who you are," I laughed. "Arresting me on bullshit wasn't enough, *Cooper*? You got a lot of nerve breaking into my house."

Reaching behind his head he swiftly removed the ski mask from his face and threw it on the floor. "I'm a fucking cop! I can do what the fuck I want to do and get away with the shit. Who do you think they'll believe, you or me? All I have to do is give a statement saying I was here to arrest you for the murder."

"How are you gon' explain the dead muthafucka upstairs, bitch? See you didn't think this thing through before you rolled in here tonight. Planting drugs in my crib is hoe shit for you to be a cop. Shid, I feel like a hoe standing here casually talking to yo' punk ass but I know if anything other than talking takes place, you'll shoot my black ass and get off for sure," I laughed.

"Knowing how you muthafuckas roll, you'll just say you thought this was yo' crib and I was the one trespassing."

I was making him and police in general look like shit and it pissed him off. Cooper aimed his gun at my leg and squeezed the trigger. Shooting me in the middle of my thigh, I fell to the floor but not before I whipped my Glock out and shot him twice in the chest. He staggered back and brought his arm up again and I planted a bullet right between his eyes without thinking twice about my actions.

The day Cooper pulled that bullshit getting me arrested, I knew I would be the one to end his life. Taking my shirt off, I tied it around the top of my leg and hopped upstairs to get my phone. Walking slowly down the steps, I went right out my front door and sat in the chair on the porch and called Sin.

"Rodrigo, what's up, baby?" She asked when she answered.

"I'm about to go to jail. I just killed Cooper."

"You did what! Where are you?" she asked as sirens wailed in the distance.

Before long, there was blue and red lights flashing up and down the street. There were about ten squad cars scattered about the cul a sac while I sat on my porch talking on the phone. "I'm at home but I'll be gon' before you get here," I said quickly.

"Did this happen inside your house, Rodrigo?"

"Yeah."

"Please tell me you still have the cameras set up in your shit."

"I do," I responded as several officers walked up the driveway.

"That's all I needed to hear."

The police were at the bottom of the stairs with guns in their hands. "Get off the phone and let me see your hands!"

"Sin I gotta go, the bullshit has begun." I dropped the phone in my lap and clasped my hands behind my head. I could hear Sin screaming she was on her way before the officers rushed me and threw me on the ground handcuffing my hands behind my back.

Chapter 29
Sin

"Who the fuck was that and where you think you're going at this time of night?"

Beast was getting on my fuckin' nerves playing twenty-one questions. All I was trying to do was get to Rodrigo before the police found out who he shot and killed him for what he'd done. "Stay with Gio, Rodrigo killed Cooper and I have to make sure he's good," I replied while buttoning my dress shirt with shaky hands.

"I'm going with you! What happened?"

"Beast, I'll be fine. It's too cold for the baby to be out and I'm not waiting for you to get him ready. Rodrigo didn't go into detail because the police swarmed him. All he had time to say was he's going to jail for killing Cooper."

Rushing to pull up my black dress pants and rushed to pull on my low-cut boots. I wasn't trying to get spiffy but I knew I had to represent as Rodrigo's lawyer and that meant dressing the part. I grabbed my keys off the dresser and threw my phone inside my purse heading for the stairs.

"Sin, be careful and please don't go out there getting yourself locked up. You won't be any good to him if you're behind bars with him. I will be there shortly. Love you," Beast said to my back because I was on the move.

As I got into my car, I retrieved my phone and called Ricio putting it on speaker as I backed out of the driveway. "Yeah, Sin. What's up?"

"There's a situation at Rodrigo's house. He called me saying he killed Detective Cooper and he was going to jail. I'm on my way there now and hopefully I can get more information. I wanted to give you a heads up but there's no need for you to come all the way out here because it will be too late. Keep your phone on, I will call you back soon as I can."

"Damn! What the fuck, man! That racist muthafucka was out to get him and now he going down for murdering him. How the fuck did he know where he lived anyway? His crib ain't even in his name!"

"When I request to talk to Rodrigo, I'm quite sure Cooper said some shit that would bring everything to light. Stay by the phone, Rico I'll call you back." Hitting the button to disconnect the phone, I drove a little over the speed limit to get to Cambridge Circle.

When I turned on the street Rodrigo resided, it looked like the entire Country Club Hills police department was on the scene. My car was parked on the side street because I wasn't going to be able to get through all the cars that were blocking entry to the cul de sac that led to Rodrigo's house. Walking briskly down the street, I was immediately stopped by an officer.

"Ma'am, this is a crime scene, you aren't allowed beyond this point," he said holding his hands out towards me.

"I'm trying to see what's going on with my client. Mr. Vasquez called me informing me about what happened and I would like to make sure he is okay."

"Who may you be?"

"I am Attorney Sincere Westbrook."

"Mrs. Westbrook, Mr. Vasquez has been transported to Ingalls hospital because he sustained a gunshot injury to his thigh. What exactly did he tell you about what transpired here tonight?"

"He told me someone broke into his home and shot him. Before he could say anything more, I heard officers demanding him to put the phone down and the line went dead. Now can you tell me what's going on and why are there still police in his home and he's no longer there?" I asked crossing my arms over my chest.

"There are two deceased males in the home and it's officially a crime scene. Mr. Vasquez is going to be charged with two counts of murder, ma'am. There's nothing more I can tell you at this time."

"Explain to me how he's being charged with murder when there were two people in *his* home in the middle of the night? You mean to tell me he is being found guilty because he is alive and well? What about the investigation? When will that take place?"

"Mrs. Westbrook, I won't discuss this case with you any further. I'm only doing my job," the officer tried to explain. "Mr.

Vasquez is at Ingalls and you can speak with him there. I will call ahead so you will have no problems gaining entry since he is in the custody of the police."

He turned away and walked toward Rodrigo's house before stopping to speak with another officer. Both of them looked back at me and continued to talk. I had no clue what was being said but I knew I needed to get to Rodrigo and find out what the hell happened.

The hospital was about two or three miles from Rodrigo's house. It didn't take me long to get there the way I was driving. I found a parking spot and hopped out and rushed inside. Giving Rodrigo's name, the nurse stood and went to the back. She came back and officer Bradley was right on her heels. I didn't know how he was able to find out about this incident so quickly but it had the hairs standing up on the back of my neck.

"Sincere, it's good to see you," he smirked.

"Cut the shit, Bradley and take me to Mr. Vasquez," I sneered through clenched teeth.

"He won't be seeing anyone tonight. You will have to wait until he's processed at the County jail."

"The County? Under what grounds?"

"Mr, Vasquez is being charged with two counts of murder, possession of narcotics with the intent to sell, and possession of a firearm. There were large quantities of cocaine and heroin in his home, along with an arsenal of weaponry. Not to mention, two dead bodies and one being a cop. He is going down Sincere and there won't be anything you can do to help him.

We all knew that he had it out for Cooper when he was arrested a couple months back. I just didn't think he would set him up to kill him."

There was no way they found drugs in Rodrigo's home. He didn't keep that shit on him for this reason alone so I knew something fishy was going on. Ricio's words rang through my mind 'how did Cooper know where he lived? The house is not in his name.' Which was true because Beast's name is on the house.

As far as the guns, I wasn't worried about that because I knew for a fact every gun Ricio and Rodrigo owned were registered and they had their Conceal and Carry license. None of the guns that were used in any of the shootings would be found in that house. These pigs had absolutely nothing and I wasn't worried one bit.

"Mr, Vasquez didn't have it out for Cooper, it was the other way around but that's neither here nor there. Cooper was way out of his jurisdiction so why was he at my clients place of residence in the first place?"

"We have been investigating both Mauricio and Sosa Vasquez for some time and we have proof they are responsible for many deaths that has occurred around the city. There's also proof of their drug operation that is flooding the streets of Chicago with the product that is tearing the communities apart."

"You didn't answer my question Bradley! Why. Was. Cooper. At. My. Clients. Home? Did he have a warrant?" By this time, I was pissed because this clear muthafucka was dancing around my question.

"I believe he did."

"You believe? I think you should know because if he didn't, I will be suing the fuck out of the department and your ass too. You racist muthfuckas have found the right black man to fuck with this time and he has a strong black woman that's ready to stomp down on the necks of the Chicago Police Department with stiletto heels on. Now I need to make sure my client is getting proper care and is still breathing. The last thing I need to see on the news is that he died from a gunshot wound to the thigh," I said cutting my eyes at him.

The nervousness was evident because he was sweating around his neck like he was in hell instead of the lobby of a hospital. Bradley breathed deeply and rubbed his hand down his face before turning back around toward me. "You get fifteen minutes to say whatever you have to say then you have must to leave."

"And when I leave, Mr. Vasquez better be in the same condition I left him in or there will definitely be bigger problems."

Bradley led me into the examining room where Rodrigo was being held and there were two officers standing outside the door. They moved to the side and allowed me to enter. Bradley tried to enter behind me and I put a stop to that shit immediately.

"This is a private meeting. I don't need you to sit in on the discussion between my client and I."

"Sincere, he is in my custody and I need to be in the room to keep an eye on him."

Rodrigo was lying in the hospital bed with his leg raised on a mound of pillows with his left wrist handcuffed to the bed. Directing my rage back to Bradley, "Where the hell will my client go? He is restrained to the bed and he is not a threat to anyone. Get out now! I don't care about you being a police officer, my client has rights and I will be here to enforce them."

"You have fifteen minutes. Nothing more." Instead of responding to his ignorance, I pushed him out of the room and slammed the door behind him.

"Sin, this is bullshit," Rodrigo yelled.

"I'm going to need you to lower your voice because I'm quite sure his goofy ass has his ear plastered to the door trying to listen very hard to hear what's being discussed in this room. Tell me what happened tonight?" I said pulling a chair up to the bed.

Rodrigo told me what took place from the beginning to the moment the cops told him to get off the phone. He was quiet for a spell before he started talking again and I sat listening taking everything in. When he started talking about what Cooper revealed to him, I was shocked.

"You mean to tell me Fats is a snitch?"

"That's exactly what I'm saying. I called Ricio after Cooper pulled me over as I turned onto my street. It never crossed my mind that he would try to take my ass out. Angel should be trying to find Fats because without his testimony, they don't have shit and everything that happened tonight screams self-defense and I have the video with sound to back it up. They broke in my shit and I protected myself.

Cooper even planted drugs all around my living room and said I was going down. You got to get me off Sin. I know it's gon' take a while and I'm cool with that, but I don't want to sit in the County until it's figured out." Rodrigo was up to something and I didn't put two and two together until he explained briefly what he had in mind.

"I need you to talk to Beast and tell him to get everything worked out. I'm taking this shit to trial and I hope you're ready to fight, Sin."

The plan Rodrigo came up with was going to be one for the books. My cellphone rang just as Bradley entered the room. "Yeah, I'm on my way home now," I paused listening to Beast bitch about me not calling to let him know I wouldn't be at Rodrigo's house even though I specifically told his ass not to bring the damn baby out. "I'll be there soon, love you."

I looked at Rodrigo's leg, "how bad is it?" I asked.

"It was a flesh wound, nothing major. I'll live. I think that's what the pigs are worried about," he laughed looking directly at Bradley. "Get home so your husband don't think you're out in these streets trickin' off.

"He better take his ass to sleep, I'm working. Take care of yourself call me soon as you get to your next destination. I have a lot of work to do."

"Thank you for coming to check on me. I really appreciate it."

"No problem. I'll see you soon," I said walking out the door. Fats was going to wish he had gotten in touch with one of us before he turned into a rat. He would find out sooner rather than later how a pussy gets its prey.

Chapter 30
Nija

I woke up with a splitting headache and a queasy stomach. Tomorrow was Nihiyah's homegoing and wasn't ready for it at all. My mama was still being the strong woman she raised me to be but I found myself being strong for her because she was going to break. A couple days ago Rodrigo was locked up and the police was trying to send him up the river for killing the cop that broke into his house.

The judicial system was fucked up when it came to African Americans. Our people received football numbers while the privileged folks got sentenced to ten years but are back with their families in five. That won't be the case for bro though. Sin ain't playing no games and she was working hard on his case. Rodrigo didn't have to worry about a lawyer doing half the job or getting paid off to do him dirty.

Swallowing repeatedly, I tried my best to stop the bile from rising. I got up and went into the bathroom to perform my morning ritual of throwing up. These twins were kicking my ass and I wanted this pregnancy to be over. Flushing the toilet, I turned the water on to brush my teeth. My mind went back to earlier in the week when I'd called my father. He never made it to Chicago like he said he would.

It was alright with me because at the moment it was fuck him! I really didn't give a damn if he showed up or not. A real father would've made sure his daughter was put to rest beautifully. The nigga ain't gave a dime, hadn't called to see what was needed, nor gave any indication that he was hurt about what happened. I was playing mediator the day I talked to him and he lied, he was on his own from here on out.

"Nija! Where you at?" Kimmie was screaming my name like the house was on fire. "Nija!"

"If you don't stop screaming like it's an emergency," I said walking out of the bathroom. "What's the problem?"

"Nothing," she laughed. I just wanted to be a pain in your ass this morning. We have to go shopping, girl! Why you ain't ready?" she asked sitting on the side of my bed.

"I just woke up and if you forgot, I'm five months pregnant with twins. My life as I've known, is no more. Kimmie I'm tired of being sick and sleepy all the time. I want this shit to be over. I'm fat and my stomach's too heavy."

"Nija, stop exaggerating, you are all baby. There's not an ounce of fat on you. Well, u have gained weight but it's not a lot at all. Get dressed so we can go, boo. Oh yeah, mama cooked breakfast so I'm going to eat while you sulk over being fat. Hurry up before I eat your shit too."

"I'll beat yo' ass Kimmie, don't play with me."

I went into the closet and grabbed a green Nike jogging suit along with my green and white converse sneakers. Kimmie left out laughing but I didn't see nothing funny. Throwing on my clothes, I was ready in less than ten minutes. As I made my way down stairs the doorbell rang. I watched my mother walk to the door and looked out the window before opening it.

My father stood at the door with a smile on his face as his eyes traveled up and down her body. "Hello, Mark," she said with her hand on her hip. Standing up straight my mother's stance became sort of defensive so I hurried to the bottom of the stairs. "Why did you bring her here?" she asked glancing at him.

"Patricia, she is my wife."

"Well, your wife is not welcome here. You should've dropped her off at the hotel instead of bringing her here."

"I thought it would be better if we stayed here actually," he said with a straight face.

"You thought wrong, Mark. Not only is your wife not welcomed to stay in my home, neither are you. I don't know how you even had the notion to let that shit fall from your lips. It would be a cold day in hell before I allow either of you to sleep under my roof. I wouldn't trust me enough to close my eyes around me if I'd did the shit you did. Get her the fuck away from my house."

Walking up behind her I whispered in her ear, "this is about Nihiyah, ma. Let the bitch come in. I agree with you about them sleeping here, it's not going to happen." Mom moved to the side allowing him entry. His petty ass didn't even wait for his wife before he stepped inside.

Tina sashayed to the door and turned her nose up rolling her eyes as she waltzed past us. My mother's fingers drummed the door in a rhythmic fashion as she clenched her teeth together. Gently rubbing her back, mama closed the door and bowed her head for a few seconds.

"Come on, ma let's get this over with," I said leading the way into the living room. Motioning for Mark and his wife to have a seat, I took a deep breath and sat on the loveseat across from them. "I'll start by saying there will be no disrespect tolerated in my mother's home." My eyes were trained on Tina the entire time I spoke.

"Just like you don't want to be here, we don't want you here either. My mother isn't the one you should be upset with, this muthafucka should get *all* the blame," I said pointing at my father.

"Nija, watch your mouth when addressing me."

"In case you haven't noticed, I'm grown. It's a little too late for you to chastise me. I'll be a mother soon and my child will never endure the pain I did growing up. What you should've done was left and still took care of your responsibilities. We didn't ask to me be brought in this world."

My father didn't hear anything except I was about to be a mother soon. His eyes dropped to my round belly and his demeanor turned cold as ice. His chest heaved in and out but I wasn't worried about his reaction one bit.

"When were you going to tell me you were pregnant? As your father I should've known about it day one!" he snapped.

"You got your females mixed up. This bitch is the one that reports to you," I said motioning toward his ugly ass wife. "While you're hollering about being a father, I haven't seen you since I was twelve. I can count on one hand how many times I've talked to you in that time frame. If it wasn't for my sister passing away, your deadbeat ass wouldn't even be here today. So, miss me with your bullshit and tell me why you're really here."

My father jumped up from the couch and raced around the coffee table and hovered over me as if he was about to swing. "You will not disrespect me, lil girl. I'm your daddy and I will knock your fuckin' head off!" Mark was foaming at the mouth and only got madder when I didn't flinch. "I'll still kick yo' ass, Nija!"

"Then where the fuck you gon' live, nigga?" Kimmie came out of nowhere with her Nina in hand. "I don't' know you but get the fuck out her face. This ain't what you want, daddy."

Mark turned around glaring at Kimmie but he knew not to approach her while she held that heat. "Who the fuck is you?"

"It don't matter! You'll be a distant memory if you don't sit the fuck down!" Stepping to the side of Kimmie's gun, Mark sat down next to his wife. It was obvious that he didn't appreciate Kimmie pulling a gun on him.

"Kimmie, put the gun down, baby," my mama said calmly. Doing as she was told, Kimmie lowered the gun but she held it by her side locked and loaded. "Mark, like Nija asked before, why are you here? I sent the funeral arrangements to you via text, there was no need for you to be here."

"Nihiyah is my daughter too, Pat! I have a right to be here."

"You know exactly what I meant when I said you didn't have to come here, meaning to my home, Mark. Now, again, why are you really here?" My mother asked once more.

"Okay, we need to discuss the insurance policy," he had the nerve to say. "I was the one who took the policy out on all three of y'all. I should get something in return."

"You are out of your fuckin' mind! My daughter is laid up at the funeral home and you're worried about money! Not one time have you asked what happened, what her life was like, nothing!"

"Pat, don't make it seem like I don't care about what happened. Obviously, you didn't keep an eye on her and let her run wild in the streets of Chicago."

"The reason she was doing the things she did was because of the lack of communication and love from you! Don't you dare come in my house criticizing my parenting skills. I didn't stop working when I moved here. That shit made me work harder and instill independence into my daughters. Mind you, all without your help!

If you would've taken your head out of your wife's ass for a few minutes to keep in touch with your firstborn children, we might not be sitting here mourning today. You are a poor excuse for a father and you can kiss my whole ass," my mother said with tears rolling down her face. "What is it you think you deserve, Mark?"

The room was silent for a few minutes while we waited for him to respond. Kimmie stood tapping her gun against her leg with her eyes trained on my father. I prayed he didn't do anything stupid because she wouldn't think twice about popping his ass.

"I deserve half of whatever is left. I paid for that policy—"

"Mark, come on! You paid for the policies up until Nihiyah was ten years old. If it wasn't for me, every one of them would've lapsed. The least you could've done was kept up with the payment. But me as a mother, I did what needed to be done and made sure it was taken care of. I'm here to let you know, you don't deserve shit! Not only didn't you pay child support, alimony, or buy a pair of shoes, you couldn't even pick up the fuckin' phone! Get the fuck out of my house, Mark!"

"I'm not going nowhere until you agree to give me half of the two hundred fifty thousand. It's either you give it to me willingly or I'm gonna sue your ass and have the judge force your hand."

I couldn't believe my father was threatening to sue my mama. There was no way I was going to allow him to profit off my sister's death. Tina was smiling hard at what he said and it was sickening.

"Baby, I don't think—"

"It doesn't matter what you think! Your best bet is to sit there and shut the fuck up! This don't have nothing to do with you. If you would've been his hype man to be there for his kids, I would have some type of respect for you. Unfortunately, I have none!"

The situation as a whole, I was over it. Me and my mama had to endure the hardest thing in the world to do, and that was to bury my big sister. We didn't need the negativity that Mark brought to our doorstep.

"Nija, that's my wife and I'm tiring of telling you to slow your roll," my father sneered.

"If you're tired, get out like my mama told you to do. We are done discussing this shit," I threw back at him.

"You really want me to fuck you up, I see." My father jumped from his seat but before he could approach me, Ricio walked through the door with a grimace on his face.

"Patna, you puffin' at the right one. I stood outside the door and heard the pussy ass shit you was talkin'. You may be her father, but I'm her babies' daddy. Miss Pat asked you to leave, I'm telling you, get up and get the fuck out now!" Mark and Tina both got up and headed toward the door. Standing in the opened door for a spell before he turned glaring at my mama. "If you say anything out of the way you gon' meet yo' maker today, nigga," Ricio said smoothly.

Clearing his throat, Mark's demeanor softened a little bit when he stared at my mama. "Look out for the legal papers in the mail, Pat. I'm getting what's owed to me," he said slamming the door behind him.

My mama wailed loudly and my heart broke at the sound of her cries. I'd been waiting all week for the moment she would break, it finally happened. She needed to let the pain out before the service because I thought it would've been worse if she hadn't. After a while she calmed down.

"I'm okay, baby. Thank you, Ricio for getting him out of my house. He's going to be a problem."

"Nah, there won't be a problem. Don't give him shit. He don't have a leg to stand on with this insurance mess. Dig out your receipts, you gon' need 'em. I'll get you the best lawyer around to help you spit in his face from a distance. If he comes back call me and his ass will die," Ricio said giving her a hug.

"Mauricio, I don't need you in any trouble because of me. Mark isn't stupid enough to come back to my home. I'm not worried about him taking me to court because there's no way he'll win. No amount of money can bring my daughter back but the money that's left over from this ordeal won't go to his grimy ass. I'm going to lay down.

Nija, let me know if you decide to go out," she said leaving the room.

My father showing up in Chicago just to bring more drama into our lives, pissed me off. I was ready to forgive him for not being there for me and my sister, but I would never forgive him for the shit he pulled with my mother that day. Mark Foster was officially dead to me.

Chapter 31
Slim

Ricio set me and Jake up in a hotel and this muthafucka was tweaking. He'd been pacing back and forth for the past hour mumbling to himself. Scratching like he had fleas and chewing on his tongue. If I looked like that when I was using, I'm glad to be done with that bullshit. From the outside looking in, the shit was a sad sight to see.

"Aye, buddy, when are we leaving? I'm feeling sick and need a hit."

"Soon as my people gets here, we out. Here, suck on this candy," I said tossing him a couple pieces. "For a muthafucka that ain't got a pot to piss in, you sure know how to get your fix. Sit back and calm yo' nerves, I'm gon' get you right."

Knock knock

The sound of someone knocking on the door was music to my ears. This nigga needed to get some air and I was glad Ricio sent somebody at that precise moment. Quickly going to the door pulling it open, there was a swollen ass nigga standing on the other side.

"Nicholás?" I questioned.

"Yeah. Ya'll ready to roll?"

"Fo sho. You showed up at the right time, this muthafucka was working my nerves. I'm glad you're here. Let's go, Jake!" I yelled over my shoulder as I reached behind the door grabbing my coat.

"Ricio sent this for you to cop with. I'll be sitting on the block waiting for you to come back out. Slim, you got to sell this shit and make it happen. This mission is sitting on your shoulders, don't fuck it up. Floyd gots to be stopped and the cards is on your table. Don't fuck up because I would hate the outcome if you do. It's not a threat, it's a promise. You signed up for this shit so we expect you to deliver."

"No doubt, I got this and I want to avenge my nigga Reese's death just as much as his sons. I've waited on this moment for months. Actually, I thought Ricio and Sosa would've handled this shit by now but I see there's been a lot going on since I went to rehab."

"Shit's been hectic but it was nothing that couldn't be handled. Things like this takes time without getting caught. We had to be smart about everything and patience was key. Do what's expected of you and we will be one step closer to living normal lives again. I don't know you, Slim but for some odd reason, I have faith in you. Don't make me out to be a liar," Nicholás said walking away from me.

Jake eased by me and followed Nicholás to the parking lot. As I climbed into the passenger seat of the Range Rover, I glanced over at Nicholás, sizing him up. If you didn't know he was kin to Ricio and his brother, there was no way of knowing they were related in any way. Nicholás was fair skinned with thick eyebrows. He was about six feet even with muscles that protruded out showing he worked out diligently.

Reaching in my pocket, I retrieved the piece of paper Ricio gave me with Floyd's address scribbled on it and a plan came to mind immediately. I knew exactly how I would get to Floyd without him becoming suspicious. Nicholás drove as I directed him to the street Floyd rested his head.

"Park behind that red car right there. Floyd lives in that brownstone building on the right. His apartment is on the second floor. Over there across the street is where they made the most money selling their shit. I don't see nobody out here so I have to figure out how to get into his crib."

Just as the words left my mouth, Floyd emerged from the building and sat on the steps and lit a cigarette. "It's not going to be hard at all. My target just came outside to me. Sit tight, Youngblood, it's time for me to work my magic.

"Y'all be careful. My eyes and ears are open and I will come running at the first sign of danger," Nicholás said as I got out the truck.

"It's time to get your medicine, Jake. I'll do all the talking, don't say shit, understood?"

"Yeah, buddy. I hear you," he said getting out and closing the door. As we got closer to where Floyd was sitting, he still hadn't noticed me and he seemed kind of spaced out.

"Aye yo, Floyd! What's up, fool?" I yelled out. He squinted his eyes trying to figure out who was calling his name.

"Slim, that's you?"

"Yeah, nigga it's me. It's dead as fuck around here, where is everybody?" I asked walking up the steps dapping him up.

"Man, shit been crazy out in these streets. Hold up! Where the fuck you been? I ain't seen you around in a minute."

Shaking my head, "I almost died, nigga. Somebody found me passed out from an overdose and called the ambulance. If that person hadn't did that shit, I wouldn't be here today. An angel was with me. But I don't want to talk about old shit. They put me in rehab but you know crack has been my best friend for too many years to turn my back on it."

"Slim, if you have been clean this long, don't go back to that shit. It ruined your life before. This is your second chance. Take it and live your best life."

Floyd was spitting real shit but I had to keep the façade up and keep pretending. "Are you gon' sell me some dope or what? I just want to get high," I said irritably.

"I have one question for you, Slim. Who the fuck is this muthafucka?" he asked pointing at Jake.

"That's Jake, he good."

"Aight, I don't want no shit. Yo' ass been gone and come back with a white muthafucka in tow. His ass could be a pig for all I know," Floyd said skeptically.

"Floyd, I'm a muthafuckin' addict. I don't fuck with the cops and you know this shit. How long have I been around this muthafucka giving yo' ass a heads up when the law was riding down yo' shit?"

"I just want you to know it bet not be no bullshit on yo' part. I'm still the same muthafucka," he said puffing on his cigarette. "I don't have no work right now but I do have my own personal stash I'd be willing to share. It's only coke if that's cool. We can kick back and catch up for a minute."

Floyd raised up from the step he was sitting on and flicked his cigarette into the bushes. He led the way to his apartment and we went inside. I was surprised by how far he had fell off. His apartment had an old table with four folding chairs, a worn couch, a small box tv and an air mattress. All in the living room. I was ready to get all in his business as I took a seat in one of the chairs.

"Damn, fam, what happened? I ain't never seen you down like this and you fuckin' with the white girl. Talk to me man."

"I'm gon' get us something to drink and we can definitely talk. Get this shit ready for us," he said tossing a couple baggies on the table with a single playing card.

"Where's your bathroom, Buddy?" Jake asked.

"I'll show you," Floyd responded leading him down the hall.

They left me alone sitting at the table and I took that opportunity to put my plan in motion. I took the package Nicholás gave me from my pocket and poured it on the table. Mixing the substance with the coke, I rushed before either one of them returned to the room. I was for damn sure leaving the apartment alone. Separating the coke between the two of them, I had no intentions of snorting any of that shit.

Floyd came back from the back of the apartment and went into the kitchen. "You want anything to drink, Slim? I have Heineken, MGD, Henny, Remy, and tequila," he asked with his head inside the refrigerator.

"I've been thinking about what you said earlier and I'm going to take this ride on the sober train. I'll take one of those MGDs and a bottled water if you have it," I said putting the empty baggie in my pocket.

"I got you. Slim you doing the right thing. Man, I feel bad for even thinking about doing this shit around you."

"It's all good. When I was getting the coke ready for y'all, I didn't even have the urge to partake in that shit. Enjoy yourself, Jake can party and I'll still be here to shoot the shit with you."

Jake appeared and his eyes lit up at the sight of the powdery substance on the table. He sat across from me and his body language was pretty jittery like and his upper lip perspired profusely in the dimly lit room. I shot a stoic stare in his direction and he piped his ass down whipping his face.

"You want something to drink?" I asked him.

"Nah, I want that candy right there," he said smiling.

"So, Jake. Tell me about yourself, homie," Floyd said walking back to the table sitting a Heineken in front of Jake.

"I was married with two kids, a dog, a big house with the white picket fence. Making eighty grand a year, I let my job control my life," he said taking a sip from his beer.

I said a silent prayer that this muthafucka didn't reveal he had killed his family. My plan would go to shit because Floyd would beat his ass and put both of us out of his crib. Nobody had respect for anybody that harmed kids in any way. That was the reason I wanted Jake and Floyd to enjoy themselves one last time on earth. Both of them were scum in my eyes.

"What happened? It sounds like you had it made out here," Floyd asked.

"When you're working in Corporate America and the hours are long and strenuous, there's little time to spend with family. My job became my wife and dope became my mistress. My wife tried to steer me on the road to recovery but it was out of control by that time. I didn't give a damn about anything but finding my next hit.

Bills starting piling up and my wife couldn't afford to keep up the household payments the way I did. When I was fired from my job because I fucked up with a prestigious client, everything went downhill from there. My wife washed her hands of my bullshit and left me. I had nothing after that and didn't give a fuck about my life anymore." I knew Jake spoke truthfully about his life and was glad he left out the critical pieces of the puzzle.

"Why wouldn't you get yourself together to get your family back?" Floyd asked.

"It's easier said than done," Jake said sadly taking a sip from his beer.

The room was quiet for a few minutes before I broke the silence. "Floyd, what happened around here? It's like a ghost town on this block. Rain, sleet, or snow it used to be crunk on 26th Street!" I screamed throwing my hands in the air.

"We lost a lot of people in the last couple months. Ricio and Sosa ran through this muthafucka and a couple of our other spots and fucked shit up. They burned down Big Jim's crib along with money and drugs forcing me to start over from scratch. Big Jim kicked me to the curb once he found out about my coke habit. I fucked up."

Floyd looked pitiful after giving a quick version of what had taken place. He started preparing himself to hit the coke by chopping at it with the playing card even though I had already lined it up for him. Pulling out a cigarette, he lit the tip with a lighter and took a pull before continuing his story.

"Everything that happened stressed me out to the point I tried coke to cope with the loses and couldn't stop. It caused me to make bad decisions that spiraled out of control. Every death was my fault because I wasn't on my shit. I believe karma played a major part in our downfall and it hit with a vengeance. It was because of what we did to Reese. Sometimes I wished I could turn back the hands of time, he was good to us but I followed Big Jim's lead and ran with it."

Floyd didn't realize, bad karma was about to finish him off and it wouldn't be long before he found out firsthand. Jake was salivating at the mouth waiting for Floyd to tell him dinner was served. Floyd look across the table at Jake and smiled. Passing him a dollar bill, they both rolled up and got in position.

"You ready, Jake from State Farm?"

"Hell yeah, I am! I've been waiting for this all day," he said excitedly.

"To new beginnings," Floyd said before he and Jake snorted the coke nonstop until all the coke was gone.

I was beaming with pride on the inside because I had literally killed two birds with one stone and I didn't have to lift a finger. Both of their heads fell back and it was like time stood still. Sipping my MGD, I glanced around the table and Jake started clenching at his throat. His eyes bulged wide as he struggled to breath because his windpipe closed up. Foam formed in the corners of his mouth and he tried his best to cough but he couldn't.

Knowing he was dying before my eyes, I turned to Floyd and he opened his mouth but nothing came out. he toppled over onto the floor and seized violently. The same foam spewed from his mouth and it was a beautiful sight to see. Floyd clawed at his face scratching the skin off to the white meat. I stood over him with a sly grin on my face as he took his last breath.

"That's for Reese and Max, bitch ass nigga!" I sneered as I left them both lying in feces and piss to rot in hell.

The rat poison and cyanide laced coke I mixed up for them worked faster than I anticipated but it did what I set out to do. Killed two dirty muthafuckas that didn't deserve to walk around the streets of Chicago another day.

Chapter 32
Ricio

I stayed with Nija at her mother's house in case her punk ass daddy decided to pop back up. Miss Pat slept the rest of the day and we watched movies with Kimmie for most of the day. Sin called to fill me in on what was going on with Rodrigo and it wasn't looking good for bro at the moment.

The Chicago Police Department Superintendent was trying to throw football numbers at him without doing an investigation. He was immediately moved to the County Jail and placed in Division 11. It was bullshit because there were white cops out here killing innocent people in their own homes and getting ten years with the possibility of parole in five. But Rodrigo killed a racist cop that broke in his home and planted drugs and they want to give him life without parole. That's what you call white privilege, it will never be fair for a black muthafucka.

Kimmie was taking it hard because she'd formed a bond with my brother, something I'd never thought could happen. She went to bed early and left me and Nija alone sitting on the couch. It was the first time in months that I'd been able to hold her in my arms. Moving my hand to her round belly, I caressed it softly.

"Ricio, what are we doing? "Nija asked interrupting my thoughts.

"We're lying here watching tv as I bond with my babies."

"You know what I'm talking about. You're here with me instead of being out with one of your many women."

"Nija, baby there are no other women. I've been in the streets dealing with what happened to my brother and recouping from being shot myself. Now I have to deal with what's going on with my Rodrigo and find out what the hell happened to your sister. Not to mention, I have to find Madysen's ass because no one has heard from her since the day she left Gio in the house. At what point have I had the time to deal with another bitch?"

"All of that didn't stop you from having sex with the correctional officer chick. You can't tell me you haven't been in contact with her, Ricio."

"I've talked to her only because she called me after getting assaulted by one of Big Jim's workers. I went to her apartment and called for an ambulance. I even went to the hospital and stayed to make sure she would be okay. She knows I'm happy with you and want my family. There's nothing going on with us. Latorra has decided to leave Chicago because she feels her life is in danger and I agreed to help her out so she can start over.

"Why do you feel compelled to help her? You don't owe her anything, Ricio," Nija asked moving out of my grasp.

"The only reason she was put in the position she's in is because of me. I feel obligated to help her. Big Jim used her to get to me, Kind of the same way Floyd used Nihiyah. The only difference is, me and Latorra started talking before she even knew his intentions. But that's neither here nor there, I'm telling you that shit is a done deal, Nija. This has been going on long enough.

We have babies coming soon and I want my family together. The love I have for you is strong and always has been. I've made many mistakes by taking your love for granted, I'm sorry. Let's make this right," I said pulling her back between my legs. Nija rested her head on my chest and my hand automatically went back to her stomach. One of the babies moved and my heart skipped a beat.

"Did you feel that?"

She chuckled at the amusement in my voice. "Every day for the past week or so. They've been acting up in there doing somersaults like *Simone Biles*. I think we may have a couple of future gymnasts on our hands." Nija covered her hand with mine and it felt as if an electric current shot up my arm. The closeness we once had was nonexistent and it was good to feel her warm touch. Gently pressing my fingertips into her stomach, she continued to probe until she found one of our babies. I was amazed because I'd never felt such a thing in my life. As I pressed harder, the baby kicked with force, disappearing from the area.

"Damn that was a mean kick. Let me find out you breeding little ninja's in there," I laughed. "What am I going to do with not one, but two daughters? I'm definitely going to buy a couple of guns just for their boyfriends."

"You are going to be an alright daddy, Ricio. The only thing I ask is that you don't be anything like my father. Be active in the girl's lives and make sure they are okay financially, mentally, and physically. My door will always be open for you to come see them, pick them up, and take them for however long you want. All I ask of you is do your homework on the female that will be in your life."

Nija was pissing me off because I'd just told her I wanted my family and she was still planning shit as if I agreed to the co-parenting idea she came up with. That shit was dead and was never going to happen as long as I had breath in my body. Caressing her stomach slowly, I adjusted the pillow behind my head and sighed.

"Speak your mind, Ricio we need to discuss this. I don't want us to be at each other's throats because we couldn't make it work in a relationship. Regardless of it all, you are still my best friend and the love I have for you is still strong. I just don't think forcing ourselves to be together is the right thing to do. It's time to move on. Our friendship can't be broken, we have that special kind of bond.

"Nija, I'm not trying to hear all that. You have been a special part of my life throughout the years and until this day. Everything I've been through you have been there for me. Did I take you for granted hoping you would always stay by my side without a commitment? Yeah, I did.

We told each other we loved one another on a daily and I meant it every time it left my mouth. But at what moment did you ever tell me you wanted more from me? You haven't, Nija! Now we have not one but two beautiful daughters coming and you want me to be a daddy part-time. I won't agree to that,' I huffed.

"I'm glad you acknowledged the fact that you took me for granted, Ricio. The things I did for you in itself should've told you how I felt about you. We won't say anything about the loyalty I held only for you. Spoken words ain't shit without action to back it up. I've shown you that I loved you for years but you couldn't see it.

The other females were your priority and I was one of your fillers. How long did you think I would sit stagnant in the position you provided without being upgraded? There's more to life than being in a one-sided relationship when there's a man out there that wouldn't have a problem loving only me," she said removing my hand from her stomach and attempting to get up.

"Where are you going? I thought we needed to talk about this," I said grabbing her arm to prevent her from going further.

"It doesn't matter, Ricio. I've been singing the same tune for far too long and I'm good on the what ifs. We can be very good parents without being together," she snatched away and walked up the stairs slowly.

Sitting in the quiet living room I didn't want to follow her upstairs because trying to resolve the situation right now would only stress her out more than she already was. With Nihiyah's funeral being the next morning, I'd hold off on bringing the topic up again. Instead, I grabbed the remote and turned the tv on. Surfing through the channels a news segment caught my attention.

We are live at Bufferington Harbor in Gary, Indiana. Witnesses reported seeing a black Toyota Camry veered into the harbor and attempts to get the unidentified woman out of the car were unsuccessful. The car quickly sank into the dark waters before rescuers could arrive. Divers are searching for the car as we speak.

I watched as the cameraman focused on the water and one of the divers emerged from the water yelling but I couldn't understand what was being said. An extractor device was on standby waiting for a sign that the vehicle was found. Reaching for my phone, I dialed Beast's number and he answered on the first ring.

"Ricio, what's good?"

"Turn to Channel 9. Don't Madysen drive a black Camry?" I asked never taking my eyes off the screen.

"Yeah, why you found her dirty ass?"

"Nah, but the fish did. I think she may have driven her car into the harbor by the casino. There's live coverage on it right now," I said staring at the tv as the car was raised out of the water. Leaning forward, I tried to see the license plate on the back but it wasn't clear enough. "Are you watching?"

"I think that is her car, nephew. You see the yellow sticker in the window, it says baby on board. I bought it for her before she had Gio. And the deep dent on the left side of the bumper is the one she wouldn't allow me to get fixed for her. It's definitely Madysen's car. Let's pray she wasn't in it."

"Beast, there's witnesses that said there was a female in the car and they tried to get her out but couldn't. She's in that muthafucka, fam. Be ready for the police to show up because she changed her address to yours, right?" I asked still watching the tv screen.

"Yeah, she did. Hold on, they are saying something."

"The car has been successfully pulled from the water and there are reports that a body is indeed inside. The doors are being pried opened because they are jammed shut. Paramedics are removing the body from the driver's seat. Let's pray for this young lady and hope everything will be alright. CPR is being administered and the paramedics are working hard to save the life of this woman."

After about ten minutes, a sheet was pulled over the body and the very somber scene that unfolded for all to see came to an end. Madysen was a good woman but she let the death of Max pull her into a black hole she refused to get out of. I didn't feel an ounce of sadness for her death because in the back of my mind, she was going to die anyway for what she'd done to Giovanni.

"Damn, that shit is sad. I tried to help her the best I could, nephew. She didn't have to go out like that. All she needed to do was accept the help. What she did to Gio was fucked up and I guess she knew there was no coming back from it. I'll tell Sin but she won't give a fuck one way or another. Nija is the one I'm worried about," Beast said getting quiet.

"I'll let you go so I can go spring the news on Nija. You will be at the funeral in the morning, right?"

"I got the arrangements in the text. Don't worry, we'll be there for Nija no doubt. Oh, I'll be meeting up with Sam tomorrow afternoon. I'll keep you posted on that."

"Aight, cool. get some rest and I'll see you tomorrow, Unc," I said ending the call.

Before I could get up off the couch, my phone was ringing in my hand. "What up, Slim?"

"It's done. Both of them muthafuckas laid up with their tongues hanging out the side of their mouths."

"Wait, what the fuck did the white dude do? I thought you were trying to save his ass," I said laughing.

"That nigga killed his whole family and the dog. He was on the run but I put a stop to that shit. Fuck him. I'm heading back to the hotel, talk to you soon. It's time for me to get my shit together, young blood," Slim said.

"I'll be by there sometime tomorrow. Hit my line if you need anything, aight?"

"No doubt. Keep your eyes open because there's a couple more of them niggas lurking about."

"Trust me I know. Our job ain't done yet."

"Well, goodnight, Ricio. I have a warm bed waiting for me. I appreciate you looking out, man. I really do."

"This is just the beginning, Slim. My father told me to make sure you were straight and I plan on doing just that. I'll see you later, Old Timer."

"Bet."

So much had happened in my life in just a short timeframe and I was tired. My life hasn't been my own since I lost my little brother and I couldn't wait to see brighter days in the future. Getting shot and living to tell the tale was a blessing in itself and it changed my outlook on life. I thought I would want to be the next Kingpin of Chicago but I've had a change of heart. Being on this Earth to raise my daughters was my future and that meant more to me than being out in these streets being the plug.

I didn't know what I would do with the hundred bricks I had stashed at the warehouse, but it really wasn't a concern of mine. There were a couple niggas I had to get at first though and I hated to do it, but the shit had to be done. Rodrigo was locked up and I had to do this shit for the both of us as well as for Max and my father. Eliminating Fats was going to be the hardest of them all but he made his bed and he will lie in it for eternity.

"Are you okay, Ricio?" Miss Pat asked walking into the living room.

"Yes, I'm okay. Just sitting here thinking about many things."

"Do you want to talk about it?" she asked sitting next to me on the couch.

"There's so much that has transpired in the past couple months and it's taking a toll on me. Not to mention, things with me and Nija are basically over according to her. I have done so much to her that I didn't think affected her the way it has. Miss Pat, I love your daughter with all my heart. I want to be a full-time dad to my children and a husband to her."

"Ricio, let me tell you this, Nija loves you and I do believe you love her too. What you have to understand is this, we as women are very sensitive and know what we want in life. You're all she has ever talked about from the day y'all met. Her love is real and whatever you did to turn her heart cold, own that shit. You have a lot of making up to do if you know her like you say you do.

She'll only turn a blind eye for so long and right now is not one of the times. Nija is grieving and pregnant, bad combination, baby. You have to give her time and show her that you are serious about being with her and only her. After tomorrow I don't know what her mindset will be, but get ready for whatever she throws at you because this was your doing. There's not many loyal, dedicated, and genuine women out here that's loving a man for who they are versus what they have."

"I hear you and thanks for talking to me. For some odd reason you said some of the same things Nija said but it came off differently coming from you. I'm going outside to grab my clothes from the car then I'm calling it a night."

"I'm always here if you need to talk. Fix it, Mauricio," she said as I went down the stairs to my car.

Miss Pat stood in the doorway until I gathered my bags. Giving me a big hug when I came back inside, I made my way upstairs to hopefully cuddle with Nija.

Chapter 33
Beast

There was a dark cloud lingering over all our heads. Death was surrounding us like a plague and I didn't like it one bit. The police showed up about three in the morning to inform Sin and I about Madysen's passing. I had to take the trip to the morgue alone to identify the body because Sin refused to accompany me. When I laid eyes on her, Madysen looked like she was at peace and had a slight smile on her face.

My heart was hurting for her but it didn't last long because of what she had done to Gio. The drive back to the house was quiet and I thought about the call to the funeral home I would have to make later that morning. Planning a funeral for her was out of the question because I'd be the only person present so I decided to have her cremated. When I pulled up to the house I went in and took a shower then laid next to Sin to get a couple hours of sleep.

"Erique, get up," Sin said shaking me awake. "We have an hour to get dressed and out the door. We can't miss this funeral because there's no do overs when it comes to this. Nija needs our support today."

"Okay, I'm up." Rubbing my eyes, I blinked several times trying to focus. Sin was sitting on the side of the bed feeding Gio. He was dressed in a little button-down shirt with a pair of black jean pants and white socks. Sin had brushed his hair back neatly on his head and he stared up at her while clutching her gown in his little fist.

The sight of Sin cradling the baby put a smile on my face but in my mind, I thought about how Gio had to grow up without both of his parents. It was happening more every day and it was sad because the kids didn't ask to come into the world but they had to live in it the best way they could. Gio was going to be alright though because I was going to make sure I raised him right.

Getting out of bed, I walked to the bathroom and stood over the toilet with my head held back thinking about how I didn't want to go to yet another funeral. Knowing Sin wasn't going to allow me to back out, I flushed the toilet and washed my hands before brushing my teeth. Choosing a black Armani suit when I walked back into the bedroom, I got dressed and took over for Sin so she could get herself together.

We were out the door in no time and every song that came on the radio was sad and dreary. Sin finally hit the button and turned the radio off completely. "What are your plans after we leave the funeral?"

"I have to go holla at that nigga Sam about who he sold then bricks to. They didn't just jump in Nihiyah's car and wherever she got it from will lead me to whomever killed her. Why, what's up?"

"I wanted to work on Rodrigo's case and get some air without Gio interrupting what I have going on. But I'll make it work somehow," she said looking out the window as we cruised on the expressway.

"Sin what are u really trying to do?" I asked skeptically knowing she was up to some sneaky shit. Rodrigo is locked up and them muthafuckas ain't trying to give him a trial no time soon. He is guilty as charged in their eyes so I knew Sin was on bullshit.

"I just told you what I wanted to do, Beast. Don't question me like I'm a teenager trying to go hang out and do wrong. I said what the fuck I said."

Not wanting to start an argument with her over what she had planned, I turned into the parking lot of the church and quickly found a spot and cut the engine. The church parking lot was full and there were a few people lingering outside. I spotted Ricio standing off to the side consoling Nija and I opened the door before getting out. Walking around to the passenger door, I opened it so Sin could get out and went to the back door to get Gio. I handed Sin his diaper bag removing the car seat from the seatbelt and covered his face with the blanket from the cold.

The Vasquez boys were standing outside the church in case somebody decided they wanted to show up and show out. I walked up and dapped each of them up then turned and handed the baby to Sin before walking over to Ricio and Nija.

"Hey, babygirl, you okay?" I asked. Nija shook her head no with tears rolling down her face. "Come on so we can go inside."

"I don't think I can do it. She's lying there and don't look like herself. That's not my sister!" she wailed into Ricio's chest. Glancing at Ricio, he shook his head back and forth holding Nija tight as he rubbed across her back.

"Nija, your mom is looking for you," Sin said walking past me to get to her. "It's going to be alright, baby. The funeral is about to start."

"That's not my sister in there! Nihiyah was light skinned, beautiful with a head full of hair. That person lying in that casket is dark skinned and looks like an older woman."

"I can understand your concern but that's your sister in there, Nija. The drugs she was taking is the cause of her appearance. I've seen this reaction many times in my years and it's a hard pill to swallow but it's how things are at times," Sin tried to explain.

"Well, tell my mother I'm not coming inside until the casket is closed and I don't want it to be opened again."

We were finally able to get Nija to go inside and the funeral was beautiful. Nihiyah was sent home beautifully. After the service we all gathered in our cars and went to the cemetery where Nija and her mom were able to say their final goodbyes. Their father was a pussy nigga because he didn't shed not one tear the entire time. All he did was snarled at Nija and her mother while his wife wore a smirk on her face.

Seeing Nija breakdown even though her sister betrayed her, touched me in so many ways. It took a strong person to still have a heart for someone that betrayed them. Family or not, I wouldn't have given two fucks, but that's just me. She fainted as she kneeled down peering in the hole and I was glad Ricio was there to catch her before she tumbled inside.

Everyone gathered back at Miss Pat's house and majority of them only came to eat free food. I was holding Gio when I heard loud voices coming from the back of the house. Looking around the room I noticed Nija's mama wasn't in the room and neither was her punk ass ex-husband. Ricio eyes connected with mine and I swiftly handed Gio to Kimmie.

"I'll be right back," I said following Ricio in the direction of the voices.

"You gon' give me my fuckin' money, Pat. What the fuck was Hiyah doing out in these streets? Did you see my daughter lying there looking like she was eighty fuckin' years old and she wasn't even twenty-five?"

"I'm not about to do this with you, Mark! Don't act like you give a fuck because what Nihiyah was going through is your least concern. She's in a better place and finally resting in peace. I just buried my daughter. The same one you turned your back on years ago and never looked back. Fuck you!"

"No, fuck you! I know you received that money and I want what belongs to me! If I have to, I will beat your ass in here and leave you lying here for everybody to see." Ricio stormed through the door and in two steps punched Mark hard in the face. He stumbled against the dresser and bounced back quickly.

"Didn't I tell you the last time you were here not to come back?" Ricio yelled grabbing Mark in his collar. Punching Mark repeatedly in the face, he didn't stand a chance of getting away from Ricio.

"Ricio, let him go," Nija said walking into the room.

Instead of complying with Nija, Ricio snatched his tool from his waist and pointed it at Marks head. "This is my last time telling you, stay the fuck away from this family, nigga. You will get the opportunity to walk out this bitch off the strength of Nija! But if it was up to me, I'd kill yo' punk ass right now! If I hear about you harassing my mother in law about some bullshit ass money again, you gon' die and that's a muthafuckin' promise."

Ricio slung Mark toward the door and a bloody trail followed with every step he took. Turning toward Pat, he smiled spitting blood at her feet. The loud sound of Ricio's gun cocking was the only sound that was heard. Nija kept her eyes trained on Ricio begging him not to shoot her father.

"It's not worth it, Ricio. Put the gun down," she said quietly. "Just let his evil ass leave with the little bit of dignity he has left."

"Nija I will—"

"You'll what, nigga?" Ricio asked throwing the gun on the bed and walking up on Mark. "You ain't gon' do shit, say shit, none of that to her. Act like a stranger when it comes to her nigga. Now get the fuck out and take your bitch with you!"

"Who the fuck you calling a bitch?" Tina asked appearing in the doorway. "Ya'll in here jumping my husband!"

I tried to get to the door soon as I saw Sin kicking off her shoes but I was too late. Tina's head connected with the doorframe and Sin started whooping her ass like She was *Claressa Shields*. Sin was giving that bitch the business but I had to stop her because she had dragged Tina into the hall and a crowd had gathered.

"That's enough, Sin!" I said pulling her up.

"Bitch you came at the right one today. This woman just buried her daughter and y'all on this stupid shit. Money is the root of all evil and it's sad. Even if y'all didn't come here to mourn, this mother will for the rest of her life! Y'all are two of the sorriest muthafuckas I've ever met in my life. Get the fuck out before I beat yo' dumb ass again!"

Angel and Alexander grabbed Tina and Mark and escorted them out of the house. I was able to let Sin go once they had them out of sight. Nija sat on the bed and cradled her face in her hands.

"Nija and Pat, I'm sorry about what I did in your house. But after the shit I heard they did the other day, I couldn't let that fly. Don't give him shit because he doesn't deserve a penny," Sin said snatching her shoes up and walked off.

"Okay, the show is over people. As a matter of fact, everybody go home. I'm tired and over this day already," Pat said walking through the crowd of people.

Kimmie made her way into the room and sat on the bed next to Nija while still holding Gio. Nija looked up and took the baby from her friend's arms and cuddled up in the bed with him. Ricio crawled in the bed behind her and held her tight.

"Ricio, I'm about to go handle that business. I'll hit you once I'm done. I'm sending you my location just in case something happens," I said.

"Beast don't go meet that nigga by yourself, take my cousins with you so they can watch yo' back. We don't know if Sam is in on this shit or not. Don't be stupid, fam."

"I'll gather up the troops but I don't need them. They can come along because you want them there. I'll hit you up later," I said leaving the room.

Sin was standing by the window talking to Angel when I walked into the living room. She still had a scowl on her face and I knew she would wear it for a couple hours because that's how long it took her mean ass to calm the fuck down. The image of Sin beating the hell out of Mark's wife was fresh in my mind and it reminded me of the woman she used to be. Sin City was the woman I tried to leave in the past because she was vicious.

"Babe, I'm about to head out to handle some business. Have Kimmie give you a ride when you're ready to go home," I said kissing her lips. "Angel, I need you and the rest of the clan to take a ride with me. I'm going to hook up with Sam to talk about that package that was sold on the streets."

"Say no more. Aye, y'all let's roll out with Beast. I'll explain as we're driving," Angel yelled out to his family.

"Be careful, Erique," Sin said with a gleam in her eye.

"When you leave here, Sincere, take yo' ass home!"

"Alright, Ike," she chuckled as she walked into the kitchen where Miss Pat was. Sin was up to something but I didn't know exactly what.

***

Sam agreed to meet at the lagoon in Washington Park on South King Drive. The location he picked was a peculiar one but I was ready with my nine locked and loaded on my hip. The setup didn't feel right to me but I wasn't the type of nigga to back down from shit. My phone rang and Angel was the other end.

"What type of shit is this, Beast?"

"I don't know but I want y'all to park on 59th Street and sit in wait. I'm going to park in the lot, I will be in your line of vision from where y'all will be waiting. My gut is telling me this is a setup and he has others watching his back from afar. At the first sight of bullshit, come out guns blazing."

"Okay, gotcha but stay on the line to make sure you can see me," Angel said.

Putting the phone in my pocket, I put my Bluetooth earbud in my ear and connected it to my phone. "You still there?" I asked.

"Yeah."

"I have you in my ear so you can hear what's going on. Pay attention to what's being said and move in if necessary," I said as I drove into the parking lot of the park and killed my engine. I checked my tool, ensuring it was fully loaded and grabbed a couple clips from the glove department and pocketed those as well.

"Beast, I see you. There's one nigga standing by the water, no other movement at this time," Angel informed me.

"Aight, cool."

Getting out of my ride, I closed the door softly and made my way across the grass toward Sam. His back was turned and the sound of the rustling leaves made him turn abruptly with gun in hand. "Damn, Beast, you can't be sneaking up on a nigga like that!" Same exclaimed.

"Always check your surroundings is what I was taught early on. It's cold as hell out here so let's get to the problem at hand. Word on the street is one of the bricks Ricio sold to you was found in a dead woman's car. Who did you sell that shit to?"

"It doesn't matter who the fuck I sold it to. Let his bitch ass take the fall for that shit. Those two crackhead hoes stole the lil homie's work and he did what he had to do. Somebody should've taught them to keep their hands off shit that didn't belong to them. As for Ricio, I don't give a damn what happens to him or his brother. My uncle was found dead in his apartment with another muthafucka and I think they had something to do with it."

"Who the fuck is your uncle?" I asked knowing damn well who he was referring to.

"Floyd, nigga! They've been after him for months and finally caught him slipping. He was the only family I had left and they will pay for this shit."

"Let me ask you this, Sam. What makes you think Ricio had a hand in Floyd's death?"

"My uncle hasn't had a problem with coke because he only used his own shit. All of a sudden, he overdosed with a muthafucka I've never laid eyes on a day in my life. That's bullshit!"

"An addict takes risks every time they consume any type of drugs, Sam. You sell the shit. You should know there's a chance of death with every hit. The way you're talking, it sounds like you had plans to get at my nephews from jump," I said staring daggers at his ass.

"Your nephews? Since when, Beast?"

"From day one, nigga! You should've done your homework on the nigga you cop from because I sure did mine. I've been following you since the sit down you had with Ricio. I didn't see anything suspicious from you until the day after the two women were killed. Rello is the person you sold the bricks to, right?"

Sam nodded his head while rubbing his hands together. "Beast, there's movement to your right. Get ready to use that tree to your advantage. I'm about to take this muthafucka out," Angel said.

As soon as Angel gave me the heads up, Sam raised his gun and with a smirk on his face. "You fucked up coming here on behalf of them fuck niggas. Fuck you, Beast!"

A bullet tore through the right side of his neck and blood squirted from the left. Jumping back, I snatched my tool from my hip and took cover behind the large oak tree I stood beside. Bullets flew through the air and it was like I was back in Iraq. Sam's body fell face first onto the grass and several of his men came out of hiding. The Vasquez Boys started blasting their asses before they could get close to me.

Angel and his family ran into the park in different directions. I came from behind the tree and a nigga was running toward me full speed busting at my ass. Bullets from his weapon bounced off the tree sending woodchips flying into my face. Mateo aimed and fired several shots from his AR-15 opening the nigga's chest in a matter of seconds.

Seeing movement out of my peripheral vision, I aimed my Nine at the nigga that snuck up on me. I let off two shots hitting him in the arm knocking the gun from his hand and once in the chest. He rolled over trying to retrieve his gun but I ran over to him and emptied my clip in the back of his head. When I looked up, two niggas were hightailing it out of the other end of the park and jumping into an old school Chevy before peeling off.

Angel jogged over to where I stood, "We gotta get out of here. A couple of them got away and I know for a fact one of them was Rello."

"They won't live too much longer. Getting away today, doesn't mean they can hide forever. Let's go. Thanks for having my back, it's a good thing I listened and brought y'all along. I wouldn't have been able to shoot my way out of this situation alone."

"It's all good, we have to end this shit, Beast."

"The end is near, fam. They don't have a leg to stand on," I said walking back to my whip.

Chapter 34
Sin

After Beast left to handle business, I helped Pat clean up after everyone left. I had changed into an all black jogging suit with my black Airmax sneakers so I'd be comfortable. Sitting at the kitchen table, I was thinking about the information Angel gave me. It was time for me to get to the bottom of the particular bullshit at hand. Standing to my feet I walked down the hall to the room where Kimmie was with Gio. Nija and Ricio were lying in the bed with the baby between them.

"Kimmie, would you mind giving me a ride home?"

"Yes, I can do that for you. I'll get Gio ready with his handsome self," she said standing up from the chair as she pulled down her black sweater that had risen up a bit.

"Kimmie, leave him alone, he's sleeping soundly," Nija spoke without opening her eyes. "Sin, I want to keep him for the night, if that's alright."

Nija opened the door for me to go out and do my dirty deed. There was no way I would let this once in a lifetime chance pass me by. I wanted to jump for joy but I held my composure so I wouldn't raise suspicions.

"He has enough pampers and milk in his diaper bag. The powdered milk, bottles, and another outfit is in there too. Be sure to apply the ointment on his burns after each diaper change. Call me at any time if you want me to get him."

"My nephew will be cool, Sin. If Nija wants him here, then we got him," Ricio said rolling over. "The only thing I want to say to you is this, auntie, be careful out there."

"What you mean, Ricio?" I asked playing stupid.

"Sin, you ain't slick. I'll act like I don't know what's going on but stop playing me for a fool. I want to know your every move just in case I have to pull up."

"My location will let you know I'm at home. I'm not dropping nothing, Kimmie come on so I can get home," I said walking out before Ricio could say anything else. I heard Kimmie tell him to lock the door as I made my way to the entryway.

"Sin, I'm serious. Hit me with your location, man," Ricio yelled from the porch as I sat in the passenger seat of Kimmie's car.

Ignoring him I put on my seatbelt and thumbed through my phone to get the address to my destination. Kimmie backed out the driveway and pointed her car in the direction of the expressway. When I found what I was looking for in my phone, I added the address to the GPS system and glanced at the side of Kimmie's face.

"You strapped?"

"I stay strapped. What's up?" she asked keeping her eyes on the road.

"We're making a detour. I got some business to take care of in Capentersville. You ready to cause havoc with me?"

"Hell yeah. Who we about to body?" she asked smiling.

"That nigga Fats is the muthafucka that snitched on Rodrigo. His ass knows the code of the streets and for him to go against the grain is an instant death sentence. Fats been hiding out with the help of Cooper, but he's all alone now so his ass is mine."

"Damn, I never thought Fats would turn into an informant after all Ricio and Sosa did for him. Everybody in their circle ate good, what the fuck was he thinking?" Kimmie asked picking up speed as she merged onto the expressway.

"I don't know what he had on his mental, but he's going to wish he'd never betrayed the muthafuckas that have been there when he didn't have shit."

Kimmie was quiet for a moment before she took a deep breath. "Sin, what's the odds of Rodrigo beating this case? I mean he killed a cop—"

"Rodrigo may be a shoot first ask questions later nigga, but he killed in self-defense. Cooper was trying to bring him down since he made him look like a pussy the first time he took him in for questioning. CPD is trying to throw the book at him but I won't let that shit happen sitting on my ass. I'm going to fight hard because what they don't know is everything is on video and it will be seen even if I have to leak that bitch to every social media outlet available.

Rodrigo won't be confined to the prison system because they want to protect a corrupt officer that got laid down for the dirty shit he tried to pull and failed. There's too many of our black men locked up for bullshit and dying by the hands of trigger-happy police officer's that's trying to eliminate the African American race. We ain't safe in the comfort of our own homes, our babies and women are dying because they ain't training these muthafuckas properly and covering the shit up saying the shootings were justified.

I'm tired of this shit and Rodrigo's case will be one to remember because this black bitch is going to make sure of it. I want everybody involved and I'll make sure he gets a huge settlement out of this shit. I bet they start training these bitch made ass baby clan members before they put their asses on the street from now on. I may be an African American lawyer but I'm a muthafuckin' goon in the streets of Chicago and they got the right one."

"Sin, I just want him back home," Kimmie said sadly.

"Let me find out you let Rodrigo get the pussy and you fell in love with the D. That muthafucka is only here for a season, Kimmie. When all this shit is over, Sosa will be back. They are two different niggas living in the same body. Check ya feelings because shit may not be the same when his mind gets right. I had never seen this side of that man until Max died. Prepare yourself, baby. That's all I can tell you."

The car ride was too quiet after about ten minutes and I reached out and turned on the radio. We were forty minutes from our destination according to the GPS and I wasn't for the silence. *If I ruled the world* by Nas filled the car and I sat back bobbing my head and grooving to the tune. Hit after hit passed the time as we drove further away from the city. Kimmie even got into the groove of the music when *Gin and Juice* came on.

The voice indicator on the GPS instructed Kimmie to get off on the next exit and she signaled to get over to the right lane. I turned the radio down because we had it bumping inside the car and our presence didn't need to be known once we approached the house. According to the GPS, the house was ten minutes away. Exiting the expressway, Kimmie made a right hand turn on a dark street following it for six miles. She made a left on another street and the house was on the left side of the street.

The sun had set and it was barely seven o'clock in the evening. The house that we were looking for was dark with the exception of the glow from a tv downstairs. "Park a little bit past the house. We have to scope this muthafucka out first before we make any moves," I said to Kimmie.

She parked in the driveway of a house that had a for sale sign on the lawn and we got out. Kimmie checked her gun and put it back in the small of her back. I threw my black shoulder bag over my head and was set, ready to pop shit off.

Creeping to the side of the house Fats had been living in for God knows how long, I put my finger to my lips to tell Kimmie to stay silent. She nodded her head in understanding and I proceeded forward. The lack of lighting worked in our favor because we blended into the darkness. Staring through the opening in the curtain, there was no one in the room and I made my move.

There was a side door further down the walkway and I stopped in front of it as I pulled my tool pack out of my bag. Taking out what I needed, it took a couple seconds for me to pick the lock to gain access inside. Both of us eased inside and closed the door quietly. Throwing the tools in my bag, I tiptoed around the room with my Glock in hand. Walking slowly to the room off the kitchen, it was empty but was decorated for a little girl.

That detail alone worried me because I wasn't into killing kids. My mindset was in overload trying to figure out what to do with the child if she was in the home. The lower section of the house was empty so we crept up the carpeted stairs to the second level. I went to the left and Kimmie headed to the right. The bedroom was empty and I left after checking the closet to be sure no one was hiding inside. I met Kimmie in the hall and she shook her head back and forth indicating she didn't find anything.

The last door in the house was closed but as we got closer, the sound of lovemaking could be heard. Fats had the nerve to be knee deep in pussy while my nephew was locked up because of his diarrhea mouth ass. There was no way the child could be on the other side of the door with the noises coming from the other side.

"Fuck me harder, baby!" The female screamed out in ecstasy.

"Hold yo' muthafuckin cheeks open and hold that arch like I told you!"

His fat ass sounded like he was about to pass the fuck out. Fats was well over three hundred pounds and wasn't cute at all. He had to be finessing this bitch to have her faking the funk at that moment. My stomach was churning listening to the sounds of sex coming through the door and it was time to put a stop to the ghetto Pornhub that was taking place. Screwing the silencer onto my Glock, I looked over at Kimmie and she had her shit ready too.

Kicking the door damn near off the hinges, Fats rolled over and reached for a tool he had on the nightstand. Firing off a shot, I took off two of his fingers causing him to withdraw his hand immediately. "Arrrrrghhh!" Fats howled holding his hand rolling back and forth.

"Oh my God, what have you done?'" The female screamed holding the sheet over her chest.

"Bitch shut the fuck up! You got two seconds to save yo' muthafuckin' life," Kimmie snarled pointing her Nina in the female's direction.

I almost laughed at how fast she closed her mouth and stifled her cries as she held the sheet for dear life. Fats was holding his hand with tears rolling down his face. Blood was oozing between his fingers rapidly. If looks could kill, his head would've exploded the way I was glaring at his big ass.

"Sin, Sin why are you doing this? What did I do?"

"Nigga, did yo' fat ass just ask me that stupid shit? You know exactly what you did for me to pay you a visit. Stop acting clueless because you are far from a blonde, bitch!" I spat back.

"I swear to God I don't know," he cried.

"Darren, who do you think you're talking to, Detective Cooper?" I laughed. His eyes got big when I mentioned the cop's name and his girl gasped loudly, letting me know they knew exactly why I was in their shit. "I'm going to give you one chance to tell me how you got yourself caught up in the position to go against family, Fats."

"Sin—"

"Say my muthafuckin' name again, bitch!" The only thing I want to hear is why you betrayed us!"

"He didn't do shit to y'all! Darren did what *had* to be done to save his family and to keep himself out of jail. I don't think he was wrong for what he did!"

"Baby girl, that's called snit—" Before I could finish my statement, the hoe had a hole in the middle of her head and was slumped over with a pair of perky titties playing peekaboo with me.

"Kimmie, what the hell!" I laughed loudly. "I wanted the bitch to explain the logic behind the bullshit she stood by."

"Oh well! Ding dong the bitch is dead now! Your turn crybaby Cobbs. What made you tell the pigs where my man laid his head at night?

"I—I got caught with some dope and a gun. Cooper pressured me to tell everything I knew about Rodrigo and Ricio. I folded when he threatened to lock me up with a mandatory twenty-five-year sentence. I have kids to take care of. They put them in CPS custody and I want them back."

"So, you turned informant and didn't have the decency to call and give a heads up? Cooper didn't have that much of a hold on your nut sack, nigga," I shot back at him.

"I have a phone but Cooper monitors the shit out of it. Believe me, I wanted to say something but didn't know how. Speaking of Cooper, he should be calling at any moment and I need to get to the hospital. you shot of my fingers, Yo!"

"Fuck getting you to the hospital, take that pain, nigga! I'm sorry to inform you, Snitch of the year. Ya boy Cooper won't be calling nobody ever again. He's residing in hell wearing gasoline draws and you'll be joining him shortly," I said walking closer to the bed he laid on. Placing my gun on the bed, I pulled a mini machete out and grabbed his small member with my left hand.

"Sin, hold on! I'm sorry!" he cried out trying to push my hand away.

"I warned your fat ass not to say my name again and you had the audacity to touch me! Fuck you, snitch ass muthafucka!" My arm went into the air and I swung it swiftly slicing his dick off at the base.

"Arrrrghhh! God noooooo!"

Fats screamed like a bitch and it was music to my ears. I held his joint in my hand and shoved it down his throat to shut him up. He struggled to breathe, I grabbed my gun and shot his ass between his eyes. Fats' chest was still moving up and down slightly indicating he was till amongst us in the world we lived. I pulled the trigger hitting him in the heart and the nigga was a goner.

Fats laid motionless with his eyes open and I was satisfied with the results I'd delivered. Kimmie started wiping down everything we had touched as we made our way out of the house the same way we entered. The ride back to the city wasn't like it was when we started our journey. Another nigga down made me smile because this shit was coming to an end rather nicely, if I could say so myself.

Chapter 35
Ricio

For the past couple weeks, I'd been making sure Nija ate and wasn't mopping around falling into depression. The death of her sister took a toll on her and her health was suffering from it. We went to her doctor's appointment and she had lost a substantial amount of weight and that wasn't good for the babies per Dr. Hayes.

I put off going after Rello to make sure she ate right, got sleep, and exercised to stay fit. Things have been going great between the two of us because I showed her that I could be the man she needed me to be. Hiding things from her was a thing of the past. When I hooked Latorra up with a few bands to bounce out of Chicago, I let Nija know. After that, all communication came to a halt with her and we were able to move forward. She eventually moved in with me permanently and I had a huge surprise in store for her.

It was time for me to trust that she would do right without being under my watchful eye, I had work to do. I called Face's mother because I hadn't heard anything about his funeral and she informed me that he was cremated. The shit pissed me off because I didn't get the opportunity to tell my nigga I'd see him on the other side. My anger didn't stop me from giving her a lump sum of cash but I was hurt just the same by her decision.

Beast called me after finding out Sin and Kimmie went out the night of Nihiyah's repast and killed Fats. I didn't see anything wrong with it but was glad he got in her ass for being sneaky. Fats got what he deserved because the nigga could've implemented anyone other than one of us. Now my bro was locked in a caged behind his punk ass. My phone rang and I looked down and answered knowing who was on the other line.

"You have a collect call from an inmate at the Cook County correctional facility. Press nine to accept the call," the automated system blared in my ear. Pressing the correct number, I waited for the call to connect.

"What up, brah. What's shakin'?"

"Bro! How ya' holding up in that muthafucka?" I asked glad to hear my brother's voice.

"Man, these nigga's wild in this shit hole. I've had to beat the fuck out of a couple of 'em because they throwing their weight around. Somebody should've warned them about the kid."

"Be easy, brah. You don't need to be getting caught up in that hell hole. We working to get you out of that bitch. It's going to be a long fight. A lot's been going on and you know I can't discuss it over the phone. Just know, shit is looking up and we gon' be straight. It's good hearing from you. Call Kimmie, she misses you, bro."

"I'm not calling her because I don't know how much time I have in this muthafucka. I don't expect her to hold me down while I'm in here. She needs to live her life because I wouldn't want her to put nothing on hold for me. Let her know I think about her every day but this is the way it's going to be."

"I'm not telling her that, brah. You will have to call and deliver that news on your own. Kimmie is bad as yo' ass when she's pissed."

"Aight, scary muthafucka," he laughed. "How's Gio?"

"He's cool. Growing more every day. Time is flying and he's looking more like Max as time passes. I hate he won't get to know either one of his parents as he grows up."

"Ricio, Gio is gon' know all about his daddy and Madysen. We're all gon' make sure of that shit. Sin and Beast will give him the best life any kid would ever want. Not to mention, he has two of the coolest uncles in the muthafuckin' world. Gio gon' be straight, stop worrying about nothing. This phone is about to cut off soon, but I called to let you know I'm going to be transferred in a couple days."

"Where the hell they shipping you off to?" I asked sadly because that meant he wouldn't be coming home anytime soon.

"Don't sound so sad, brah, I'm good with leaving this dirty ass place. I'm going to Danville," he responded cheerfully.

"Word!"

"Hell yeah, man! Anywhere is better than the County. I'm happy to be going elsewhere even though I'd rather be coming home."

"You have one minute remaining for this call," the automatic recording cut in.

"Aight, bro, keep your head up and your eyes wide open. Make me proud and come home safely. I love you."

"Get out yo' feelings. Over there sounding like Nija's sensitive ass," he laughed. "Tell sis I say hello and—"

Rodrigo's words were cut short as his time expired. I stood from the bar stool and went into the kitchen to whip up lunch for Nija. Deciding to make turkey panini sandwiches, I removed everything I would need from the refrigerator and placed them on the counter. Along with the sandwiches, I made fruit bowls and a green smoothie. Of course, that was for Nija because I wasn't drinking nothing that looked like baby poop.

Thirty minutes later I had everything on a tray walking into our bedroom. Nija was sitting in the middle of the king sized bed browsing the internet on her laptop. Glancing up, she smiled as I entered the room.

"You must've heard my stomach growling. I thought you were on the phone, not cooking for me."

"Nawl, I didn't hear anything but it is time for my three favorite girls to eat," I responded placing the tray on the nightstand until she moved the laptop out of the way. "I did talk to Rodrigo and he told me to tell you hello," I said placing the tray on her lap.

"Awww, how is he holding up?" She asked taking a sip of her smoothie. "You made this just right, thank you."

"No problem. He's okay, I guess. He is being transferred from the County jail in a few days. I can't wait for this to be over and he's back home."

"I know. It's going to be a long road for all of us but I think Sin will pull a rabbit out of her hat and get him out of that damn place."

"What were you doing on the computer?" I asked getting comfortable on the bed.

"I was looking for items for the nursery. We should decorate the room down the hall for the babies," she said taking a bite of her sandwich.

"Nija, I think we should wait on decorating for now."

"Why wait, Ricio. These babies will be here before you know it and I don't want to wait until the last minute. There's no better time than now," she said finishing off the last bite of her sandwich. She looked at me and then back down at my sandwich that I hadn't touched yet before taking another sip of her smoothie.

"I've been working for months on something and it's finally completed. With two babies coming soon, I wanted us to be able to live comfortably. We are the only ones still living in the city and I want to be closer to the rest of my family. Nija, I purchased a five-bedroom, three bath home in Flossmoor. Before you say anything about your mother being in the city, I thought about her when making this purchase.

Mama Pat is more than welcome to come with us. The property has a guest house that I will gladly open up for her. She wants to put her home up for sale anyway because of what happened to Nihiyah on the very street where she has to live. We can decorate the nursery in our new home," I explained as I handed her the deed.

Nija read over the paper and looked up at me. "Ricio, I haven't agreed that we'd be together."

"Baby, please. Miss me with the bullshit. If you weren't willing to give us a chance, you wouldn't be here. Things have still been kind of rocky but I've done all that I could in the past couple weeks to prove you are what I want. If I have to fight for the rest of my life, it will be well worth it. Our children will be raised in a loving two parent home by both their mother and father.

Nija, we will not be part of the statistics that are paved for black families," I said opening the nightstand drawer. Dropping down on one knee I grabbed her hand and kissed the back of it. "Nija, would you be my wife?" I asked opening the black velvet box exposing the five-carat cushion diamond ring.

I waited for her to respond but she didn't utter a vowel. Nija stared at the ring while rubbing her round belly with tears in her eyes. A few minutes passed before I stood to my feet and placed the ring on the tray beside her plate. "You don't have to respond now. I'm going to handle some business and hopefully you'll let me know what your answer is when I return. Kissing her softly on the lips, I turned to leave the room.

"I love you, Nija. Don't ever forget that."

Grabbing my keys from the bar as I made my way to the door. I was pissed and someone was going to pay for the way I felt at that moment. Taking the elevator to the garage I jumped into my vehicle and pulled off. I hit the radio button to eliminate the silence that tried to smother me inside my ride. Scarface's old school hit *Murder by Reason of Insanity* boomed through the speakers and I knew exactly where I needed to be.

65th and Loomis was where I was headed and hopefully, I didn't have to sit too long for my target to show its face. In spite of the cold weather, there were many people out and about. Driving down Loomis, I saw Rello coming down the steps of his home and my mood changed for the better. I slowed my car down until he pulled his car onto the road.

Rello wasn't told to always know what's going on around him when he had wronged someone. I was on his ass all the way to 75th and King Drive. He parked outside the *Harold's Chicken Shack* and two other niggas waited for him to exit his car. I parked a couple cars behind him and let my window down to hear what they were talking about.

"Rello, what the fuck going on? How the fuck is everybody coming up dead?"

"On the real, it's fucked up. Sam was popped, Floyd was caught slipping, we still haven't seen Erv, and many more are gone. We are the only ones left other than Big Jim and we know he's safe because of where he's at. Who can touch him in prison?"

"I think we should leave while we still have a chance," one of the dudes said.

They were going back and forth scared as hell because none of them knew who the hell they were fucking with. *I had something for them though,* I thought as I pulled away from the curb. All three looked at my whip as I drove past but they couldn't see inside. I bent the block and jumped out to grab my tool from the trunk. Throwing the case on the passenger seat, I opened it up and pulled off.

The Steyr SPP 9mm submachine gun that I held on my lap was one I bought for this occasion alone. Checking the thirty-round clip, I turned onto to King Drive to get back onto 75th Street. Rello and what was left of his crew were still congregating outside the chicken shack and it was on from there. I let my passenger window down and gripped the tool in my right hand as I sped down the street I stopped abruptly in front of the restaurant.

Before anyone could react, I let my bitch sing to them niggas without missing my target. I jumped out and made sure they were all dead by emptying the clip. Running back around to the driver's side I got in and took off. Police sirens were wailing in the distance and I got lost in the wind. Pulling my phone out of my pocket, I called my nigga that ran a chop shop.

"What up nigga?"

"Yo, I got one for you to get rid of, I'm on my way," I said slowing down at a red light.

"I got you, fam. See you when you get here."

Ending the called I dialed Beast's number. "Hey, nephew."

"I need a favor. Meet me on 159th at the shop. I'll fill you in when you get there."

"Aight, see you in a minute," he said ending the call.

It felt good to know that our troubles were over in these streets. The only obstacle we had to get through was Rodrigo's trial. After that, we wouldn't have anything else to worry about. I made it to the shop in record time and when I pulled up, Beast was already parked outside. I got out of my car and started taking all of my personal items out of the vehicle.

"Ricio, what the hell is going on?" Beast asked getting out of hid ride.

"I killed Rello and his crew on 75th. The shit is over Beast! We finally got our lives back," I said throwing my shit on his back seat. "We can live, Unc."

"It's not over, Ricio. Big Jim is still a major piece of this puzzle and it's not complete without that piece. Once that's done, we still have a black cloud looming over our heads. Have you talked to Rodrigo?"

"Yeah. He's getting transferred to Danville soon," I said closing the door.

"Who do you think made that shit happen? Me. I called Fitzgerald and told him what the deal was and he drew up the paperwork. When he gets to Danville, he will be in a cell by himself, a cellphone will be waiting for him, and Big Jim will be taken care of however Rodrigo decides to make it happen. We will just have to wait until he comes home to find out all about it."

"Do you think he will be able to win the case?" I asked seriously.

"I don't know to be honest. The way the judicial system is today, who knows. But I do know that Sin has a great defense team in place because she won't be able to tackle these muthafuckas by herself."

"I don't give a damn about the dollar amount, we will pay. Enough about that, I need to go to the dealership to buy another ride," I said.

"Aye, Ricio! What you got for me, fam?"

"I got my BMW for you. I need you to get rid of it completely," I said reaching in my pocket.

"I don't want your money. You know I got you," he said. "Get outta here and I'll take care of it. What's going on, Beast?"

Beast threw his head back in a what's up gesture and got into his car. I walked around to the passenger side and got in. We went to the Mercedes Benz dealership and I browsed the showroom floor and fell in love with a black GLE Coupe SUV. It took a couple hours to finalize the purchase and I ended up driving away with a silver E-Class silver sedan. I had a couple adjustments made on the vehicle so I had to wait until they were done.

After loading my belongings into my new whip, Beast and I parted ways and I headed home. When I inserted the key into the lock, the door opened suddenly and Nija stood before me beautiful as ever. “Hello, gorgeous,” I said bending down kissing her on the lips.

“Hey,” she said pulling back. Nija placed her left hand on my chest and I noticed she had the ring on her finger.

Pulling her into my chest, I held her tightly and didn’t ever want to let her go. The feeling of knowing we were going to be okay, made me the happiest nigga alive.

Chapter 36
Rodrigo

The first couple days that I was at Danville, these muthafuckas put me on a Block designated for them transgender niggas. I'm far from homophobic but I didn't belong with their asses. There were certain things that a straight man like myself shouldn't be subjected to. The shit I saw had me thinking about killing on purpose by mistake.

Laying back on the bottom bunk I was contemplating if I wanted to go out and eat the bullshit that was being served in the mess hall. It had been a couple days since I'd eaten anything other than junk food. My phone vibrated under my pillow and I didn't recognize the number but I answered anyway.

"Yeah," I said when the call connected.

"Chuck is on his way to you with an Italian beef, dipped with hot peppers and mozzarella cheese along with fries and a drink. I also sent a special package for you as well. Just make sure you put a towel under the door and open the window. There's already air freshener in your locker, use it. Delete this number but keep it in your mental," the caller said hanging up.

I had a good feeling that was Warden Fitzgerald but I wasn't sure. Memorizing the number, I deleted it and put my phone back under my pillow. There were a couple rapid knocks on my cell door before it opened. "How you holding up, fam?" Chuck asked closing the door before walking over to hand me the greasy bag of food. Getting up from the bunk, I sat at the desk and ripped the bag open.

"I need to get the fuck away from this side of the building," I laughed stuffing a couple fries in my mouth. "These niggas wild! I hope y'all giving their asses some condoms while they're fuckin' like there's bitches in this muthafucka."

"Man, that's on them. I'm only over here because I came to make sure you were cool. But check it, Sinnamon may be able to help you get at Big Jim. That bitch owes me for bringing him a philly cheese steak and ain't paid me yet. The Block you will be going to is where Big Jim is housed.

If you plan on doing anything, do that shit before you get transferred over there. Getting in without being seen won't be a problem. The warden already knows what's up but it's the other officers that need to think you were in this cell during the hit."

"Which one is Sinnamon? There's a stocky nigga with French braids that walks around with his t-shirt tied in a knot behind his back. That shit looks weird as fuck because he looks like a whole nigga but walks like he's on a runway."

Laughing hard as hell, Chuck almost coughed up a lung while holding his stomach. Once he got out his giggles, he cleared his throat. "Yeah, that's him. He has a whole entourage around this place. Word is, Big Jim been in here fuckin' all the newcomers and got at the wrong one. The latest was Sinnamon's nephew and he's already planning to get back at Big Jim in the worst way."

"Still on the same shit, I see," I said with my face balled up. "Aight, set that shit up. As a matter of fact, tell that nigga to come see me instead of going to the yard tomorrow." Taking a bite of my beef sandwich, I barely chewed before swallowing and took another bite. "Damn this shit slammin'! Good lookin', I needed this," I mumbled with a mouthful of food.

I finished eating and washed it down with the cold drink. "I want to thank you for getting that video of my brother, man. It gave us closure and explained a lot of shit that Max couldn't before he left this fucked up world."

"Sosa, I don't know the dynamics of the video but getting it to y'all was my main objective. So—"

"Chuck, that nigga Sosa been MIA for a minute. You didn't get the memo, fam, this Rodrigo you rappin' wit right now. Don't make me repeat that shit again."

Chuck looked at me for a quick second and hunched his shoulders. "No need to thank me. Yo' daddy was there for me and I'm going to do the same for you while you're in here. Big Jim needs to be dealt with." He stood and started collecting my garbage to take with him.

"I have to raise up outta here. This should last for a couple days. I'll hook you up right once you're moved to D Block. Sinnamon will be to see you about noon. Strategize accordingly, fam," he said handing a paper bag to me.

Chuck bounced and I secured my door and put a towel underneath it. Breaking down the wood, I stuffed it with green and sealed it up for dessert. Opening the tiny window, I blazed up, got high as fuck and passed out.

Count time came sooner than I would've liked but I got my ass up so they could see me and moved the fuck on. Going to the sink to wash my face and brush my teeth, I was lucky enough to have a real toothbrush and muthafuckin' Colgate toothpaste. Warden Fitzgerald had a nigga feeling like I was housed in a luxury prison for the stars and believe it or not, I was comfortable.

After getting myself together I went back to the bunk and slowly took my phone out. Kimmie had been on my mind and I just wanted to take that time to hear her voice. I had to fish around in my brain to remember her number and I was drawing a blank. Nija's number popped in my head and I hurried entering the digits.

"Hello," she said hesitantly.

"Hey, sis. It's me."

"Rodrigo? How are you calling me?"

"I got a phone. How you and my nieces doing?"

"We're okay. They are getting bigger and weighing down on my bladder. I have to pee every five minutes, bro. I want this to be over and my feet are swollen all the time. The doctor put me on bedrest, making me take off work and everything."

"It's what's best for you, Nija. Listen to everything those doctors are telling you, ma. Cut back on the salt and increase your water intake. You taking your vitamins, right?" I asked.

"Yeah, and I'm not eating a lot of salt. Your brother got me on a strict diet."

"How are y'all doing, Nija? You and Ricio, I mean."

"We are taking things slow. Bro, you know how much I love your brother."

"I do."

"I had to humble his ass and not give in to him the way I had done in the past. Ricio needed a taste of reality and if that meant losing him in the process, I was willing to allow that to happen. I was ready to raise my babies on my own with him being there part-time. The bullshit I was accepting from him had to end. The love I have for myself is far more important than running after a man and trying to force him to love me the same way I loved him.

I'm giving him another chance to get it right. So far, it's been going well, he even put a ring on it, bro. But I won't travel this road with blinders on, Rodrigo. I've turned a blind eye for too many years when it comes to Mauricio. Walking away would be hard if it leads to that, but it will be something I'd have to do for me."

Listening to Nija speak showed me how much she had grown from the young girl I met years ago through my brother into the woman she was at that time. I'd always told Ricio that he had a gem in her but he had to learn the hard way. Hopefully he'd realize she's the one for him and cherish her forever.

"It seems as if you have it altogether, sis. I'm proud of you. Stay strong and always know your worth. We got into other shit and I almost forgot why I called. I need Kimmie's number."

"(773) 555-7254. Rodrigo she is so worried about you."

"I got this, sis. I'm about to holla at her about this right now. Save this number and text me some time, it's lonely in this bitch."

"Will do, bro. Love you."

"Love you too," I said disconnecting the call.

Wasting no time, I dialed the number Nija gave to me and listened as it rang. I was about to hang up when Kimmie's sultry voice came through the speaker. "Hello."

"Hey, ma. How you doing?" I said lying back on the flat as pillow.

"Sosa!"

"Aht, Aht, you know better."

"Yeah, yeah I got the wrong nigga, I know," she laughed. "I'm doing okay, thanks for asking. How are *you,* is a better question?"

"I'm straight. Word is you're out there worrying yourself about a nigga. Kim, I'm fine so I'm not what you should be concerned about. These muthafuckas trying to give me big boy numbers behind the shit that happened. The last thing I want you to do is put your life on hold for me. There's no telling how long it will be when I get out," I told her truthfully.

"What you not gon' do is bring negativity into your life, you gon' win this shit. As for me moving on with my life, not gon' happen. See, we started something that will get finished because I'm one of few women that's built for this shit. We ride together, we die together, just like Bad Boys. If you like it or not, I'm gon' hold you down for as long as I need to until you step foot out of that prison.

Kimille Sutherland is going to be your peace, and calm during and after the storm. I was bred to be a different type of ride or die chick and I choose you to, as you say, put my life on hold for. We got everything under control out here, now you have to get back out so we all can breathe normally."

The way she said that shit was gangsta, made my dick hard in the process. I didn't even have a comeback for her to be honest. Kimmie was a different type of lady but I couldn't quite figure her out. She was going to do what she wanted regardless of what I said so I was ready to welcome the conversations until I got out.

"Is it okay for me to call you on this number?" she asked.

"Yeah, but text me first and I'll call you back instead."

"Okay, I have to get back to work. Thanks for calling and we will get through this together," she said hanging up. Kimmie had me thinking about the sex session we had and I got up and got the jar of Vaseline and jerked my dick before falling asleep.

The sound of knocking woke me out of my slumber. Glancing around after opening my eyes I forgot where the fuck I was because in my dream, Kimmie's body was wrapped around mine. The dream seemed real but reality hit me in the face when I focused on my surroundings.

Knock! Knock!

"Yo, hold on!" I yelled out getting up from the bunk with my dick hanging freely. Tucking my joint in my pants, I grabbed the Vaseline that I'd used earlier and put it in my locker. I washed my hands and walked the short distance to the door and opened it. Sinnamon stood with a smirk on his face. I knew then I had to shut whatever the fuck he was thinking down.

"Hey, I'm Sinnamon. I heard you wanted to see me," he said batting his eyes.

"It ain't that type of party, partna. What the fuck is yo' real name because I'm not calling another muthafuckin' Sinnamon."

"That is my real name. I legally changed my name a few years ago—"

"Save that bullshit, homie," I hissed.

"Since you're offended, the name I was given is Patrick. He rolled his eyes and leaned against the doorframe with his hand on his hip.

I wanted to punch his ass in the throat for standing in front of me acting like a bitch that shot her shot and failed. Shaking my head, I turned and left his ass standing there. "Come in and close the door. Sit yo' ass over there," I said pointing to the chair by the desk. Sitting on the bottom bunk, I waited for him to sit down before continuing.

"I asked you to come holla at me because there's a mutual nigga in this prison that we both want to cancel out. I figured we could work together to make it happen."

"Big Jim. He has fucked over many people, I see. I've been waiting for the chance to give him a taste of his own medicine for months. I'm down with making his life miserable. What's the plan?"

"That's what we have to discuss. I don't know how this place is operated so I need to know a good place to formulate this attack."

"Jim usually approaches his prey in the showers. I heard the willing participates are taken to the laundry room to get complete privacy. The CO on duty after dinner don't check back there because he don't give a fuck apparently."

"Alright, the laundry room it is. You can be the person to lure him in."

"That wouldn't work because he already suspects me and my crew of gunnin' for him. he would never trust one of us. There is someone who Jim has been trying to get at though. Pee Wee don't run with us but I know he would do the shit for a price. He'll do it for a couple packs of cigarettes."

"I can hook him up, that won't be a problem. The one thing I don't need is you or your crew runnin' ya'll mouth. This shit has to go under the radar and smoothly. Make sure all your people understand this shit because I'm not the nigga you want to cross, Patrick. My reach is long, remember that."

"I'm a lot of things but a snitch ain't never been one of them. I'm doing life in this bitch and will never see the light of day. I'm all in with this shit because that nigga violated my family. This conversation never happened between us, cutie."

"That shit will get you choked to death. My name is Rodrigo and don't you ever forget it. Ain't shit cute about me. Keep that shit on reserve for all these sweet niggas in this bitch."

"I'm just bullshittin' with you," he laughed. "I know how to respect a muthafucka that don't indulge in the lifestyle I lead."

"Here's the plan," I said dismissing the garbage he said. We spent well over an hour going through the plan of how we were going to end Big Jim's life.

Chapter 37
Big Jim

I was informed a couple days ago that my empire was no more. All I had left was the money in the bank and my sister. My house was burned to the ground, Floyd was dead, all my foot soldiers, dead. Shit, after Rello delivered the news to me, I hadn't talked to that nigga since and he couldn't be reached.

The bitch named Karma was out to get me and she was winning. The shit that I'd done years prior had finally caught up with me. Never in my wildest dreams did I ever think Ricio and Sosa would be able to conquer all they had. Everything that happened was solely my fault because I should've been more involved and not put the responsibility on Floyd alone. I shouldn't have under estimated Reese's bloodline.

"Aye, Big, man is you gon' pay attention to the cards, or you gon' keep spacing out?" Snapping me from my thoughts, Doug sneered at me because there was money on the game of spades we were playing.

"My bad, I have some shit on my mind and it's eating at me. I'm cool, let's come back from this shit," I said looking at the cards in my hand.

The cards worked in our favor and we won the game right before it was time for chow. I walked my half of the winnings back to my cell and left right back out to get something to eat. Going through the line, I had my tray in hand and went to sit down. One of the sissy niggas walked through the door and I couldn't take my eyes off his ass. I had been checking Pee Wee out for a while and I had plans for him.

Pee Wee ignored all my advances but I had a feeling he was going to stop playing hard to get one day. While eating my food, my eyes stayed glued on Pee Wee until Sinnamon and his crew entered the room. Sinnamon was a nigga that had beef with me and didn't know shit but my name.

One of the homies told me that he was mad at me because his nephew gave up the ass to me. Obviously, the lil nigga went back and told his uncle how it really went down. I took that shit. Being the muthafucka that I was, I didn't give a fuck, none of them niggas shook me by any means.

Sinnamon walked by the table I was sitting at and looked down at me like I was a little nigga. Dropping my fork on the tray, I raised up but Sinnamon kept moving with his bitches right behind him. Watching their every move, I was cool once they sat in the back of the chow hall. As I sat down there was someone standing next to me and I looked up with an attitude. Peewee was holding his tray standing next to me with a goofy grin on his face.

"Don't get your blood pressure up because of that fool. Sinnamon ain't on shit and he's not going to do nothing. Is it alright if I sit with you today?" He asked with a smile.

"I'm not worried about that nigga! Sit down and stop standing over me," I said picking my fork back up. The imitation meatloaf, watery mashed potatoes, and soggy carrots were already nasty when it was hot, so I already knew the shit was disgusting cold. Putting a piece of the meat in my mouth, I felt Peewee staring at me.

"What is it, man?" I asked.

"Big, I been thinking," he paused. "I want you to fuck me."

"What made you change your mind, Peewee?" I asked chewing slowly.

"I've been contemplating about it for a minute and I think it's time I stopped running from what I really want."

Glancing around the chow hall, I put another piece of the meatloaf in my mouth and turned back to Peewee. "Meet me in the laundry room at seven thirty," I said finishing my food.

We sat eating in silence until Peewee finished eating then he got up with his tray in hand. "I'll see you later. You're going on the ride of your life tonight, Daddy," he smiled and walked away.

I waited until Peewee was out of the hall before I got up and dumped the remaining food in the garbage. Something was telling me not to show up to meet Peewee but my dick had other plans. He was about the same age as Max and I knew he'd give me the feeling I'd been missing since the last time I had Max. When I got to my cell, I sat down on my bunk and fished my phone out. The urge to talk to my sister was strong.

"James! How have you been, brother?"

"I'm alright, sis. I had to fire the lawyer that was working on my case. He told me there's no way I'll be able to beat this case. I believe he just doesn't want to put in the work the way Rod did."

"James, Rod was a friend of yours. He did what he had to do to get his *friend* back on the streets. In other words, he was willing to lie and do whatever he had to do in order to get you off. Don't get me wrong, his arguments were very believable but you and I both know they weren't true. Every lawyer you hire is going to go by the book. You were lucky to have Rod on your team and y'all fucked it up."

"Lynetta, I know I fucked up! You don't have to throw this shit in my face, okay? My life is a mess and here you are trying to make me feel worst. Everybody in my circle is dead because of something I started! I'm only alive because of where I am. I don't care if I get out or not."

"You're giving up, James. We weren't raised to give up! Fight to get out of there and leave Chicago. There's life after this shit, brother."

"I don't think there is. Lynetta, thanks for being there for me through this time. Go out and do something for yourself, on me. Buy whatever you want and I'll talk to you later. I love you, sis."

Ending the call before she could reply, I got up and left the cell. With every step I got an eerie feeling but I shook it off. The CO on duty was watching the tv that was mounted on the wall and I eased down the hall to the laundry room. As I entered, the air felt thick and stuffy but I continued inside. Peewee was waiting for me as he said he would and I wasted no time taking him in my arms.

"I've waited a long time for this," I whispered in his ear.

Peewee stepped back and pushed me against the wall and dropped to his knees. Freeing my member from my pants, he swallowed me down his throat. My eyes closed instantly and my head fell back.

"Suck that shit, bitch!" I moaned grabbing the back of his head. The way Peewee was sucking me off had my toes curling tighter than they ever had. I felt my nut building up but I didn't want it to end. Rocking my hips back and forth I picked up the pace and I was going to explode even though I didn't want to. "Fuck, Peewee!" I growled.

Soon as I released my semen down his throat, I felt something sharp against my temple and the suction stopped. "You just busted the last nut of your life. I knew you would be a dumb ass and get caught slipping." I opened my eyes and was staring Sinnamon in his evil eyes. "The way I see things, Big Jim, you have always been the giver, never the receiver. Today is your lucky day, muthafucka." Sinnamon's voice sent a chill up my spine and Peewee smirked at me as he walked toward the door.

"You set me up!" I yelled at Peewee.

"All dick ain't good dick, Big. You fell for the banana in the tailpipe, now you gon' get fucked," he laughed as he left the room.

I was slammed to the floor by my neck and a couple of Sinnamon's homegirls held me down by my arms. Squirming around, a hard fist connected with the back of my head dazing me for a short period of time. Feeling my pants being pulled off my ass, I yelled out but something was stuffed in my mouth to muffle the sound.

"You're about to feel what it's like to get fucked, BJ," Sinnamon said nodding his head at one of the dudes.

Rolling a condom onto his dick, he got behind me. I bucked trying to free myself from the hold I was in but there was no use. My hips were raised, lifting my ass in the air before a sharp pain shot throughout my asshole. Screaming out loud, tears sprang from my eyes as I was violated over and over. Everyone in the room took turns assaulting my asshole and I was ready to pass out.

I had thrown up several times but swallowed most of it due to being gagged and damn near choking to death. Tears mixed with snot covered my top lip. Praying to God to make it all stop, the door to the laundry room opened and I thanked the Lord for hearing my cries. I knew for a fact the CO had decided to finally do his job and check the room. But that thought was short lived because the person I saw standing there was no other than Sosa.

The way my heart was beating in my chest, I thought I was having a heart attack. “That’s enough,” Sosa said from the doorway.

How he got in this prison was beyond me but I was glad he intervened and stopped the assault on me. Sosa walked toward me and Sinnamon passed something to him. He looked down at me with a frown on his face.

“You a shitty mess, Big Jim,” he laughed. “Getting’ that ass beat up don’t feel good, huh? Now you know how the fuck my brother felt when you violated him in the same manner,” he said snatching the cloth from my mouth. He grabbed a broom and broke the stick over his knee.

“I’m sorry, Sosa,” I croaked out.

“Nah, homie,” he laughed as he snatched me up by the collar of my shirt. Feces dripped down my legs and the smell was horrible. I could barely stand but the hold he had on me kept me upright. “You wish you were apologizing to that nigga. Since yo’ ass killed our brother, Sosa’s been away. Rodrigo is who you’re attempting to apologize to and I’m not trying to hear the bullshit!

The things you did to Max were foul as fuck and you gon’ pay for that shit. I guess you thought the worse that would happen was you getting fucked in the ass then off to the infirmary you go, right? Wrong, nigga!” he yelled shoving the jagged stick up my rectum.

“Arrrrrghhhhhh!” I screamed bloody murder as he snatched the stick out and rammed it inside me again. I felt every prick of the wood attaching itself to the inside of my canal and I fell onto my stomach on the floor.

Sosa kneeled beside me and planted the makeshift shank into my side. Blood filled my mouth and I knew I wouldn’t live to see another day. I don’t know how many times I was stabbed but I tried my best to make peace with God before he slit my throat from ear to ear.

Chapter 38
Sin

After Killing Fats, I went to work gathering as much information I could on Rodrigo's case. Once the police gave clearance for us to go into Rodrigo's home, I went straight to his surveillance equipment that was hidden in a secret compartment of his basement and got the footage. When I saw what took place, I knew there was no way he would be convicted for killing Cooper. The police Commissioner was calling Rodrigo a cop killer not knowing that the cop he was defending wasn't doing the job he had sworn to do.

I had two high powered attorneys to help me with the case and we were determined to win. Rodrigo's trial was finally here and I was walking into the courtroom with a lot of confidence. The courtroom was packed to capacity and it would be televised. I knew they were only doing that to try to make an example out of yet, another black man.

Everyone was sitting in wait for the trial to begin. Beast, Ricio, Nija, Kimmie, and Pat was holding Gio sat behind the defense table. The Vasquez Boys, Psycho, AK, and Felon all sat close to the back of the courtroom. As I walked to the defendants table, Rodrigo was being escorted into the courtroom. The Grey Armani suit fit him well and he looked like he was ready to pose for GQ Magazine.

He sat in the empty chair between me and the other attorney's that had helped me on this case. I tapped him on the shoulder and gave it a tight squeeze letting him know everything would be okay. The bailiff stood in the front of the courtroom and everyone quieted down.

"All rise. The state versus Sosa Vasquez is now in session, the honorable Judge Ivy Higgins presiding." The Judge entered the courtroom and took her seat at the bench.

"Everyone but the jury may be seated. Mr. Staples, please swear in the jury," the Judge stated.

The bailiff turned to the jury. "Please raise your right hand. Do you solemnly swear or affirm that you will truly listen to this case and render a true verdict and a fair sentence as to this defendant?"

The jury as a whole responded, “I do.”

“You may be seated,” the bailiff replied.

“Mr. Staples, what is today’s case?” The Judge asked.

“Your Honor, today’s case is the State of Illinois versus Sosa Vasquez.”

“Is the prosecution ready?”

The prosecution attorney stood and answered, “yes, Your Honor,” back down.

The judge then turned to me and asked the same question and I replied, “yes, Your Honor,” taking my seat. The prosecution was first to give their opening statement and I sat back to listen to what type of bullshit they were going to present.

“This case is about an honorable Police Officer that took an oath to serve and protect with the Chicago Police Department. He was a father of three and a great husband that loved what he did for a living for the past twenty years. His life was taken from him by a man that refused to surrender himself to the officer. Instead he took his life in order to stay out of jail. That’s why we’re here today, ladies and gentlemen of the jury. My name is Matthew Sutherland, and I represent Detective Gary Cooper. In this trial, we ask you to grant our request for Capital Murder in the first degree.”

I stood from my seat and walked around the table as I positioned myself in front of the jury box. “On October twelfth at approximately two in the morning, my client was sleeping in the privacy of his own home when he heard movement downstairs. He went to investigate and was approached by an armed masked intruder. Mr. Vasquez protected himself in self-defense and we will prove that here today. He is described as if he’s a monster and that’s not the case. You will here testimony about what his late father did for a living, but that’s not who my client is. There will be testimony about his younger brother’s death as well during this trial but what I want you to do is listen to the facts that’s presented along with the evidence to back them up. My name is Sincere Westbrook and I’m representing Sosa Vasquez. We are asking that you grant a not guilty verdict in this trial.”

I sat down after seeing the reaction of the jury after I finished my opening statement. These muthafuckas painting a picture of Rodrigo that may count against him but I have the trump card to slap their asses in the face and make them look stupid. The judge shuffled through her paperwork and glanced up at the prosecutor's table.

"Prosecutor, you may call your first witness."

"Thank you, Your Honor. I call to the stand, Detective Colin Bradley."

Detective Bradley made his way to the witness stand and was sworn in by the bailiff. Once Bradley took his seat, the prosecutor stood and walked to the middle of the room. Sutherland paced back and forth before he asked his first question.

"Detective Bradley, what was your relationship with Detective Cooper?"

"Cooper and I had been partners for the past fifteen years. He was like a brother to me," Bradley stated.

"On the night of October twelfth, were you aware of what was going on with Detective Cooper and Mr. Vasquez?"

Bradley looked nervous but held his composure. "I knew there was a warrant for Mr. Vasquez's arrest but I didn't know my partner was going to the house that night."

"What was the warrant for, Detective?"

"The warrant was for drug possession and suspicions of murder, Sir."

"Thank you. No further questions," Sutherland said taking a seat.

"The defense may cross examine," the Judge said.

"Detective Bradley, you and Detective Cooper were partners, correct?"

"Yes, I already stated that," he said smartly.

"If the two of you were partners, why didn't you accompany Cooper to the residence of Mr. Vasquez instead of a civilian that wasn't part of the police force?"

"I object!" The prosecutor shouted.

"Overruled. Detective Bradley answer the question," the Judge replied.

"I didn't get a call from my partner so I don't have an answer to your question."

"Did Cooper have a personal vendetta against Mr. Vasquez, Detective Bradley?"

"I wouldn't call it a personal vendetta but he didn't like the way Mr. Vasquez disrespected him during an interrogation."

"And since Cooper felt there was disrespect, he took it upon himself to break into Mr. Vasquez's home and plant drugs so he could present the warrant and lock him up?"

"Objection!"

"Withdrawn," I said with a smile. "Is there a copy of the warrant against Mr. Vasquez on file, Detective Bradley?"

His eyes dance back and forth between me and the prosecution before he dropped his head slightly. "No. I believe my partner forgot to enter the details of the warrant."

"Did he forget or he never had one to begin with? That's the reason you knew nothing about Cooper going out of his jurisdiction, correct?"

"I object!" The prosecutor yelled once again.

"No further questions, Your Honor," I smirked as I sat down and folded my hands on the table.

"You may step down, Detective," the judge said. "Prosecutor, call your next witness."

"Your Honor, all of my witnesses seem to have died before this trial. We believe that Mr. Vasquez and his gang may have arranged it that way."

"That's hearsay, Your Honor," I spoke up.

"So, you mean to tell me that you have no one else to testify today?" the Judge asked.

"I would like to call Lynetta Carter to the stand, Your Honor."

An older woman I'd never seen a day in my life walked into the court room. She strutted down the aisle and glared at Rodrigo as she passed our table. After being sworn in she sat quietly with tissue in hand.

"Miss Carter, do you recognize anyone in the courtroom today?" The prosecutor asked.

"I wouldn't say I know the young man sitting right there," she said pointing at Rodrigo. "But I know he was the one that killed my brother!"

"Who is your brother, Miss Carter?"

"James Carter. On the street he was known as Big Jim. He was killed in the Danville Correctional Facility last month," she said wiping a fake tear.

"I'm sorry to hear that, Miss Carter. What makes you think the defendant had anything to do with your brother's death?"

"My brother told me that Sosa and his brother Mauricio were out to destroy him for the death of their brother Maximo. James loved those boys and would never hurt them."

I was fuming because the bitch was lying through her teeth. Big Jim didn't love them boys, he loved the money that came along with them. Breathing through my nose, I sat back and listened to the rest of her testimony.

"How did your brother pass away, if you don't mind me asking?"

"He was found in the prison laundry room. My brother was raped, sodomized with a broomstick, and stabbed over thirty times. Mr. Vasquez was present at the jail at the time according to Detective Bradley. I know he got revenge on my brother. There was no one else that wanted him dead."

"Thank you, Miss Carter. No further questions."

"Miss Carter, is it?" I asked walking to the witness stand.

"Yes, that's correct."

"If your brother, James Carter loved Mr. Vasquez and his brothers so much, why did he forge documentation to get custody of them after their parents were killed?" I asked.

"As far as I knew, the paperwork was legit. James went downtown and had the paperwork done himself with the notarized document that Maurice Williams gave him before his death."

"Your Honor, I would like to present that notarized document along with bank statement with Maurice Williams signature on it. The signatures don't match and it is evidence showing the document was forged," I said passing the papers to the bailiff.

"I knew nothing about that, Your Honor. All I can say is, James took care of those boys like they were his own! They didn't want for anything while in his care."

"You speak about all the love your brother had for these boys and how he loved them as his own. Would your brother have sex with his son?" I asked.

"Where are you going with your line of questioning, Miss Westbrook?" The prosecutor asked.

"Answer the question, Miss Carter," the Judge demanded.

"Of course not!" she exclaimed. "Even if James had a son, he wouldn't do anything like that."

"Your Honor, I would like to present this evidence to the court," I said submitting the disc to the bailiff.

"What is this, Miss Westbrook?"

"Your Honor, what I just presented to court is the evidence of Mr. Carter admitting he raped Maximo Vasquez."

"My brother would never have sex with the same sex! Bitch you are out of your mind and lying through your teeth!"

"Order in the court!" The Judge yelled banging her gavel repeatedly. "We will break for thirty minutes. I will look over the evidence with the jury and we will resume at twelve thirty. Court is adjourned."

The case got off track but it was good to see that the prosecutor thought bringing Big Jim's sister in was a smart move. But it actually wasn't. I know for a fact they were trying to pin Big Jim's murder on Rodrigo too but he had a strong alibi for his whereabouts in the prison. I watched as Rodrigo was taken to the back and I met my family in the hall.

"Sin, they are going after Rodrigo hard. They are going to try to pin Big Jim's murder on him."

"I know, Ricio. It's cool, I promise, I got this. I'm going to throw everything they lay on the table right back at them. Even the bullshit about the murder of Cooper. My nephew is coming home. Let's go grab something to eat," I said taking Gio from Kimmie.

We ate quickly and made our way back to the court house. Pat took Gio back to her house because he was fussing. Entering the courtroom, everyone was seated and Miss Carter was back on the stand. The Judge walked out with a grim look on her face and I sat patiently waiting on what she had to say.

"I watched the footage and what I saw was very disturbing. Mr. Vasquez, I'm sorry your brother had to endure such pain. The evidence is submissive in this case. Are there any more questions for Miss Carter?"

"No further questions, Your Honor," I stated.

"You can call your next witness," the Judge said to the prosecutor.

"Your Honor, I would like to call Sosa Vasquez to the stand."

I glared at the prosecutor because I didn't expect them to do that. It was okay though. "Keep your cool, nigga. This is not the time to be who you've been on the street. If you can't contain yourself, let Sosa the fuck out now!" I whispered in his ear.

"I got this, Sin. Sosa wouldn't know how to answer none of the questions because his ass ain't been through shit. This is my fight and I'm about to win, trust me," he said rising to his feet.

Rodrigo was sworn in and he took his spot on the stand and Sutherland didn't waste time going at him hard. "Mr. Vasquez, is it true that you wanted Mr. Cooper dead after he took you in for questioning a couple months ago?"

"Nah, there's no truth to that. Detective was upset because I wasn't willing to sit back and say yes master as he repeatedly called me a nigga. The so-called arrest was bogus, the only reason I was taken in was because his ego was bruised when I stated facts to him and he was sent to the car by Detective Bradley like he was a child."

"Why didn't you comply with Officer Cooper and let him arrest you after he presented the warrant to you?"

"If there was a warrant presented, I would've gone to jail willingly. But at two in the morning I was sleeping in my bed and my doorbell did not ring once. I stepped out of my bedroom and was met by a masked man with a gun. I got to the assailant before he got me because he obviously broke into my house to kill me. I didn't know there was another person in my home until I got to the bottom of the staircase and saw a second masked man planting drugs around my living room."

"Mr. Vasquez, are you trying to say Detective Cooper was trying to frame you?" Sutherland asked.

"At the time I didn't know who the person was and yes, that's exactly what I'm saying."

"Cooper nor the other victim had masks on when Detective Bradley arrived on the scene. What happened to them?"

"That's something you need to ask the officers on the scene. I am being accused of being a cop killing when in reality, I saw two burglars in my home and I was defending my place of residence. I'm not the one that compromised a crime scene. That would be the crooked officers that's covering up corruption on the part of one of their fellow officers."

"There isn't any proof of what you claim, Mr. Vasquez. It's your word against two dead people and one is a cop. I have no further questions." Sutherland stormed to the prosecutors table and sat down in a huff.

"Mr. Vasquez, at any time did Detective Cooper identify himself as an officer?" I asked raising to my feet.

"No, not at all. When I went downstairs, Cooper was expecting the guy he referred to as Jasper to be the one to come down stairs. He turned and saw me and immediately pulled his gun. Me on the other hand, put my hands in the air and I asked him who sent him to my house. His response was that I was going down and I had to die that night. As he continued talking, I recognized who he was.

I figured it out myself, not because he identified himself as an officer. Cooper stated that he could kill me and give a false statement and get away with it. He shot me in the thigh after I told him with my hands behind my back that he was trying to make me do something to give him reason to shoot me. That was when I pulled my gun and shot him twice in his chest and once in the head when he raised his gun to shoot me again."

"Your Honor, I would like the court to see the footage from Mr. Vasquez's home on the night of the shooting," I said going to the table to retrieve the evidence.

"I object! The evidence was not presented beforehand and should not be admissible here today," Sutherland argued.

"Overruled. Mr. Staples, insert the disc please," the Judge said.

The bailiff started the footage and turned the volume up on the television. The footage showed how Cooper and his accomplice entered Rodrigo's home through his patio door. Even though Sutherland claimed there was no masks involved, it showed clear as day on the screen and there were murmurs throughout the court room. I looked over at the jury box to see their reactions. The look of surprise was on all of their faces and I was glad Rodrigo had surveillance.

As the video came to an end, Sutherland's face was red and embarrassment was etched all over it. He knew they had fucked up royally. "I have no more questions, Your Honor." I smiled because I knew we had won that round hands down.

Both sides gave our closing arguments and court was adjourned so the jury could deliberate on the case. There was no telling how long it would take for them to come back with a verdict. I had a good feeling about Rodrigo's trial. There was no way he wasn't walking out of the court room and back home after everything I presented in the court room that day. It was a waiting game for now and Rodrigo was escorted from the court room and I left to go home with my family.

Epilogue
One year, 2 months later
Nija

It was New Year's Eve day and Ricio and I were putting the finishing touches on the twin's party. I went into labor December thirty-first at six forty-five in the morning. Fraternal twins Siona Kimille and Maritza Simone Vasquez. I had to pay homage to Ricio's mother and my best friend and what better way than with my beautiful daughters.

The doorbell rang and I went to answer it quickly so I could hurry back in the kitchen to finish mixing the punch. "Heyyyy, bestie!" Kimmie screamed as she came in with an armful of gifts. "Where my babies at?"

"They were sleeping but if you keep using your outside voice, they're going to wake the fuck up before I want them to," I said closing the door.

Kimmie sat the gifts on the table that I'd set up for that purpose and followed me into the kitchen. My mama was finishing my punch and I was grateful for her. She had agreed to move into the guesthouse and sold her home not too long after. Evergreen Park was a place where people rarely moved away from. The minute she put it on the market, offers started coming in immediately. Mama got a nice profit from the sale and she was happy living close to me and her grandbabies.

"How are my babies doing?" She asked over her shoulder.

"Mama, I'm so tired. I want this party to be over and it hasn't even started yet," I said sitting down at the table.

"Hey, mama I'm doing well. I can't wait to turn up with my nieces," Kimmie said twerking her booty.

"Girl don't you be in here dancing like that with the kids now. They are one years old, save that shit for the party tonight." I laughed.

We had chips, hotdogs, and hamburgers that Ricio grilled the night before, coleslaw, macaroni and cheese, beef ribs, chicken, and Italian sausage for the adults. I had a custom cake with a Baby Shark design. The girls loved that damn song and it drove me crazy every time we listened to it. The entire dining room was set up with the Baby Shark theme.

"Where's Ricio?" Kimmie asked.

"He went to make sure everything was set up at the venue for the party tonight. He claimed he wanted to be there to ensure everything is perfect. You know he has been promoting this party everywhere for months. He has some big names lined up to bring in the New Year with us but he refused to tell me who they were. I wish Rodrigo could be here to celebrate with us though."

"Me too," Kimmie said sadly. "I still can't believe they still charged him with possession of an ounce of weed and the only gun out of many that wasn't registered. The shit didn't smell right then, and it still don't. Excuse my language, ma."

"Don't apologize. I know it was bullshit but he will be home soon. He's tough and he will be better than ever when he gets out. Now forget all that sad shit, it's my grandbabies' day and it's a day of happiness."

"Ma Ma," I heard one of my daughters calling from the top of the stairs. Both me and Kimmie went to the stairs and little Maritza was standing in front of the security gate waiting to be rescued. She looked like a female version of Ricio, down to his chocolate skin. Siona looked more like me. Maritza saw Kimmie and squealed while clapping happily. "Mee-Mee!"

"Hello, beautiful!" Kimmie said reaching down to pick her up. "You got a wet butt, Simone. We have to get you cleaned up." Kimmie decided to call my baby by her middle name for reasons unknown and everyone followed suit.

Removing the gate, I placed it in the closet and followed Kimmie and Simone to the nursery. Siona was awake sitting up on the pallet I had made for them to sleep on while watching Paw Patrol. She rubbed her eyes and started whining. I walked to the closet and took their blue jeans and Baby Shark shirts with their names on the back placing them on the dresser.

"Kimmie I'm going to run them a bath so we have to tag team because we have about forty-five minutes before the guests start arriving."

"I'm all for it, sis. Let's get these little beauties ready to enjoy themselves. Who's all coming anyway?" She asked.

"I invited the kids from the daycare, Sin, Beast, and Gio, Psycho is bringing his kids, AK, is coming, Slim and of course, the Vasquez Boys. Oh, Tangie from my job is coming with her family too."

I scooped Siona up and took her down the hall to the bathroom with me. I turned on the water and started undressing her. After a few minutes, I turned the water off and Kimmie brought Simone in and placed her in the tub. We sat watching them splash around for a few minutes before we washed them up and took them both out wrapping them in their matching bath towels.

Kimmie and I had both of my princesses dressed in a matter of ten minutes. I gave both of them three ponytails and added colorful ribbons in their hair. Kimmie went to the closet and got their pink Uggs out the boxes and put them on their feet. At that moment, the doorbell rang and the first guest had arrived.

Thirty minutes later we had a house full of people and Ricio wasn't back. I took my phone out of my back pocket to call him and there was another guest at the door. Rushing to answer, I disconnected the phone and put it back in my pocket. When I answered the door, Angel was standing there with boxes so high he had to peek around the side so I could see who he was.

"Y'all spoiling the hell out of these little girls!" I exclaimed taking some of the packages off the top.

"That's what we do. We come from a family of men and this nigga Ricio produces the only girls. They will be protected and spoiled for life. Get used to it, cuz."

I sat the boxes on the floor because the table was full. Mateo walked in with just as many gifts as his cousin. Nicholás, Alexander, and Javier followed and the scene was the same. All I could do was smile as I shook my head. Each of them hugged me after freeing their hands of gifts. It was a race with who would get to my babies first. Siona and Simone was showered with love and I had to get it on camera.

Javier ran to the stereo and changed the music to the Baby Shark song and all the kids started dancing around trying their best to sing along with the music. I continued to record and it was hilarious watching all those grown ass men dance and sing that damn song with the kids. Moments like the one that was before me, were what I lived for.

My front door opened once again and Gio ran in shouting, "Baby Shark doo doo doo doo doo doo, Baby Shark!" Beast came in singing the damn song and I was ready to pull my hair out because I was over it by that time. Sin looked at me and laughed because she knew how irritated I get when that song played continuously.

"It will be over soon, boo," she said giving me a hug.

"Nija!" I turned to see who the hell was walking into my house and noticed the door was already open so Sin knew someone was coming in behind them.

"Hey, Tangie! Thanks for coming."

"Ya'll having fun up in here," she said shaking her hips. "Where do I put these?" She asked holding up several gift bags.

"Yes, they are. Find I spot by that table. It's filled to capacity," I laughed. "Where is the husband and the kids?"

"Both kids are sick and hubby decided to stay with them while I dropped the twins gifts off. I'm staying for a while because these kids turning up!" My phone vibrating in my pocket. I took it out and there was a text from Ricio.

Ricio: Bae, open the garage door and come help me with these gifts.

Instead of responding, I went to the garage and hit the button to let the door up. When the door rose all the way up, Ricio stood outside his truck and Slim got out the passenger seat. He looked good in his button-down shirt and leather coat with fur in the hood. I was so proud of Slim because he had really gotten himself together and left the drugs alone for good.

I could see that the truck was filled to capacity through the front window. I politely went into the house and got all his cousins. Several trips later, all the gifts were inside and the party was in full swing.

Ricio grabbed me around the waist and kissed the side of my neck. "I had to give you that before my babies saw me. You know they only share me with each other," he laughed turning me around kissing me deeply on the lips. Soon as we pulled apart, the twins spotted their daddy and started crying for him to get them.

The party lasted another three hours and the girls had a grand time. They partied so hard that they fell asleep along with Gio on the living room floor. The last of the guests left and it was time to clean up the mess that was left behind.

"You look so tired, Nija. Go on upstairs and sleep before it's time to hit the streets,' Ricio said hugging me from behind. "I have to make a run and will be back shortly."

"Baby, I have this mess to clean up. I can't go to sleep until it's done."

"Nija, take your ass upstairs," Sin said walking up behind us. "There's enough of us that we can get this shit done. Go get some rest, we got this. Ricio get out so you can get back here and get a few hours of sleep yourself."

"Sin, Gio is staying the night with me and the girls, right?" My mama asked coming out of the kitchen.

"Of course, he is. Tonight, I'm gonna party like it's nineteen ninety-nine," she sang out loud.

"I'll get up with y'all later. Bae, put the girls in the bed before you leave," I said going up the steps.

"Don't touch them! I'm not walking up those stairs and I live across the way," my mama fussed and I let it be, plopping in my bed face first soon as I walked into my bedroom.

***

We were hours away from a New Year and I was ecstatic with the way my life turned out. Ricio and I got over the bump in our relationship and we were looking forward to spending forever together. I was still working at the Department of Human Services, we moved into a bigger house in the suburbs, and we had the perfect family in my eyes. Ricio decided to invest some of the money his father left him by opening a barbershop, a music studio, a lounge called Reese's, and two laundromats. He also bought a court way building on the Southside that had twelve units.

I thought he was lying when he said he was done with his illegal dealings in the street. Ricio was completely done once he found someone to purchase the hundred bricks he had left. Everything has been going well but I could tell Ricio really missed Rodrigo but he covered the way he felt well.

I had been awake for a few minutes and still didn't want to get out of bed. Ricio had been planning this event and there was no way I could tell him I didn't feel up to going. Swinging my legs out of the bed, I went into the bathroom and put on my shower cap to protect my hair from getting wet. I turned the water on in the shower and walked to the sink to brush my teeth.

Stepping in the shower, I washed my body quickly and got out. I grabbed a towel and wrapped it around my body as I walked back into my room. I opened the closet door and grabbed the dress bag that Ricio brought in a couple weeks ago. Placing the bag on the bed, I unzipped it and pulled the dark green dress out.

Oiling my body with shea butter, I slipped the dress over my head and it fit like a glove. The dress was off the shoulders, with laced long sleeves and the bottom of the dress had a long, sheer, mermaid train. I walked back to the closet and got the silver, strappy Louboutin's out the box and slipped them on my freshly pedicured feet.

Ricio had bought me a diamond chandelier necklace with matching earrings. It looked great with the dress and the nude makeup I lightly applied to my face. I pulled my Brazilian weave into a bun with curls cascading down the sides of my head. As I slipped my engagement ring on my finger, the doorbell rang. Rushing down the stairs, I looked through the side window and Sin was waiting patiently for me to open the door.

"Oh my God, that dress is stunning!" she exclaimed when I opened the door. "Are you ready to go?"

"Ready to go? Ricio hasn't even been back home since earlier. I don't know where he is."

"Damn, I forgot to call. Ricio told me to come by and scoop you up. He said he would meet us at the venue."

"What is it that he had to do that kept him away most of the day, Sin? I swear if he is out there playing around again it's going to be over!" I said angrily.

"Girl, if you don't shut yo' ass up! That man loves you and you want to accuse him of doing something he said he would never do again. I thought you let the past go, Nija."

"I did let it go, but I will never forget. You know what, you're right. I'll go upstairs and get my wrap then we can leave to bring in the New Year," I said faking a smile. I grabbed my fur wrap and put my phone in my silver clutch before walking back downstairs.

Sin was still standing by the door and I got a good look at the sequin dress she had on. It was the same color as my dress but the sparkle of the sequins set it off. "You are beautiful yourself, Sin. Sorry I didn't notice when you complemented me."

"Lil girl, it's okay. Now, are you ready to go?" She asked looking at her watch.

"Yes, yes, we can leave," I laughed.

Sin opened the door and I was right behind her so I could lock up. When I turned around, there was a black Maybach sitting in my driveway with a chauffeur waiting to open the door for us. My heart warmed knowing Ricio put a lot of thought into this New Year's Eve party. I felt like a celebrity for the moment and I took it all in.

"Your man's got style and he can arrange for me to pick you up anytime," Sin said laughing. "We have to make one more stop to pick up Kimmie."

"Why the hell didn't Kimmie bring her ass out here! Now we have to go all the way to the city to get her when the venue is out here on Lincoln Highway," I said rolling my eyes.

"For your information, Miss know it all, Kimmie is at Rodrigo's house. So, stop complaining so much. You have been really grouchy lately, let me find out you're with child."

"I am not having any kids anytime soon. My girls just turned one and they are a handful. What is Kimmie doing at Rodrigo's house anyway?" I asked.

"She said she was missing him and wanted to be close to him. She asked if she could have the keys to his house. After you went to sleep, she left and went to take a nap of her own in Rodrigo's bed," Sin explained hunching her shoulders.

The chauffeur pulled up to Rodrigo's house and Kimmie came out wearing a dress the same color as mine, similar in style, but her dress didn't have a train. She had on the exact same shoes as me too. She looked stunning but I had a feeling something was up and neither one of these heifers told me about it.

"Hey, Divas!" Kimmie screamed as she got in the back of the luxury car. "Y'all ready to party?"

"It's about to be a good night," Sin said staring at me.

"What's going on that y'all ain't telling me?"

"What you mean?" Kimmie asked.

"We are basically dressed alike and this is just a New Year's Eve party and we're dressed like we going to meet Barack and Michelle Obama."

"Well it is a formal affair, Nija. What did you expect us to wear, leggings and t-shirts?"

"Ha ha ha, Sin. I thought y'all was hiding some shit from me, that's all."

"We would never do no shit like that," Kimmie said grabbing the bottle of Moet and popping the top. We drank a couple glasses of champagne as we cruised to the venue.

The parking lot was filled to capacity so I knew the party was live. Sin had been tapping away on her phone for the past fifteen minutes and I had to be nosey. Leaning over trying to read what she was typing, she pulled away and nudged me back.

"Stay out of grown folk business, Nija. What Beast is talking about is for my eyes only," she chuckled.

"Ewww, y'all nasty," I said scrunching up my nose. The chauffeur got out of the of the car and walked around to open the door for us. "I can't wait to see all this work that had my man away from home for countless hours."

"Well we're about to see firsthand how beautiful this place is," Sin said linking her arms between mine and Kimmie's.

We entered the venue and everything was beautiful. There were green, white, and silver streamers flowing wall to wall. All the décor was the same colors and it hit me at that moment that Ricio had a color scheme for this party and it was a wonderful idea. It was strange because I didn't hear any music coming from inside the main room of the venue. Angel, Mateo, Javier, Nicholás, and Alexander came walking out in white tuxedos.

"Oh, y'all clean up nicely and look good too," Sin said playfully.

"Ricio went straight formal with this party. I hope he didn't choose formal music too because I need to shake my ass for the New Year," I said popping my ass.

"You ladies look lovely as well. Ricio is about ready for y'all to come in," Angel said looking around.

"Angel, why do we have to wait to go inside of a party?" I asked. "What's going on?"

"We're waiting on somebody. It will be about another five minutes."

"Well, it's gonna be New Year's Day in about, what time is it, Sin?"

Looking at her watch, "it's eleven thirty."

"In thirty minutes, Angel."

"I know, I know," he said.

Beast walked out and whispered to Sin and Kimmie. They walked off and I stepped to follow but was stopped mid stride by Beast. "What's going on, Beast?" I asked puzzled.

"I'm gon' walk you in, Nija."

"Nah, I got this one, Unc." Turning around I looked into the eyes of Rodrigo and ran right into his arms.

"Rodrigo! When did you get out?" I asked stepping back.

"Hey, sis. Rodrigo didn't make it back this time. I heard he was acting a whole fool out in these streets and I had to send him back where he came from. Sosa is back. You ready to do this thang, baby girl?"

"I don't know what's going on but okay, I'm ready," I said taking his hand pulling him along.

"Okay, nephew since you're here, I'll go let them know you're here." Beast left the room and all the guys did too, leaving Sosa and I alone.

"Sosa, what's going on?"

"You are gon' find out in a few minutes," was all he said. The music for *A Couple of Forevers* by Chrisette Michele flooded through the speakers and I looked around. "That's our cue, sis. Let's go we have a party to attend." Sosa said grabbing my hand.

I see it clear, my heart is here
We got each other let's take it from there
And if I could I'd love you all forever end of time

What we've been through, no one else knows
Cause all that matters is how far this goes
And it will go until it starts again

Me and you are built like armor
Nothing can stop love from loving on us
And I'm not asking for much

Just a couple of forevers
A couple of forevers
I'm the only one, you're the only one
Together 'til never
I'm talking about forever
Just a couple of forevers
I'm the only one, you're the only one
Together 'til never

Mateo was making his way down the aisle and when I saw Ricio standing at the other end, the floodgates opened. Tears fell from my eyes because I'd accused him of hoeing around when all along, he was putting this surprise wedding together for us. My nerves were all over the place and I didn't even write my own wedding vows. I always said if I got married, I wanted to recite my own words. Ricio set my ass up and good too.

Sosa placed my hand into Ricio's when we made it to the front of the venue and kissed my cheek before stepping to the side. The preacher stood between us as Ricio caressed my face gently. I looked around at the crowd and saw my mama and the babies sitting in the front row and I started balling harder. Everyone knew about this and no one told me a thing.

"Baby, it's okay. This is our special, forever." Ricio whispered in my ear as he held me close.

"Dearly beloved, we gathered here today to celebrate with Mauricio and Nija as they proclaim their love and commitment to the world. We are gathered to rejoice with and for them, in the new life they now undertake together.

Mauricio and Nija, the relationship you enter today must be grounded in the strength of your love and the power of your faith in each other. To make your relationship succeed it will take unending love. It will take trust, to know in your hearts that you truly want what is best for one another and to learn and grow together. It will take faith, to go forward together without knowing what the future holds. If you both come freely, and understand the responsibility and work involved to make your relationship thrive, and are committed to not only each other but your family, please take each other by the hands and reply 'we do'."

"We do," both of us said in unison.

"Who gives this bride to this groom in marriage?" the preacher asked.

"We do!" Everybody in attendance shouted. That alone started another flow of tears from my eyes.

"Amen," the preacher said with a huge smile. "Do you all have your own vows to recite?"

"Yes," we both responded. Ricio looked shocked that I said I had my vows.

"Nija, ladies first," the preacher said gesturing toward me.

"Mauricio Williams, you have been my best friend, mentor, playmate, confidant, and my greatest challenge since I was twelve years old. But most importantly, you're the love of my life. In the past year, you have made me happier than I could ever imagine and I am more loved than I've ever thought possible. You have made me a better person, a mother to our beautiful daughters, as our love for one another is a reflection in the way they see us. So I am truly blessed to be a part of your life, which of today becomes our life together. I love you."

Ricio wiped the tears from my face with his thumb before taking a deep breath. "Nija Foster, you've put up with so much of my nonsense throughout the years and held me down just as long. I've seen your kindness which at times I took for weakness and your strength. I promise not to take you for granted ever again. You are my favorite person in the world, and I choose you to be my wife. My heart is and has always been yours. I see these vows not as promises but as privileges. I get to laugh with you, cry with you, care for you and our daughters, and share eternity with all three of you. I love you, baby."

"And so, by the power vested in me and the state of Illinois, I now pronounce you husband and wife. Mauricio You may kiss your bride." As soon as our lips connected, the clock struck twelve and we were officially married on New Year's Day.

We filed out of the main room and into another room to party. I was having the time of my life dancing with all my family and friends. Sosa and Kimmie made me laugh as we filled him in on how his life had been over the past year and he couldn't believe the things Rodrigo had him doing. Kimmie revealed that the two of them were in a relationship and kept pleading the fifth until she whispered something in his ear.

"Oh Yeah, that's how we were getting down? Come take a walk with me because I don't believe you. If you live up to what you just said, I'll move yo' ass in tomorrow," he smirked.

"Don't worry homie, my shit already in the drawers on the left. Rodrigo had plenty of conversations with me before you took your body back. Like I told him, you two muthafuckas is the same nigga. I'm just lucky enough to have the best of both worlds. Come on so I can blow yo' muthafuckin mind since you want to be tough and shit." Needless to say, Kimmie and Sosa is now a couple and engaged.

Sin and Beast came over and congratulated me once again on being Mrs. Mauricio Vasquez. They went to the center of the dance floor and danced slowly together. Peeling my eyes away from the happy couple that I've grown to love, I saw Angel rushing to the balcony with his phone to his ear and he didn't look happy at all. Flagging down Ricio, he came over to see what was wrong. "What's the matter, Wifey?"

"Something is wrong with Angel. He went out on the balcony."

Ricio took me by the hand and we went to check on Angel together. by the time we made it outside, he had ended the call and was rolling up a blunt. "What's going on, cuz?" Ricio asked.

"Shit is fucked up back home. We got to take a trip to the Dominican Republic," Angel said putting fire to the spiff.

The End

Submission Guideline

Submit the first three chapters of your completed manuscript to ldpsubmissions@gmail.com, subject line: Your book's title. The manuscript must be in a .doc file and sent as an attachment. Document should be in Times New Roman, double spaced and in size 12 font. Also, provide your synopsis and full contact information. If sending multiple submissions, they must each be in a separate email.

Have a story but no way to send it electronically? You can still submit to LDP/Ca$h Presents. Send in the first three chapters, written or typed, of your completed manuscript to:

LDP: Submissions Dept
Po Box 870494
Mesquite, Tx 75187

DO NOT send original manuscript. Must be a duplicate.

Provide your synopsis and a cover letter containing your full contact information.

Thanks for considering LDP and Ca$h Presents.

Coming Soon from Lock Down Publications/Ca$h Presents

BOW DOWN TO MY GANGSTA

By **Ca$h**

TORN BETWEEN TWO

By **Coffee**

BLOOD STAINS OF A SHOTTA **III**

By **Jamaica**

STEADY MOBBIN **III**

By **Marcellus Allen**

BLOOD OF A BOSS **VI**

SHADOWS OF THE GAME II

By **Askari**

LOYAL TO THE GAME **IV**

By **T.J. & Jelissa**

A DOPEBOY'S PRAYER **II**

By **Eddie "Wolf" Lee**

IF LOVING YOU IS WRONG… **III**

By **Jelissa**

TRUE SAVAGE **VII**

MIDNIGHT CARTEL

DOPE BOY MAGIC

By **Chris Green**

BLAST FOR ME **III**

DUFFLE BAG CARTEL **IV**

HEARTLESS GOON **II**

By **Ghost**

A HUSTLER'S DECEIT III

KILL ZONE **II**

BAE BELONGS TO ME III

SOUL OF A MONSTER III

By **Aryanna**

THE COST OF LOYALTY **III**

By **Kweli**

THE SAVAGE LIFE II

By **J-Blunt**

KING OF NEW YORK V

RISE TO POWER III

COKE KINGS IV

BORN HEARTLESS II

By **T.J. Edwards**

GORILLAZ IN THE BAY IV

De'Kari

THE STREETS ARE CALLING II

Duquie Wilson

KINGPIN KILLAZ IV

STREET KINGS III

PAID IN BLOOD III

CARTEL KILLAZ II

Hood Rich

SINS OF A HUSTLA II

ASAD

TRIGGADALE III

Elijah R. Freeman

KINGZ OF THE GAME IV

Playa Ray

SLAUGHTER GANG IV

RUTHLESS HEART II

By Willie Slaughter

THE HEART OF A SAVAGE II

Available Now

By **CA$H & Coffee**

LOVE KNOWS NO BOUNDARIES **I II & III**

By **Coffee**

RAISED AS A GOON I, II, III & IV

BRED BY THE SLUMS I, II, III

BLAST FOR ME I & II

ROTTEN TO THE CORE I II III

A BRONX TALE I, II, III

DUFFEL BAG CARTEL I II III

HEARTLESS GOON

A SAVAGE DOPEBOY

HEARTLESS GOON

By **Ghost**

LAY IT DOWN **I & II**

LAST OF A DYING BREED

BLOOD STAINS OF A SHOTTA I & II

By **Jamaica**

LOYAL TO THE GAME

LOYAL TO THE GAME II

LOYAL TO THE GAME III

LIFE OF SIN I, II III

By **TJ & Jelissa**

BLOODY COMMAS I & II

SKI MASK CARTEL I II & III

KING OF NEW YORK I II,III IV

RISE TO POWER I II

COKE KINGS I II III

BORN HEARTLESS

By **T.J. Edwards**

IF LOVING HIM IS WRONG…I & II

LOVE ME EVEN WHEN IT HURTS I II III

By **Jelissa**

WHEN THE STREETS CLAP BACK I & II III

By **Jibril Williams**

A DISTINGUISHED THUG STOLE MY HEART I II & III

LOVE SHOULDN'T HURT I II III IV

RENEGADE BOYS I II III IV

By **Meesha**

A GANGSTER'S CODE I &, II III

A GANGSTER'S SYN I II III

THE SAVAGE LIFE

By J-Blunt

PUSH IT TO THE LIMIT

By **Bre' Hayes**

BLOOD OF A BOSS **I, II, III, IV, V**

SHADOWS OF THE GAME

By **Askari**

THE STREETS BLEED MURDER **I, II & III**

THE HEART OF A GANGSTA I II& III

By **Jerry Jackson**

CUM FOR ME

CUM FOR ME 2

CUM FOR ME 3

CUM FOR ME 4

CUM FOR ME 5

An **LDP Erotica Collaboration**

BRIDE OF A HUSTLA **I II & II**

THE FETTI GIRLS **I, II& III**

CORRUPTED BY A GANGSTA I, II III, IV

BLINDED BY HIS LOVE

By **Destiny Skai**

WHEN A GOOD GIRL GOES BAD

By **Adrienne**

THE COST OF LOYALTY I II

By Kweli

A GANGSTER'S REVENGE **I II III & IV**

THE BOSS MAN'S DAUGHTERS

THE BOSS MAN'S DAUGHTERS II

THE BOSSMAN'S DAUGHTERS III

THE BOSSMAN'S DAUGHTERS IV

THE BOSS MAN'S DAUGHTERS **V**

A SAVAGE LOVE **I & II**

BAE BELONGS TO ME I II

A HUSTLER'S DECEIT I, II, III

WHAT BAD BITCHES DO I, II, III

SOUL OF A MONSTER I II

KILL ZONE

By **Aryanna**

A KINGPIN'S AMBITON

A KINGPIN'S AMBITION **II**

I MURDER FOR THE DOUGH

By **Ambitious**

TRUE SAVAGE

TRUE SAVAGE II

TRUE SAVAGE **III**

TRUE SAVAGE **IV**

TRUE SAVAGE **V**

TRUE SAVAGE **VI**

By **Chris Green**

A DOPEBOY'S PRAYER

By **Eddie "Wolf" Lee**

THE KING CARTEL **I, II & III**

By **Frank Gresham**

THESE NIGGAS AIN'T LOYAL **I, II & III**

By **Nikki Tee**

GANGSTA SHYT **I II &III**

By **CATO**

THE ULTIMATE BETRAYAL

By **Phoenix**

BOSS'N UP **I , II & III**

By **Royal Nicole**

I LOVE YOU TO DEATH

By Destiny J

I RIDE FOR MY HITTA

I STILL RIDE FOR MY HITTA

By **Misty Holt**

LOVE & CHASIN' PAPER

By **Qay Crockett**

TO DIE IN VAIN

SINS OF A HUSTLA

By **ASAD**

BROOKLYN HUSTLAZ

By **Boogsy Morina**

BROOKLYN ON LOCK I & II

By **Sonovia**

GANGSTA CITY

By **Teddy Duke**

A DRUG KING AND HIS DIAMOND I & II III

A DOPEMAN'S RICHES

HER MAN, MINE'S TOO I, II

CASH MONEY HO'S

By Nicole Goosby

TRAPHOUSE KING **I II & III**

KINGPIN KILLAZ I II III

STREET KINGS I II

PAID IN BLOOD **I II**

CARTEL KILLAZ

By **Hood Rich**

LIPSTICK KILLAH **I, II, III**

CRIME OF PASSION I & II

By **Mimi**

STEADY MOBBN' **I, II, III**

By **Marcellus Allen**

WHO SHOT YA **I, II, III**

SON OF A DOPE FIEND

Renta

GORILLAZ IN THE BAY **I II III**

DE'KARI

TRIGGADALE I II

Elijah R. Freeman

GOD BLESS THE TRAPPERS I, II, III

THESE SCANDALOUS STREETS I, II, III

FEAR MY GANGSTA I, II, III

THESE STREETS DON'T LOVE NOBODY I, II

BURY ME A G I, II, III, IV, V

A GANGSTA'S EMPIRE I, II, III, IV

THE DOPEMAN'S BODYGAURD

Tranay Adams

THE STREETS ARE CALLING

Duquie Wilson

MARRIED TO A BOSS… I II III

By Destiny Skai & Chris Green

KINGZ OF THE GAME I II III

Playa Ray

SLAUGHTER GANG I II III

RUTHLESS HEART

By Willie Slaughter

THE HEART OF A SAVAGE

By Jibril Williams

FUK SHYT

By Blakk Diamond

DON'T F#CK WITH MY HEART I II

By Linnea

ADDICTED TO THE DRAMA I II III

By Jamila

YAYO

By S. Allen

TRAP GOD

By Troublesome

BOOKS BY LDP'S CEO, CA$H

TRUST IN NO MAN

TRUST IN NO MAN 2

TRUST IN NO MAN 3

BONDED BY BLOOD

SHORTY GOT A THUG

THUGS CRY

THUGS CRY 2

THUGS CRY 3

TRUST NO BITCH

TRUST NO BITCH 2

TRUST NO BITCH 3

TIL MY CASKET DROPS

RESTRAINING ORDER

RESTRAINING ORDER 2

IN LOVE WITH A CONVICT

Coming Soon

BONDED BY BLOOD 2

BOW DOWN TO MY GANGSTA

www.ingramcontent.com/pod-product-compliance
Lightning Source LLC
Chambersburg PA
CBHW070550260626
47161CB00002B/559